OFF THE DEEP END

R. JAYNE REVERE

ISBN: 978-1-7369025-0-9 (Hardcover)
ISBN: 978-1-7369025-1-6 (Paperback)
ISBN: 978-1-7369025-2-3 (Ebook)
Library of Congress Control Number: 2021936396

Cover art by Dan Van Oss, CoverMint
Character Illustration by J. Petersen DarcArt
Line Editing by Anne Victory
Proofreading and Oops Detection by Annie and Crystalle at Victory Editing
Formatting by Tami at Victory Editing

Printed in the United States of America
First printing edition 2021

Untamed Originals, LLC
PMB #150
132 West Columbus Ave
Bellefontaine, OH 43311

www.rjaynerevere.com

For all those who have inspired me and encouraged me along the way.
You know who you are. Thank you.

TABLE OF CONTENTS

CURIOUS ENCOUNTER

CHAPTER 1

ALEX

BOY, HAVE I GOT A story to tell...

Well, that's one way to start off a journal. Alexandra Thomas established her vantage point on the topmost deck of the large research ship. Cross-legged on the rooftop of the bridge, she surveyed her surroundings. Her new notebook lay open and waiting. She chuckled at her first line entry.

Her brother's invite had come at the perfect time. With the past eighteen tumultuous months behind her now, this quest would help satisfy her yearning for adventure. Time away. A refreshing change to occupy mind and senses, to close the door on that rough period and renew her zest for life. Reawaken her soul. This excursion also showed the distinct possibility of a lengthy trip and was already an undertaking far out of her ordinary. A jump start for better things to come. She'd barely contained herself at his request to join one of his assignments. Did he have any idea what this meant to her? A good probability. His intuitive abilities were uncanny.

On what should be a quick search mission, she would also help watch out for her nephew and provide extra hands on board when needed. Enjoy time on the ocean, an expedition with her family. Get away for a while and just be. This time with her brother and nephew came as a welcome respite too. Seldom anymore did they achieve quality togetherness, with her and her brother now residing on opposite coasts. This voyage would be good for them all as a family, including the delightful bonus of new friends in the making. A journal of their voyage along with plenty of photographs would hold a pleasant record of their shared experiences.

What destinies lay ahead? A commissioned discovery mission, the vaguest of details. The entire crew and all on board interviewed and vetted. No personal cell phone calls, and computers and cameras inspected upon return. These particulars lent a considerable aura of mystery to the whole operation. So clandestine in nature, the objective must contain classified material of immeasurable consequence to its proprietors.

Already the core ingredients for a great story.

Alex's brother, Jimmy Thomas, geographical engineer, deep-sea researcher and professor, had introduced her and his eight-year-old son, Will, around to the captain and crew over the past hour or so. A wide variety of personalities among them, the troupe was cordial and personable even if a bit eccentric. A fun and tight-knit group. The galley personnel stood out to her with their endearing wit, and a laughing Will had remained in their stead when she made her way to her current position.

Under normal circumstances, visitors in unofficial capacity were not permitted. Only crew and researchers. This was not an official research voyage, however, thus allowing her sibling some leeway in the people he chose to bring aboard. The task and trip had come on short notice for Jimmy and therefore to her, and four days later, here they were.

Their vessel still at port but nearing readiness to get underway, the crew continued to prep the ship. Raucous, spicy banter wafted up to Alex's ears. She clamped a hand over her lips to catch a sudden giggle. *I think you guys forgot you have visitors.* Light waves lapped against the hull and dock below as early-morning sunlight did its best to moderate the invigorating breeze. She adjusted the towel underneath her to better protect her bare legs. Cold steel roof decking was like sitting on a block of ice! Maybe not the best decision to start the day off in shorts. At least she'd brought a warm jacket.

Her decision to climb up here was rewarded with an encompassing view of the entire bay area. The opposite end held shipping docks, cranes, and tall stacks of multicolored containers that stretched into the distance against a backdrop of low, coastal mountains. Beyond the harbor, pearly ocean and marine layer blended into an esoteric haze. Seagulls squawked as they glided by on their lookout for breakfast. Fishy brine of ocean air filled Alex's lungs, a deep, relaxing breath aiding her desire to soak up all the sensations of this experience. *This should be fun!*

As she sat there enjoying the scenery, an indescribable perception washed over her. A strange, exhilarating tingle flushed her skin and made her heart pound. Pleasant in one sense, it also made her shiver. Butterflies. Harmony. Unity. Coupled with… extreme loneliness? What a paradox! *What the heck was that?* Weird. She pulled her jacket tighter around her as her brows came together.

That jolt of hollow desolation. The "alone" sensation carried her thoughts straight back to childhood. A little girl, awakening in the night. Crying. Wailing.

The dreams and intuitions had been repetitive through her younger life, but her grandmother had always come to her room in those wee hours to console her.

"Gramma, I feel so sad." A young Alex had sniffled through sobs. *"I feel alone. Like a little kid is lost and alone. He just wants to go home. It hurts, Gramma. I don't know what to do! I need to help him! I want to hug him and tell him he's safe!"*

Grandma Ann's words floated into her mind, just as when the older woman had held her protected in gentle arms and rocked her to help ease her small child-self back into slumber. *"You have a gift, little one. You are safe. So safe and loved. But you feel things. What others feel. It can help you well in life when you learn to understand it."*

"But I don't understand, Gramma."

"You will in time, sweetheart. You will in time."

Alex shook herself back to the present moment. She hadn't experienced that intensity of forlorn missing, what she could only term a homesickness, in years! It had lessened throughout high school, and with work and life stress in general since, she'd all but assumed that part of her childhood was the result of a fantastical imagination. Occasionally it would surface, but to a much lesser degree. Why she'd had those wistful connections in the first place remained a mystery. And why all of a sudden *now*? Her recent independence? No, that development was working out well for her. It was something else. Aside from expected novelty, this trip held a peculiar air about it, an undercurrent she just couldn't put her finger on. Likely just anticipation of unknown adventure ahead. Even with family here, this trip embodied a journey far from what she called home.

She removed her sunglasses. Sailboats, small craft, and other larger vessels occupied this portion of the port. Sparkling water, seagulls, and bustling activity on the lower decks also caught her attention. A couple of pelicans sat atop pilings. Nothing out of the ordinary for a place like this. She smiled and wiggled, a small, seated dance in place as excitement melted away the lonely, and she picked up her camera. Twenty or so pictures later, she set it back down beside her, replaced her sunglasses, and pulled her long hair back into a ponytail. Layered ends too short for the tie fell loose at her cheeks. She flipped the tail forward to fall in front of her left shoulder, a position that helped cover a small, heart-shaped scar behind her ear.

The sea breeze kicked up. She zipped her jacket and secured her notebook to write, but before pen hit paper, the sound of more voices drifted to her from below. She glanced down at the dock.

Three men in black tactical gear waited at the plank. All carried large duffel bags.

She slid her sunglasses down her nose to peer over the top as her brother jogged down the plank to greet them. He shook hands with each in turn. *Who was this group?* Jimmy hadn't mentioned anything about others besides the crew. And these guys looked military.

Her high perch granted the perfect place to study them from. A tall man stood easy as he listened, a rifle bag slung over one shoulder, black ball cap shading most of his face from view. Beside him, a bulky blond man chewed the stub of a cigar, head cocked, stance wide, meaty hands on hips. On first impression, all appeared quite capable of governing a mission, but it was clear to her that the man at the front, speaking with her brother now, commanded the lead. Just shorter than either companion, his relaxed yet precise movements told of a controlled confidence. This man projected a calm that bound secrecy. Deviating from that observation, he shared a hearty laugh with Jimmy, and the two shook hands again.

That laugh! Oddly familiar. Those strange butterflies kicked at her stomach once more. Was it something about *him* that was bringing up these old feelings? And why a few minutes initially before she'd even seen or heard him? *Huh. Weirdness continues.*

Curiosity piqued, she leaned forward as they followed her brother on board. As she struggled to see more of the lead's face, he confirmed a fleeting smile at some comment the tall one whispered close to his ear. At the last possible second before disappearing from her sight, the tall man with the rifle looked up, met her gaze, and offered a casual nod. No weird butterflies, but adrenaline jolted her gut and she nearly jumped. Busted. She giggled to herself. Hadn't figured on anyone actually noticing her way up here. Well, okay, interesting, but who and why? She would find out from Jimmy later. Pushing her glasses back into place, she continued writing.

CHAPTER 2

ALEX

"WELL, ACCORDING TO CAPTAIN MAC, it looks like smooth sailing for maybe… he said up to two weeks or more!" Jimmy's brown eyes sparkled as he glanced out at the smooth ocean surface. A thick mist of marine layer had burned off an hour prior, transforming what began as a dreary cool morning into bright sunshine and warmth. A long stretch of good weather and calm seas would be most helpful to the search. Tall and slender, he pushed back his dark brown hair as it shifted in the light breeze that wafted through open hatches. He chuckled and winked. "You should appreciate that, sis. Catch some rays 'n' stuff."

"You know I'm not just here for the cruise-ship experience," Alex shot back. The younger sibling by two years, she was used to his teasing. Her hazel eyes flashed back at him. "Although… a nice sunny deck *is* very appealing. I may just take you up on that." She bent down and wound her sun-streaked dark blond hair into a long ponytail. Flipping her head back, she straightened to eye her brother. "I still wonder what's on it though."

"Don't know, don't need to know. All we gotta do is find it. Military will send out their own recovery team. When they won't say, it's always better to not ask too many questions."

Alex nodded a wise smile and blew a piece of wayward hair from in front of her eye. "I know. But you know me. Always curious." She turned and headed toward the hatch. "I'll go see if Will is finished with his breakfast."

"Okay. I've got a lot of work this morning since we've reached the search site, but we'll have lunch later, and I'll spend time with him this afternoon." Jimmy shifted his attention back to the charts on his laptop, which held down copies of the paper versions underneath. "And he can hang with me for some of this chart work too if he wants."

"I'll tell him. He'll be excited." Alex looked over at her brother and moved back to stand beside him, laying a hand on his shoulder. While the more technical aspects of his work eluded her understanding, she did know the basics and let her gaze roam over the topographical lines of ocean-floor elevations that overlaid the real-time scans of that murky surface miles below them.

Jimmy's reputation well preceded him among his colleagues and really anyone even remotely interested in oceanography. Her brother's abilities, some joked, bordered on a near supernatural quality, his intuitive sense at times appearing more accurate than sophisticated multimillion-dollar equipment. "If you want it found, call Jimmy" had been said on more than a few occasions.

Alex admired how he managed to stay humble in the presence of such praise too. He would just shrug it off and joke back about the sea talking to him and such.

She squeezed his shoulder and leaned closer against him. "Thank you again for inviting me. Sincerely. I'm *really* excited. And to be able to spend this time with you and Will means so much."

Jimmy smiled back at her. "You're very welcome, sis. I'm just glad I was able to get the chance to bring you guys. Don't normally get an off-the-official-record assignment like this. Glad you're here too."

"Thanks. It's been a while since I've really gotten away. I think I'm ready for another complete change of scenery in my life now too, you know?"

"Sounds like a plan. New boyfriend in the cards too?"

"Oh, come on! Seriously? Between you and Lou, I'd be dating half the world by now. You guys have got to lay off it!"

Jimmy laughed and dodged as she made a motion at slugging him. "Just want my baby sis happy."

"Well, I'm quite happy, thank you," she replied. "I'm doing just fine on my own. And… I'm kinda liking it right now. I'm not that little kid anymore. I *can* handle things by myself, you know."

"I know you can. Really." Jimmy nodded at her scolding sarcasm. His tone softened into seriousness. "It has been well over a year now. And I am really sorry about Brad. I liked the guy. Still can't believe he just up and left."

"Yeah, I know." Alex sighed. "I thought he was a great guy too. But I knew for a long time it wasn't working."

Truth be told, from the beginning the relationship wasn't right. Good, even great at times, but not *right*, at least not in the way she felt it should be. Not the soul-felt connection that would bind them together across all space and time no matter the challenges that showed up along the way. But was that type of bonded closeness just fantasy? A hopeful promise of a disillusioned mind, the product of too many fairy tales from a pleasant youth? Which in turn had set the bar far too high for the real world to deliver?

Despite those observations, there had existed an awareness ever since childhood of something out there, of an elusive pull to oneness. There had to be more… didn't there? Did such a reality truly exist? Maybe it never could. *Maybe I'm just a crazy, hopeless romantic. Or too damn independent.* She chuckled internally. She didn't expect perfection, but the feeling, that indefinable something—whatever it was—had to be there. And right or wrong, no matter how hard she'd tried, it hadn't been with Brad, not in the way it needed to be for her. Painful as it was, the time had come for them to end.

Her brother's voice brought her back from her musings. "Well, like I've said before, even though I liked him, better to end it than to live a lie and not be truly happy."

"Yeah, I know. You're right. And I should have ended it long before anyway," she replied. "And thanks. Thanks for being there for me. Through all that mess."

"That's what family's for. We've got each other's backs." He eyed her. "You've had a bad stretch, hon. Don't let it haunt your life." He grinned. "Plus now you can just go wherever you want. I know you've been wanting to travel. You always were the adventurous one."

"Yeah. In my own mind," she replied with a chortle and an eye roll. "You ended up with the more adventurous job."

"Sometimes it is." He chuckled back. "But you've got more flexibility and time freedom with yours now. And nothing tying you anywhere. You've been setting yourself up just for this, to be more mobile with your work. Just go and do it."

Alex shrugged. "I know. I should." She reflected a moment. "I do kinda feel like I'm right on the edge of something. I just can't quite... It's strange, you know? Like something big is about to happen? Maybe that's my cue. Maybe I should just book some random long vacation when we get back and see where that leads me."

"Do it. Be bold." Jimmy gave her a nudge with his shoulder. "Go find your adventure. You've got more courage in you than you give yourself credit for, little sis. You'll step into it, then look out, world!"

"Very funny." She gave her brother a quick hug. His encouragement meant a lot to her, but she couldn't help feeling that it came off as a bit over the top now.

Always the protective big brother, wanting to keep her safe when they were growing up, holding her back from the risky ventures she'd been prone to in her headstrong youth. *You never let me do anything!* she'd screamed at him on too many occasions when he acted like she was too delicate for her tomboy ways. Was pushing her now his way of trying to make up for overprotecting her then?

Though she'd held fast to her daring ways at heart, it would be a lie to say that her spirit hadn't been dampened by those quashing experiences. She'd chosen safety one too many times over what she really wanted. Let go of dreams that others told her were too fanciful, that she'd get hurt if she tried. No more. Her newfound alone time was bringing back that venturesome girl and transforming her into a fearless woman. She hoped. She never wanted to settle again.

"Thanks for the pep talk. And you never know. Might surprise you. I just might."

He chuckled at her again, his knowing eyes warm. "I got faith in you." He winked at her and added, "And don't worry. You'll find somebody too. Somebody who's actually right for you, and you for them. I know you will. You know... maybe on your travels?"

"Will you stop trying so hard?" She giggled at his persistent teasing but offered an acute stare to accompany her bold insinuation and now forced laughter. He'd just *had* to add that in. He liked to pick at times, but this was beginning to get tiresome. Was he trying to get her married off as another "safe" option?

She sighed. Maybe she was overreacting. Her friends and family just wanted to help, and she had to keep that in mind. But they also needed to understand it would be on her terms. And her timeline.

"Geez, I keep telling you, *not* exactly looking right now."

He grinned at her and turned his attention to his charts to jot a couple of notes. After some quick scribbles, he tucked his pen behind his ear and picked up his coffee mug.

ELLA'S VANGUARD. Alex read the name engraved into the polished teak wood that adorned the space above the instrumentation panel, just below the forward viewing windows. The ship was named for the wife of the founder of the university's oceanographic studies division—Ella Winston's boundless support of the exploration and protection of the world's oceans had become the matriarch's cause. This ship would reflect her vibrant spirit and curiosity of the unknown. That brief history lesson, conveyed to Alex earlier, reminded her a great deal of her own sister-in-law. Six years now since the accident, the woman's twinkling brown eyes and infectious laugh came to her mind's eye as if she'd just spoken with her the day before.

Alex rested her arm across her brother's shoulders and gazed out the window at the endless gray-blue of the ocean surrounding them. Hundreds of miles from the nearest landmass, their ship's current position was classified, though she'd been told it was roughly in the middle of the mid-Atlantic, northwest of the Cape Verde Basin. She was officially farther away from home now than she'd ever been. Sunlit sparkles danced atop small rippling waves like a million shimmering camera flashes. "Molly would've loved this trip too."

"Yeah, she would have. You two would've had a great time." He paused, clearly reminiscing. "She always loved the ocean. And she loved it out here on assignments too before Will was born." Jimmy smiled. "She'd be quite happy he's now getting some of this open-sea experience too, you know? She always wanted that for him."

"I know he sure loves when you take him out on the sailboat."

"Yeah, he does. But this is one of Daddy's big work ships. He's *really* excited about that."

Alex gave Jimmy's shoulders a comforting squeeze and turned to go. As she reached the hatch, she caught sight of the three men who stood conversing near the bow. A slight frown crinkled her forehead, and she paused in the opening. "I still don't know quite why you had to hire mercs for this." She moved back closer to her brother, who'd resumed his study of the digital maps. "Was that necessary? What do you really know about them?"

Jimmy glanced up from his charts and toward the bow, back to his work again. Having stressed to her the importance of discretion for this mission and the fact that he and their captain had handpicked their entire crew for it, her unease should be understandable at the seemingly unusual aspect of them taking on veritable strangers.

"Yeah, they're cool. They come highly recommended by Lee. He knows guys who've worked with them before." He looked up at her, reached over, and put a hand on her arm. "Really. And just because they're independent, don't think of them as mercenaries. They're not. They're our protection detail. I want the best to protect us. Remember, we are close to pirate waters. Even most of the crew are armed. We shouldn't have any trouble, but I'd rather be as safe as I possibly can on this. *Especially* with Will and you here."

"True," she said after a moment. Though she was still conflicted, she broke into a reserved grin. "And if Lee recommended them, that's good enough for me. He won't work with *anybody* he can't trust."

"Yep. Exactly why I'm good with it. Honestly, I wouldn't have considered having them on if it weren't for him. But after he and I talked the other day? His advice means a lot." Jimmy paused and studied her, combing nimble fingers through his dark hair. "We've only been out a couple of days. You should talk with them more. Might ease your mind a bit. They won't bite. Will seems to really like the sniper, Care Bear, I think."

Care Bear. The man her brother spoke of *had* impressed her with his mindfulness in explaining his weapon and himself to the eight-year-old boy. Will's eyes had been fixed and attentive as he'd studied the companionable sniper, hanging on every word in complete awe, enthralled by the large rifle and its operator. That recollection brought a smile to her lips, and with a nod to her brother, she headed below toward the dining quarters.

Still, unease remained. Why have hired guns on board when they had a perfectly able and experienced, not to mention armed, crew?

She herself had some weapons in tow, though she'd not made it known. Her brother would *not* be pleased about that. She'd been the one to take after their father in that pursuit, her dad's encouragement and teachings at her curiosity bringing her confidence and a skill level at shooting that would rival many a marksman. Even though she'd continued her training and practice over the years, Jimmy carried a more "let the professionals handle it" attitude when it came to weapons. He'd never been enthusiastic concerning her interest in firearms. Too dangerous, he'd always said.

Jimmy and this crew had spent time in the region on research assignments several times before with no incident. However, in the past year, reports of attacks had seen a dramatic increase. It concerned her too that Lee counseled they have extra backup. In addition to serving in the military, their friend possessed an extra-keen sense about possible trouble and always stressed the importance of being prepared. Plus, friends of Lee's or not, these guys wouldn't come cheap. If her brother was being paid enough to afford *them*? That spoke even *more* profoundly to the actual object of the search.

She had to admit she'd not given the three a real chance yet. Beyond their initial acquainting at the brief security meeting the team conducted explaining their presence on board, she'd kept her distance. Her usual approach to meeting new people was more open and accepting. They presented as professional and kind. So why did she feel so conflicted this time? It was as if there was an equal attraction and repulsion concerning them. A strange alluring appeal, yet something off that shouldn't be. But this whole experience was far different from her norm, *and* she had spent most of her time so far in keeping her active young nephew corralled. And in familiarizing herself with their new temporary home.

She pushed the troubling thoughts out of her mind. It would be fine. She would take her brother's advice and engage more. And stop overthinking. Additionally, judging by Captain Mac's weather report, the immediate future foretold of many beautiful sunny days ahead. Alex intended to enjoy them all.

Scents of various cooked breakfast meats wafted from an open hatch, a yummy approach to her destination. Her mood lightened more as she entered the galley. Her blond-haired nephew, Will, stood laughing with Mario, the ship's cook. Sporting a classic pompadour of jet-black hair, the stocky, golden-bronzed Mario took nearly as much pride in his deft sense of humor as he did his culinary skills, and he and Will had taken an immediate liking to each other upon introduction.

They'd also commenced straightaway into a game of Will guessing Mario's home country. Will munched his last piece of bacon as he watched his new friend chop onions and peppers and add them to a large pot for the evening meal. Still immersed in their mirth, they both continued with hilarity as she walked up to greet them.

CHAPTER 3

AARON

"SO... THINK WE'LL SEE ANY action this trip?"

Les LeBeau's casual tone and British accent matched his relaxed stance as he checked over his weapon. The Barrett M82, fitted with custom scope and stock, his own retrofitted design, rarely left his side. More than proficient with said rifle, the tall, wiry, dark-haired man's service as medic had gained him the offbeat moniker of Care Bear. Piercing blue eyes squinted against the sun's glare, and he glanced over to the man next to him.

"Mmmm... don't know. Hope not." Standing just a couple of inches shorter than his lanky associate, trim athletic frame resting against the ship's rail, Aaron Donovan made a meticulous scan around the area as he peered out at the surrounding horizon. High-powered binoculars showed only turquoise sky melting into blue-gray ocean. Endless. A drop of sweat tickled its way down the length of his backbone. The cloudless day and a black T-shirt were not proving the best combination. "Doesn't look like much. Absolutely *nothing* out there." He gave the horizon another scan. "But… you know that can change in a shake."

"Yep." Care Bear raised his rifle and sighted out over calm water through the scope. "Nothin' now can turn into all bloody hell breakin' loose in an hour."

"Boyeez!" The third member of the group strode up and dropped a large arm across each of their shoulders. "What's the verdict today?"

A broad, muscular hulk of a man, Shane Harrison would transform to all business when it came to warfare. When not in combat mode, however, he delighted in his habitual persona of self-proclaimed ladies' man and all-around goof. He craned his neck, looking from one to the other and back, bright blue eyes flashing. "Well? Hey, no reason to be so serious till it's *time* to be serious." He stepped back, pulled out a cigar and lit it.

Aaron lowered the binoculars and gave Shane a sidelong squint. A smirk touched his lips. He shook his head before turning his blue-green gaze back through the lenses.

"Aww, c'mon, my Psycho brother. Ya gotta lighten up 'n' enjoy!"

"In a minute."

Psycho. Two reasons had earned Aaron that namesake years prior. First, his deeply observant nature and extensive studies of behavior and the human condition. Those coupled with a natural propensity and curiosity provided him the ability to establish a swift, accurate read on most personalities and intentions. The second? A long history of taking extreme chances in battle. Many others, even the well trained and seasoned, considered him unhinged in his daring. Weapons expert. Lethal marksman. Hand-to-hand combat skills that bordered an unsettling side of effective. All those qualities made for deadly efficiency. Time had now honed the brash self-sacrificing to shrewd intensity. A more discerning courageousness. And so far, he remained alive and well, no matter if others considered him psychotic. It worked.

Shane, or Loverboy, a nickname that he embodied with zeal, spread his arms open. "A gorgeous day, a ship on the water, and a potential date in sight." A toothy grin flashed, and he inclined his head up to the upper deck. Alex had just appeared there next to the captain as their skipper took a break from his post. Shane's eager inspection lingered over her willowy form, which was covered by white capri pants and a mint-green tank top. "What more could a man ask for? Ha!"

Satisfied that no threat was imminent, except maybe from his jolly companion, Aaron stowed the binoculars and ran both hands through his tousled brown hair. He turned to rest his back against the railing and folded his arms.

Les, the consummate master, decent, professional, calm and cool in most any situation thrown at him, always presented a positive example. Having worked alongside the man for many years and countless missions, were Aaron to have a best friend, Les LeBeau would be it.

On the other hand, Shane could be a hothead. A scattered and unpredictable personality. Never their first choice for this job, he had been available last minute, though with only two prior assignments worked together to judge him on. But Shane *had* proved his worth during those as a strong and skilled combatant. The man just needed to exercise some self-control and keep his head in the game.

Dark blue-green gaze narrowed and intense, Aaron's eyes warned Shane: *Don't* cause problems.

Les reproved Shane too. "You know, we *are* here to do a job, not hit on the only chick on the boat. Plus you do remember the dollar aspect and just how much we're getting paid, don't you? And that it is her *brother* who is doing the paying?"

"Well of *course!*" Shane's retort faked injury. Playing up hurt feelings, he continued in an exaggerated wistful tone and hung his head. "You can't blame a guy for tryin' though." He perked back up with a hearty guffaw and turned to Aaron. "Speakin' of which, whatever happened to that last chick you were with, that hot brunette... You screw that up too?"

Les laughed at Shane. "Damn, man. I know we ain't pulled a job together in a while, but that's been a bloody *long* time ago. Keep up."

"Whatever." Shane sniffed and eyed Les before turning marked attention back to Aaron. "So? What about it?"

Aaron sighed. "It just didn't work."

"What, this lifestyle not her cup of tea?" Shane's lips twisted up as he persisted, continuing his dig, his payback for Aaron's silent reprimand. "Or was it just you?"

"You could say that." *To either point.* Whether in jest or not, his companion liked to bait and push, sometimes too far. And Shane well knew Aaron was not one to discuss his personal life. Or maybe the man had forgotten. His expression didn't change, but Aaron's jaw clenched and his shoulders tightened along with a growing pit in his stomach. That ending was *not* something he cared to bring to mind again.

Shane had struck the correct nerve. At the sudden tension, he puffed up his chest, took up a defensive stance, and arched an eyebrow. "Ya wanna try me? Could be fun."

Was the man actually serious? Aaron considered this as he noted the other's expression and subtle body language. That certainly wouldn't go well, though he could sense Shane was ready should he decide to vent any frustration. But Shane was dragging up old news. And Shane liked to play.

Shane's bluff of an attempt at intimidation left his face veined and ruddy, a sharp contrast to his buzz-cut blond hair. The platinum spikes caught the midmorning sun and caused Aaron to picture a sputtering volcano capped with snow. One corner of his mouth twitched upward. Irritation checked, he kept his gaze fixed on Shane, a look that still said *back the hell off.*

"Okay, okay. Geez! Not that big a deal! Damn, you guys are no fun at all!" Shane shook his head but laughed, turning more amiable. "Think I'll go find me some *prettier* company." He slapped Aaron on the arm and walked off to the nearest hatch.

"Boy doesn't have a chance." Les glanced over to Aaron. "Wanna take a bet on how far he gets?"

"No."

Aaron's short, matter-of-fact answer and mischievous expression made Les crack up. "Yeah, I know. Bloody crap bet."

Shane appeared several minutes later on the upper deck next to Alex and Captain Mac. His usual animated self, he smarted off, a little too loud, trying to make an impression. After a few more minutes, Alex laughed and walked away, leaving Loverboy to stand with the captain. Looking confounded. Typical.

"You know," Les observed in a low but humorous tone, "she is cute. You should…" He trailed off and backed away a step, feigning fear.

Quiet amusement laced Aaron's voice. "You guys *really* need to get lives."

Les laughed. "Just lookin' out for ya, mate."

Aaron gave Les a sly smile before turning more reflective. "Yeah, I know. It's just… not a good idea."

They stood in silence, Les tinkering with his rifle, Aaron lost in thought and staring at the deck.

After a time, Alex walked up. "You guys may want to come see this," she said, her voice conveying dread. She turned and walked back to the hatch.

Aaron watched her go, and Les watched him watch her.

"You were saying?" Les commented as they both took off to follow.

DISCOVERY
AND FORTUNE

CHAPTER 4

ALEX

CAPTAIN MAC, HIS FIRST MATE, and Jimmy stood on the bridge, examining the radar screen. It showed a blip—a small one—and it came and went. Something that could be another vessel and just within detection range.

"What do you think?" Jimmy asked.

Aaron studied it. He looked at Les.

"Could be nothing. A lost fisherman or floating junk," Les said. "Or... these guys will sometimes put out a scout disguised as just that."

"Keep an eye on it," Aaron instructed. "If anything changes, we're in earshot." He nodded at Les, and they both left for the foredeck.

Seconds later, Shane poked his head in the door. "Did I miss the party?" When Alex pointed forward, he said, "Thanks, darlin'!" He winked and scurried off after his companions.

AARON

THIS QUEST WAS MUCH MORE than just finding the downed plane. It had carried something or had surveillance data of something that somebody wanted pretty bad. Aaron didn't think Jimmy really accepted the details as is—according to what Aaron had been told, they'd been downplayed. And Jimmy had been brought in by the military for the express employment of his expertise in deep-sea exploration.

Jimmy figured, as they all did, that whatever lay below held incredible importance. Just the fact that Jimmy had brought on Aaron and his crew spoke to how much more seriously Jimmy was taking it. Still, the engineer felt comfortable enough to bring his sister and young son along, so he clearly wasn't extremely concerned.

Aaron drummed his fingers. Of course, the man probably hadn't been told everything. Just go find the plane, record the coordinates, get some pictures, call it a day. Pretty easy. Pretty standard. Only, they neglected to inform anyone just how perilous these nasty little jaunts could be.

ALEX

ALEX APPEARED AT AARON'S SIDE as he scanned the horizon. "Do you see anything?"

"Just… barely. It's way out. Miles." He lowered the binoculars and handed them to Shane.

Les sighted through his rifle scope. "They'll hang out there like that, sizing things up. Wait a few days till they think the time is right." He trailed off. "It could be serious. It could be junk. Just have to give it a wait and see."

Alex and Aaron exchanged a glance before she turned and walked off. Did the small smile and nod she'd offered him cover her alarm? And her sudden bashfulness at being that close to him? Unable to reconcile how those surges of disquiet threw her, she walked faster. She just needed some solitude.

The return path to her cabin stretched unusually long this time. Hatch secured behind her, she leaned back against the cool steel with a deep sigh. *Damn. What is it with all these oddball feelings? What is it about Aaron Donovan?*

She pushed off the door and went over to pull a duffel bag from under the bed. A quick probe through folded tops and she removed her pistol. The 9mm SIG, a gift from their father when she'd turned eighteen and planned to leave for college.

He'd surprised her with a trip to their local range, and they'd spent the day having her try out various pistols to see which felt best to her. The SIG P226 provided the perfect combination of grip, weight, and accuracy. Having watched her shoot his old Army 1911 at targets for years, her father had told her that no matter what she held, she could shoot a fly off the top of a telephone pole and leave the legs. That analogy had made her laugh and exclaim eww at the same time, especially as they'd been enjoying a spaghetti supper when he said it.

She giggled again at the memory as she looked over her chosen weapon. A quick check; full magazine, nothing chambered. She attached her holster inside her back waistband, tucked the pistol in, and pulled her shirt down over it. Maybe a hasty move on her part, but with the possibility of dangerous, unwanted visitors, she would rather be prepared. She went back out and up to the bridge to talk with her brother.

CHAPTER 5

AARON

ALEX'S CARRY CAUGHT AARON'S EYE as soon as he saw her again. This woman embodied much more than appearances held. For the present he resolved to just keep an eye on her. Would she handle it in a professional and careful manner? Or would she pose more of a danger to herself and others, being armed? He would wait and see, act in accordance if needed.

He didn't mention his insight to his team either, choosing to see how long it took each to pick up on this new facet. Les always used discretion in his observations, a word in private or directional nod his preferred method, likely coming in short order. Shane, however, could be more publicly vocal. The fact that she was armed was something they had all missed. He was certain no one else on the ship knew either as her brother would have been sure to inform him at the outset. One of the conditions for the job, for everyone's safety, was that he and his team have knowledge of all weapons on board, all personnel trained and using those weapons if trouble arose, who would be a continual carry. Otherwise, this oversight wouldn't constitute a big deal.

A day later, after dinner, Shane called him out on it.

"Great. Just great. That's *all* we need! A woman with a gun. Might as well slap a goddamn bow on it and *gift* it to the enemy!" Shane's tone became accusatory as he voiced his growing displeasure to his companions. He confronted Aaron, all but demanding an explanation, and rested a hand on his own holstered pistol. "Thought you checked everybody out, knew who all had the guns on this bucket."

All three were now aware of the pistol Alex wore at her back. The average person wouldn't notice, but to them the concealment shone obvious.

Aaron traded a knowing glance with Les, spoke to soothe Shane. "It's no problem. I'll talk with her and see what's what." He held Shane's gaze until the other shrugged and looked away. Aaron watched him a moment longer. *Man sure has some issues. But then I guess in one way or another, don't we all?*

He sighed and rubbed the back of his neck as he turned and strolled closer to the edge to peer down to the next level. Alex Thomas, what a conundrum. Contemplating now what could end up a confrontation with her, his gut took a jump and a constrained tingle slid through his veins. These sensations were not a normal part of his existence, and they caused him to hedge with reflection.

In general, he found social interactions with women easy and enjoyable, and he had no problem with someone considering him attractive, whether the attention was wanted or not. Sometimes that interest was a good thing… other times, not so much. Long gone were the days that he'd blow off comments, and at times loathe allusions to good looks. That awkward aspect in youth had transformed. His sweet boyish smile and well-timed wink could be quite disarming, a distraction tactic if the situation called for it, but always the best when he found himself engaged in a natural, honest connection.

This woman. Why was she shy and elusive with him? And were those aspects drawing him to her? At least he now allowed himself to acknowledge the fact existed. Was it an attraction of perceived mystery, a desire for something appearing kept away, a challenge? No, it was greater than that, otherwise he'd have already made an effort. He was also reserved, and it wasn't just because of it not being a good idea to get involved with a charge, as he'd told Les. Nor despite a personal decision he'd made some time ago to take a big step back from any attempt at a relationship for a while. But what *was* this weird entangling essence? Hell, they'd only been on the water three days!

Three days… More than enough time for him to trust in his instincts about her that he *did* want to know her. She intrigued him.

Her energy was almost palpable as they'd approached the ship's plank to board, and he didn't need to look when Les confirmed her bridge-roof position to him. Could it have just been his natural keen awareness? No, this was a captivation. Lucky for him, banter with her brother created enough distraction to hide any confusion. Only later as he stowed his duffel in his cabin could he get a handle on centering and calming himself. He had to figure out that something more that he couldn't quite grasp. That strange pull that at the same time felt maybe just a little… frightening? It made him unsure of how he should approach her. So far. This little diversion, however, if not so common for the average woman, would be a perfect icebreaker.

He admired her lithe form, cross-legged on the deck, immersed in the sunset. To prevent strands obscuring her view, one hand attempted to restrain waves of hair against the light sea breeze. Her other arm rested across shapely thighs. She carried a gentle presence about her that overshadowed a tangible independent streak. That innocence was what he saw now, and he almost hated to disturb her serenity. Almost. After observing her some moments more, he hopped the rail.

CHAPTER 6

ALEX

THAT JUMPY YET EXHILARATING INFLUENCE had continued to permeate Alex since they'd left port. And it wasn't caused by whatever lurked on their horizon, though that discovery *had* upped the level of unease for all on board. At this point she still just passed it off as a product of her foreign surroundings. The inspiration of this unusual adventure. This conclusion did not, however, take away the underlying current of an indescribable *something* that coursed through her. If anything, that force was intensifying. At least it wasn't a bad feeling. Rather an excited, anticipatory joy, like the nervous butterflies of waiting in line for a roller coaster.

Gazing at the sunset, she allowed her thoughts to drift. Watercolor wisps of magenta, tangerine, yellows and purples of cirrus clouds glowed their reflection as the sun kissed the ocean's cool gray horizon. The camera beside her already contained its array of photos. The enchanting sight calmed her, and her eyelids developed a heaviness as the bright globe slid lower. Maybe she'd call it an early night tonight.

The form landing several feet from her jerked her from reverie. Aaron Donovan. Alex greeted him as he approached. *Um...* that look on his face! Was she in trouble? Stern and cool, hard to read. But no, there shouldn't be anything wrong. Besides, his regular prevailing facial expression *did* tend toward the more serious.

"Hey," Aaron replied to her greeting as he walked over from his landing point. He dropped to sit beside her. With a brief inclination of his head and a flick of his eyes to her waist, he got right to the point. "So, I see you're carrying."

Taken just a little aback at the abrupt statement and still recovering from his unexpected appearance, she eyed him. "Wow. You... really are a straightforward kind of guy."

His steady stare never wavered as she met his gaze.

She'd had yet to experience substantial personal contact with any of the protection team. Well, except for that big blond one's less than tactful overtures of affection. One of those pesky types that refused to take no for an answer. *Yikes.* Was that Shane guy serious or just having fun? Likely both if she were to give in. *No. Way.* At least he wasn't aggressive about it. Just persistent. Yep, Loverboy fit him to a T. He had a funny, if raunchy, sense of humor and always seemed to be joking, but there was an edge there that gave her an odd feeling. And not the good kind.

The tall sniper, Les LeBeau, a genuine good guy judging by the way he interacted with her nephew, was always polite. An easy jovialness. Friendly and respectful, like a protective big brother. Care Bear was a perfect nickname for him. That man exuded a calm confidence while remaining utterly laid-back. Everyday stressors wouldn't give him the slightest concern. Maybe that just came with the territory.

And Aaron Donovan? *Psycho?* Wonder where he'd picked *that* name up? It didn't seem to fit his personality or actions. He came off with that same cool assurance as Les, just not quite as low-key. Maybe a play on that? Maybe there was something more she would learn about him to justify it. *If* she got to know him. Up until now he'd barely spoken to her, though he'd always offered an honest and affable smile in passing. Along with their several mutual covert glances. This would be a first of any real conversation with Aaron. For what *that* was looking to be worth…

She studied him as he waited for her response. With the late-evening sun highlighting his features, a sudden awe swept through her at just how handsome he was. Even with that sober countenance. Blue-green irises rimmed and flecked with deep gray, green and gold striations at the pupils; those steadfast eyes held her with complete immersion. *Wow, how beautiful…* Yet *another* seeming paradox to a tough exterior. That mesmerizing kaleidoscope of focus, a curious intensity, yet somehow… heartbroken? Familiar misery of ancient childhood forlorn longings jumped to mind with a swift kick to her chest. Just like at the dock. Right before… *What the…? Why?*

She ripped her focus from his face, breaking their visual connection, hoping he would judge the confusion that flashed through her as just a reaction to his question. Plus her scrutiny had done nothing to persuade further dialogue from him. She pulled herself together, swallowed at the burning in her throat, and in one motion removed the pistol from her waistband, ejected the magazine into her lap, and checked the chamber. With that, she flipped it around and presented it to a somewhat surprised Aaron.

Aaron took the weapon from her, raising an eyebrow at how deftly she'd handled it. He looked over her choice of sidearm, turned his gaze back on her, and handed it back.

"Just like to know who has what. And that you know what to do with it. Can't take chances." He was dead serious but offered her a warm grin.

She grinned back. It was the first time she'd seen genuine lightheartedness from him up close. The mischievous, slightly crooked smile and the way the lines at the corners of his eyes and mouth crinkled gave him a childlike quality that contrasted the usual stoic visage. Waning sunlight cast a reddish tint to medium brown hair that held maybe a hint of silver creeping in at the temples. A faint half-inch heart-shaped scar impressed his left cheekbone. The odd energetic charge surged again. She concealed a shiver. An excited shyness she hadn't felt in some time threatened to overtake her, and she averted her eyes back to the orange horizon and setting sun.

Alex reset the magazine and returned her pistol to her back. *Good Lord, this man's gonna think I'm a nervous wreck.* As she regained her wits and corralled the hair that now drifted across her face, her thoughts turned back to the initial reason he had approached her at this moment. Having dealt with more than enough derisive comments over the years, from boys and men alike, concerning females and weapons, she was not at all unsettled by the questioning. "Gee, and I thought it was just because I'm a girl."

Another lopsided grin and a wink did nothing to help her composure.

"Nope. I know girls can shoot. Just not all girls. And not all guys, for that matter."

CHAPTER 7

ALEX

ALEX STOOD AT THE SHIP'S rail, eyes closed. A brief morning meditation time by herself to set intentions for her day… interrupted by the scrumptious scent of coffee and croissant… close! Her lids snapped open to rising steam. A cup of coffee and a small plate of pastries just in front of her chin were held by strong hands at the end of arms extending from behind her. She twisted around to see who was displaying this surprise postbreakfast offering.

"Aaron! Hey." She blinked at him.

Aaron responded with an almost shy boyish, lopsided smirk. "Morning." He brought his arms back and held the items between them. "Um, I thought you might like a little breakfast... dessert?"

Alex couldn't have held back her grin if she'd tried. After their unexpected talk about her concealed carry the prior evening, she'd gone to sleep wondering what he thought of her, thinking about his smile, if or when they would talk again. Hoping...

"That's so sweet of you. Of course. Thank you." With that she leaned forward to take in a large whiff of the steaming coffee.

Aaron's smile widened. "Great. Uh, here." He handed her the plastic mug and small plate. Once they were secure in her grasp, he bent to retrieve his own mug from the floorboards. "Follow me."

They walked forward to the ship's bow and took seats on the deck at the rail. Neither spoke at first, just sipped their coffee. Alex wasn't sure what to say. This complete reversal from his perceived avoidance to him now seeking her out left her flummoxed. She grasped a coherent question at last and opened her mouth to speak just as he did also. They giggled at each other.

"You go first," Aaron said and took a bite of croissant.

"Okay. I was just gonna ask you what happened to your morning meeting? Don't you guys usually reserve this time for, I don't know, your daily strategizing?"

Aaron swallowed his bite. "We were. Don't really need to now, I mean not beyond a 'hey, if anything looks weird, check in.' We're all set, no need to repeat every day. We hang out enough. Hash out anything we need to then."

Alex nodded. "So you decided to bring me treats instead?" *Okay, that sounded kinda dumb.* She sipped her coffee and kept the mug close to offset any redness in her warming cheeks.

Aaron chuckled and looked at the plate in front of him. "A peace offering. Thought I might have been a little less than tactful last night. Maybe prove that I am a nice guy. At times." He fiddled with his coffee cup as he looked back up at her.

"At times." Alex grabbed her lower lip in her teeth to keep her smile from getting too big.

"Sometimes." He winked at her.

Alex giggled. That was a loaded *sometimes*. She didn't know him well enough to respond with spicy wit. Not yet. Not that she would have come up with anything on the fly anyway.

"So, what brings you out here?" Aaron asked between sips of coffee. "I mean, I know your relation to our researcher. But otherwise, why did you want to come?"

It took Alex a few moments to reply. She hadn't spent much time thinking about the reason beyond adventure and family time, though that deeper logic existed. From the inflection in his voice, he was looking for that something more from her, the underlying why. "Family of course. A fun adventure. I guess, other than what you already see, I wanted something completely different from what I've experienced before. I needed to… get away, see my life from a different perspective." She stopped and stared at her mug. "I've chosen safe and ordinary, at least what seems ordinary to me, too many times."

"Well, you're here now. You're doing something. That's the first big step if you really want change."

Alex looked up into his eyes. They shone with a kind softness. *Wow, he really does care.* "Yeah, I guess I am."

"Don't take that for granted." He went on. "Not everyone will take action when they need change. You're braver than you may think."

She shook her head. "That's what my brother said the other day."

"Well, it's true. I've seen too many people just sit and complain about their lives and never lift a finger to change anything. It's too bad really. They'd rather stay stuck in what they think is safe even if it makes them feel like shit every day. But that's their choice. Change can be hard, but it's also rewarding. And when you know it's right, you need to go after what you want."

"Thank you. Really."

"You got it." He patted her knee. "What do you do back home?"

"My best friend and I run a small shop. Art and photography. I'm the photography half."

"Where at?"

"West Coast small town. She moved out there a while back. I just did last year."

"Sounds nice. You like it?"

"I do," she replied. "Someday I'm gonna move to the middle of nowhere though. I've always wanted to. Lou, she's my best friend, and I have camped a few times in the mountains, and I'm hooked. But in all honesty, I've been hooked since I was little. Nothing like being surrounded by tall pines and amazing views."

"I won't argue with that one bit."

"What about you?" Alex asked. "How did you get started in this, and how long have you been doing what you do?"

"Yeah, well, that's a long story. For another time. The getting started part anyway." Aaron chuckled into his coffee cup before taking a drink, then looked out at the ocean. "For now, I do like what I do. We keep people safe from the worst. Lots of travel. It's been good, as it can be, for quite a few years."

"So, is there anything exciting you can tell me?"

A dark, side-eyed smirk from him. "If I tell you, I'll have to kill you." He finished with a quick eyebrow hike.

Alex burst into laughter.

"No, really."

"Right…" She rolled her eyes at him. "You mentioned travel. How many continents have you been on?"

"All of 'em."

"Okay, yeah, that's… Wow, all?"

He nodded.

"How many countries?"

"Name some."

Alex stared into his humor-lit eyes. What would be the more obscure or improbable places she could come up with? "How about Siberia?"

Another nod.

"How many times?"

"Just once thankfully. At least for the reason I was there. Beyond that, it's a beautiful place."

"Uh-oh. The reason you were there wasn't good?"

A pained look flashed across his face before a naughty smirk replaced it. "Remember, I'll have to kill you…"

"Oh geez." She smacked his knee. A sigh and she took a big bite of croissant. "What about…" *Think out of the way here.* "Antarctica? Staying with the cold theme."

A lighthearted look this time. "Once also. And I will say a little about that. Protection detail. It was an educational expedition. One of the students was a kid with high-profile parents. Parents who from time to time received threats. Nice people, mind you, just that that more exposed life sometimes attracts the wrong element. It was a little like this." He gestured, indicating their current voyage. "No team though, just me. I went as a chaperone. It was a cool trip really, no pun intended." He laughed. "Ten days. And no complications. My charge and the others loved learning about the ship and the continent."

"Aww, that sounds so fun!"

"It was a good assignment."

"Have you ever had to do that other times, pretend you're someone you're not? I mean *we* all know that you're here for protection on this trip, and I guess, well, you're *you*. But like on that trip where you were a 'chaperone' and they didn't know the truth?"

Aaron opened his mouth and shut it, turned to look out at the ocean.

That pained look again. *Oh God, I upset him!* Alex shoved the last of her pastry into her mouth as her chest started to feel tight. She finished and swallowed the bite. "I'm sorry. I shouldn't ask so much."

He offered her a brief smile. "Don't be sorry about being curious." He looked down at his coffee cup and spun it a couple of times. "All right, this one is from *way* back in the day. Before… anyway, this team I ended up with, they needed access to certain individuals. That was part of my skill set. So, it's a black-tie affair in…" He halted and sighed. "Let's just say on the European continent. My objective is to get the high-profile target away from the event and as secluded as possible so the team can have a chat with him." Another pause. "In that case, the target might have deserved some of what he got. At any rate, my assignment is to get this guy alone for them. He has this poodle that he's just obsessed with. And when that poor little creature isn't with *him*, it's tended to by his mistress. And she had her own proclivities that didn't just pertain to him. Ahead of time, we researched these people, looking at likes and dislikes, searching for patterns of activity. As it turns out, she has a thing for hooking up with new partners in secluded outdoor settings at lavish events. And get this, knowing all the while that he will come find her in said compromising position and fight it out with the unfortunate new lover."

Alex sat back and raised an eyebrow.

Aaron shook his head. "I know. Weird game. So I'm the new guy in this scenario. I make contact, flirt, boost her ego. We sneak out of the party and head for a spot she's used before in a tall growth garden, pup in tow. I keep her attention on me, target shows up, the team shows up, my job is done."

Alex sat with a wide-eyed, dubious stare. What an unconventional story! "Uh, so did you, you know…?"

"You mean did I sleep with…? God no. Not that…" His nose wrinkled in distaste. "No."

"Sorry. I mean that's good. I mean…" She stammered as heat flushed her cheeks. Why was it important for her to hear that? She barely knew him. Why should it matter what he did?

"Well, which is it? Sorry or good?"

"Good." Her cheeks grew hotter, and she shook her head at him. "Just please, go on."

He laughed at her. "Remember, you asked. Okay, well, the whole funny thing about this is, the target is more worried about his *dog* than her. No matter what these guys do to him, he's yelling the whole time about getting that dog back inside and safe."

Alex still couldn't come up with accurate words to express the mixed emotions swimming through her. "I don't know what to say. That's… not at all the kind of story I expected you to tell me." She tried to collect herself. "Do you still, um, do those things?"

"No. No, that was way before. These protection details we do now are nothing like… We don't deceive the people who hire us." He paused and rubbed the back of his neck. "That wasn't a good scene back then. Something I *never* should have gotten mixed up in. And what I told you, even as bad as it may come off, was one of the lighter moments."

"Well, it was a funny story. In a way. Was the little dog okay?"

"Oh yeah, that dog was *very* well cared for. The one good thing about those people. They genuinely *loved* that dog. Last I saw of it, it was being carried back to the mansion by the mistress. After she got done screaming and cussing me out."

Alex laughed. "You obviously made quite the impression."

Aaron side-eyed her. "Yeah, just not the kind of impression she was hoping for."

"At least you did the right thing in that respect."

Aaron nodded but said nothing and turned a haunted gaze out to the water again.

Alex watched him. The look in his eyes told of a darker aspect he avoided. What was going on in that head of his? A fascinating if oddball story that last one, and he seemed deeply troubled by things that happened in that time period of his life. Her heart ached for him for whatever might have occurred that hurt him.

"Thank you. For breakfast dessert. And for the stories." She laid a hand on his knee.

"You're welcome." He turned back to her. "You're really interested in this stuff?"

"Of course," she replied. "It was fun. And intriguing."

"Well, I've got tons more. If you want to hear. I don't usually talk about it. Most I won't. But there're some cool places. And a few other scenarios you might like." He tilted his head. "You want breakfast dessert tomorrow?"

Alex's heart skipped. *Really?* This man was interesting, well-traveled, and had a widely varied history. Not to mention how she felt being around him. And he was also interested in her! He genuinely wanted to spend time with her, know her thoughts and feelings, share his stories. *Yes!*

"I'd love that."

"It's a date then."

Oh shit, a date? Alex's grin overtook any thought of playing it cool.

CHAPTER 8

ALEX

"FRISBEE!"

"Frisbee?" Alex's eyebrows shot up. Her questioning of her nephew on what fun things he might want to do for the day had elicited that as his first choice.

"Yes!" Will replied, jumping in place. "I *love* Frisbee!"

Alex winked and shook her head. "I love Frisbee too, bud. But remember, we are on a ship. We can't throw it very hard or it'll go over the side."

"I know. I promise I will try not to. *Pleeease?*"

"Okay," Alex agreed. "I'll try too. Let's go get it."

They retrieved the toy from the mess lounge and returned to the main aft deck to play. While not being a comfort for the hot weather they'd experienced over the past week, the near nonexistent breeze proved very helpful toward not carrying away the Frisbee. They were able to get in about thirty minutes of throwing and laughing before an errant toss by the young boy sent the bright turquoise disk over the rail and into the ocean.

Will's frolicsome eyes transformed to enormous brown orbs, and he clamped his hands over his mouth, staring at his aunt.

Alex bit her lip and smiled back at him. "Oops."

They made their way over to the railing.

"Aww, man," Will said, his cherubic face falling into dejection. He and Alex looked over and down at the smooth water below and the Frisbee drifting away. "Epic fail."

"Well, it did work out for a while," Alex said and ruffled Will's blond hair. "We'll let someone know and get a new one for the crew when we get back if they don't recover it. Any other ideas before it gets too hot?"

He turned to her, his studious look exaggerated as he tapped his chin with one finger, his other hand resting on his hip. "Hmmm... Well... What about... baseball!" His eyes lit up as he came to his decision.

"We can't hit, but we can throw," Alex said. "And we'll have to be careful to not let the balls go over too."

"Yeesss!" Will exclaimed as he took off, Alex in tow, to retrieve the bag of baseballs from the room he shared with his father. "And don't worry—it's okay if we lose a couple 'cause I have a lot!"

After a quick stop to inform about the Frisbee situation, they gathered the balls and a duffel with several gloves and headed back up to the aft deck. Will played ball back home, and it wasn't often that he went anywhere without his gear if he could help it. He grabbed his glove as Alex sifted through to find one for herself. The closest fit flopped a little loose but would work.

They threw for a time, high flies, grounders, pitches, and some just tossing back and forth.

"Can I do some fast pitches?"

"Bring it," Alex replied with a wink.

Will threw a couple. They zipped fast but a little wide, and Alex had to run after and retrieve them. Then one clapped solid in her glove.

"Nice one!" she called out to him. Another good one. The next slapped hard, stinging her palm. She tossed the ball back to him and removed her hand from her glove, rubbed it, and shook it out before replacing the protective cover. "Ow," she said, and Will giggled.

The next throw went wild, and she ran to collect it. Next one in the glove. The pitch after flew outside again and she dove for it but missed. The small sphere bounced away behind her. She rolled onto her back and lay there on the deck, resting her gloved hand across her eyes to block the sun. The scent of worn leather filled her nostrils.

A little out of breath now from chasing the strays, she called out to Will, "Just a sec!"

Sun-drenched floorboards warmed her back, too heated for comfort, and a few seconds later she moved to get up and go retrieve the ball. Brightness flooded her eyelids as she took the mitt away from her face. Ah, sunny days. About to roll to stand, an eclipse flickered across her sight as the missed globe sailed above her, back to Will.

"Hi, Aaron!" Will called out.

Alex blinked at Will and followed his line of sight back the other way.

Aaron walked toward her. He waved to the boy as he strolled up to stand beside her, his shadow protecting her from the sun's glare. Luminous radiance streaked out around the sturdy outline of his body in a halo effect.

He gave her a quick eyebrow raise in greeting. "Want some help?" He extended a hand.

"My hero."

She reached up and grasped strong fingers. A warm, sparking rush surged through her digits and up her arm, and she nearly let go. His hold remained firm, and she reasserted hers. Maybe catching all those fast pitches had affected her nerves? But... that was her other hand... He pulled her on up to her feet.

"Thanks."

The briefest of frowns and a fleeting hint of question flashed through his eyes. He nodded to her. "Got room for a couple more?"

"Sure," she replied as Shane strode up to join them.

"Hey, sweetie!" Shane made a show of a lingering touch to her back and his purposeful move between them as he passed through, not hiding a risqué wink to Aaron. He headed for the bag of gloves and greeted Will as the boy ran over and began pulling more out.

Alex shared a near simultaneous eye roll with Aaron. She removed her glove and handed it to him. "You can take my place for a while actually. I'm gonna sit out for a bit. You may want a different glove though," she added as Aaron glanced over to the two rummaging through mitts.

He stuck the glove she'd given him on his hand, flexed his fingers, shrugged, and smiled at her. "It'll work." He stepped out a few feet from her and whistled to Will, punching his fist into the glove once and holding it up. "Right here!"

She watched the two men and her nephew throw for a few minutes. *Aaron Donovan... why can't I get you out of my head?* A rather intimate dream had roused her from sound sleep that morning, in turn leaving her with a warm fuzzy aftereffect and the distinct recollection of his eye color. Their now regular after-breakfast hangout had been postponed as he'd had a meeting with Jimmy and Mac, but a near-miss collision with him later in one of the passageways resulted in shared laughter, a borderline flirtatious quip from him, and her thankfulness that, as he'd had some errand or other, she hadn't had to hold a coherent conversation. She blushed again at the recollection. *That'll teach me to daydream and not pay attention.*

She turned away and made her way down to the galley to select a pack of water from the refrigeration unit. Cold air against overwarm skin caused a chill when she opened the door, and she lingered a few extra seconds in its invigorating embrace. As she walked back, Alex inspected her hand, folding and extending her fingers a couple of times. Had she bent her wrist wrong and pinched a nerve as Aaron grabbed her hand? No odd tingling now. She rotated the joint. *I think I may be losing my mind.*

Upon returning to the deck, she moved over to a large storage crate. It lay tucked in the shade, and she positioned herself there, sitting cross-legged on top. She pulled out a water and twisted off the cap. Refreshing liquid slid down her throat to cool her insides. Over half was gone before she recapped it and set what remained beside her on the crate. Aaron glanced over to her, and she held up the water bottles for him to see. He nodded before sending the ball back to Will.

Watching the two men throw and catch pitches with her nephew, Alex contemplated just how wrong her initial thoughts were about having the hired guns on board. Though they were, beyond any doubt, all business when it came to tactics and weapons, they had integrated well with the crew and her family. Taking the time to carefully familiarize everyone with plans in case the worst happened, they did so in a way that was instructional, to the point, reality based, and at the same time not upsetting for Will. They made sure Will felt secure while still understanding what he would need to do in case they were boarded by hostiles. Aaron had even met alone with Captain Mac, her brother, nephew and her on a separate plan just for their family. Just in case.

Will took to them right away, and they regularly spent some of their downtime with him in various activities. Alex appreciated that for Will more than she could say, since there were no children for him to play with on board. And for all of them. Instead of being the complete hard-asses she'd first expected, she found them to be just regular guys with a rather irregular profession. Maybe they could be cold, tough, and terrifying when it came down to a situation, but otherwise she found them fun and interesting. A warmth filled her heart. She'd uncapped her water to finish it when Les appeared next to her.

"Hey, Les," she said. "You ready to play too?"

"Absolutely," he replied and gave her a quick smile. "I think your brother is on his way down too in a bit."

"Good," she said. Jimmy was putting in long hours and more than deserved to get in some relaxation time. "I take it all's well?"

Les took a water, swallowed a mouthful, and nodded. "Yep. Whatever's out there on the horizon is still out there. And they're still just runnin' sweeps below." He nodded down as he spoke to indicate the continued scanning of the ocean floor. "No change."

Shane hollered at him from across the deck.

"Have fun," Alex told Les as he trotted off to choose a glove and join in.

Will was in heaven having so many to play with, and it showed in his glowing grin. Alex smiled again and finished her water. As she laid the empty bottle down beside her, she discovered that Les had deposited a small cooler behind her on the crate. She opened it to find twelve beers and a couple of sports drinks inside. About to close it up again, she stopped when Jimmy walked up. He pulled out a beer, popped the tab, and took a drink.

"Hey, sis."

"Hey, you." She nudged his arm. "You look like you're ready for some time off."

"Oh yeah," he replied with a hearty sigh. He set the half-finished beer down beside her. "Definitely ready." He jogged out to his son, who greeted him with a hug and Jimmy's regular glove.

CHAPTER 9

ALEX

IT HAD BEEN TWO AND a half weeks since the first sighting of the mystery vessel, almost three weeks into their mission. Having determined the object on their skyline was not trash, as said garbage would have either floated out of range or closer to them soon after initial discovery, the radar showed it maintaining a too precise, even distance from their position. All had settled into the uneasy routine of going about their business and trying to get in some occasional relaxation, all the while keeping a watchful eye on the horizon and that blip.

Soon after breakfast, Alex stood on the upper deck at the rail. Warmth of the early-day sun refreshed her where it touched her skin. For the moment anyway. Another hot day lay ahead, and with any luck the current light breeze would remain to help comfort them. Sea air, soft and tranquil, swaddled a perfect morning. Swirling, invisible zephyrs shifted her hair and shirt. Closing her eyes for a time, she allowed the feeling of that present coolness to wash over her.

A stronger flurry gave her a chill, and her eyelids fluttered open to reveal Aaron on the deck now, farther forward. Sitting at the rail, legs over the edge, he leaned on the middle rung, chin resting on crossed arms. His feet dangled, swaying like a child daydreaming in a tree house, as he stared out over the steel blue of the water. Now-familiar black tactical clothed lower extremities. Lean muscles the length of his relaxed back contoured refined yet powerful lines into the thin gray material of his T-shirt. Sunlight glinted gold on tanned, sinewy biceps. The gust that had startled her ruffled the tousled top of his hair.

Wow. Momentarily transfixed, she blinked herself back and rubbed her eyes.

Though seeming distant at first, since he'd opened up more to her, their now-frequent talks highlighted her days. He was quite fun if still somewhat mysterious. While eager to share stories with her, he always held back. Like he wanted to say more but couldn't. Purposely vague descriptions of assignments past, many radically different than their present, only scratched the surface with just enough detail to provide intriguing tales while still not revealing murky truths. Deep secrets that would cloud cheery smiles from time to time. He was always quick to disguise the less savory details with humor, but the implications didn't evade her notice when those sufferings escaped his eyes.

She marveled at the variety of assignments he shared with her, the many specialized portrayals he'd taken on. An ease of transforming to what was required of him. Handsome, in a rugged sort of way, he was a man who would be just as comfortable in a flannel shirt and Levi's or a Tom Ford suit, depending what the situation called for. So many places he'd been, so many experiences. Despite the harsh conditions and dramatic events that had long been his life, he had a way of making her feel at ease, in a way she'd never known. A calmness, a soft side that brought her a sense of comfort and home.

After this trip, would she see him again? Would this go anywhere? Or was it just a sweet, passing friendship? For all her intent to avoid romantic entanglement for a good long while, this one had sure changed up that scenario. Alex found herself more and more longing to stay in touch. There was something different here, about him, a curious and unusual pull. The depth of their connection had grown so fast it at times left her mind reeling. Could this be real?

What am I thinking? Would he even have room for her in his life, for a real relationship? Or the time? Much as she would love to find out, he would have to be the one to express such an interest. He would likely be off to another part of the world after this, then another. But if he did show the sentiment, she would make a go of it. She had to. This felt... right. Her imagination guided her through several of his more daring adventures and ended with her visualizing him in a tux. And less. Heat grew in her cheeks. *Oh stop! We're not even close to that yet...* She pulled herself together and walked over to join him.

Aaron looked up as Alex approached. "Hey."

"Hey." She sat down next to him, swung her legs over alongside his, and scooted up to lean on the rail. Sunlit ripples sparked the water's surface, cheerful and carefree. "Anything new today?"

He shrugged. "No change in them," he said and nodded out in the general direction of the distant vessel. After a moment, he spoke again. "It's just odd though."

His furrowed brow was obvious, but the deep concern in his dark eyes struck her most.

"What's odd?"

"Well," he continued, "generally—and I do just mean generally as there are really no hard-and-fast rules when it comes to pirates—they only watch and wait a few days max before they make a move. They're greedy. And impatient." He shook his head. "These guys, you know, it's been over two weeks since we first saw 'em. It's like they're waiting for something. They know we haven't moved much. That makes us an even easier target for…" He trailed off as he caught her gaze. "Hey, it's okay." He put his hand on hers. "They're still way out there. It may stay that way." He gave her a wink and a smile. "No reason to worry unless they head this way."

Alex breathed the care off her face, glanced out at the ocean, back to him. *Guess I must've looked a little more freaked than I thought.* "So you say," she commented, sarcasm edging her tone. "But you guys are what, ex–Special Forces or something?" She eyed him. "If you're worried, I'm worried. Just sayin'."

Looking back out at the ocean, he chuckled. "Well, I guess you do have a point." He returned his eyes to her. "But seriously, try to not let it bother you too much. We've all gone over what to do. You, everyone, know exactly what to do." His hand still covered hers on the rail. The tenderness of his touch and his steady eyes helped comfort her concern. "It will be all right. Trust me."

She shook her head and smiled back at him. "Okay. If you say so." His words and confidence brought her more to ease, but that little edge of worry remained. Well, maybe not so little.

"We'll just take it day by day," he said. "Do what we gotta do and make the best of it." He eyed her. "Hey, where's your camera? You're never without that."

"Will's still got it. I gave it to him again for the day yesterday," she replied. "He *loves* taking pictures. He was so excited."

"Yeah, he was bugging us pretty bad for pics yesterday," Aaron recalled. "Well, good. He should've had fun then."

"Yep. I told him not too many, but I know he burned through the rest of my card," she said with a laugh. "Luckily I always bring a spare."

They talked for a while, about things, about nothing. After some time, Alex's curiosity got the better of her. She'd held off so far, but with their incessant daily chats, grew brave enough to ask. "You've told me some really amazing stories. So, what *did* you do? Officially. Before this, being for hire."

Something flashed in his eyes that was just as quickly shut down with a tight smile and shake of his head.

Aaron once more turned his gaze out over the ocean. He didn't answer, his vision now seeming focused on the distant line of the horizon, that subtle demarcation of hue that differentiated sky from sea.

Oh God, did I just piss him off? "It's okay, never mind. I just assumed military, Special Forces, special ops, something like that. You don't have to talk about it."

He chuckled, gave her a warm grin that put her back at ease, and after a moment replied. "Well… special *something*. You're kinda right. It's complicated."

"Hmm. 'It's complicated,' he says. Now I'm *really* wondering." She nudged him with her shoulder, relief flooding through her that she hadn't upset him.

He looked over at her, one corner of his mouth still turned up, the creases at the corners of his eyes deepening as he squinted against the brightening sunlight.

"Okay then," she said, studying him. "So… what do you do *now* when you're not doing this? Or is that some big secret too?"

He laughed at her question. "No, no big secret. Just planning, really. Kinda hoping this will be my last job, at least doing this type of stuff." He stretched and pulled one knee up. Resting an arm on it, he began picking at chipped white paint on the rail with his thumbnail, all at once lost in his own world. "Then I know exactly the where and the what. Pretty much off the grid. But…" He gazed out at the ocean again before bringing marked attention back to Alex. "There are still a few details I haven't quite nailed down yet."

"Well, that's still a little vague. But off the grid is sweet. Sounds intriguing," she replied, curious.

He raised an eyebrow. "You actually *like* the idea of off the grid?"

She just smiled and leaned on the rail again, resting her chin on crossed arms. "You have no idea."

Alex waited for him to offer more detail of his retirement plans or question her further on her reply, but he remained silent. She turned her head to face him, resting her cheek on her arms. For all his seeming straightforwardness, he remained a mystery. And it was so hard to tell from his expression sometimes what he was feeling. But his eyes were still showing her a genuine curiosity and lightheartedness at their conversation.

After a minute, she said, "Got anyone waiting on you to get out? Wherever home is?"

"Um, no. It just... doesn't work out for me. This lifestyle's not really conducive to what I'd call a real relationship. How 'bout you?" He bounced the question back, quick to get the focus off himself.

"No. Bad split a year and a half ago. Then a friend tried to set me up six months later, under extreme protest, I might add." She groaned. "Then lucky me, that turned into kind of a stalker. So I've pretty much just said screw it for now."

"Well, saying *that* isn't gonna turn off some guys."

His roguish comment didn't register right off, but the humorous sparkle in his blue-green eyes at last brought her to understanding. "Oh! Crap. I guess that really didn't come out quite right, did it?" She blushed at her poor choice of words.

He continued to stare at her, clearly trying to stifle a full-on laugh as he took in her rose-red face, her lower lip now in her teeth, her bashful eyes peering back at him.

"Quit!" she exclaimed and smacked his knee with the back of her hand.

"Hey, you're the one who said it," he shot back, actually laughing now, and grabbed her hand before she could whack him again.

She gave him a stern but playful pout as she yanked her hand back in protest.

They sat there a few moments, recovering from their giggles in silence before Alex asked him another question. "Do *they* know you're getting out?"

"Les does," Aaron replied. "I've worked with ol' Care Bear off and on for years. Shane? I doubt it. This is only the third job he's been on with us." He snickered as he shook his head. "Loverboy wasn't even supposed to be on this one. Our other regular, Simon? Had a sudden illness pop up. Shane was available, so we picked him up. Boy can be a little questionable with some of his methods, but he is awful handy in a firefight."

Her hand rested on the deck beside her and he put his down next to it, his pinky finger covering hers. His gaze was once again on the ocean. *Not that subtle there, bud.* Her heart raced. Even without the sparkling rush of his physical contact, she'd have been drawn to him. This just enhanced the connection she felt even more. Now used to the curious sensation that emanated when he touched her, she put her attention on that warm, pulsating current. If he noticed it too, he wasn't saying. And she wasn't ready to address that subject just yet. Maybe a roundabout approach?

"So, question for you: What's your opinion of paranormal?"

He looked over at her. "What, like ghosts, or more like destiny and fate?"

"Um… maybe both?"

"I'm open-minded. You have to admit, there's plenty that goes on in the world that can't be explained. I believe there's more. A lot more to life than what we see."

"Okay. Can I tell you something? And will you promise me you won't be freaked out and you'll still talk to me?"

He laughed and cocked his head at her. "Hmm. Don't know. Might have to throw you overboard."

"Fine. I'll keep it to myself."

He chuckled again and brushed her hair back off her cheek and shoulder. "No, tell me. Seriously."

Where to begin? Could she really tell him at this moment about what his physical touch did to her? How weird would that sound? She racked her brain for what to say, now faced with his intense focus. Maybe not that yet. Maybe...

She took a long breath. "When I was little, like three to five years old, I would wake up in the night with this horrible alone feeling. Not every night, but a lot. I have no idea where it came from, and I had no reason to feel that way. My family was close, and I always felt loved. But it was like I was, I don't know, feeling someone else's feelings? It always seemed like it was a little boy, like someone I knew but yet didn't, you know? I couldn't see him, but I could feel him, like a best friend I'd never met." She stopped as tears started to form, and she rubbed her eyes. She refocused on him. "What do you think that means?"

Aaron stared, his look a mix of shock and understanding. "Wow. Well, I can't say for sure. There's the theory on quantum entanglement. There are plenty of myths and stories of people having an extraordinary connection. You... might have a strong connection to someone you hadn't met." He wrapped his pinky into hers. "My own take for myself? I used to wish for... when I was younger. Wished stuff like that was real. There were times growing up that I felt incredibly alone. Later on too." His gaze clouded and he looked away to the water.

Oh my God. "Aaron, right when I first saw you guys at the dock, I felt—"

A flurry of activity erupted on the lower deck, excited shouts and called-out orders drifting up to them, interrupting the intimate solitude of their conversation.

"C'mon," Aaron said as he jumped to his feet. He held out a hand for her. "Let's go see. They might have found something."

CHAPTER 10

ALEX

"WE'VE GOT A GREAT SIGNATURE!" Jimmy exclaimed, jubilation lighting his face as Alex and Aaron walked up. He turned and spoke to the crew near him on deck. "That's good. Let's get sub two in the water and have a look!"

Several crew members who had surrounded one of the two submersibles on board continued prepping it for launch. If this was it, all they needed were confirmation pictures to go with the coordinates and they could all go home.

"Vacation over?" Shane made his appearance to stand with them.

Jimmy looked up from his screen again and nodded. "Maybe so. Here's what we're seeing."

He handed his tablet to Aaron, and he and Shane studied it for a moment before handing it back.

"Looks good to me," Shane replied. He craned his neck around in a rather dramatic, abrupt search. "Where's Care Bear? I'm gonna go fill him in." He slapped Aaron on the back and strode off at a quick pace.

Shane disappeared through a hatch, and a shadow crossed Aaron's features before he turned his attention back to present company. Alex caught his look. *What was that all about?* They continued to chat with her brother and several crew members. As the launch neared readiness, Aaron went to help steady a line. Alex and Jimmy stood together.

"We may be headed home tomorrow. You still glad you came along?" Jimmy asked. "I know it's been a little worrisome here and there."

"Absolutely!" Alex exclaimed and hugged her brother. "And thank you *so* much. Really. You know I've told you for years that I wanted to come on one of these trips. It's been fun!"

"Good. I hoped so. And I know you were ticked about these guys being here at first." He nodded over at Aaron and Les, the latter who'd now shown up and stood speaking with his companion. "But you seem pretty good with it now. Sorry I couldn't tell you ahead of time."

Alex smiled at him. "I know. It's okay." She paused and glanced over at Aaron and Les helping out the launch crew. "And let's just say it's been very interesting. Hey, I'm gonna go track down Will and my camera!" She hurried off, giving Jimmy a quick wave before he could reply.

AARON

"SO, SHANE FILL YOU IN?" Aaron asked as Les approached.

"About what?" Les asked. He grabbed a line near him while the man holding it stepped in closer to the sub to check instrumentation.

"Well…" Aaron pulled hard on his rope, helping realign the sub's track. "He took off in an awful big hurry to find you. Figured he did."

"Nope. Haven't seen him. What's up? They find it?"

"Maybe so," Aaron replied, again with a quizzical knitting of his brows. *Where the hell is ol' Loverboy always running off to?*

"Cool," Les said. "Maybe some easy money after all."

REVELATIONS

CHAPTER 11

AARON

WITHIN AN HOUR OF CONFIRMING the pictures displayed on the screens and cheers of success going up, the mood took a distinct turn. That distant blip that had been just a ghost on their periphery all at once took on purpose. It now came straight for their position, bright and unwavering.

"Well, here they come," Captain Mac stated, his gruff voice almost a growl.

He'd just ordered everyone off the decks and the crew to general quarters. They'd barely had time to clear the submersible from the water and chain it to the deck. Not built for speed, there was no way the research ship could outrun whatever type of vessel now sped toward them.

Still, Mac was unwilling to remain a stationary target. "Let's just make 'em *work* for it… put as much distance between us as we can."

Jimmy glared at the monitor as if to will the approaching red dot from existence. "Well, of all the… What perfect, *shitty* timing!"

"Yeah, that's a little *too* perfect." Les looked over at Aaron, who watched the screen with intent. "Man, it's like somebody just called 'em up."

Aaron approached the captain. "Have there been any communications go out? Anything?"

"Not on my watch. And not my crew." Mac narrowed his eyes, defensive. "They're loyal to a fault."

Aaron searched the older man's face. No deception, no hint of contradiction to what had been stated. At last satisfied with the captain's answer and opinion of his fellow sailors, he clamped a hand on Mac's shoulder and moved to the hatch, Les joining him. "Follow the plan. We'll see how it plays out."

"Aye." Mac nodded, his voice rigid.

Aaron and Les paused in the hatchway to share a weighted glance at his next remark.

"You boys may want to check your own house. You gents got the only equipment other'n me that'd reach that far."

CHAPTER 12

AARON

TWO CANNON SHOTS HAMMERED ACROSS the port bow. "Turn off your engines! All on board assemble on the foredeck! *No exceptions!*" The shouted demands over the loudspeaker were meant to intimidate. "Do it *now*! Any attempt to deviate from our orders will be met with swiftly and harshly!"

Proximity revealed detail. The severe, distressed look of the hull and upper exterior of the pirate ship, which was nearly as large as their own vessel, served as a partial disguise. Most would see it as an old junk trawler or salvage freighter and not give it a second glance. The throaty rumble of engines disclosed retrofitting for interception. Several strategic placements of machine gun stations decorated the upper levels. Scruffy men with well-used AK-47s, AR-15s, and varying sharp-edged weapons patrolled the decks.

The protection team took up predetermined positions, still in sight of each other yet hidden from view of the hostile ship. Les picked out several targets through his rifle scope, setting up his order should he need it. Aaron sighted in his own rifle, an AR-15, as did Shane. Aaron noted the actions and subtle communications between the raiders he could see. *These guys seem pretty well organized.*

His eerie sense of concern that they were dealing with more than just average pirates was confirmed as the quiet of waiting shattered in automatic-weapons fire. Wood decking erupted into splintered fragments all around them, and sharp pings cracked off railings and bulkheads as bullets streamed from one of the upper gun turrets.

The firepower was executed with a little *too* much accuracy. Les rolled out of range and cursed. Aaron ducked and dove for more cover, wincing at the sting of a round that nicked his arm. Another slammed his rifle, rendering it useless. He pulled the magazine, tossed the ruined weapon aside, and pulled his SIG P320. Shane began return fire as best he could. More projectiles thundered into the floorboards.

"We're pinned down!" Les yelled. "How the *bloody hell* do they know our positions?"

Damn good question. Aaron scanned for retreat. He motioned to Les, who moved, and Shane glanced back at them.

"Go, go, go!" Shane screamed as he unleashed a hail of lead toward the enemy vessel.

CHAPTER 13

ALEX

"Y'ALL NEED TO GET BELOW." Captain Mac spoke with a reserved panic to his gravelly voice.

Alex had located Will in his usual spot, in conversation with Mario, and the protective cook escorted them both back up to the bridge. The barrage of traded automatic-weapons fire they'd all heard had now ceased.

Mac watched the vessel floating just off their port bow, sky-blue eyes narrowed, the deep, weathered creases on his tanned face defining apprehension. He traded a nod with his first mate and began powering down the engines. "This ain't normal."

"What *is* normal about getting hijacked?" Alex asked.

"Definitely not this. It's overkill. Get below." He turned to Jimmy. "Do what we talked about 'n' be *quiet*. Go. *Now!*"

Well away from the cargo hold and storage areas that would result in an obvious search, the four hurried down to mid deck, back past guest sleeping quarters. Just after that and before the crew's quarters resided a small access panel. Jimmy unlatched it, peered inside, nodded to the rest of them as he ducked and entered. A dimly lit, cramped space, it housed some of the mechanicals and main secondary electrical junctions. Jimmy scanned the ceiling as Mario reset the panel in place.

"There." Jimmy pointed.

Above them, a malfunctioning light panel flickered in subdued strobe effect. His fingers probed the edge until they reached their objective, and he pressed a small flexible screw. The whole panel popped and released downward, hinged on one side.

"Will, let's go."

Will stepped forward to his father.

"It'll be okay." Jimmy reassured his son as he lifted him at the waist.

The child grabbed the edges of the opening and pulled himself up with a push from his dad.

"You're next." Jimmy motioned to Alex.

She looked from her brother to the dark passage above, took a deep breath, and jumped. Strong hands of her sibling and the cook boosted her on up. Her legs disappeared through the opening. Jimmy motioned for Mario to go ahead of him. The man began to protest but thought better of it, grabbed the edge, and hoisted himself through the overhead.

Jimmy gave one last glance around the small mechanicals room. *"As secure as it's gonna get."* He hauled himself up. Once sure in his balance, he reached back down, grasped the pull handle, and brought the light panel up, latching it into place.

The four found themselves in a small but seemingly secure hidden compartment. Approximately five by eight feet and not quite tall enough for the adults to stand, the hideout appeared to be part of the ventilation system. Mesh air grates arranged on three sides and the top alluded to cage panels, stark woven metal illuminated by a tiny amber service light buzzing in an upper corner. Before they could even think about a spot to rest and wait, a thunderous shock wave pitched them all to the floor.

Will whimpered as the booming rumble subsided, and his father pulled him close.

"What the... What was that?" Jimmy whispered.

"I believe it was the bridge," Mario offered, nodding in the general forward direction. "It came from up that way."

The three adults looked from one to the other. Dilated pupils shone black in the murky light. They needed to remain strong for Will.

Oh no... Mac. Alex lowered her forehead onto her hands, which rested on the cold metal floor. They would wait... and hope.

CHAPTER 14

MAC

CAPTAIN MAC STOOD ALONE AFTER the group left him, having sent his first mate below to join the rest of the crew. The pirate vessel floated in eerie stillness off their port bow. Too quiet. Mac's seasoned eyes squinted further as a sudden sense of dread gripped him.

Aw, hell... He backed away from his controls, wheeled and dove headfirst out the hatch. He rolled and bounced down the steps as the bridge all but disintegrated behind him, concussion from the deafening fireball blasting him the remaining distance to the bottom. Sprawled out, bruised, silver hair singed, Mac regained his bearings. Sickening flames lashed at him from above. He clawed at the floor and launched himself down the passageway, desperate to escape the growing inferno that chased him…

CHAPTER 15

AARON

"WHAT THE HELL WAS *THAT*?" Les steadied himself by grabbing a nearby rail as Aaron, who'd been thrown to the deck by the blast, regained a crouching defensive stance.

Arid sarcasm laced Aaron's reply. "Well, they obviously don't care about a *working* ship."

"Yeah, this is messed up."

They crept to the bridge area, keeping out of the sight line of the pirate vessel. Acrid smoke and embers swam around them. Shane had disappeared after the shoot-out, but he could take care of himself. They would reconnect with him later. Moving closer and somewhat obscured by the smoke, they peered out from the upper deck as pirates began boarding.

Lines were attached, a crude plank laid, and men with assault rifles spilled onto the main foredeck, a dozen in all. Ten were dressed in worn and grimy street clothes. The other two caught Les and Aaron's attention. They wore military-style clothing and moved with more precision and purpose than the others. One of them spoke with two of the pirates, and the three of them took off aft. The other barked orders at the remaining eight on deck.

"Gather up the crew and bring 'em up here," he said. "And try not to kill anyone—not yet. We may need them for a bit." When the eight nodded, he continued. "The captain and that family are our best bet, so make sure you just detain them." He glared at his charges, dark gaze conveying the consequences should they fail to follow orders.

Six of the men were altogether held by that. Subtle reactions from the other two indicated they weren't too keen on just taking prisoners.

The leader glanced around before speaking again. "And if you run into that protection team, don't engage. Radio it in. You know what to do. But…" He grinned at one of the two more ruthless-appearing pirates. "If you do get a clear shot, take it."

The men confirmed and scattered in twos, leaving their commander alone on deck. He pulled his radio and spoke, but he'd turned his back in their direction, and they couldn't make out his words.

"Wish we coulda got a listen on that," Les commented.

Aaron nodded and motioned for retreat. Les was already moving as Aaron turned to follow to a safer location. A moment later, the three intruders who'd left the deck first appeared near the bridge area.

Safe and out of view, hidden behind crates, Aaron and Les watched the three pick through charred remains of the bridge.

Most of the flames had dissipated, but one man stomped and swatted at the few that remained.

After several minutes of poking through rubble, the lead grunted into his radio. "Nuthin'! It's all gone. Leon really screwed this up." He listened to the reply and nodded. "Confirmed." He spoke to the two with him. "C'mon."

The three left the bridge, heading down. Aaron's mind flashed to the armed crew holding defensive positions belowdecks. Les nudged Aaron's arm and shook his head as Aaron met his gaze. This was bad. Pirates wanted to loot or kidnap for ransom. This group, without a doubt, had come for whatever information Jimmy had been sent to discover. And when they got it, there would be no negotiation. All the lives on this vessel would mean nothing to them.

"Let's find Shane," Aaron said. "We're gonna have to take out as many of these guys as we can." His concern heightened for the safety of the crew and for Jimmy and his family. Their initial consultation told him the crew were seasoned and able to deal with pirate attacks, having fended off several over the years. But with this more organized assault, would they be as successful?

"That's why we're here." Les nodded and checked his weapon.

Commotion echoed from below and yanked their attention back to the main foredeck.

Their captain, first mate, and a dozen more of the crew were being herded onto the deck by the three from the bridge encounter. Languishing in rough formation, they obeyed an order to kneel and keep their hands in open view. There had been no shots. No defensive firefight. And too short a time between occurrences.

One pirate screamed for information while the remaining five and one of the mercenaries kept their weapons at the ready. After watching his comrade get nowhere, the commander approached the agitated man and motioned for him to stand aside.

Standing over Mac, he leaned forward and spoke in a low, brittle tone. "Where is your engineer and his family? And where are those three hired guns you brought on board?"

Mac just stared back at him, glaring death.

Aaron and Les gaped from their vantage point.

"This is falling apart fast," Les said, deep concern edging his tone.

Aaron nodded slowly, not wanting to accept what his eyes showed him.

Les continued in a hushed voice. "How'd they find the cap 'n' crew so fast? I thought the concealment plan we all came up with was pretty good. And they never even fought back? That don't make any bloody sense!"

"Yeah, it was good. And you're right." The plan in its originality, even with the chance of unforeseen circumstances, played out better than good. He frowned. Too many things were adding up the wrong way…

"And what about the family?"

Aaron eyed Les. "Mac 'n' I were the only ones who went over their plan with them."

Les narrowed his gaze toward the scene below. "That's probably a good thing at this point. Unless Mac can't hold out."

Aaron rubbed his chin. Any decision he made was risky. But riskier still was leaving people in the bowels of a ship where a haven could now become a death trap. "I'm going for them. We'll just have to fill Shane in whenever he decides to show up."

Les agreed. "What're you thinkin'?"

"These guys have already destroyed the controls to most everything. If anybody cracks and they're able to get the info they want, they won't hesitate to sink the ship and everyone on board. Jimmy, Alex, and the kid may not be able to get out in time where they're at."

Les and Aaron hashed out a rough scenario. Les would hide his sniper rifle near the ruined bridge, where it would come into play later. They would try to hook back up with Shane, then separate, each hunting as many wandering intruders as they could. In the process, they would confirm the location and condition of the family, trying to get to them before the pirates did. If all were okay, it would continue to be a hunt and destroy until the pirates were overtaken, outmatched, and repelled. The wild cards were the mercs and what they might do to the captured sailors. And there was still a company on the pirate vessel, estimating from earlier observation of at least three or four roaming and probably a skeleton crew belowdecks to man the engine room and other mechanical necessities. Aaron would go after the family, and Les and Shane would try to mop up any roving miscreants on this ship. If they could find Shane.

A silent form dropped in behind them. Almost silent. Les spun, sidearm up, as Aaron in one fluid motion unsheathed his knife and pressed it and his forearm up against the newcomer's throat. In that instant, he recognized Shane.

"Whoa there, Psycho, I'm a friendly," Shane rushed out in a harsh whisper.

Aaron kept his knife in place a moment longer before removing it and jamming it back in his boot sheath. He gave his companion a narrow-eyed glare. Mac's cryptic words popped into his mind— "Check your own house." Shane *had* been disappearing conveniently… But anyone they worked with was supposed to be vetted. *Supposed* to be…

"You got a bloody death wish there, Loverboy?" Les asked, a sharp vein to his usual calm demeanor.

"Sorry. Had a little trouble of my own," Shane replied.

CHAPTER 16

ALEX

WITH THE VENTILATION SYSTEM DOWN after the destruction of the bridge controls, the small hiding space grew warm and stuffy. The group of four sat facing each other, backs against the walls. Waiting. Though little over an hour since they'd barricaded themselves in, it might as well have been half the day.

"I wish we could see what's going on," Will said.

His father brushed sweat-soaked blond hair off the young boy's forehead. "Yeah, I do too."

"How long should we wait?" Alex fidgeted and chewed at her lower lip. Restless images threatened to consume her thoughts. *What's happening out there?*

Jimmy shook his head. "I don't know. Aaron said they would come for us when it's safe. Maybe we should—"

He fell silent as a rustling scuffed the panel above. A rattle and the top grate jiggled. Alex pulled her SIG from her back, aiming toward the grate. Jimmy shot her a glare of reprimand. He'd told her not to carry on board. Of course she hadn't listened.

The grate popped open and swung on its hinge, and a dark form dropped landing almost silent in their midst. Alex kept the barrel of her pistol leveled at the newcomer.

"Crap!" Will exclaimed as they all recognized their new addition.

Alex sighed and lowered her weapon.

"Everybody okay?" Aaron glanced around to confirming nods. "Good. We're gonna go." In brief, he explained the current situation. "First though, we could use a few more weapons." He nodded at Alex and locked eyes with her. "The rest still hidden in your room?"

She started, trying to blink away her surprise. "Uh… yeah."

"Alex!" Jimmy exclaimed. "More?"

"Later. Right now it's a good thing," Aaron stated.

Jimmy quieted with a tight-lipped nod and looked away.

"You come with me." Aaron motioned to Alex again. "The rest of you be ready to go when we get back."

They crawled as soundlessly as they could a good distance through the narrow ductwork, past the crew quarters to the second guest compartment. Aaron held up a hand, signaling to wait as he peered down through the air grate. After a few moments of silence, he nodded back to her that all was clear and began unfastening screws. As he worked the last one, the grate gave way.

Lightning fast, his hand shot out and snagged it, thumb and forefinger just catching onto a corner. Under guarded breath, he pulled it back up into the duct and with care, laid it on the other side. He indicated for Alex to follow and he dropped down into her room.

She crawled ahead and peered in. Aaron stood below her, glanced around and up to her. He motioned for her to come down. She scooted forward and swung her legs over the edge. A deep breath. She pushed herself off and dropped.

Aaron caught her at the waist and lowered her to her feet. "Okay, let's get them and get back. Ammo?"

Alex pointed to the small closet. "Bottom. Pink purse," she whispered, almost giggling, partly from stress, partly because of her own choice of concealment. Who would *ever* look in a pink handbag for ammo?

He headed to the closet and she to the dresser. The bottom drawer issued a minute squeak as she eased it open to remove her other two pistols from a hidden bag. She stood and turned toward the bed, almost crashing into Aaron, who had come up behind her.

"Where's the rest?" he whispered.

"Here," she replied and moved past him, plopped her handguns onto the blanket, and reached under the mattress. She'd just stowed some there the night before to be within easy reach.

As she retrieved the three boxes, it occurred to her what he'd just asked. Along with knowing she had multiple weapons? The implications of these questions sank in. *How did he know?* She hadn't told him. Her back remained to him and she clenched her jaw. *He couldn't be that deceitful... could he?* All their shared time and conversations, getting to know each other. Hurt vised her chest. Was all that worthless? Did she really know him at all? A sick heat snaked its way up to redden her face. He *had* spoken on more than one occasion about using charm and deception in his earlier work. Had he just been playing with her all this time? She turned and eyed him, her focus fierce. "How did you know there were more?"

"It's my business to know. Besides, I checked," he replied offhanded as he took a box from her, picked up one of the pistols, and began loading the mag.

Her mouth dropped open, but she couldn't come up with words.

He froze. With a muffled curse at himself and a deep sigh, he turned to face her. "Look, when we do a job, we don't need any wild cards. When I first saw you carry, I could tell you didn't want anyone to know. And..." He shrugged. "For whatever reason, I thought there might be more. So I checked."

"You went through my room?" Alex forced herself to keep to a loud whisper. *Did you have fun with that?* She held her tongue, biting back the urge to curse or scream at him, suddenly glad it had been him and not one of the others. "I would have told you if you'd asked!"

"Would you have?" Aaron shot back. "Besides"—he went back to loading, now jamming rounds into the mag—"it doesn't matter right now. You can be pissed at me later."

"Uh, yeah, it matters a lot." Alex moved over to stand in front of him, put a hand on his to stop him loading and force him to look at her. "This"—she gestured around at her room—"this may not matter in this very moment, in this particular situation." She swallowed hard against mixed emotions, needing truth. "But I need to know I can trust you. That my family can trust you. *That* matters."

"Okay. I should've asked and I'm sorry about that. But with what I do, there's no room for mistakes. No room for missing things. It was just a safety precaution on my part." He took hold of her shoulders, and his look softened. "Trust me. You can. I will do absolutely everything in my power to get you and your family and everyone on this bucket out of this mess alive and well. That's why we're here, in case it went bad." He resumed loading but kept a sympathetic gaze on her. "I don't know what else I can do or say to prove it to you."

Alex searched his face. His answer seemed forthright. It wasn't like she'd revealed her stash after the initial safety briefing either. And he'd never given her reason to mistrust him before. His skilled fingers poked round after round into the magazine, and his gaze never wavered from hers. The shroud around her heart began to unravel.

Finally accepting the sincerity and apology in his eyes, Alex spoke with conviction. "That's twice now you've told me to trust you. Just do what you just said."

CHAPTER 17

AARON

WITH RECOVERED WEAPONS AND AMMO stowed in a duffel, they headed back to the center of the room. Thank God Alex seemed to have accepted his apology. *Besides, I checked? Really Donovan? Dammit!* Why the hell did that have to slip out? And he'd had no time to explain it with any kind of tact. Though early on in the voyage, he should have owned up to his search of her quarters long before this. He just hadn't figured out how and therefore let it slide. Would she find him creepy now? Dishonest? His gut twisted at the possible consequences of his secretive actions. Violation of privacy had never been his intention. Would she understand that? *Fuck.* That look she'd had on her face, those accusing eyes had crushed his heart, that sincere questioning, more than any words or demanding tone could convey. She'd made clear he'd breached her trust and that it went way beyond her room. She really had suspected his loyalty overall—something he didn't need in this predicament and the last thing he ever wished her to doubt.

Aaron tossed the bag up into the ventilation shaft and turned to Alex. "Ready?" he asked as he grabbed her at the waist.

"Yeah," she replied and bent her knees to jump.

Voices and footfalls. Aaron let go of her, put a finger to his lips, and pulled his pistol. The sounds grew louder. A door slammed. Commotion in the next chamber. Jimmy and Will's room. Back in the passageway outside.

Aaron scanned the room and indicated for Alex to follow him. While collecting ammo, he'd noticed the small closet concealed another door at the rear off to one side, likely an access panel for mechanicals. A narrow opening large enough to step through, there should be enough room for them both to hide inside. Hopefully.

He shoved clothing aside, carefully and quietly turned the latch. A quick check. He motioned for her to enter, eased the closet door shut, and backed in behind her. Before closing the panel hatch after him, he reached out and pulled the clothes back toward it, taking a pair of pants and hooking the hanger through the ventilation slats. A leg would cover the handle from the closet side. If the pirates searched the closet, with the handle being concealed, hopefully they wouldn't recognize the ingress and look further. He peered out through the small slats, pistol held ready.

The cramped space was the size of a small broom closet. Alex pressed tight against his back, and Aaron could feel her chin against his shoulder, probably trying to see what she could through the slats, which wasn't much. The voices outside grew louder, and the door to the sleeping compartment opened. Aaron glanced over his shoulder to see a look of panic in Alex's wide eyes. He moved his free hand back to take hold of one of hers and squeezed.

Aaron felt a jolt of fired electricity ascending from their laced fingers. There was an immediate flex of muscles up the length of his arm where it lay in contact against her body. Stronger than the now-normal tingling of their casual touches, even more than the sensation when he'd pulled her from the deck during the ballgame. He was at a loss as to what it was, but he'd never felt such a thing with anyone else. Regardless, the warm, pulsating ripple remained, a solacing reprieve in the crisis.

Alex squeezed back, and her eyes met his. They both turned their attention back to the ventilation slats, closet, and compartment beyond.

Boorish voices. Shuffling feet. Items crashing to the floor. An angry voice, a heated discussion. Silence, and the closet door opened. Alex's body went rigid against Aaron's back, and he squeezed her hand again.

A man rifled through clothing, kicking aside shoes and a bag. He crouched down, grabbed the bag and dumped it, then slammed it to the floor, unsatisfied with its contents. He stood again, scanning the inside of the closet, and paused. Beady eyes fixed on the back wall.

Had the pirate spied the door that concealed them? Too long to just be curious. Shit. Aaron tensed, readying.

The intruder whirled and stomped out, slamming the closet door behind him with a ferocious bang. Voices continued in the room, murmurs, a few chuckles. Abrupt silence. The men hadn't left, and Aaron's mind flashed to the missing ventilation grate in the ceiling. Had they noticed it?

Seconds later the men spoke to one another. A bawdy laugh at something said, and they exited the room.

CHAPTER 18

ALEX

ALEX LET OUT A BREATH she'd been holding almost since they'd entered the closet as the firmness of Aaron's back muscles relinquished their tension against her chest and abdomen. Her eyes closed as her body relaxed in mirror to his. She opened them again to find his reassuring gaze on her. She shook her head and rested her forehead down against his shoulder as he gave her hand another comforting squeeze.

They stayed still and quiet, nestled together in the tiny access as the pirates ransacked the next room down and moved on. Soon no voices or footsteps reached their ears. Abiding in the lull a while longer, Aaron holstered his weapon.

Alex maintained confidence in her own abilities and in the man beside her, but this little incident had shaken her more than she wanted to admit. Behind the barriers of a closed door and a language she didn't understand, the arrogance in the harsh voices spoke to men with devious desires. Used to getting what they wanted, enjoying whatever cost that might exact. The danger now upon her family and new comrades boded far worse than she'd allowed any imaginings to venture.

Dammit, this is not a time for tears! Her body seized up again, and her teeth clamped against the welling tightness in her throat.

Aaron squirmed around to face her and took her shoulders in his hands. "Hey," he said, his voice barely above a whisper. When she lowered her lashes, he moved a finger under her chin, bringing her face up to his so they were eye to eye. "You know, if you wanted to get me alone in a dark closet, you didn't have to wait on this bunch of yahoos to make that happen."

Alex shuddered and bit her lower lip as she tried to keep her composure. The sharp transition from nearly being discovered by killers to Aaron's playful remarks threw her. *Is he seriously flirting with me right now? Now?* Were their close quarters affecting him as much as they were her? Or was he just playing to make her feel better and alleviate her fear?

Her damp eyes lit with laughter at his choice of tactics. If only she could come up with some witty comeback to that, but coherent words refused to form in her mind. He certainly knew how to defuse the frightful aspect of their situation. His blue-green irises were mere inches in front of her, his pupils dilated in the dark, his warm breath on her face.

Oh God. She couldn't maintain the eye contact. Any longer and she'd either cry or kiss him. All remaining doubt from earlier fled. She looked away and melted into his arms, now not because of confined spaces. Would he mind? Almost in answer, his arms encircled and tightened about her. Tension released from her body again.

"Well, this still wouldn't've been my first choice of how to get you in a secluded place"—he gave her a quick wink—"but… you know you really need to get better at this."

Her lips brushed the side of his neck as she tucked her head in and stifled giggles, her cheek now snuggled under his ear. That charged touch raced through her. She felt his face expand in a grin and he squeezed his arms even tighter about her. *He has to feel that too! He has to!* She sighed against his overwarm skin as he cuddled her and rubbed her back. Did she just feel him tremble a little?

"C'mon. Your brother's probably worried himself sick by now." He removed an arm from her and grasped the handle of the hatch. Slow and careful, he opened the door.

She lifted her chin from his shoulder and looked back into his shining eyes. He let out a sigh and grinned at her, then led her by the hand into the main closet and back out into the room.

CHAPTER 19

AARON

"WHAT HAPPENED? ARE YOU GUYS okay?" Worry from their extended absence showed heavy on Jimmy's features as Aaron and Alex reappeared at the vent opening through which they'd left.

"Had a close call." Aaron handed Mario a pistol and ammo.

Alex nodded at her brother in confirmation.

When Aaron offered Jimmy a pistol, he refused it. Aaron shrugged and tucked it and the ammo for it in his own pockets.

Will scooted over to Alex and hugged her.

Alex ruffled her nephew's hair and kissed him on top of his head. "It's okay, bud."

Aaron gathered everyone close and gave a quick and efficient explanation of the plan. They would all meet up with Les and Shane, and while he and his teammates executed some kind of diversion, the family would be taken to the launch area where a stowed transport skiff waited. With any luck, the protection team—with some help from the captain and crew—would then be able to overpower their attackers.

Aaron led Jimmy, his family, and Mario out to reconnect with Les and Shane. In the time he'd been gone, the situation with the other crew members had seen rapid deterioration. Remaining forced on their knees, they formed a disjointed row, all now bloodied and bruised. Caesar, the first mate, looked to have sustained the worst of it so far, likely an attempt to get their captain to talk.

"We have waited enough! We grow tired of this stalling! Five minutes and we start killing!" The pirate snatched the shirt collar of a crew member, dragged him forward as he floundered on hands and knees, and jammed a pistol to his head. "I know you can see this! Five minutes! No more!"

Les leaned in close to Aaron, the sniper's brow deeply furrowed. "Somebody's gotta get out there or they're dead!"

"I know," Aaron agreed.

This disturbing turn of events, not unexpected at this point, would still prove tough to solve. Just how did their attackers know *so much* of the objective of this mission? That remained to be discovered. Add the additional fact that they were informed about Aaron and his crew. *No one* had previous knowledge they were to be on board except one person. And that person would never put his family in jeopardy.

Aaron stole a glance at Alex as she bent down to help her brother reassure Will. *Dammit. Why did this all have to go to hell now...* "I'll go," he told Les. "You're a better shot with that rifle.

Just make sure you got me covered too. Just like the Christensen job."

Les cringed and nodded, giving Aaron a dubious side-squint. "Aye, as that was such a smashing success."

"Hey, we got the assets out. We lived. Your point?"

Les could only shake his head at Aaron's smart-ass smirk. "And you spent the next week in infirmary if I remember correctly. What about McGregor Cross?"

"That one *was* an experience, wasn't it?" Aaron replied. Yet another job that had served to solidify his nickname. "Yeah, but no time. Half these guys are scared of something, the other half are just itchin' to kill. It's goin' down now."

"You're right," Les responded.

Aaron knew Les didn't like it, but the Christensen scenario *would* play best for shutting down the pirates' actions in the short term. Les laid a hand on Aaron's shoulder, squeezed, and started for the ruined bridge where his rifle lay stowed.

"Okay. You got it. But that's bullshit on the shootin' man. *And* you're still bloody nuts. Just give me a good distraction and I'll cover everybody." Les winked and disappeared toward the bridge.

"Shane, get them down and out of sight," Aaron instructed. "Go for the launch. If this goes bad, get 'em outta here."

Shane saluted Aaron. "You got it, boss. Trust me."

CHAPTER 20

ALEX

ALEX'S BREATH CAUGHT IN HER throat. That overheard conversation and what it meant froze her in place as she stood. The diversion was *him?* Going out *there?* A chill prickled her skin, and she shifted her awareness back to him.

Aaron glanced over in the direction of the forward deck, one hand rubbing the back of his neck as he tilted his head to crack it. His shoulders and chest expanded and fell in a heavy sigh. This was his job, and she'd spent enough time with him, listening to his narratives, to know the risks involved. But still.

She stepped over and took hold of his arm. "You're not seriously doing that, are you?"

He cocked his head at her as he holstered his pistol. "Yeah."

"But *why?* Can't he just pick them off from up *there?*" She waved toward the direction of the bridge and Les.

"Not quite that simple. We gotta get their attention off the crew right now. Stop them from killing them. Because they will. And Bear might initially get a couple of good shots off... but eventually the gunners over there will pin him down. This way," Aaron said and checked around the corner before turning back to her, "it'll keep those guys busy. It's the art of diversion. Their attention will be focused out there, on the deck. On me. With that distraction, it'll give you guys time to get away. And by the time anyone actually realizes what's *really* happening, he should have the ship's gunners down and then hopefully check these goons before they do too much damage to me. At least that's the plan anyway."

"You're takin' an awful big fuckin' chance, man," Shane told him. "Sounds like a damn suicide mission to me."

"Well, what other choice have we got? Tell me that?" Aaron shot back at Shane's irksome remark. "We gotta do something *now.*"

"Are you *crazy?*" Alex exclaimed. She didn't much care any longer what any of them thought.

"Not like I've never been accused of *that* before." Aaron half chuckled the remark as he knelt next to Shane and passed him some ammo, his extra mags, and a second pistol.

His half-hearted humor was not reassuring in the least.

"We do call him Psycho for a reason, sweetheart," Shane added. "If it's crazy and dangerous, he's all in, balls in."

"You're not helping, man. That's enough." Aaron side-eyed Shane as they finished swapping ammo.

"What the hell, dude. It's the truth, and you know it!" Shane snapped back. "And to think you actually question the way *I* do shit."

Aaron sighed and clenched his jaw.

The biting smell of gunpowder and acrid smoke drifted about. Screaming invaders, fear, and blood. The crew lined up for execution on deck. Tears streaking glossy ribbons down her nephew's cheeks, creases that stole hope from her brother's face... *To be able to snap my fingers and whisk us all away from this hell!*

Alex glared at Shane and looked back to Aaron, the harsh and deadly reality of the situation pressing hard on her. Someone could die here. An overwhelming sense of loss and sorrow swept over her, constricting her heart. "But... but what part of this doesn't... involve you getting yourself killed?" She sucked in her lip, crossed her arms, and looked down at the deck, blinking back the wetness that stung her eyes.

"Hey, come on now." Aaron stood and turned to face her. "Give me *some* credit here." Reaching out, he put a finger under her chin and tilted her head back up to him. "They're not likely to kill me. They still need information. Till they actually get it...?" He offered her a half smile. "This isn't the first time we've done something like this. It'll work out. Don't worry about me."

Alex stared at him. Just exactly *how* was this plan supposed to "work out"? Sudden uncontainable emotion overcame her, the consequence of the upcoming gambit solidifying in her mind just how much his surviving this meant to her. How much *he* meant to her. She stepped forward and grabbed him in a tight hug.

"*Please* be careful," she whispered to him. "It matters."

AARON

AARON RETURNED THE EMBRACE, STARTLED at just how much comfort her firm hold provided him in the midst of this impossible situation. "Be careful." When *was* the last time anyone had said that to him? The urgency those hushed words held as she breathed them against his ear gave him a rush. The warmth of her body, holding him close, her touch imploring him to come out of this safe. He pressed her tight to him and rubbed her back, their recent moments in hiding replaying in his mind. And the method he'd chosen to calm her fears. Shit, really? At least it had worked. Levity always came in handy and for multiple reasons. Being that close to her had affected him for sure, but really it was just her in general. Her soft giggle at his remark. Those petal-soft lips and her deep sigh against his neck. Holy hell. Right then he'd known she'd be fine. Him, however? Emboldened by her reaction, his heightened senses from battle, and for the sudden need to calm his own nerves, he'd continued his mischief, and in his joking way he'd put his affections out there. She was used to his humor. And she hadn't smacked him.

She'd melted into his arms. Just like now...

Nice job, Donovan. You should've told her before that you wanted to see her again after this voyage. But now sure the hell wasn't the time.

After a moment, he whispered into her hair. "C'mon, you gotta go now." He resigned to give her one last hard squeeze before releasing her.

She stepped back, turned, and paused.

"C'mon!" Shane called in a loud whisper. He shouldered his rifle and motioned for the four to follow him.

"Alex!" Jimmy called to her. "C'mon!"

Aaron moved toward the corner. He looked back over his shoulder to find Alex's eyes on him and gave her a nod. "I'll see you after."

God, that look; he *had* to make it through this. *Back to business, son. Now.* He returned his attention to the path ahead of him, took a deep breath, and stepped out.

TRUST AND VENGEANCE

CHAPTER 21

AARON

NO DEFENSE, NO RESISTANCE. A play of submission to the pirates to convince them they had control. Let them punish him and make a scene so their comrades would turn their attention. There was never a guarantee of it going as planned. No assurance of success. Just a judgment call that violent men would enjoy a good torture show... Maybe it *was* a good thing he'd never discussed anything about after. In this mess he might not make it anyway.

"I'll see you after"...if I'm still alive. Fuck...

"Don't shoot! I'm coming out!" Aaron called from behind the bulkhead.

"Show yourself!" a voice ordered. "Now!"

Aaron emerged slowly, hands up as he stepped into view.

The pirate commander nodded to a subordinate, and the scruffy man trotted over. With a rough search, he came up with the pistol, one extra magazine, and knife. His menacing smile revealed a sad lack of dental care as he stowed the recovered weapons in his own belt. He grabbed Aaron and shoved him hard over toward his boss and the captive group.

"Where are the rest?" the commander demanded.

"I'm it. They're dead."

"I don't believe you!"

"Well, believe what you want, it won't change anything."

The chief nodded to his second again.

The man yanked Aaron's arms back and zip-tied his wrists. "Down!" he growled into his new prisoner's ear and kicked the back of one of Aaron's legs to push him to his knees.

As Aaron hit the deck, he looked over to the crew and found Mac's defiant eyes. The discreet, slow turn of Mac's head said "don't do this." Aaron read the concern on the older man's face and responded with an almost imperceptible, reassuring nod.

"We will get what we want, or you will pay dearly!" The man in charge moved to stand behind Aaron, pointing a pistol at his head. "What are the coordinates? Now!"

Aaron shook his head. "What coordinates?"

Impact from the butt of the weapon sent a jolt of pain slicing through Aaron's skull. "You know them! You will tell us!"

Aaron shook his head, driving the stars out of his vision. *And so it begins…* His ear throbbed from the shock of the blow, and warmth trickled down his cheek.

He slumped and shrugged his shoulders, groaning out his reply. "Don't know what to tell you, man. I don't know any coordinates."

CHAPTER 22

ALEX

SHANE MOVED THE SMALL GROUP several hatches back and down to the next level. Emergency lighting cast eerie shadows as they hurried along, shoes scuffling intermittent mouse squeaks on gray-painted steel decking. As they reached the last compartment in that hallway, a walkie crackled to life.

Shane snatched it from his pocket and hissed into it. "Not now!"

The others, farther ahead, missed that response. Alex didn't. Her heart might as well have fallen to her feet, each step now feeling like lead weights were in her sneakers as the meaning behind that short reply hit her. She stopped short and spun to face him.

A wicked glint crept across his narrowed cerulean gaze. By now the others noticed the two unmoving behind them, and they also paused in inquiry.

Shane brought up his rifle, motioned toward the last compartment's hatch. "Get in."

"What the...?" Jimmy's question halted on open lips, and he took a step toward Shane. "Just what the hell's going on here?"

"Dad?" Will moved closer to his father and twisted to follow the direction of that demanded question. His brown eyes grew wide as they met with Shane's frosted ones. "Hey! You're s'posed to be the good guys!" the young boy shouted.

He stared at Shane, someone he'd shared laughs and playtime with just a day earlier. Respect drained from his indignant face. Small fists clenched as his glare bored into the turncoat.

"So sorry, kid." Shane's flat tone revealed his lack of compassion. "Now do what you're told and get in!"

Alex backed away.

With the group not reacting quick enough for Shane's liking, he lunged out and grabbed her arm, pulling her against him. He shouldered his rifle and snatched her pistol from her belt. "Get the hell in that doorway or she's dead!"

"Aunt Alex!" Will cried.

Alex jerked against Shane's rough grip. Shane thrust the barrel of her gun against her head, and she stopped struggling.

"You asshole!" she hissed under her breath. "We trusted you!"

"Yeah, I know. Whatever," he replied, voice cold and controlled. He tightened his grip on her arm and glared at the others. "Last chance. Get in. Now!"

Jimmy offered Shane a withering scowl and continued to hold his black look as he steered his son's shoulders and eased toward the hatch. Shane just inclined his head along with a sick sneer. Reluctantly, Mario stepped through the hatch first, followed by Jimmy shielding Will. The disillusioned small boy still stared daggers through his tears.

Shane half dragged Alex over. "Shut it," he ordered, indicating the hatch.

How could you! Furious at him for his treachery and at herself for feeling so helpless, Alex eyed him like she would a filthy toilet and reached out to close the hatch. Had she been correct in questioning her brother's hiring of this bunch? It broke her heart to think that Les or Aaron could be involved in such treason. The constriction in her chest and the lump now clogging her throat threatened to choke her. Praying that the two were not in collusion with Shane's duplicitous scheme, her fingers had barely touched the cold steel when there was a sudden shriek from within.

A cacophony of reports exploded the terse silence, and flashes strobed the shadowed oval. Mario burst from the room, weapon snapping off rapid fire. He launched himself at Shane.

Shane jerked away, nearly dragging Alex off her feet again as a round sprayed blood from his thick bicep. He cursed and spun.

For the unfortunate cook, the mercenary's reflexes proved too fast. A sidestep and then a single shot dropped the poor man in a heap to skid past Shane's feet. His head thudded to the deck, and the pistol bounced from his now lifeless fist to clatter across the passageway like an unlucky die.

Will's shrill scream echoed from beyond the hatch.

A cold sweat encased Alex at the shock of their friend's undue demise. *Mario, no! Oh God!* And what an awful thing for her poor little nephew to see! Her horrified stare came to rest on their captor. Gloating twisted his lips into a vile bow, and he loosened his grip on her arm, too engrossed in his own sick world.

You absolute sonofabitch! Alex broke free and dove for Mario's dropped gun. Her fingertips made the grip just as the weight of Shane's boot crashed into her side. She slammed into the adjacent wall.

He scooped the pistol up himself, tucked it into his own belt, and stepped forward to slam the hatch shut.

Alex pulled herself to hands and knees. Rising bile from both the blow to her body and the ugliness at hand tickled at the back of her tongue. She rubbed at a growing bump on the side of her head. Her left shoulder ached and her right side throbbed. Spots and dullness dissipated and her eyes regained focus as Shane grabbed her arm again, hauled her to her feet, and pushed her stumbling ahead of him.

"You're comin' with me. Back up top, sweetheart." Shane sneered. "Got a nice little show for ya up there."

CHAPTER 23

ALEX

"OH GOD, THEY'RE GONNA KILL him!"

Shane had returned Alex to the main foredeck where the pirates held Aaron and the others. The position he confined her in kept them mostly hidden in the shadow of a bulkhead while giving her a clear view of the actions on deck.

Interrogating. Taking a bit too much pleasure in inflicting pain. Most of the attention was focused on Aaron at present. Just as he'd told her would happen. On his knees, hands secured behind his back, he turned toward her. Bruising now marred the line of his jaw. A trickle of bright crimson snaked down his left cheek from matted hair just above his ear.

Planned or no, this was not what she'd expected, and the sight nearly brought her to tears. Locked in Shane's viselike grip, there was nothing she could do. Another sick chill needled her skin.

You fucking pricks! Leave him alone! Every breath she took burned like fire in her lungs, and her stomach twisted into knots.

A disheveled little man paced in front of Aaron. The stunted vermin alternated between yelling and short, quacking guffaws, occasionally providing a taunting jab to Aaron's ribs or shoulders with the barrel of the rifle he waved wildly in one hand. A pistol was clutched tight in his other.

Where the hell was Les, and why didn't he *do* something?

More screaming from the rat. Aaron remained motionless, head down, just keeping his balance as he received a hard boot to his back. The pirate commander positioned behind Aaron leveled his gun at his captive's head.

Horror gripped Alex, scrambling her senses. She couldn't make out the hateful words, but that deep baritone voice spewed pure rage. The small scruffy one who stood in front of Aaron let out a cackling laugh.

"That's the idea, sweetheart." Shane's menacing words were edged with excitement, his sour whisper a grating abuse in her ear. He tightened his clasp on her arm, twisting until it hurt. "It's part of the bargain. Guess you made the wrong choice."

Alex gave him no satisfaction from any reply. It would be impossible to find words to counter the nightmarish hell of events playing out in front of her. The iron grip on her arm grew so tight she felt he would break it, and she couldn't quite stifle a whimper.

At that, Shane let out an evil giggle and his restraint eased a bit.

Right then, three successive thunks preceded respective sonic cracks. The two captors with Aaron glanced up. Faint shouting drifted from the other vessel. Another thunk-crack. Silence.

Clearly unable to determine the origin of presumed shots, the commander returned his attention to Aaron. *Oh God!* What if he tortured him? Alex hiccupped a sob. What if he killed him, thinking it would get the others to talk?

The commander licked curled lips, displaying a toothy grin as he lined up his kill shot again.

CHAPTER 24

AARON

HEAD STILL BOWED, AARON FELT the whiz above his skull blow an icy kiss on the back of his neck. A crunching, aqueous thwack came from behind him, like a melon dropped from a high-rise, followed by the sharp crack of pistol fire, and the bullet meant for him drove into the deck next to his knee.

Fine red mist speckled the floorboards. Ringing in his ears from his captor's missed shot muted the thump at his back. Aaron risked a peek up to see the man in front of him gasp, eyes dilated and mouth agape at having witnessed the disintegration of his commander's chest.

'Bout damn time, Les...

Aaron dropped to his side and kicked out. A successful aim landed a crushing blow to the forward man's knee, and the bones crunched and separated under his boot.

The little man screeched as he slammed down, impact with deck boards bouncing both pistol and rifle from his fists. He clutched at his ruined joint, screaming and cursing Aaron all the while. Eyes locked on the semiauto, the pirate let go of his knee with a howl and scrabbled to close the short distance between them to recover the fallen handgun.

Just as the pirate's fingertips tickled the grip, Aaron booted it out of reach. The scrawny man swore and drew a fist at him. Aaron rolled closer. The pirate's wild punch missed any solid contact, and Aaron swung his legs, locking them around the cur's head and neck.

Trapped in the crush of contracting thighs, the diminutive hijacker flailed arms and legs in an attempt at escape, grasping and clawing at both decking and his captor's pants as he squirmed to regain his freedom. A tight grimace contorted the swinelike face, and a last rasping squeal escaped through bared teeth.

Aaron arched his back, twisted, and squeezed until there was a loud pop. The pirate went limp.

Releasing his leghold, Aaron spun and scooted close. He snatched his knife from the fallen scum's waistband. Behind his back he worked it up his wrist. The sliced zip tie flopped to the floor, and he slammed his blade back home in his boot. Aaron flipped over to crouching and grabbed the pistol off the deck. His gaze darted over his surroundings, a quick assessment of his new situation.

"Well, well, well… Now it's a party!" Venomous sarcasm from a familiar voice. Shane moved out into better view, hauling Alex with him, knife at her neck. "Nice show!" he spat out. He barked orders at the three pirates guarding the remaining crew members. "Get them outta here! Lock 'em up below somewhere!"

The trio fidgeted but did as instructed and began herding the group off the deck. A thunk-crack and the one bringing up the rear slumped. Several of the captured crew took advantage and subdued their two remaining captors, commandeering weapons.

"Care Bear, you get your ass down here right now, or you're gonna lose two more!" Shane shouted.

Focus locked on Shane and Alex, Aaron clenched his jaw tight. More? What the hell had gone on? He blocked out hurtful images before they could take hold. Not now. Get this done. And Alex? The sight of her trapped in the hold of a madman didn't help his frame of mind.

Purposefully positioning Alex between himself and Aaron as a shield, Shane walked her farther into the open.

Aaron kept his aim on Shane, though he had no clear shot. He waved off the crew, hoping they wouldn't try to intervene, wouldn't cause Shane to act out in haste. They stopped and backed away, headed below, their restrained captors in tow.

Knowing Shane's methods and skill, having him as an opponent rather than an ally definitely altered the equation. Another man down, a new enemy. *Why the hell didn't I see this coming sooner?* Shane had always been a little off, but Aaron had never thought the man would flip like this.

Treading slowly and cautiously, Aaron eased around Shane and Alex. "Bear, you got this?" he called out. Nothing. "Les?"

A sudden scuffle and several small-arms shots sounded from the bridge area. Still no reply from anyone.

"Shit," Aaron murmured under his breath. From bad to worse to hell. His mind raced in overdrive to come up with a solution to this mess.

"I think ol' Care Bear might have gotten himself in a pickle." Shane offered an exaggerated chortle, then turned severe. "And if you want this little chicky and the rest of 'em to live, you'll drop your weapon and give up. Right now!"

"You know that's not gonna happen," Aaron replied, keeping his voice calm and resolute. "Think about it, man. You're outnumbered now. No way you make it out."

Shane shrugged. "Maybe I don't make it, maybe I do." He shifted his stance so Aaron could better see the knife his left hand held pressed against Alex's neck. "But I can sure as hell cause you some serious shit in the process. I know how you can't stand to lose any oh-so-precious people under your watch," he snarled. "It's your worst fear. That'll cause you more pain than anything I can do to you. But still…" He shrugged again, took the pistol from his belt, and pointed it at Aaron. "This is my show. I decide the entertainment value. You'll drop that weapon. And you'll do it now!"

Aaron didn't budge, remaining laser focused on Shane and Alex. If Les was down, he would have to take the chance and take the shot himself. "You know me better than that."

"Yes, unfortunately, I do." Shane sneered. He crushed Alex closer, wet lips skimming her cheek. "Let's have some fun first," he whispered. He aimed low and pulled his trigger.

The bullet caught Aaron on the outside of his left thigh, and he staggered down to one knee.

"No!" Alex screamed and jerked against Shane's hold. The tip of the knife blade scraped at the side of her neck.

Aaron steadied himself and sucked in a breath. Dammit, Shane knew where to put a bullet that would hurt like hell but still not incapacitate. He'd seen him do it once before, string a captured assailant on, torturing with round after round, neither immobilizing nor outright killing. Aaron had finally had to intervene, but at least in that case the target had been an enemy. And according to the incident report, Shane had supposedly received disciplinary action. This current wounding was more than likely just the start of Shane's intended persecution of him.

As long as he could keep Shane's attention fixed on him however, the man's aggressions wouldn't be taken out on Alex.

Just keep him talking and figure this out. "So," Aaron asked, doing his best to ignore the searing pain in his leg, "what are they paying you?"

Shane's menacing laugh echoed across the deck. "Well, one helluva lot more than I could ever get hangin' with *you* assholes! Besides, getting paid to find it was just the tease… What we can sell it for to the highest bidder is a whole 'nother level." He pulled Alex in closer to him, nodding at Aaron. "Plus a nice little added bonus to sweeten the deal."

There it is. Shane's overconfidence. His weak spot. He would make a mistake at some point, let his guard down.

"So it's all about the money with you now, huh?"

"Ha!" Shane exclaimed. "Always *has* been! What the hell you think I been doin' these jobs for? Ya see, with enough cash, you can get anything in life you want. You just have to get past the whole 'not making certain sacrifices' thing." With that he clutched Alex even closer in his grip. "The money is everything that matters, man. *Everything* has a price."

Aaron gritted teeth against the pain but never took his aim off Shane. Shane had incredible reflexes… but his own were better. If only he could get a clear shot, and…

Just. Shoot. Perfect.

He locked eyes with Alex for a brief moment. "Not everything."

An evil smile spread across Shane's features. "So there *is* something between you two! Oh, I'm *really* gonna enjoy *this!*" he spat out.

He took aim at Aaron again, thick finger squeezing the trigger.

Thump-crack. Shane's arm jerked and his shot missed wide. His gaze followed his pistol as it clattered across the deck. Deep creases etched the space between his brows. He folded his elbow, slow-motion rotating the arm as he inspected what absurd circumstance had interrupted his intended sport. His pupils dilated as his hand flopped over at a severe odd angle. He gaped at the oozing shredded tissue, and the ivory of visible bone protruding as jagged daggers from his shattered forearm.

"What the hell...?" Cursing split the air and he howled out his trauma.

Les emerged from a far corner, a wisp of smoke rising from the barrel of his rifle suppressor. The man moved with a limp but was alive.

Shane constricted his grip on Alex and backed up. Knife dimpling her neck, he attempted restraining her with that same limb, his damaged arm hanging all but useless to any task.

"Stay still, bitch!" He crushed her to his chest.

Alex kicked back at his legs and kept struggling against his grip, but that muscled arm remained like a steel trap.

"Just shoot him!" she screamed, any remaining fear clearly relinquished to her fury.

The knife dragged down her neck as Shane battled to keep his hold on her. Blood trickled from the scrape. With his struggle of keeping that blade in place, she might have a chance. *Please, God*, Aaron thought as her gaze met his again.

Alex drove an elbow into Shane's gut and slammed her head straight back. Aaron could hear cartilage crack and crunch. The knife slipped away from her neck, and she dove for the deck. She pulled as hard as she could against her captor, squirming in his grip and making him hold all her weight.

Shane shrieked and cursed as he yanked her back but couldn't keep adequate leverage on her to still defend himself. Blood bubbled from his wrecked nostrils. He grabbed and clawed at her in an attempt to keep her hugged in place.

The knife slid across her collarbone. She cried out when it gouged her, and Aaron's heart seized, but she twisted away to wrench from his grasp, and Shane was exposed just enough.

Aaron fired twice.

Alex yelped and fell forward, now released from Shane's hold. Her hands slammed the decking, and she collapsed, sprawled on her stomach.

Shane stumbled backward behind her. Gasping, slipping in his own gore, he stared down at two jagged openings in his abdomen. Crimson fluid spilled to soak his legs.

"Those... rounds... weren't meant for *me!*" His knife tumbled from slack fingers, clattering to stillness in the puddle of red. With a burbled moan, he sank to his knees, swayed in place a few seconds, then crumpled to the deck and lay still.

Alex—safe from immediate danger. A moment longer of focused attention to make sure. An exhausted Aaron dropped back on an elbow and slowly lowered his weapon.

CHAPTER 25

AARON

ALEX SCOOTED AWAY FROM SHANE'S fallen body and pulled herself to her feet as Les limped across the deck toward them. She pressed a hand to her side. Pain flared in her eyes, and her fingers came away with blood.

Aaron got to his knees.

Les shouldered his rifle and reached out a hand to help him up. "You all right, buddy?"

"Been better." Aaron grasped Les's arm and winced as the man hauled him to his feet. His head throbbed. The aching in his thigh ramped back up, and various contusions began to make their presence known as his adrenaline subsided. Between the bullet wound and the beating he'd taken at the hands of the pirates, his body would soon be hard-pressed to not feel like one giant bruise.

"Think we shoulda negotiated extra hazard pay on this one," Les said, half joking. "Li'l more rough than usual."

"Yeah, a little." Aaron groaned his reply. He shifted his attention to move toward Alex, but she had already closed the few yards to join them. He nodded to her. "You good?"

Alex took a deep breath. "Yeah, I'm good. I hope. But you?" She couldn't keep profound worry from her eyes as she stared into his.

Her extreme care touched him, and he flashed her a quick smile. "I'll live."

He reached out and took hold of her jaw. Fingers firm yet tender, he gave her chin a quick caress with his thumb and turned her head to the side to inspect the knife wound she'd received, courtesy of Shane. Even though it wasn't deep, he frowned. His gaze lowered to the slice on her collarbone, farther to her bloodied hand and the dark red on her side.

Oh God. Had he hit her? A razor-close shot even without the moving target, but he thought he'd shot clean. His brows lifted and knit. He swallowed hard and his insides convulsed at what could have ended in disaster…

"It's okay. Really," Alex said. "I think it just barely—"

"I thought I missed you," Aaron told her, his eyes stinging. "I thought…" His voice cracked, and he stepped forward and grabbed her.

She rushed into his hold. His clutch neared desperation, and he couldn't keep his weight from pulling on her. The embrace she returned him, a comfort he could find no words for. He gathered her close. Fatigue took over, and he collapsed against her, shuddering in her arms as she cradled him closer.

"I've got you, bud." Her soft whisper breathed reassurance in his ear. She held him against her and braced her legs, supporting them both.

Les moved over to lock an arm around each of them. "Yeah, you'll both live. C'mon. Let's get everyone over and get the hell outta here."

CHAPTER 26

ALEX

SEVERAL TRIPS WITH THE SKIFF and across the planking got everyone, some salvaged equipment, and all their remaining personal gear transferred to the pirate vessel. Mario's body was recovered, a heartbreaking discovery for Aaron and Les upon learning of the cook's murder at the hands of their team member. Shane's midsection wounds were wrapped to contain excess leakage, and his corpse was put into cold storage in the sketchy refrigeration unit, along with but well away from Mario's, for the trip home. Weapons and munitions of the pirates were confiscated and stored nearby. The few pirates that remained alive had surrendered and were locked in a cabin, two of the crew guarding the door. Towlines were attached to the damaged research ship. It would be a slow voyage back to port.

Captain Mac surveyed the bridge of the pirates' ship and communicated with the engine crew below decks. He swiped at the sweat on his brow with a bloodied arm. "Well, she's seen some rough years, and sad care, but she'll get us home," he remarked to Jimmy. "I'll make for Lisbon; we'll find safe port there."

Les and two crew members stood nearby.

"Good." Jimmy's voice choked. He swept at his eyes and cleared his throat. "The sooner, the better."

With the complete disaster of this whole ordeal, the priority now was to get everyone home safe. Jimmy and Les left to return to the foredeck.

Alex, Will, and Aaron rested near the bow. Les had patched up Aaron's and Alex's wounds earlier, along with his own. To Aaron's relief, the bullet graze to Alex's side proved just that; a stinging flesh wound.

Aaron's thigh received antiseptic too, and a few stitches, the through-and-through near the skin's surface with minimal trauma to underlying muscle. He'd have a good ache for a while, but no lasting infirmity. Painkillers from Les's medical goody bag helped for the time being.

Aaron and Will sat talking and eating melted ice cream. Alex stood some yards away where she'd walked to the railing, head inclined to the water below. Jimmy went to her and hugged her tight.

"I'm so sorry about all this," he said into her hair.

She squeezed her arms around his shoulders. "It's not your fault. None of it."

They released each other and moved a bit farther away to talk.

"I'm so very sorry about Mario. I know you've known him and this crew for years. He was a good man." Alex's voice hitched as she tried to keep away forming tears.

Blinking back his own, Jimmy nodded, clearly not able to come up with words.

"And what about all that information and the coordinates you needed, why we even came out here?" Alex asked after a time.

Jimmy shook his head.

He'd told her before that the details were so secretive the only knowledge supplied for this mission was a general area within a few kilometers of where the military had conducted their search. He'd succeeded, then had it all ripped away with the destruction of the bridge, and now he was left only with that with which he'd started: a general location.

Even with his knack for locating things at extreme depths, Alex knew he probably couldn't recover anything. All the instruments, his notes and charts, his laptop and tablet, were all gone.

"I don't know, sis. Since the attack, we've likely floated a good distance. And this pirate ship is nowhere near as up to date on the technology side. We're not lost by any means, but exact location of anything at depth, in any kind of quick fashion, would be impossible. Also, wrong to attempt at the moment. We all just need to get home." He gave a heavy sigh and shrugged.

"What will you tell them?"

"I don't know. The truth, I guess. It's all gone." He ran his hands through his hair, rubbing his head. "One of the submersibles is damaged, the ship's a mess..." He dropped his hands to his sides and let out a frustrated chuckle. "But I'm pretty sure as far as the job goes, they're not gonna give anything for information they already had. If only I at least had the numbers. I even wrote them down on... but I didn't put it in my pocket," he said, sober. "The last time I saw that piece of paper? Tucked under the edge of my laptop on the bridge."

Anguish returned to his features. "And you guys… If I had thought anything like this would really happen… I would never have let Will and you come along. What if…?" He slumped against the railing. "And poor Mario."

Alex laid an arm across his shoulders. "I know. But we're okay. Will's okay. And you had Les and Aaron here. You thought enough ahead to do that. They saved us."

"You're right." He took hold of her hand on his shoulder, and after a few moments straightened and wiped his eyes. "You seem to be handling all this pretty well. Better than me," he said. "You sure you're okay?"

Alex hugged his arm. "Yeah… I'm okay. I guess. Maybe still in shock. But you know me. Deal with it now, cry later." She shook her head. "Remember, I did learn a lot from Dad. And my best friend Lou and I have taken those weapons and self-defense courses. I've been around more than a few guns in my life. Obviously not like this… but don't worry, I'm sure I'll bawl my eyes out before too long."

Jimmy gave her another quick hug. "Yeah, I'm still not entirely thrilled about all that gun training even if you say it makes you feel safer. And I don't even want to know how you were able to get them here. But I guess it did pay off for this."

They both turned to find Will standing there.

"Dad?" The boy's question came soft with hesitation.

Jimmy knelt and grabbed his son in a tight embrace, cuddling the child close. "I'm so sorry, buddy. So sorry." He released his boy and stared into his face.

"It's okay, Dad. I love you," Will said, and Jimmy hugged him tight again.

"I love you too, son." After a moment, Jimmy stood. "C'mon," he said to Will and Alex. "Let's go."

As they made their way back over toward Les and Aaron, Jimmy holding his son's hand, the young boy spoke up. "Dad? I heard you say you lost a paper with numbers?"

Jimmy squeezed Will's hand. "Don't worry about it, son. It's okay."

Adamant, Will stopped, pulling Jimmy to a halt along with him. "But *Dad*," he insisted. The child fished around and pulled a wadded paper from his pocket. "I'm sorry I took it. It was by your computer, and I wanted to draw something. It was before we had to hide. It has numbers on the other side."

He held it out to Jimmy, who slowly took it from his small hand.

Jimmy glanced to Alex, straightened the sheet. A pencil-drawn picture of a boat with happy fishermen adorned the page. He turned it over. Smudged, but still intact, his handwritten coordinates remained.

Tears glistened in Jimmy's eyes as he shoved the paper into his pocket and ruffled his son's hair. He cradled the boy's chin in his hand.

Alex grinned. "Is that…?"

Before Jimmy could answer, Alex spotted movement in her peripheral vision, drawing her attention back the way they'd just come.

CHAPTER 27

AARON

AARON AND LES STOOD ENGROSSED in conversation. A guttural wail silenced them and made both men jerk their gazes toward the trio still several yards from them.

"What the hell?" Les gasped under his breath. The sight that met their eyes nearly brought each of them to their knees. "I knew he felt too damn warm. But I checked him, I bloody checked him! He had no pulse! He should've been dead!"

Aaron responded in little more than a whisper. "I know you did. So did I."

Shane. Wet and bloody. Monstrous. A wild, deranged scowl contorted his pallid face.

"It's not... that... easy!" he snarled, his gurgled threats hitching and struggling to emanate through clenched teeth. Grisly saliva drooled from curled lips as he lurched to one side, attempting to maintain balance. The epitome of a rabid beast. "You don't... get to get away... that easy!"

Cerise-tinged droplets pooled in his boot prints. A couple more jerking, unsteady staggers toward the small group of survivors brought him within mere feet of them. He opened his clenched fist. A grenade. Pin gone. An evil, warped sneer defined his features and intent.

ALEX

JIMMY HEAVED HIMSELF BACKWARD, PUSHING Will behind him, away from Shane. Alex grabbed Will, pulling him to her. Shane released the spoon and hugged the grenade to his chest. He was so close!

No! You can't do this to us! Powerless to do anything to prevent the loss of her precious family, Alex was gripped by horror as events unfolded for her in a slow-motion purgatory. Her eyes found Aaron's and locked with them. Just for a moment. The heartache in her soul meshed with his anguish and resolve reflected there. Jimmy and Alex hit the deck, shielding Will underneath them.

"You won't make it!"

Alex jerked her head up at Les's shout, just in time to see Aaron in a flying leap tackle Shane with enough force to take them both over the railing and the side of the ship. Mere seconds. No time to think or scream. A deafening explosion rocked the vessel, sending gallons of seawater up to rain down on them.

Stunned, ears ringing, soaked, they regained their feet.

Les ran to them. "Everybody okay?" he asked, giving each a quick check.

He nodded and jumped to the railing.

Scanning the water.

Searching…

Les hung his head and stepped back from the rail.

Will broke into a sob and flopped down where he stood. Jimmy joined him on the deck, attempting to comfort his young son.

Alex just stared at Les. He wouldn't look at her, his blank gaze fixed on the deck. Strong hands fell open and slack at the end of limp arms. The usual sturdy shoulders wilted. His sides caved.

She backed away from him. Stumbling to the railing, she grabbed on to steady herself and leaned out as far as she possibly could. Not wanting to see. But needing to. Just frothy water, bubbles, and foam in slow dissipation in the shallow waves. She scoured the surface. Nothing.

Shouts. Boots clomping across decking. Ship's crew rushing to their aid. Captain Mac's voice reached her ears, several others, but she paid no attention to any of them. The cold of dripping steel under her hands permeated her spirit, injecting a numbness as though it meant to drain away her very life force. Hollow, icy fingers wormed their way around her heart. A desperate pang of desolation, unlike anything she'd ever experienced enveloped her.

This can't be real… it's just cruel!

She lifted a foot to the bottom rung, and Les's hand closed on her arm. The sadness in his damp eyes told her everything she didn't want to know. At last forcing herself away, she turned and sank to wet floorboards, back against the rail, and buried her face in her knees.

139

"Craziest, bravest son of a bitch I ever knew." Les slumped down next to Alex, put a comforting arm around her, and held her while she cried.

Captain Mac spoke up then, loud so all could hear. "That man saved your lives. Saved all our lives. We owe him *everything*."

FATED
REMEMBRANCE

CHAPTER 28

ALEX

AN OVERSEAS FLIGHT BACK TO the States. Two days of debriefing and counseling meetings with Jimmy and some officials. Another flight across the country to the West Coast. Eight days now since her return home. Time to try getting back to normal.

Normal. Alex remained unconvinced she would *ever* feel normal again. What part of that word could hold any real significance for her now? And did she want it to? She should at least make a solid attempt to rejoin what had been her life. Before. Shouldn't she? Or should she just chuck it all and take off, start over, find distractions for her reeling mind? Would that provide relief?

They had all been advised to seek professional help to cope with their traumatic experience. Alex had yet to make any appointment. She had, however, confided as much as she could bring herself to say to her best friend and had spoken with her brother several times by phone and text. Their compassion and counsel had helped keep what remained of her sanity intact.

A quick check through emails. She answered several, deleted most, got up and went to the kitchen to pour a second cup of coffee. After a shower, she completed phone calls, setting a couple of business appointments for the following week. The day before the trip, she'd taken canvases and photography prints to the local gallery to show. Though Lou had attended them, along with her own artworks for the showing, Alex should put in a personal appearance within the next few days. The last thing she wanted to do at the moment, however, was chat with the public even if it was about one of her passions. A groan accompanied knuckles rubbing weary eyes before she grabbed the remote. Her flat-screen snapped to life.

Glued to news sites and channels for days after returning, she'd lived in a hope that maybe there would be something. Anything. A lone survivor washed up on shore? An unidentified man in a hospital? But no word would ever come. A plain brown package two days prior had given her hope, but it ended up containing her pistols that Mac had retained as part of the crew's arsenal and had now returned to her. Glad to have them back, she still couldn't help the feeling of letdown. She'd never know the true objective of the search either. Jimmy couldn't tell her even if he were made privy to those details. So many unanswered questions tormented her mind.

Just as she started flipping channels, a knock pounded on her front door. The remote dropped from her fingers and coffee sloshed from her mug. *Dammit!* Too many things made her edgy these days. She jumped up and grabbed a paper towel off the bar to swipe at her shirt and calmed herself as she crossed the room.

A peek from behind the curtain. Jimmy! She undid the lock and threw open the door.

"Hey, how ya doin', sis?" He stepped forward and engulfed her in a hug.

"Oh my goodness!" She returned his warm embrace. "What are you doing all the way out here?"

"Flew in yesterday. Had to wrap up a couple of things at the university out here, so I thought I'd stop by and surprise you."

She stepped back and let him inside. "I'm so glad you're here. It's good to see you. I'm okay, I guess," she told him in answer to his initial question. "How about you? And how's Will doing?"

"I'm all right. And he's doing good too. It's funny, but he really likes going to his meetings," he continued as they made their way to the kitchen table and sat down. "Says his psychiatrist is fun and likes sports too." He chuckled. "I think he's doing better than me. But we'll be okay."

"I'm so glad," Alex said, putting a hand on her brother's arm. "I've been worried about you guys. Especially him. Because of Mario." She looked down at the table, shook her head, and looked back up at her brother.

"I know. But he seems good. Even been talking about him. And the other guys too. Oh, I almost forgot." He reached into his jacket pocket and produced an SD card, which he put on the table in front of her. "I found it in the bottom of my bag. They must have missed it when they searched everything. I'd forgotten about it, but it's yours."

Alex picked up the small item and gave him a questioning look.

Jimmy continued. "That day when you let Will have your camera? Well, he took more than a few pictures and he came to me, worried about filling it up. I didn't have the time to go through and see if I could delete some of his, so I just gave him one of my cards to put in. It was empty, so you'd have plenty of space, and I just shoved this in my bag. But I wanted to make sure you had it back if you want it."

She looked at the SD card in her hand and back to her brother. "So what they took from my camera was only from... the day of the pirates?" *Oh thank God...*

"Yeah, I guess. Just whatever you took after Will had it. I think he might have taken a few more on it too, but I told him just a couple."

She closed her hand around it. "I'll look at them later. Thank you. When they confiscated all the equipment and computers and stuff, I thought everything was gone." She shook her head. "But I don't think I can do it right now."

"Of course. If you want to throw it away too, do it. Just destroy it first if you do. Just for safety's sake. And don't worry, under the circumstances, I did take the liberty of looking through it. Didn't find anything that would be considered sensitive info, at least in my professional opinion. I just wanted you to have it. I know how you love your pictures. But I know it may be hard to go through them."

Alex nodded. It would be difficult. She slid the SD card into her pocket. "How'd it go with your personal debriefing? Did they ask about Les?"

Jimmy stretched back in his chair. "It went well. No unusual questions. Mac had added Les to the crew roster, so that was thankfully covered. Man, do I owe Mac. And we must've been convincing enough about the attack being random pirates. Plus"—he leaned forward, resting his elbows on the table and lowering his voice as if to tell her a secret—"they recovered the plane!"

"That's awesome!" Alex sat up straight. "When?"

"Three days after we got back to the States."

"Wow, that's fast!"

"And... they were *very* pleased with my accuracy. I guess other consultants had said it'd be damn near impossible to find, so they weren't even convinced I could do it. Gave Mac and the crew a nice bonus. Sent extra for Mario's family." He looked down at a napkin on the tabletop and pushed at it. "It can never compensate..."

Alex reached out and laid a hand on top of his.

Jimmy cleared his throat. "Les is off the grid. There's a post office box in Montana under a woman's name. Only contact info I have for him. I sent him the team's fee, plus. Least I can do. He can handle what to do with it from there."

It pained her seeing her brother so dejected. Shifting to a happier topic, she said, "I'm glad you're taking a leave. You deserve the time off. And Will's gonna love it."

Jimmy's countenance brightened. "I've been considering it for a while. This whole ordeal drove it home. The universities will be fine without me. I don't want to miss any more time with him. Think we'll sail for a while. Some short trips at first. He says he's ready to be out on the water. At least what happened didn't scare him off from that."

They talked for a while and had lunch before he got ready to leave for the airport and his flight home.

"Are you still planning on moving?" Jimmy asked as Alex walked him down the sidewalk to his rental.

"Yeah, definitely. Just not sure when, or where exactly." She smiled at him. "I've been holding back way too much in my life. Time for some major changes. And I've gotta make up my mind sooner or later. This place has always just been temporary for me, but it's been nice. And I know Lou wants me to at least stay in the area." She paused as they got to his car. "We've done some hiking and camping up north. It's gorgeous up there. And I've done some searches on cabins and properties. We'll see. But the pine trees, oh my God, you wouldn't believe how big! And the smell!"

"Know that old pine tree in our front yard when we were kids? You had so many cones!" Jimmy laughed as he glanced skyward. "I think Dad secretly got rid of some every now and then. He didn't think you'd notice."

"Oh, believe me, I noticed. And I still have a few." She nudged her brother's elbow.

"Sounds like a great spot for you then."

"Yeah. But stick me in the middle of a pine forest like that and you may never see me again. I can work remotely now, you know."

"What, no Christmas invite?"

"You know I'm kidding! Mostly." Alex offered a sassy grin. "Of course you and Will are *always* welcome wherever I live."

Jimmy gave her another hug before opening the door, then said as an afterthought, "I still think you should travel first. Go on an adventure. Go see the world 'n' stuff." His tone was half joking, but he turned more sincere. "Like I've said before, you've got the perfect job for it. You can go anywhere. As you say, work remotely. And now you've got opportunity. You should. Just go."

"You're always telling me that." She crossed her arms and cocked her head at him. "Okay. I'll take it into consideration. But I think maybe I've had quite enough adventure for a while. I'll be sure to let you know though. Call me when you get home?"

"I will," he said. "We'll talk more soon. Love ya, kid."

"Love you too."

Jimmy got in, started the engine, and drove away.

CHAPTER 29

ALEX

LATER THAT EVENING, ALEX SAT at her computer, card in hand. Was she ready to see the pictures? Relive those memories so soon? She squeezed her eyes shut and inhaled, held, opening them again on an extended exhale. Best go ahead and go through them. Get it over with. She stuck the card in the slot and began her download.

Scenic photos, the dock, the ship, the ocean, several sunsets and sunrises. Random pictures of the crew, her brother, her nephew. A group shot of the three of her family and the crew. One of the protection detail. Though reluctant to have any taken, the three agreed to pose for one. And one of Will with Les at the rail. A couple of her being silly that Will had taken.

Another she took of Les and Aaron at the rail. Looking back now, had they been discovered, these photos would have raised unfortunate questions as to the identity of unregistered parties aboard. Unless Mac had a cover for that too. A couple more snapped of the submersibles and crew at work, Captain Mac at his post. She wiped her eyes as recent memories came flooding back through the images on her screen. She had taken quite a few, but those were what she remembered. The rest were from Will's hand.

There were a lot; her brother was not wrong. She always loaded the larger card first, expecting to take way too many herself.

Will had a good eye for photography, though sometimes a clumsy finger. A couple of shots showed only deck. Unless there was some small bug that she just couldn't see. She chuckled. He was also sneaky. The few of her relaxing on the upper deck she hadn't known about. She'd located the most secluded spot she could in order to remain discreet while getting some sun. Will had obviously found her.

Also, more of the three hired men. They had likely not known either as they appeared in various states of horsing around. Fun and informal. Aaron's smile. *Oh God.* She fought back the growing lump in her throat and her stinging eyes. Some silly ones of Mario holding a fake carrot mustache balanced on his upper lip. She looked away, and the tears came as she recalled in all too vivid detail his heroic last stand.

After a few moments she wiped damp cheeks again and continued. There was one of Shane from a distance, talking on his sat phone. A sickening punch to her gut. Exactly *who* had he been speaking to? She almost deleted it, not wanting to look at him, but didn't. More of the crew, some of Jimmy, one of a seagull on the roof deck of the bridge. A couple of attempted selfies with Will making a silly face. She smiled.

The next one made her breath catch. She and Aaron sat on the deck, facing each other, laughing. She tried to remember what had been said in that exact moment but couldn't.

Movement beside her. Sami, her friend's cat, jumped up on her legs. She hugged him tight and buried her face in the black fur on his back. A happy rumble of purrs, and she let him settle onto her lap.

Alex looked up to the screen. Would she ever know for sure, ever *really* gain closure? No body had been recovered. Excruciating as it had been to hear, Jimmy explained to her that that wasn't uncommon in ocean environments. Especially with the explosion. And Les's hug at the dock, encompassing and drawn out. The salute to her as he walked away before disappearing into the crowd. That distant look in his eyes; the same as just after the explosion when he'd been at the rail of the ship. When he could barely bring himself to look at her. The desolate suffering. So final.

Why was she still so caught up with this? Why did it still affect her so? Why did *he?* Was it just the extreme situation that had come to such a dramatic and violent end? She had known Aaron for less than a month, but the pain she experienced felt like she'd lost someone close whom she'd known her entire life. The depth of emotion seemed absolutely ridiculous!

Her first day back, after Lou left her apartment, she'd cried herself numb. The next four, she'd sobbed herself to sleep each night. Now she just tried to keep him off her mind. To no avail. Maybe she did need to talk with a professional. Maybe just more time was needed to get past it all.

Aaron. That signature half smile, sometimes sarcastic or whimsical, but a reaction more representative of the friendly, interested, and inquisitive side of his nature. He was unique and kind with an undertone of sadness. A lot more existed under the surface than he let show.

They'd shared great conversations on that short voyage, plans and dreams, past remembrances. Sitting and talking with him about life in general and hearing the stories he *was* willing to share from days gone by had become her daily guilty pleasure. He possessed a wonderful, contemplative take on many things. *God, I miss that. Miss him.*

How in the world had he ever wound up in such a hard profession? His thoughtful, bright, and at times downright silly personality, when he did let that surface, appeared in extreme conflict with the stringency and combat skills, the violence sometimes required in protection work. That was the key though. Protecting others. That was the aspect that made it work. And he was damn good at it. The precision of his movements. His quiet intensity. Sharp and controlled. Everything with intent and purpose. Always deliberate, never sloppy. Some of it had to be a natural athletic ability, but however else he'd come by his expertise, the man had known his stuff.

Just the right hint of cologne. The first time he'd passed close by, the memory of a childhood family trip to the mountains had jumped to mind. Surrounded by pine trees. Never overpowering, his subtle, enticing woodsy scent enchanted her. Even sweaty and dirty as they'd stood hidden in that tiny compartment off her room, his body pressed to hers, fingers intertwined, she'd been captivated. That moment had imprinted the essence on her soul forever.

And that crazy weird electricity in his touch, whatever cool oddity that was. Aside from that, just being around him magnetized her far more than any physical presence could account for.

Musings wandering too far now, she snapped herself back to reality and the present moment. Yeah, meet someone that exceptional, whom she'd also experienced a real connection with, and he ended up getting himself killed. And even though that act involved him doing a thing utterly selfless and brave, saving her family's lives, it still hurt like hell.

Why does this have to feel so bad? What is *this? Yep. I've officially lost it…*

She let out the breath she held and continued through the remaining dozen or so photos. The last few were of Aaron and Les. Will must have taken it as a personal challenge when they said no more pictures. Them at the railing, talking and laughing. A couple of Les by himself, looking out over the ocean. The last three were Aaron. Leaning on the railing, one foot propped up on the bottom rung. Facing out toward the sunset, the soft orange glow highlighting deep introspection. An exquisite capture. The next, he stood looking down at the deck. The last brought her a surprised and eerie charge. Standing tall, eyes fixed out of frame, hand on the grip of his holstered pistol. Downright handsome, but serious. A little *too* serious, even for him.

Reflecting on those photos brought her tears once more. The beauty in them just enhanced the sense of loss. Why, oh why, did things have to end the way they did? *I'm so tired of feeling shitty! This hurt needs to stop!*

She jacked in a fresh USB drive and backed up everything. She would not leave them on the computer. Flash drive and the SD card stowed in a safe place in her desk, she turned out the light and carried Sami in to join his feline sister Mia on the corner of her bed. Flannel sheets that should have snuggled her in coziness were cold and lonesome. Sleep would not come easy again tonight.

CHAPTER 30

ALEX

"BYE, YOU GUYS! AND THANKS!"

Lou and Alex waved as the red Audi A5 convertible containing two of their friends drove off. Louise Christmas, or Lou, and Alex had been best friends since high school. Lou's move west and her subsequent enticing invitations had prompted Alex to embark on her own childhood dream to the area after her breakup. The laid-back coastal town of Intention Point, California, was nice though not her ultimate end goal. But it would do for now. The two made their way up the sidewalk to Alex's apartment as Alex got out her key.

"That was so much fun! I just *love* that band!" the taller girl exclaimed, long brown curls bouncing as she skipped along behind Alex, hands on her friend's shoulders. She gave Alex a quick squeeze. "And it's so good to see you laugh again too, sweetie."

Over a month now since the ordeal on the ship, Alex had somewhat settled back into her everyday routines. And some evenings out with friends helped too.

The following morning, the two chatted over coffee and breakfast before Lou had to leave.

"We've got to do that more often," Lou said, referring to the previous evening's outing.

"Yeah, it was a good time." Alex smiled back at her friend. "Kinda forgot how much I love dancing. It's been a while."

"I know!" Lou replied. "Now you're back to being you again too." She eyed Alex. "You seem a little different though. Braver. And not as reserved in speaking your mind anymore either. I still can't believe you told Miller to go fuck himself. Remember Eddie at the next table? Think he 'bout choked on his beer over that one." She giggled. "He was still talking about how badass you were an hour later with his crew."

"You're funny," Alex replied with a smirk. "Well, being held captive by a madman and then getting shot does change the perspective a bit." She ran her hand down her side to the place where Aaron's bullet had grazed her. To tell Lou that she considered the nearly healed wound a badge of honor because the scar would be a permanent reminder of Aaron? That might make her friend think she'd really gone over the edge. "Plus Miller deserved it. Joking around is one thing, but what he did? That was over the line. Sorry, guess I just don't have time for the bullshit anymore."

"Don't be sorry," Lou replied. "I like it. My girl out to kick some butt!"

Alex laughed. "Not out to. But not gonna deal with what I don't have to. And *shouldn't* have to. I guess the whole ship thing is making me look at life a little different now. Need to get out there and make it count, you know? Take some bigger chances."

"Absolutely! I agree!" Lou clapped her hands together. "Right there with ya, girl." She picked up her mug and took a sip of coffee. "Speaking of that, Chad seems nice. I think he really likes you too."

"Don't try to fix me up!" Alex's sharp retort was out before she could think. Her thoughts flashed to Aaron again, and she just as quickly shut them down. She'd found her mind being drawn to him more in the past several days, and she couldn't control it. Every time she looked at a man, she saw Aaron's face. No way could she attempt a date. Would she ever be over him? And what was there to be over? *Oh Lord, I've fallen for a dead guy...* Lou would assume she was still just upset about Brad or Chip. Alex squeezed her eyes tight and, after several deep breaths, recovered. "Sorry. You know I'm just not ready for that yet."

Lou apologized and reached across the table to give Alex's hand a hasty grip. "I know, sweetie. And again, I'm so sorry. I shouldn't keep on it like I do. I just want you to be happy."

Alex nodded. "I know." Conversational again after her own sip of coffee, she offered her observation. "Yeah, he is nice. He's so funny too. I wouldn't have thought that. I always thought he was quiet."

Lou giggled in relief at the acknowledgment. "Well, give him a couple of beers and he becomes a silly mister jabber-jaw."

Alex giggled back. "What, like you?"

"Shut up!" Lou feigned shock and threw a piece of her toast crust at Alex.

Alex ducked, and the piece of bread skidded across the linoleum to stop against the counter. She stuck her tongue out at her friend and got up to go retrieve it to the trash. "You missed."

Lou faked another hard throw with her last piece and then popped the toast into her mouth. "Maybe we should go to the range. Think my aim is suffering."

"Sounds like a plan. I need to work on mine too."

"If we go Wednesday night, we can listen to Billy's comments about how girls can't shoot." Lou smirked. "Sound fun?"

"That sounds *especially* fun." Alex's eyes took on a devious glint. "And we'll show him just how *bad* we really are. Wanna challenge him? You *know* he'll go for it."

Lou smirked again as she got up from the table. "Oh yeah."

"Call me later?"

"Will do."

"Cool. And I am sorry for yelling at you," Alex said as they walked toward her front door. "I just… It has to *feel* right. I don't want a repeat of Brad, and I *definitely* don't need another Chip." She rolled her eyes at the latter. "I just want some time. And before you say it, I'm *not* looking for perfection. I don't care if he lives in a shack or if he's a billionaire, if he's a hit man or a preacher. I just need the right feeling."

A snort issued from Lou. "Girl, the examples you come up with. Hit man or preacher? One extreme to the other, eh?" She flopped an arm over Alex's shoulders and squeezed. "It's okay. You don't need to apologize to me," she said. "I know I can go a little overboard sometimes."

Alex winced at that last remark but hid it with a tight grin and shake of her head. Her friend had no idea…

She had just pushed open her door for Lou when she heard her name. Both turned to look.

Alex's neighbor and landlord, Betsy Wilcott, hurried across the small courtyard toward them, her silver hair almost glowing in the morning sunlight. Her short, squat form moved with a grace that would be unexpected to someone who didn't know her.

Rosy cheeks dimpled as she greeted them, and she stuck out her plump hand to Alex. Fingers clutched a small envelope. "I wanted to make sure you got this. A nice young man stopped by last night and was going to leave it in your door. But I told him I would get it to you."

Alex took it from her and thanked her. Ever since her move here the year prior, the vivacious landlord had kept an attentive eye on Alex and her activities. To some, that attention could come off as nosy, and maybe to a degree it was, but to Alex she seemed more watchful and protective. Betsy had never overstepped any personal boundaries, retaining a grandmotherly respect, and Alex appreciated that in return.

"You're always looking out for us," she said with a grateful smile.

"Well, you can never be too careful. He was such a kind and decent young man." She winked at Alex. "I didn't want it to fall or get blown away and lost. You girls take care now." Betsy turned back toward her home. "Enjoy this beautiful sunny day. Too nice to stay inside!"

"We will!" Lou called after her.

Alex turned the envelope over, but the only thing written on it was her first name. She frowned and was about to toss it on the entryway stand when Lou stopped her.

"Aren't you gonna open it and see who it's from?"

"Nope. Later."

"Seriously? Come on!" Lou beamed. "Maybe it was Chad."

Alex shot her a critical eye. "Couldn't be. We were all out together last night, remember?"

"Oh yeah. True. Duh. Well… okay… but you *better* fill me in, Miss Popular. See ya later!" Lou hugged Alex goodbye and headed for her car.

Alex closed the door behind her. Just using her first name indicated someone familiar to her or who wanted her to think that. An A2-size envelope, rose beige in color. Softly elegant yet understated. She turned it over again for closer inspection. No other markings besides her name. And it wasn't Chip. He bore down so hard when writing it was as if he wanted to engrave whatever surface lay beneath the poor traumatized paper. This was a handwriting she did not recognize. After holding it a few moments more, her curiosity took hold and she sliced it open. Removing the small matching note inside, she unfolded it. It was dated yesterday and read: JUST WANTED YOU TO KNOW. AARON

Alex's eyes felt as though they might pop from their sockets as she clamped a hand to her mouth. Her legs buckled. Gripping the note in her clenched fist, she fell hard against the door and slid down to the floor, knees drawn up in front of her, very glad she had waited and was alone now. She did not want to have to explain it all just yet. How? And that… She brought the paper to her face and inhaled. His smell! Just barely, but whatever cologne that was, it was him!

A whimper as tears came. With an abrupt swipe of her hand, she wiped them away and stood, adrenaline kicking her into action. Her heart raced. She began to pace, read the note again, and paced some more.

How is this possible? She stopped then, still clutching the small note tight.

"At least I know he's alive," she said. "And that's one helluva good place to start."

CHAPTER 31

ALEX

ALEX RETURNED FROM HER MORNING run. Showered and refreshed, she fixed herself breakfast and carried everything out to her balcony to enjoy the morning sunlight and fresh air. Birds chirped as they flitted through the trees, a melodic contrast to the light traffic noise so typical of a Saturday morning.

A bite of scrambled eggs. A text dinging on her cell phone— Lou sending a funny. A giggle and reply.

She set the phone back down and rubbed her eyes. Almost a week since the note, and it still monopolized her thoughts. Where was he? Would he come back? Was that short note just *it?* And if he didn't plan on coming back, why had he bothered with the note in the first place? What was the point? Just so she'd know he wasn't dead? Why would it matter to him? She sighed.

And where would a good starting place even *be* to find him? He, or someone he trusted, had been at her door; beyond that, she had no clue. The only solid thing he'd ever mentioned on any kind of location was wanting a place off the grid. *That's helpful.*

She stretched and groaned. Too many questions and no real answers. Unfortunately, that seemed a repeating theme with him. Leaning on the wrought iron railing, she rested her chin on crossed arms and stared down at the small parking area and green space beyond.

A motorcycle slowed on the street out front. The neighbors a few places down had bikes and lots of friends with bikes, so even though she wasn't in view of the street side, sound indicated their weekend gathering had begun. The bike's engine revved twice and zoomed off into the distance. Well, maybe not the neighbors.

Better finish eating her now-cold breakfast. She sat back and munched the rest of her bacon and eggs, collected her plate and mug, and took them inside. After pouring the remaining coffee, she returned to her balcony, flopped into the seat, and put her bare feet up on the rail. Cool metal invigorated her skin as she massaged her toes against it.

Lou texted again, speculating about the day as she waited for her boyfriend to return her call. Alex was about to reply when another text came through.

"Hey." An unfamiliar number and not one of her saved contacts. A misdial? She almost deleted it but decided to reply.

"Hey???" she sent back.

A few minutes passed. Nothing. Yep, probably a wrong number.

A walk downtown would do her good and maybe help clear her head. She went back inside, pulled on shoes, and grabbed a jacket to put on over her T-shirt and jeans. Though comfortably warm here, a light breeze drifted inland from the coast. The closer she moved in that direction, the cooler the air would get.

Front door closed and locked, she shoved the keys in her pocket. Another ding.

She pulled out her phone and read, "Would you like to go for a ride?" It was the same unknown number.

Okay, this is starting to get… a little weird.

"Who is this?" she texted back.

No reply. She looked around, and Betsy called out to her from her front porch and waved. Alex waved back, then scanned the street again. Her phone had a full charge. She would be mindful. No worries. Passing by Betsy's place on her way, Alex stopped to visit with her landlord.

As she stood to leave sometime later, a thought occurred to Alex. "I was just wondering… the man who left the note last week? What kind of car did he drive?"

Betsy was always keen on the details. Betsy would remember.

"Oh, he didn't have a car, dear," she replied. "He rode a motorcycle. It was one of those sporty ones like Ray down there has. You know, the ones that look like they're for racing? A nice red-and-white one."

Alex thanked her and stepped back out onto the sidewalk. She walked toward downtown and the farmers' market. With strange texts coming in, it would be smart to stay in a more public setting. Plus she could use some fresh veggies for her dinner later.

Her phone dinged again, and she jumped, almost tripping. *Shit!* It was Lou. Alex sighed and checked her surroundings again before replying and telling Lou about the texts. Lou was instantly on high alert. Be careful, call if anything weird happened, text when she got to the market—before she started back, halfway back, and when she was home. Lou was just being protective, but gah!

Alex had just stuck the phone back in her pocket when it dinged again. "Lou, *okay* already," she said out loud as she swiped the message into view. It wasn't Lou.

"Go to Cheeze Pleeze." The mystery number again.

Cheeze Pleeze was an artisan cheese stand at the farmers' market, the owner a friend. But this wasn't the owner messaging her. *Crap. Is someone following me?* Only about a block away from the market, and lots of people, she picked up her pace. Helena would be at her cheese stand and could hopefully provide information about just what the heck was going on. Alex entered the market gate and weaved her way through the crowd toward her destination.

A shorter, dark-haired woman, boisterous and cheerful, Helena greeted Alex as she walked up. "Hey, sweetie! Haven't seen you in a few weeks! How are you?" Expertly shaped brows came together as she took a good look at Alex. "What's wrong?"

Alex leaned across the narrow counter to return Helena's warm greeting with a hug. "Well, I really don't know," she said as she stepped back. She moved over to the side counter to speak more privately. "I'm getting weird texts."

"What *kinda* weird?" Helena's brown eyes lit with piqued curiosity. "*Good* weird or *bad* weird?"

Alex laughed at her. "Well, I'd like to think good, but I just don't know. And I don't know the number."

"Hmmm. Oh, hold on a sec, I'll be right back!"

A couple of customers needed assistance, and Helena stepped away to help them. Alex rested her elbows on the counter, scanning the crowd. A busy Saturday saw patrons meandering through as they inspected current wares available for purchase. From elderly to babies, all age groups were represented, including many different ethnicities. Nothing out of place. No one paying her any extra attention. *I'm probably just being paranoid.* She shook her head at her worries and looked back to Helena as her friend returned.

"So what *are* they?" the woman asked in eager anticipation, nodding at Alex's phone.

"Okay. Well, the last one said to come here. To you." She showed Helena the text.

"Hmm… That *is* weird." Helena contemplated the screen. "Oh!" Her mouth dropped open, and she smacked a palm to her forehead. "Duh! Oh, I'm *so* sorry! I totally forgot! It's been so busy here today. Here!"

Helena motioned for Alex to come on back, behind her counter. From a small drawer below her cash register, she pulled out an envelope and handed it to Alex.

"What's this?"

"I don't know. Some guy came by like twenty minutes ago and asked me if I knew you and if I would give it to you."

Alex threw her hands up in mock defense. "Okay, now this is getting *weirder* by the second!"

Weird was an understatement. Who *was* this? She was ready to rip open the envelope when her brain put the pieces together. Her first name only on the front. The handwriting matched the envelope Betsy had given her a week earlier. Her studious scrutiny of *that* one had committed every last detail to memory.

Helena scooted a stool up behind Alex. "Are ya okay, sweetie? You look like you're about to pass out."

Alex sat down, hands shaking. If the writing matched and the texts had led her here… She tore open the envelope and removed the note. PIER 7 COFFEE & SUDS.

Pier 7 Coffee & Suds, a small eclectic place at the head of the pier. A quaint coffee shop from early morning until midafternoon, it reinvented itself daily to open at seven in the evening as a bar and grill, including a small craft beer brewery. Well known to her, it was a place she and Lou frequented for both coffee some mornings and occasional Saturday nights for dinner with friends and to see local bands.

Alex pressed the note to her chest and turned to Helena. "Gotta go!" she said, unable to contain her excitement as hope charged her to action. She jumped up, hugged her friend, and scooted out around the counter. "And thank you!" She held up the note.

"Well, you're welcome, hon!" Helena replied with a perceptive giggle. A moment later she called out after her. "I take it it's *good* weird?"

Alex called back over her shoulder. "It's *very* good weird!"

Alex hurried through the crowd, back out to the market entrance. She jogged to the nearby corner, waited for the light to change, sprinted across the street. With three more blocks to go to the pier, she tried to calm her racing heart and mind and pay attention. She just wanted to get there. And really needed to get there in one piece.

Two motorcycles, one of them red and white, and a few cars occupied the parking lot. The antique wooden door creaked as it opened, a feature left unrepaired to add ambiance.

As she made her way to the front counter, she looked around at the various patrons. Cozy seating arrangements and booths were occupied by a few locals she was acquainted with and also several unfamiliar faces. She exchanged a wave with a couple she knew and turned to the counter as the man behind it greeted her.

"Hey, Alex!"

She returned his greeting with a bright smile. "Hey, John."

"Can I get you something?"

Alex leaned toward him, hands gripping the edge of the counter. "I think I'll pass on the coffee today—already a little too wired." She smiled again and paused as he nodded. "But can you tell me if someone is waiting for me?"

He shrugged. "Not that I know of. No one's said anything to me." He frowned at the puzzled look on her face. "You s'posed to meet Lou or somethin'?"

"No, not Lou. I was just told to come here, and I thought…" She glanced around the room again.

"Well, just 'cause I don't know don't mean they're not here. Or maybe just not yet. Runnin' late, you know." He smiled as he dried a mug. "You may wanna stick around, check out back on the pier. I saw a lotta new people out there earlier. And some of the usual locals. Fishin's been good this mornin'."

"Yeah, okay," she replied and pushed back off the counter. "And thanks."

"Yep. An' if anybody comes in a-lookin' for ya, I'll send 'em your way."

"You rock, John." Alex headed to the door to the pier.

Salty ocean air, the squawking of hungry seagulls, and the lap of light waves met her as she pushed the door open. She wound her way through the restaurant's outdoor dining tables.

Fishermen with their long rods over the rails, buckets and tackle next to them, chatted here and there. Some stood, some sat, one grandfather instructed his young grandchildren, a boy and a girl, on the finer points of baiting their hooks. She smiled as she walked by, breathing in deeply the cool, briny sea breeze.

The long pier stretched ahead. A gorgeous morning. She'd just wander all the way out to the end before turning back. *God, I hope he's here.* Her sneakers made small thuds on thick boards as she moved along. Waves broke in miniature explosions against support pilings underneath.

John was right—there really were quite a few people out on the pier, enjoying the late morning. Her phone vibrated in her pocket right before the ding. It was Lou. *Uh-oh.* She should have texted her a while ago. She responded, stuck her phone back in her pocket, ran a hand through her hair, and glanced around. The phone dinged again, and she pulled it back out, expecting Lou.

It was the "not as much a mystery" number. "All the way."

She looked toward the end of the pier, the way she'd been heading, but it was still obscured by a group of sightseers. She grinned and began walking again. *That* was a loaded remark. Hmmm, should she play with that or be good? Unable to think up a snappy reply on the spot, she just kept moving.

She approached the dozen or so tourists and picked her way through the group. The last of them shuffled past her. With another fifty-odd feet to go, only two fishermen stood to her left about halfway there. One lone figure leaned on the rail at the very end. Back to her, facing out over the water, jeans and black jacket now replaced more tactical dress. She recognized his form immediately. Someone she thought lost from this life.

Don't cry, don't cry, don't cry! Get a grip! She bit her lip and moved closer. Stuffing her phone back in her pocket, she walked the last few feet, turned, and leaned with her back against the railing next to him.

RECOMPENSE OF FORFEIT

CHAPTER 32

ALEX

ALEX LOOKED OVER AT AARON. Having assumed him dead most of this time, or at least on her holdout hope of maybe injured and holed up in some remote location to heal, her heart rejoiced that he appeared none the worse for wear. And although he had yet to acknowledge her presence, a faint smile tugged at the corner of his mouth. Eyes concealed behind dark sunglasses, he stared out over the ocean.

Alex was the one to break the silence. "You know, you're lucky I even showed up."

"I knew you'd figure it out," he replied, continuing to regard the waves. His grin deepened. He lifted his sunglasses, set them on top of his head, and turned to look at her.

Ardent blue-greens the color of a misty forest morning beheld her. Riveted, she lost everything she wanted to convey to him, the whole of any conversation she had even imagined effectively leaving her brain. After all that had happened, the shock, the loss and mourning, now the miracle of his survival, of being in his presence again, took her breath away. Her resolve was to just say "thank you," and before she altogether burst into tears, she took hold of his arm and buried her face against his shoulder. His arms were around her in an instant, the strength and tenderness of his touch a comforting assurance that the moment was real.

"Do you…?" she began through tears. "I thought we were all dead. And then you saved us, but you…" She trailed off, at a loss for words. Nothing was coming out right. She bit her lip, trying so hard not to cry.

He held her tighter. After a time, he released her and rested his forearms on her shoulders. She wiped her damp cheeks and took hold of the front of his jacket. They stared into each other's eyes for a few moments before Alex spoke again.

"How?"

Aaron shook his head, glanced out at the waves, back to her. "It's a long story."

Alex, now regaining composure after getting the tears out of the way, pulled hard on his jacket. She narrowed her eyes. "Well, are you gonna have time to *tell* me?"

"Wow. Okay, well…" He gave her his half smile. "That's up to you, isn't it?"

Alex opened her mouth to reply, shut it again. A rush of hope brought dimples to her cheeks. "Up to me, huh?" *Okay, this is good.* As her excitement grew, so did her confidence, and she made up her mind to see just where this would lead. She peered at him through her lashes, capturing her lower lip with her teeth for a few seconds. "You sure you really want me to answer that?"

He laughed aloud at her coy pretense. "I think I can handle it."

"Well." She let go of his jacket and folded her arms, surveying him. "Part of me wants to thank you. Part of me wants to punch you *really* hard. And part of me wants to kiss you."

"That's... not really an answer." He leaned his elbow on the rail. "Do I get a say in which of those options I get?"

Her face flushed and she looked back out at the water. "I did already say thank you."

"Yes, you did." The corners of his mouth edged upward again. He replaced his sunglasses over his eyes and gazed out at the ocean along with her. "I guess you might as well hit me then and get it over with."

She uncrossed her arms, her jaw falling open as she turned to stare at him. *Seriously?*

He just stood there, still and silent.

"You ass..." She took a swing, making a solid connection with his upper arm, a little harder than she'd intended.

"Oww! Damn!" He took a step back and massaged his wounded limb.

"You deserved that."

"Yeah, I guess I did. I really did." Aaron eyed her. "You done?"

She moved to the rail, leaned her arms on it, and closed her eyes, unable to hide a shy grin. "I covered the first two of my options. The last one is up to you, isn't it?"

"You sure you want me to answer that?" he asked, a clear play on her earlier question to him.

Doing the same in regard to his previous answer, she replied, "I think I can handle it."

Aaron delayed. Was he trying to draw out the anticipation? He reached over, looped an arm around her shoulders, and pulled her close, leaned in. He pressed his lips to hers for a couple of seconds and pulled back.

The protective strength of his arm cradling her, that ethereal spicy woodland scent, and his firm yet soft lips left Alex's heart racing. *That can't be... it? Just that little peck?* Attempting to reconcile whether she was experiencing astonishment at the kiss itself, something she had hoped for, or at the severe brevity of said kiss, she recovered her presence of mind.

What a comical expression. *Does he even know how adorable that half smile is? Of course he does. He's having fun with this!*

"Uh... really?" She backed up half a step. "That's it? Are you *kidding* me?" She couldn't see his eyes behind the dark metallic lenses, just that crooked smirk. Voice subdued, she rolled her eyes at him and shook her head. "Wow. Just wow. I mean, that was just so, so incredibly *unimpressive.*"

He laughed at her and she played at pushing him away as she continued. "So, *so* bad. No. I just don't even know what to say right now. Unbelievable! *Really* sad. I—"

AARON

AARON TIGHTENED HIS GRIP ON her and with his free hand removed the sunglasses, placing them back on top of his head. Mirth and sparkle showed through her determined gaze. He liked that look—equal parts challenge, curiosity, and yearning. She *was* excited to see him. *That'll work.* Green and gold flecks shimmered in her irises, and as he stared into their depths, he slid his hand up behind her neck and head and pulled her to him. He couldn't help being a tease with that first kiss; with his blood rushing and heart pounding as though it would burst from his chest at her following his instructions and showing up to meet him, he had done that more to calm himself. But this one... He kissed her again.

Tender at first, the kiss deepened as he tested her receptiveness to more. Her lips yielded to the press of his tongue. He advanced further, and she surrendered to his exploration, engaging him with her own. The nervous excitement of the unknown became, in a curious twist, all at once intimate and familiar, and the sudden longing that flowed between them threatened to take both by surprise.

As she slid her hands inside his jacket and up behind his back, he pressed himself into her comforting hold. Their embrace long and deep, her body melted against his. When their lips parted, he stared into hazel eyes again, resting his forehead against hers.

"Better?" he breathed.

Her eyelids fluttered closed as she caught her breath. A slow smile and she raised her lids to return his gaze. "Much."

His lips brushed hers, and he hugged her close once more. "That maybe make up for any of the hell I put you through?"

She snuggled him tight. "A little."

He released her and flipped his sunglasses back down. "A *little?*"

"It's a start." She grinned before continuing. "But oh yeah, you're gonna have to do a *lot* more than that." She did an about-face and began walking back up the pier toward the restaurant.

"What?" He stared after her. *Bluff called.*

"You heard me," she replied and kept walking.

She's good. With a light jog, he caught up to her and took hold of her hand, clutching it tight. She returned his squeeze, and they made their way back up the pier, past the restaurant, and out front to the parking lot.

He led her over to the red-and-white motorcycle and stopped. "You never did answer me about that ride."

"You're funny."

CHAPTER 33

ALEX

THEY RODE TO THE EDGE of town, through the countryside for a time, and started up into the hills. Emerald trees, multicolored wildflowers, and the browns and grays of stone and weathered fences blurred as they passed.

Alex reflected on their kiss. "Better," he'd asked. That was possibly the most severe understatement of the century. His urgency and tenderness confirmed she hadn't been the only one missing their togetherness. There really were no words. And to finally feel the warmth and security of his body in her arms again… this time in mutual desire and with no catastrophic danger looming?

She savored the recent memory as she leaned forward against him to speak into his ear. "Where are we going?"

Aaron angled his head back toward her. "I want to show you something."

In time, smooth highway blacktop transformed to back roads tar and chip. Elevation increased. Winding gravel roads. A secluded turnoff that ended in a long dusty trail up through tall trees. Alex clung tight, matching Aaron's movements as they bounced and jostled over increasingly rougher terrain. Soon that path disappeared into a bed of pine needles and leaf litter.

Farther into deep forest, Aaron brought the bike to a stop in a small clearing. The throaty whir of the performance engine ceased, revealing the serene quietude of nature.

Alex stepped to cushioned earth. Towering evergreens, a few deciduous trees in the mix, surrounded them. Immense granite boulders protruded from the upslope, anchoring statuesque conifers. Opposite, massive trunks framed a view of majestic snow-capped mountains that melded into woodland valleys below. Forest air, fresh and cool, caressed her face with the scent of pine. She performed a slow rotation in place before lifting her gaze through soaring treetops to the few puffy clouds and blue sky beyond.

AARON

AARON DISMOUNTED THE BIKE AND leaned back against it. Had his assumption been right? What would she think of this place? Silent in her observation, she swept her long hair back from her face with elegant fingers. Graceful arms that had encircled his waist the whole ride here now hugged her own shoulders. Her impression of this rugged natural locale lit her features. Head tilted now as she looked to the sky, her hair cascaded farther down her back.

He tugged at his jeans and made an adjustment to his stance before she could notice his excitement, then crossed one ankle over the other. *Look casual.* He grabbed his lower lip in his teeth and clamped down to keep his mouth from displaying the silly grin that his soul pushed forth. *Excellent idea, Donovan. Just don't get ahead of yourself…*

She returned her focus to him. "This is amazing! How did you find it?"

"I guess that's a long story too," he replied. "Right now, let's just say I needed to be a little more off the grid for a while."

Alex glanced around. "Okay." Finding his eyes again, she remarked, "This is beautiful."

"Good. I'm glad you like it." He walked over to a large rock overlooking the view on the downhill side and sat. "Bought it a few years back. Figured maybe someday…"

Alex made her way over to sit next to him. "Nice," she said, impressed. "How much land is here?"

"Couple hundred acres."

She pulled her legs up in front of her, hugged them, and rested her chin on her knees, staring out through the trees at the view. They sat there in silence for a time, just taking it in.

Light pressure on the outside of his left thigh shifted Aaron's attention. He glanced down at her hand, up to meet the deep hazel gaze that rested on him.

"How is it?"

The gunshot wound from the ship. The warmth of her delicate touch soothed the place that would soon become another scar. He held her gaze locked with his own and laid his hand on hers to press it tighter against him. That electric rush surged into his palm and up his wrist. *That… I gotta find out what that is! Or maybe I'm nuts. Probably am.* "It's okay. Healing."

"Good." Comforted at that reassurance, her eyelids fluttered and she leaned her head on his shoulder and exhaled. "You know, you should never have brought me here."

"Why?"

"Because now I don't want to leave."

A giddiness washed through him. *Wish we could stay right now too.* He slipped his arm around her shoulders and kissed her on top of her head. She snuggled into his hold. He rested his head against hers, and they remained like that a while longer before he spoke again.

"Well, unfortunately it gets pretty cold up here at night. Better head back down before it gets too late. You hungry?"

ALEX

ALEX NODDED BUT MADE NO move to get up. Aaron stood and stretched, turning to stand in front of her. Chill air rushed in to chase away the warmth where his body had been. She looked up into his inviting gaze. *Wow.* Sighing into acceptance, she grabbed his hands and he pulled her up off the rock.

Lengthening shadows traversed their path as they rode back down toward town. That look in his eyes, the wonder of this gorgeous natural setting, the whole scenario of the day so far was enchanting. Dreamlike. Too perfect. Rays from the lowering sun flashed between shaded tree trunks, strobing and flickering as they zipped past. Alex hadn't paid attention to just how far their destination had been. Earlier excitement had masked hours of travel time. They ate at a small, out-of-the-way diner with good food before heading back toward her apartment. She leaned against his back, arms snug around his waist, his hand resting on hers on the straightaways. This day could just go on forever.

Back in her neighborhood, he didn't drive right up to her place but parked the bike a couple of blocks away in deep shadow. They walked the rest. She wanted to ask why but didn't. Catching him scout around from time to time, she finally looked at him and raised a brow.

He shook his head. "Just used to being on guard," he said with a hint of smile, though still keeping a watchful eye.

"You're *really* gonna have to fill me in on all that at some point, you know."

"Give it some time." He squeezed her hand.

She smiled and squeezed back, gaining a spring in her step. If he was saying give it some time, that meant he would be staying around. And to have the time he would need, to be able to reach that point at which he might be able to open up and explain it to her? That could take a while. A good long while. "Time I've got," she replied and hugged his arm.

They reached her door. She unlocked it and pushed it open, took a step inside. He remained on the porch but had not let go of her hand. She put her free hand on her hip and eyed him. "There's no way I'm gonna tell you to stay out there, so that one's up to you."

He delayed a moment longer for effect, winked at her, and walked in.

She dropped her keys on the stand and closed the door behind them. "Well, okay then," she said under her breath, her stomach fluttering now in sudden anticipation of something thought lost.

Her thoughts still lingered on their kiss at the pier. Beyond it being in and of itself an incredible kiss, that strange and wonderful energy sensation remained. A tender rush. Blissful yet bizarre. It was always there in his touch, when he held her hand, caressed her face. At some point she would have to find out if he felt it too. What would he think? What if he *didn't* feel it? But it was so strong he *had* to, didn't he? To even try to explain such a thing… How to approach a subject like that? She still wasn't ready. That was a whole other matter indeed.

Alex's musings broke as she turned to walk into the room and just about crashed into Aaron, who had come to an abrupt stop. He put a hand back to halt her and removed the pistol he wore on his back waist. Pressed against him on their motorcycle ride, she couldn't help but notice its presence. Recalling those precision movements and his tense stance all too well, she felt her heart skip a beat. What in the world was wrong?

He eased back a step to whisper to her. "Is anyone else supposed to be here?"

"No. No one. Just me," she whispered back. The only light in the place emanated from the small lamp on the entry stand that she kept on as a nightlight. Unfortunately, it was also backlighting them. She stared past him into the living area but couldn't discern much in the darkened room, let alone another person.

Alex gripped the back of Aaron's jacket with one hand as he took a step forward. He stopped again. This time movement caught her eye as she looked over his shoulder, and a form emerged from a dark corner.

The man edged forward into view, his own pistol held to show, his hands up in surrender. Though also dressed in civilian attire instead of the tactical uniform donned on the ship, she recognized him right away as he approached them in the dim light.

"Les!"

Les LeBeau stepped closer and stopped. He and Aaron stared each other down.

"What're you doin' here, man?" Aaron asked, his delivery calm and even as he kept his weapon trained on his old friend.

"Actually, saving your butt." Careful and slow, Les replaced his gun in his belt holster. "And… staring at a ghost."

Deafening, awkward quiet permeated the atmosphere. An extended trepidation. The memory of Shane's deception washed over Alex, a sudden sick knot forming in her stomach as she observed in wide-eyed silence.

Aaron narrowed his eyes and gave Les a wicked smirk. "Boo."

The rock-hard muscles in Aaron's back relaxed under her fingers. Alex released her hold on his jacket. Another moment and he lowered his weapon, stepped forward, and the two men exchanged a quick embrace. Alex exhaled. *Thanks for the freak-out, Les.*

Les slapped Aaron on the back. "Man, I thought you were a goner."

"Yeah, me too." Aaron holstered his gun and moved aside, allowing Alex to step up and give Les a hug.

"Hey, Les." She squeezed and stepped back. She eyed him. "What *are* you doing here?"

"The short 'n' sweet version, milady," Les began, "is you've got two tailing you, 'bout ten minutes out." He turned his attention to Aaron, serious. "Seems you've got a bounty on you."

Aaron's eyebrows shot up. "Uh, what? How? *Why?* I thought… Everyone thinks I'm dead."

Les shook his head. "Somebody guessed it right."

"But… I eradicated any kind of trail, any evidence at all that I still existed. I covered all possible angles. I thought of everything." He stood incredulous. "How'd they find me?"

Les shook his head again. "Not you. Her."

Both men looked at Alex. Her mouth gaped open as her gaze darted from one to the other. A defensive shock wave shot through her body. That troubling knot began to reinhabit her gut.

"Hey, I didn't do anything!"

Les's stern eyes showed compassion as he addressed her. "No, you didn't. But a month or so ago, right after we got back, I heard through the grapevine about him." He motioned at Aaron. "And whoever is looking for him was having no luck. So they put up a bounty. Attracted some interest and then put a tail on you a couple of weeks ago. An' I been keepin' an eye on 'em. Figured they planned on tailing anyone from the ship. But you would've been their best bet." He turned to Aaron. "And then you show up right after, checking on her. They didn't notice you though. You're good. Till today. Lost you for a bit, but picked you back up when you got back to town."

Heartache flashed through Aaron's eyes, and his forehead creased as that alarming information sank in. He collapsed hard, back against the wall, raking taut fingers through his hair. "Dammit!"

"We'll figure it out," Les said. "But right now we got more pressing matters. Those two goons are gonna roll up in here any minute. Gotta take care of them first."

"And maybe get some answers," Aaron added with a resigned sigh. He returned in an instant to all business. "What you got in mind?"

Alex took in their conversation, only paying attention in part, the fear and anger she'd experienced on the ship flooding back. She fought those feelings away as she watched them talk, listening to their voices, attempting to keep her irritation in check. So those subtle intuitive nudges of being watched *weren't* just from residual stress.

"Two weeks? Are you *kidding* me?" she muttered, fuming to herself as she plopped into a nearby stuffed chair.

Les caught her remark as he finished speaking with Aaron. "You can be pissed at us later."

A side-eye accompanied her wry response as Aaron moved to kneel beside her chair. "Where've I heard *that* one before?"

Aaron took her hand in both of his as Les continued.

"We gotta hide you," Les said to Alex. Then to Aaron, "And we need a good distraction. They'll likely come in from different directions. If we wanna get the upper hand and not draw outside attention, we need to do this quiet. So, just in case…" He pulled out a silencer, began attaching it to his pistol, and glanced around. "There are a couple of good hiding spots we can ambush them from. If they're paying attention to something *else*, it'll be a lot easier." He paused with a pointed look to Alex. "I've got a smashing idea that gets you out of harm's way, *and* it'll provide one helluva bloody good distraction. But you may not be too keen on it."

Alex perked up. "Hey, whatever I can do to help." After all, it had been *her* that this hunter had centered on to find Aaron. Though no fault of her own, it still tore at her heart. Plus, along with providing the guys assistance, doing something other than hiding in a corner would help keep fear at bay.

Aaron and Les regarded each other. Aaron lowered his head and squeezed her hand as Les informed her of his ingenious plan for distracting their would-be assassins.

"…and just make it sound like you guys are having a rather, uh, stimulating shower together. But loud enough that it *really* gets their attention."

Alex just stared at Les. *Wait. You… want me to do what?* "Okay, that's *not* funny, guys. Really?" She stood and wrung her hands. "I don't know… I… Oh good Lord."

"Get over it," Les ordered. "We got no time. Here." He crossed to the bathroom door, opened it for her, and turned on the light. A few more quick strides and he extinguished the lamp at her front entry. "Go turn on the shower. One of us will tap on the wall when they start to break in. And then, well, you can do your thing."

Several hesitant steps brought Alex to her bathroom. She stopped and turned to Aaron as he walked in beside her.

"Sorry." He brushed her chin with his finger and gave her a quick kiss. "But it is a brilliant idea. For the short amount of time we've got."

"Yeah, but *you're* not the one that has to do it. Oh my."

Les leaned in. "Company in a couple." He nodded to Alex with a wink. "Make it good. Our lives depend on it."

"*Thanks,* Les."

Humor aside, Les was serious. But this idea of his was just, well… *nuts!* Aaron gave her a quick hug along with a few more words of encouragement before heading off to his hiding spot. Heaving a deep sigh, Alex closed the door and hurried over and turned on the shower.

A cold chill crept along her spine. *Who are these people following us? And how dangerous?* Arms crossed, she nibbled at her lower lip. Her mind reeled. Wow. Damn. This evening had *definitely* taken a turn. Now to handle the task at hand. Even alone with her thoughts, her cheeks heated. She glanced at her reflection in the medicine cabinet mirror. Yep. Red. *Unbelievable!* She psyched herself up. *Don't overthink this.* The patter of water streaming against the vinyl curtain and into the tub tapped out a chaotic rhythm. She waited for the knock on the wall.

CHAPTER 34

AARON

THE ONLY ILLUMINATION REMAINING IN the living room seeped from beneath the bathroom door. Les crouched behind the sofa, Aaron beside a chair near the wall. Minutes clicked by. Scratching sounded from the back door to the deck. More light noise at a side window.

"Here we go," Aaron whispered as he tapped hard twice on the wall with the butt of his pistol. He replaced it in his back holster and pulled a knife from his boot.

The knob of the back door jiggled, followed by a loud metallic snap and muffled curse, but the door didn't budge. Their assumption had been correct that the two would try to get in quietly and unnoticed, going for the element of surprise rather than a full-on assault.

A slight rattle from the side window, the faint swoosh of it sliding up its sash.

Moans and murmurs from Alex in the next room.

"*Damn*," Les remarked under his breath. "My plan was to bloody distract *them*, not *us*, wasn't it?"

Aaron adjusted his squatted stance and attempted to keep his focus where required. *Distraction? That's an understatement. Good Lord…* He breathed his reply in a hushed whisper. "Yeah… I'm, uh, pretty sure they're gonna believe *that*."

The back door popped, opening with a slow creak. A shadowy figure entered and made a quick sweep of the kitchen area. He soon padded across the living room to join his partner, who had made the more clandestine entry through the window. Both scanned the room.

A sensual giggle and some amative cooing hooked their attention, and they eased toward the bathroom. The two shared whispered strategy, Window Man leering and pointing, rude gestures indicating what he expected to find behind door number one. They were buying it. Gun at the ready, Door Man's teeth glinted in a bawdy smirk as he reached over to grab the knob.

In a flash, Window Man found himself disarmed, weapon hand twisted up behind his back, Aaron's knife caressing his throat. It came as a surprise to Aaron in that moment the extra restraint he had to muster to not just flip the guy around and headbutt him in the nose. Door Man gawked down the barrel of Les's silencer. Les shook his head at the man who, after a brief assessment of his quandary, thought better of trying him and handed over his own weapon.

The intruders were moved to the sofa and made to sit as they glared at Les, who held them at gunpoint.

Aaron tucked his knife back into his boot, snapped on a table lamp, and walked over to the bathroom. He paused with his hand on the knob. No time for playing around at present, but with imminent danger subdued, he could relax a bit. He rotated it just enough for the latch to release in near silence.

Resting his forehead against the cool wood of the door, he listened for just a few seconds more before pushing it on open. "Hey."

Alex started and looked over at him, clamming up almost immediately.

He beckoned to her, now fighting hard to stifle a grin. "We're good out here."

"Oh good!"

She leaned in and pushed down the lever to turn off the shower.

Moving to join him at the door, Alex peeked through her lashes. Her cheeks colored and she offered a sheepish question. "Did it work?"

"Oh yeah." He cleared his throat. The combination of what her sounds brought to his imagination and having to ignore that and keep it together for the work at hand had left him at a loss.

The second half of that equation had sure as hell *not* been on his list of options for the night. The first half? While maybe not expected in the immediate, he was hopeful for the future. That mind-blowing kiss at the pier, the warm pressure of her thighs and her tight hold on him for a good portion of the day on the motorcycle, and now this? Oh boy.

He rubbed a hand through his hair. *Come on, get your shit together, man.*

"It was, uh… Yeah, it *definitely* worked."

ALEX

"Good." Alex allowed herself a couple of deep calming breaths. What a thing to have to do on their first night of reunion. And for all the wrong reasons. The humor in it subdued her stress, and she held in a sudden giggle. *My first acting gig.*

The expected racket of a scuffle had never materialized. No stifled cries, no clunks of dislodged furniture. She'd even half expected to hear the distinctive quick thump from Les's silencer. Boy, they had done that quietly. Had there even been an actual confrontation?

The look on Aaron's face—a near quirky upturn of one corner of his mouth coupled with a pensive knit brow—told an intriguing story. Not the look of a man who had just helped disarm a couple of bounty hunters.

Aaron seemed to have relaxed now though, and he sent her a quick grin, nodding to her to accompany him. Her concern and unease were alleviated more as she followed him back out to the living room and the others.

There *were* two disheveled men on her sofa. Their downtrodden expressions at having been duped, then captured, switched to mystified stares. The two intruders gaped at Alex as she and Aaron returned to the living room. She looked them over, shrugged, and went to sit in an out-of-the-way chair to observe as Les and Aaron questioned them. This should be interesting.

The interrogation ended with Aaron and Les trading looks. It had become very clear very fast that the two young, scruffy intruders were not professionals. They had just gotten lucky. They also hadn't been in contact with anyone concerning their findings, not wanting to attract extra competition for the reward. A good thing. Little more new information, just the same as Les had heard, that someone had offered a sizable bounty. The one decent lead? A contact number the two were instructed to call if they met with success.

After a schooling that they had gotten in way over their heads and with a promise that sudden and unexpected dreadful harm would befall them should they not walk away and sever any and all ties to the whole ordeal, the two were allowed to leave.

Les palmed the recovered weapons. Only one cheap handgun each. Those boys needed a new profession.

"What was that, amateur hour?" Alex had expected those in the bounty business to show more esteem and not cave so easily during a questioning.

"Bloody good thing for us it was. *And* that they're greedy." Les looked from Alex to Aaron, his expression and dry tone the most grim and solemn she'd ever witnessed from him. He sighed. "We got some serious planning to do over the next few hours. And you know what you need to tell her."

Aaron focused a dangerous look on Les, his icy glare lost on the man as his friend got up and walked over to take a seat at the kitchen table. Aaron turned his gaze back on Alex, countenance immediately softening, fallen. He rubbed his face, rested his chin on folded hands, and stared at the floor in front of him.

Avoiding her eyes now. Silent. Thinking.

Even in the short time she'd known him, Alex could always read volumes in Aaron's eyes. That flash of regret he'd attempted to suppress—he didn't have to say a word. His slumped shoulders and hanging head told the rest. What was coming, what Les meant, sent a chill like barbed wire dragging through her being. Her perfect dream of a day and whatever future that might have sparked began to disintegrate in her mind's eye, replaced with a barren hollowness. No. Not again. *Screw this!* She exploded out of her chair.

"Oh *hell* no!" Her eyes blazed. "This is *bullshit!*"

Flaming glares shot from one to the other as both men blinked back at her.

"Today, this whole day, did *not* happen for *nothing!* I absolutely *refuse* to believe it! And I'm *not* going to have it all ripped away from me again! So whatever I have to do to—"

"You don't have a bloody *clue* what this is, what you even *think* you'd be getting yourself into!" Les broke in, admonishing her.

"Then I suggest you enlighten me!" she shot back, standing her ground. Somewhat mystified at her own reaction, she did her best to keep hyperventilation at bay while hoping her heart would survive its current tempestuous pounding. This was a huge step out of character for her, but it was too late now, and she refused to back down. Not this time.

Her ardor didn't faze Les in the least.

"Well, for starters, could you *really* walk away from your whole life? *All* of it? We'll figure this thing out, but he's got to disappear for a while. Maybe a good *long* while. Can you honestly say that you could cut contact with everyone else? Family, friends, job? Maybe for *months?*" Les rubbed his eyes and glanced up at the ceiling, reining in the combative edge to his voice. "Think about it. That's what it would mean. It's not some romantic 'run off together' thing. It's a harsh reality that you may not understand. You may not like some things you find out. And it's not safe."

"Not *safe?* It's already *not safe!* *Hello,* those two idiots just broke into my apartment a couple of hours ago. If they can find me that easily, I'm sure it's not a real hard stretch for anyone else to." She marched over, planted her hands on the table, and leaned forward to look Les square in the eye. "As for the rest of it… Since I live far away, I don't normally get together with my family more than once or twice a year. My friends will understand. And I can work from anywhere in the world."

Les leaned back in his chair and folded his arms as Aaron stood and walked over to Alex.

"Alex… it's not fair to you to have you leave everything. And I *can't* put you in that kind of danger. I can't *do* that to you."

Alex straightened and turned to face Aaron, taking hold of the front of his open jacket in her fists. "No, what's not fair is your coming here, letting me know you're still alive and well, and then disappearing again. And I don't care *what* reason you use to try to justify it."

He narrowed his eyes at her as she continued.

"You both know I can handle myself okay in a situation. And…" She looked over at Les. "If either of you are *half* as good at surveillance as it sounds like you are, then you know I can pick up and go pretty quick." She turned her accusatory gaze back on Aaron. "Since it appears you've *both* been here for a while before today."

AARON

LES AND AARON GLANCED AT each other. She had definitely registered Les's earlier remark about the timing of their arrival here.

Aaron breathed a weary sigh as he looked back to Alex. "I didn't expect this. I really thought I could finally… that I had put enough distance and steps between what was and…" He trailed off, his gaze darkening.

Not foreseeing her strong reaction to what had just happened, the response in acute contrast to her more reserved personality, he was still attempting to recover. He could understand her anger though. It *had* been a good day. Up until a couple of hours ago. But he hadn't anticipated being hunted

193

again either. *More great timing.* That turn had come out of left field and veritably knocked him off his feet.

Not only did he have to deal with the obvious feelings he had evoked in Alex, plus his own, he had to figure out just what exactly was going on with this bounty and who was after him. It *wasn't* fair. *How the hell am I gonna explain this to her?*

He shook his head. "This is serious. There's too much you don't know. If anything happened to you because of me—"

"Then it's my choice, my fault." She stopped him, pulling hard on his jacket. "Besides, you've already done the damage. You came here for a reason, and I refuse to believe that it can all just be thrown away at the first sign of trouble." Her tone softened a bit as she continued to plead her case. "After what we went through on that ship, after all that, you could have just let me go on thinking you were gone. But you didn't." She let go of the front of his jacket and shrugged, deep hazel scrutiny locked on him, refusing to allow any tear to fall. "Unless it really *doesn't* matter that much to you. Then just walk away. Tell me I'm wrong."

Aaron schooled his features to remain unchanged as Alex watched his eyes. Half a dozen different emotions shifted through him. He stood silent for several long minutes, just studying her. At last he reached out, put his hand on the side of her neck, and brushed his thumb against her cheek, searching her face.

"I wouldn't have taken the risk if it wasn't important to me," he told her, his now gravelly voice hushed. "If it didn't matter."

Aaron closed his eyes and lowered his head. This was not a good idea. But he had put her in danger, on someone's radar, just by showing up here. *Yeah, so this is what I get for thinking I can start a normal life.* And, right or wrong, he couldn't do it. He really couldn't just let her go now. Not like this. Not after this day. *After one damn day? Have I lost it?*

"What the hell am I doing?" he whispered to himself. He opened his eyes again, imploring her. What he saw there… He sighed and spoke over his shoulder to Les. "She's coming with me. Decide if you're good with that."

Another silence until Les spoke, his blithe tone unexpected. "Okay then."

Les got up, went and grabbed a duffel bag stashed in a corner and returned, pulling out maps and papers that he proceeded to spread across the kitchen table.

"You do handle strange pretty well," Les said to Alex as he worked.

CHAPTER 35

AARON

AARON WATCHED ALEX GAPE AT him and then Les, who was shuffling through the papers as he sat back down. The abrupt change in Les's demeanor and the sudden shift from her perceived loss to Aaron's affirming his own desire to have her stay with him had combined to bring her to tears.

Trying to blink them away, she looked back to him. "What just happened here?"

"C'mon."

Aaron led Alex over to a chair. She all but fell into it, and he knelt in front of her, resting his forearms on her knees. "Are you *really* sure about this? Unfortunately, I'm used to it. But I'm usually on my own. It's not gonna be easy. In fact, it'll probably be a real pain in the ass most of the time. You *really* need to fully understand what this means, what you'd be getting yourself into."

She wiped her eyes and leaned forward. "Well, let's see. Taking off with a guy I've only known for, technically what—if we count the ship—three weeks? Going who knows where. Trying to figure out who wants you gone and why, which I still, by the way, know nothing about *that* history. Hmmm..." She shrugged and gave him a weak smile. "Yeah, what's not to be sure about?"

He ignored her half-hearted attempt at humor and raised an eyebrow. "This is not something I expected. Not at all. Dammit, I would never have..." His dark gaze shifted from her to the ceiling and back again. He leaned forward and his look softened. "I know you're upset right now. I'm not thrilled about this either. But I don't want you to make a snap decision. If we do this, you can't change your mind. You need to know that. I need to know that you know that. I need you to *really* be sure. You remember what happened on the ship. There is the very real possibility, more like probability, that we'll get into something like that again. Or worse. You really have to understand what that means. It'll be hard. And there's no going back. Once we leave here, it's done. I need you to really think about that before you make a final decision."

She leaned closer. "We could call some kind of authorities, couldn't we? Or would it be the military? Somebody has to be able to help."

Aaron shook his head. "It's more complicated than that. I... I know it may be hard for you to understand, but this is all outside any conventional authority. Maybe in time I'll be able to tell you why, but right now you have to trust me when I say this is the only way for me. At the moment anyway."

Regardless of what his emotional state was telling him, why he had even come here in the first place, Aaron needed to listen to his practical, rational side now. The possibility of seeing where things would lead with her had not included ripping her out of her life. And regardless of what he had just told Les, he needed to try to convince her, make her understand just how tough a situation this would likely be. To try to dissuade her from doing this, from her desire to come with them. To be with him. Even if he didn't want it that way either.

Would she want to stay if she knew the whole truth? Although she was more open-minded about his profession than most, there was still no way he could explain it all to her at this point. And outright telling her no and just walking away wouldn't solve anything either. It would just leave her distraught and wouldn't alleviate the danger. But he had to make her as fully aware as he could of just what obstacles might lie ahead.

"I know we had some great talks on the ship. And today was, well, the best day I've had in some time too. But there's a helluva lot you still don't know about me."

"Doesn't what I *do* know count for something?"

He didn't even attempt to cover his torment this time.

ALEX

ALEX LOOKED DOWN AT HIS hands, took hold of them with her own. Strong, long fingered, a few scars. Those fingers folded around hers, warm and caring. Whatever it was he thought was so awful, she would deal with. He was not a bad person.

She let Les's words sink in. No contact with anyone in her present life. For how long? Logistically, she could cover up to six months or so without issue. She had talked about moving soon anyway. Just tell everyone she was traveling overseas or something. For an extended period.

Her brother would find great humor in that. He *had* told her to go travel and adventure, hadn't he? *Pretty sure he didn't quite have this in mind when he said that.* Her best friend Lou would be a harder sell, but she would figure out something to convince her. She would miss them all terribly, but she could do it. And it wasn't forever, right?

Swallowing against the knots taking up permanent residence in her stomach and the tightness in her chest, Alex closed her eyes. What earlier had been one of the most joyous days of her life had now shifted into one of the most bizarre. Was her current mental state rational? Of course not. Her mind scrambled and spun with how fast things were changing.

Plus the whole excitement and romantic adventure thing. And the fact that that aspect could, and *was,* clouding her judgment. *Oh boy. I really am going off the deep end here.* She mulled that over. And the danger? The very distinct possibility that things could get incredibly crazy and out of control in a bad way fast? A terrible risk, yet surreal against the backdrop of her emotions.

In the end, one true deciding factor—that unusual, strong connection with Aaron. A force she could not shake, even when she tried. Something always brought her back to it. To him. On the ship and after. In her dreams, in those days leading up to his first note. An essence she couldn't describe but was nonetheless very real. And though a past unknown to her, the man he was now was not. The man he was on the ship. Someone who looked out for them all, risked his own life. Saved them. And came back to her.

A second chance.

She would take that chance because right or wrong—or completely insane—if she didn't, she would regret it for the rest of her life.

Alex looked up and met Aaron's waiting gaze with conviction. "Remember, I have seen you work. I know what you do. I don't have any illusions about that. I wouldn't have even followed the clues and gone out to find you at the pier if I was terribly concerned that things could get a little weird at some point. Did not expect all this, but if I let you walk out that door and I don't come with you? I'll never forgive myself. There's only one place I want to be. I *am* sure."

"Not at all how I thought this weekend might turn out," Aaron commented as he stretched and looked over to Alex, who sat cross-legged next to him on her sofa.

She gave him a side-eye and they both smiled. "Nope, not exactly." She closed one eye, continuing her sideways stare. "But you are still here."

"Yep." He eyed her back, his look turning dark yet mischievous. "And you know damn well I shouldn't be." His gaze locked deep in hers. "And I know damn well I shouldn't do this." He sighed. "But keeping you with us at this point probably is the best way to keep you safe."

Alex glanced over to Les in the kitchen, in animated conversation on what she assumed was a satellite phone. She looked back to Aaron.

Eyes avoiding hers now, his expression took on a near whimsical, apologetic cast. "I hope… Please don't be too weirded out about what Les said. That I've been around here for a while."

She broke into a giggle at the abrupt fluctuation in his demeanor. "I'm not weirded out. More a little pissed it took you so long. Not like I thought you were dead or anything."

A penitent chuckle and he laid a hand on her leg, rugged fingers contracting into a consoling hold. There a silence, a reflection of recent events. "I'd like to say it's just because I'm overly cautious. Guess I wasn't quite cautious enough." His brows knit as he appeared to carefully think over his words. "I guess part of it too, is… I was just trying to get my nerve up."

Seriously? This man, usually so assured and confident, confessing to feeling on the shy side at making contact? Wow. Coming to see her again really *did* mean a lot to him. An endearing sense of awe swept over her, warming her body and releasing any lingering misgivings from earlier. She hooked her pinky finger around his, an affectionate gesture of reassurance. When his bashful eyes returned to hers, she patted him on the knee and offered him her most innocent grin. "Stalker."

They shared a laugh that nearly brought each to tears.

Aaron rubbed his face, ran both hands through his hair, and stared at the far wall, fingers lacing behind his neck. He took a deep breath, seriousness having returned. "Man, this is messed up. *So* messed up." His eyes found hers again. "I'm pretty sure I really screwed up your life though. Should have stayed away. You'd have been better off."

Alex unfolded her legs and moved over to lean across his, encircling him in her arms. Her head against his chest, his heartbeat thrummed a reassuring rhythm in her ear. "No, you shouldn't have," she told him. "I'd rather have you here, weirdness or not."

Aaron wrapped his arms around her, one hand on the side of her head, and pressed her close. He nestled his chin in her hair. "You may not always think that." His tone was soft but somber. "Things *will* get weird. And they may get real bad."

Alex hugged him tighter, comforted by the warmth of his hold. "You know, you're not doing a very good job of selling this."

"I'm not supposed to be. I'm supposed to be convincing you to run the hell as far away from me as you can get." He smoothed her hair and kissed her on top of her head before resting his chin on it again.

"Well, you're not selling that very well either."

"I guess not."

"Tell you what," she said. "When this is over? We'll go back out to the end of that pier, and you can ask me if I still want you around. After we get through all this crazy, dangerous bullshit. Deal?"

He chuckled into her hair. "Yeah, okay. Deal."

"Just gotta keep your Psycho ass alive." She smiled to herself though she was dead serious. "We do that, and I'm fine."

He chuckled again and patted her arm. "You *really* need to get some sleep."

Even though exhaustion could claim her at any second, her mind still raced. "Like I can sleep," she replied but scooted down the couch to his side. She stretched out her legs. "Okay. Good night."

He lifted his arm, allowing her to lay her head on his thigh, and rested that arm along her side as she settled in. His thumb caressed her hip.

"You know, you owe me too." Her drowsy voice reached his ears a few minutes later.

He brushed a strand of hair off her face. "Yeah? What for?"

"That," she replied and pointed at the bathroom.

He chuckled. "I do, huh?" She heard the impish grin in his voice as he patted her hip. "Well, not right now. Sleep. Long day tomorrow."

She giggled and snuggled in tighter.

"In time," he murmured, restraining a fervid sigh, as though he'd not truly intended to voice the sentiment out loud.

Alex smiled to herself. "Aaron, you're very frustrating."

"I know."

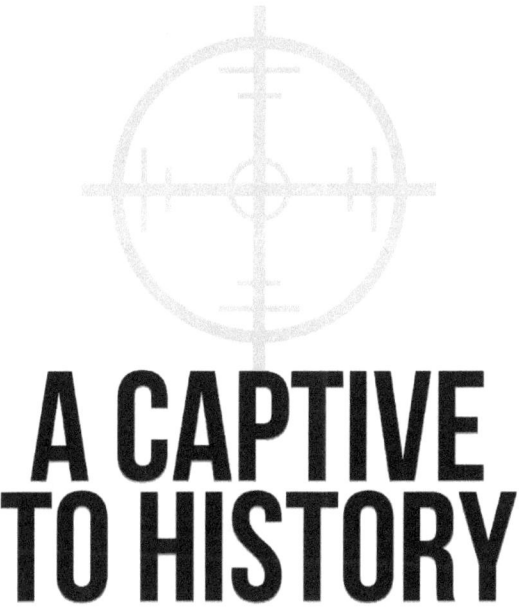

A CAPTIVE
TO HISTORY

CHAPTER 36

AARON

"WE WERE NEVER TECHNICALLY MILITARY. And I was just in the wrong place at the right time. Those people saw skills they could work with." Aaron sighed. "I wasn't exactly headed in a good direction back then, just kinda screwing off with my life. Young and dumb, working odd jobs just to earn enough dough to blow on crazy shit with the wrong crowd." He rubbed his hands through his hair.

"Anyway, it wasn't always so much the what, it's the who I ended up having to do it for. And then it became the what. Everything off the books. Shit I didn't sign up for. Decided I'd had enough, but they didn't see it that way. Guess they had too much invested in me or I knew too much. So I took off.

Disappeared. Different identities over a few years, a couple of times killing myself off. Thought I was finally good, enough time and space, enough backstops in place. Started working protection, was good at it. You know the rest. Then this one last job with you guys. One last real good payday. Thought I could finally relax, you know, just have a somewhat regular, normal life." Aaron looked over to where Alex had fallen asleep on her sofa and rested his chin on his hands.

Les sat across from him at Alex's kitchen table as Aaron opened up about some history. But his friend had a surprise of his own.

"You remember that protection detail we did in Pakistan? Third time we worked together?"

Aaron nodded.

"Kinda wondered about you then. That's when ol' Kelley started calling you Psycho, remember? We all thought you were deranged when we got in that firefight. And then having to take out those guys hand to hand? Another level indeed. I've worked with some talented fighters and marksmen over the years, but I'd *never* seen anyone *that* bloody good. So I did some digging."

Les gave an offhanded shrug before continuing. "Know a couple of guys wicked slick with intelligence. We'd stumbled across intel a few years before, on some secret black-ops-type program, but then never heard anything else. A curiosity, but since it wasn't something we were after, never gave it much thought. Until then. Just for my own interest I had them look into it. You're right. The crap that group started getting into? You *were* lucky to get away when you did."

Aaron sat passively as Les talked. None of this was news to him. Except Les's own knowledge of his past. The details, however, would be a different story. He bit down hard to keep his expression neutral. These were memories he'd buried for years.

"You don't know the half of it, man. You don't want to."

"Forget it. Don't go there. Doesn't matter now." Les stopped Aaron with a stern look, the resolve in his tone speaking volumes. "What's done is done and in the past. You left it. It's not who you are."

Aaron just nodded. There was nothing he could say. If Les said he didn't care, he knew the man well enough to take that as fact. And Les's acceptance of those events meant more to him than he could ever convey in words.

Les nodded understanding in return. "Good. Now, let's just say our merry little band has never been real agency friendly to any of 'em. And you, my friend, have had some under-the-radar backup had it been needed these past few years." He paused and chuckled. "It really is fun messing with the ones who think no one can touch 'em." He shook his head. "Anyway, we discovered one other guy came away from that mess alive. 'Bout the end of things, near as we can tell. Did some time in a max, escaped a couple of years later and vanished. Big guy. Really nuts too. But in a bad way."

Aaron's eyes shaded as he spoke a name he'd long hoped gone from his existence. "Damien Essex." *Aww, hell.* He shook his head, stared at the ceiling and exhaled slowly. "He was made for that work. A devious, twisted sort. Evil in a way that'd make your skin crawl. And he never had any love for me. Always said I was too softhearted. Yeah." Sarcasm laced his brief chuckle as he continued. "Couple of good arguments got us some disciplinary action, and he hated me after that. I honestly think there was something else behind it all too. Hell, I don't know, maybe I reminded him of somebody he couldn't stand when he was a kid. Labeled me a coward and traitor when I left. Or so I heard." He turned his eyes back to Les. "Heard he was pretty obsessed with finding me at first. Just to teach me a lesson. Wouldn't let it go. And he always loved the kill."

"Splendid," Les grunted. "Well, since you and I been workin' together, all that chatter died out after that first year. Figured anyone who gave a shit finally gave up." He nodded to Aaron.

"Think it could be this Damien character, maybe him that's involved? Seems he was a real piece o' work. Only one I can come up with that would bother enough to post a damn bounty to find you."

"Could be. I don't know. You know, we have pissed off more than a few others here and there over the years." Aaron rubbed his jaw and sat back in his chair, folding his arms. He already had resources to disappear. Would Les's take on the situation provide a better option? He'd at least hear him out. "If it *is* him, you know this is bad. What you got in mind?"

"If it is him, you're as good as dead if they get ahold of you." Les eyed him. "You know that."

"Yeah, I know. Lucky me."

"Well, once we find out for sure, we can decide the best way to do this. If it's just a fishing party, it'll be a bit less complicated." Les began folding the maps and pushed together the scattered papers they'd reviewed over the past couple of hours. "I say we turn the tables on 'em. Already got the guys runnin' stuff. Leave bread crumbs here and there. We'll find out soon enough. Draw them out and then finish it once and for all. If we need to, kill you off one last time, make it fairly visible. Then you come out the other side, complete new identity. Just another guy on the street."

"That all sounds good if it works," Aaron agreed, raising an eyebrow. "But I *have* done that before myself. Tell me one thing. Why are *you* doing all this?"

Les shoved the last of the papers back in his duffel and dropped it to the floor. "You proved to me over the years that you're one of the good guys. No muss, no fuss, get it done. But always ready to step up for those who need help, even if no one else will. Besides, we've become pretty good friends. And true friendship matters more than any bloody payday." Les eyed him. "I'd like to think you'd do the same for me."

"Fair enough. And thank you. Sincerely."

Les nodded. "Besides, if you're getting out of the protection business, what am *I* gonna do for fun?"

"True." Aaron chuckled. "Would hate for you to get bored."

They both stood and moved to the living room. Alex remained fast asleep, and Aaron took in the slow rise and fall of her back as she lay on her stomach, several wisps of hair in random abandon across a pink cheek, closed lids now relaxed and calm in peaceful slumber. A pang jabbed at his core.

He ran a hand through his hair and looked back to Les. "I wish things were different. I would never have come here if I thought it would put her in danger."

"There's no way you could've known someone would come lookin' for you like this. You been MIA from all that a *long* damn time now."

Aaron's conscience remained unsettled. "I know. But still."

"Yeah, I know." The silence of deep thought descended over Les. "Things *have* definitely worked out on the strange side on this one," he remarked after a moment. "You do realize if we hadn't picked up that last job, you might have never even met her. Then she thought you were dead. Hell, we *all* did. And you could have just left it that way. But you didn't. And now you got more than just you to be concerned about."

Les's gaze traveled over to Alex, back to Aaron. "Not that I don't think you can handle it. You'd be the one I'd go to if I needed help in the vanishing department. But you been workin' with me for what, goin' on ten years now? So it's been a few minutes since you've had to pull the disappearing act. It's been *kinda* normal." He interjected a chuckle. "As bloody normal as our work allows anyway. When I heard about the bounty, knowing how good you are at making yourself scarce, I figured if they're trying that hard, maybe you could use some extra help this time around." Les scratched his head. "I'll work out a few more details—think we're good for a couple of days without trouble. Get things with her squared away so she's ready and then meet me where we said on… Tuesday morning at three?"

"Sounds good."

"Good. An early start'll put us there in decent time." Les dropped a hand on Aaron's shoulder. "And don't beat yourself up about Shane either. I can see it in your eyes. I missed it too, and I'm usually pretty sharp on that stuff."

Aaron rubbed at his face before crossing his arms. "Deceit aside, you ever come up with any ideas on how he miraculously survived on us?"

"Ah yeah." Les frowned. "Get this. When I went through his gear after? I found his hidden stash. Had a bloody buffet of illegal pills and steroids. I'd wondered about roids but didn't expect the rest. Might account for some of his erratic behavior. Some of what he had can hype a person up or even lower heart rate and breathing depending on the amount and mix. He may've dosed himself, thinking he'd be invincible in battle. And then we wrapped the wanker up after so he didn't bleed out all over the place. All that, in combination with that half-assed cold storage, could've kept him going. A freak thing likely."

"Damn. That explains a lot." Aaron returned his contemplation to the sofa. Though a viable explanation, it still didn't bring him peace of mind. They had lost one on his watch and nearly lost much more. If there was any flaw in his skill set, it was in caring too much about the welfare of the individuals under his protection. Maybe not a true flaw, but things would be so much easier sometimes if he didn't. He just couldn't help it.

And even though what happened on the ship wasn't truly his fault, it would still take time to get past. Had he not provided Mario with a weapon, would the cook still be alive? What if he and Alex hadn't taken the time and gone after the weapons in the first place? Or, if either of those scenarios had not played out exactly as they did, would more have been lost? And how the hell had he missed Shane's deception? There was no way to know those answers. Second-guessing was never a good idea, and it never solved anything anyway.

Les spoke again, breaking Aaron's thoughts. "How's the leg, mate? You look like you're gettin' around okay."

"It's good. Healing." For the second time Aaron confirmed the fact, his thoughts drifting back hours to Alex asking him the same. A quick brow-raise to Les as he reached down and patted the spot on his thigh that now only produced a dull ache. "Helluva lot easier to train yourself outta physical pain than it is emotional."

Les nodded as his friend turned haunted eyes back to the sleeping form on the couch. "I'm still not sure it's the best option for her to come with us. This could get ugly." He exhaled and shook his head. "But she is right, you know. The damage is done. She *is* on their radar. And you know as well as I do that they'd use her now to get to you."

Aaron turned his full attention to Les, offering him a brief affirming frown.

"Crazy idea or not though, she may really be safer with us than left on her own. At least until it gets messy. But we'll figure that out later." Les tipped a salute at Alex and continued. "And she may be more up for this than we think. Kept it together pretty well on the ship. And after all that mess, she's still willing to risk that kind of crap for you?"

"I did tell her I was getting out."

"Yeah, well, she didn't even hesitate to call us out when I said for you to tell her goodbye. And that was *after* this little incident tonight. She knows. That says something. Boy, was she *mad*." Les chuckled and winked at Aaron. "*Somebody* sure made a big impression."

Aaron crossed his arms and cocked his head at Les, giving him a look.

"And then, of course, there's *that*." Les inclined his head toward the bathroom and snickered again, recalling their earlier ruse for the intruders. "You got your hands full, mate. See ya Tuesday."

"Tuesday." Aaron chuckled at Les's insinuations. "You *really* do need to get a life, man."

They shook hands and Les moved to the door. As he stepped out to the small porch, he turned back to Aaron. "Even though I think we've got a good coupla days, keep your guard up."

"You know me." Aaron shrugged as he glanced around the night-shrouded street. "Always."

Aaron locked the door behind him and checked all the windows and the back door again before moving to an oversized chair. He flopped down into it. Almost four a.m. His sore need for sleep weighed heavily on him. A few hours now and they'd start getting prepped in the morning. Resting a hand on his forehead, he massaged his temples and squeezed his eyes shut. Monday, Alex could take care of any personal accounts and affairs she needed to finalize. Then they'd meet up with Les and embark on this... insanity.

He leaned forward, elbows on knees, hands clasped. Alex slept across from him. The last thing in the world he wanted now would be to leave her. But the danger aspect caused him acute concern. People who would put up a bounty on a presumed dead man intended to get certain results, or they wouldn't waste the time and resources. And they tended to be very good at what they did. *And* very ruthless. Especially if it was Essex.

He could just leave. She'd get over it. Eventually. Maybe. Based on her reaction to Les earlier though, it would take some serious time. And then what? He'd find out later that, because of him, she'd been kidnapped or worse? Plus the fact that she would never forgive him or trust him ever again. Not an option now.

Aaron sighed. He would never be able to provide her with the kind of protection she needed from a distance either. But feelings or no, and even with Les's agreement, bringing Alex into this severe a situation seemed an irresponsible move. When it came to his own welfare, irrational actions had been the general norm practically since he could remember. But to put her through this? Whether she was willing or not, it just wasn't a good idea.

Maybe he'd sustained more of a head injury taking Shane off the ship than he'd thought? Even underwater, the explosion had caused him to hit the hull pretty hard. No, that was just an exaggerated excuse. Maybe he should have just waited and watched longer before going to see her? Should he have just tried to suppress his own sentiment and move on? The what-ifs were maddening.

Ready to leave the conflict behind, the unending tension of vigilance, the constant moving, he'd prepared for some time to step away from that life. Something else had changed in him though. These few weeks since the ship had made him take a harder look at his life and where he was now. While he could be generally engaging and friendly, he had long kept people at a distance. For their own protection… and his. Especially since his last attempt at a relationship had failed in spectacular fashion. It was just easier that way. No attachment meant nothing could cause pain. In that constant quest of staying detached, he had suppressed his empathetic side. He still cared enough in his jobs of protecting others but hadn't realized until recently just how much he truly needed that deeper connection. Until Alex.

When she'd asked him on the ship about what he used to do, he'd longed to tell her but had stopped himself and just stared out over the ocean again. What could he really say? Too much information was never a good idea. Even Les, and especially Shane, hadn't known the whole story. Pretty much anyone who did was either dead or would want him that way if they found out he still existed. Les maybe had a better idea, although the man would never say it. For all Aaron had told her, he'd always left out certain things. For a reason. Thankfully, Alex's unneeded apology for her questioning had saved him as he was trying to come up with something that wouldn't reveal much or sound really stupid.

His thoughts wandered to his best friend as a kid; Colin had had what he would consider an ideal family life. Mom, dad, a little sister. Always supper together in the evenings. Family trips. Time shared. He and Colin played together after school and over summers. Countless meals and falling asleep in front of their television when his own parents worked late. Aaron loved his parents, and they loved him. He just wished they hadn't had to work so much.

Then Colin's family moved away. Seventh grade.

That ideal situation. Something he eventually came to the conclusion he would never have. Something that wasn't meant for his life.

Or was it?

Now, with these recent events and unexpected circumstances, a different story was beginning to emerge. Plus he'd thought for sure he was off anyone's radar who cared to track him down. He would be truly free of the past. Time to make it count. Make a real fresh start. And this one was special.

This one. The reason he'd shown up here in the first place. Here was a woman, sweet and funny, with an unconventional edge, delicate yet tough as nails, and with the unique-seeming acceptance of a set of skills and checkered past that sent most others backing away. A friendship that developed fast over those three weeks on the ship. More an unspoken kinship, it held a strange familiarity. And a damn strong attachment. A mysterious pull that made it oddly impossible this time to keep any kind of separation. This was something different, something *more*. He'd made up his mind after the first few days on board that he would make plans to see her after. Take one more chance.

Long ago he'd given up ever finding such closeness. A real belonging. This *had* to be worth the risk as any thought of the alternative now left him with the sick sensation of severe loss and desolation. A cruel, nauseating knife twisting in his gut every time he even tried to consider life without her. He let out a weary chuckle. At last to find that connection, get it all together, think things could be great and go for it... and it all dissolves into chaos.

Well, wasn't this just a grand idea? Haven't been this fucked up in— another faint chuckle—*ever?* Dammit, what a mess this had become. He took an immersive breath to center and rubbed his eyes. Like it or not, she was involved and in danger regardless of what he did now. Well, just consider it a long-ass protection detail for a good cause.

After sitting and ruminating for a time and contemplating more on his own emotional state in the matter, Aaron gave up. He removed his boots, grabbed a pillow off the chair, and padded over to the couch to switch off the table lamp. The older, plush carpet welcomed his socked feet, and he curled his toes into it. As he stood over Alex in the dark, he found himself fighting back the sudden urge to wake her up and kiss her. Another unrestrained, soul-rending kiss like at the pier. Which if acted on in this present moment could also get him into trouble.

He leaned close. Soft breath warmed his fingers as he lifted a wayward strand of her hair away from parted lips. Desire rose inside him. He sank to his knees, for the moment her reposed innocence wiping away all the cares of his world. Maybe... A deep, slow breath and he shook himself out of that temptation and smiled. He could wait. The best things, right?

He set his pillow in place and lowered himself to the floor next to the sofa. He placed his sidearm just under the edge, within easy reach. He'd slept on much worse things than a carpeted floor.

CHAPTER 37

ALEX

ALEX'S EYES BLINKED OPEN. GOLDEN morning sunlight streamed through the lace of kitchen window curtains, displaying soft, bright patterns on her pillow. Sofa. She rolled over and stretched. Why she had fallen asleep there crept into the fog of her sleepy brain. All the events from the previous day hit her mind in a rush.

Butterflies erupted in her stomach, and she flipped back over and buried her face in her pillow to stifle a squeal and widening grin. Quiet enveloped her but for the faint ticking of the clock on the living room wall. Les must have left sometime during the night. She jerked her head up and searched the room, her chest tightening. The joyful butterflies disintegrated and fell like stones. Oh no…

Black tactical boots sat tucked next to her favorite chair. Aaron's boots. *Oh, thank God!* Letting out a faltering breath, she closed her eyes to recover, the tingling rush of panic adrenaline draining back out of her veins. Hopefully he had located the bedroom so he could get some decent sleep.

She moved to get up but stopped with one foot just inches off the cushion. An arm splayed out on the carpet. Right there on the floor beside her, Aaron. She eased back down to her stomach, peering over the edge at him. A warmth spread through her and her pulse quickened. Instead of finding a more comfortable place, he had chosen the floor. Next to her. What an adorable and chivalrous thing to do. But poor guy. Had he spent the whole night there?

Wow. Smiling to herself, she ducked away as he started to move. She peeked back over. On his side now, he faced the sofa. The slow rise and fall of his side, arm cradled across his chest; he remained sound asleep. Long, dark lashes edged closed lids that moved slightly as he dreamed, the calm serenity that drenched his face in slumber a sharp contrast to what he was capable of in profession. A small boy lost in wonderland.

She resisted the urge to reach out and touch his cheek, the complex reality of the past twenty-four hours continuing to wrestle in her psyche. Regardless of how mystifying it all seemed, he was here, and for that she was grateful. Captivated eyes memorized every line and feature, a couple of minute scars. That heart-shaped one.

She put her hand up to her left ear, index finger tracing her own near match just behind and below the lobe near the hairline on her neck. The lasting remnant of a childhood accident. Thrilling warmth fluttered through her chest and stomach. Wonder where he'd gotten his? She'd have to remember to ask him.

Before she embarrassed herself by staring too long and waking him, she'd better get up and go make coffee, start breakfast. Careful and slow, she pulled her legs up and crawled over the sofa arm so as not to disturb him, then tiptoed to the kitchen.

AARON

AARON STIRRED AWAKE TO THE smell of fresh coffee and bacon.

That'll work. As his mind regained focus, he stretched into a contented groan, rubbed at the stiffness in one shoulder, and rolled onto his back.

Alex was sitting on the floor beside him, holding two mugs. Two plates containing bacon, fried eggs, and sliced peaches lay on the floor next to her. Sunlight from the kitchen window backlit her in a golden, glowing silhouette.

"Morning."

"Morning," he replied, his voice husky from sleep. He rolled to face her, propped himself up on an elbow, and rested his head in his hand. *Good morning indeed.* "What time is it?"

"'Bout ten thirty," Alex replied. "Coffee?" She held out a mug.

"*Oh* yeah. Thanks." He took the mug from her and sipped, savoring the hot liquid in his mouth. A good roast. *She likes quality.* When he returned his appreciation to her, he met with the bemused twinkle in her eyes and swallowed. "What?"

She shook her head. "I don't know *why* you picked the floor. I've got a perfectly good bed in there. You could have just taken that."

He nodded. "I'm good. Didn't want you to wake up alone and think we just left."

Alex smiled at him. "I appreciate that. That was really sweet of you."

Aaron chuckled and gave her an obliging wink. "Well, you're welcome." He took another drink and nodded over toward the kitchen. "Thought you were gonna strangle ol' Care Bear last night over what he said."

"Oh yeah…" Her lips twisted sideways before she bit the lower one. *"That."* Alex tilted her head and gave him a bashful smirk. "About that… you *gotta* give me that one. I was kinda in the middle of losing my mind at that point. After yesterday? Are you *kidding*?" Narrowed eyes accompanied a firm repeat of her previous night's statement. "Oh. Hell. No."

Aaron laughed softly and moved to sit with his back against the front of the sofa. Not sure what to say in response to her sincere appreciation of their previous day spent together, his simple reply was "Thanks."

Alex scooted over to sit next to him. "Absolutely."

They sat there for a time and talked while they finished their coffee and breakfast. He looked over at her and nudged her shoulder with his own. "You ready to get to this?"

"Might as well," she replied, meeting his gaze. "But first tell me something." She touched his cheek. "Where did you get this?"

Aaron reached up to cover her hand with his own. His heart-shaped scar. The first injury he'd received from the handlers. How to say such a thing to her? Where to begin? Keeping the most severe parts to a minimum, he recounted the story for her. "Since then, it's been my reminder of survival. All through that first beating, every time I was about to pass out, thought maybe I'd made the biggest mistake of my life? That maybe my time was up and it was all over? I had the strangest feeling of a guiding light. A guardian angel if you will. A protection and comfort. I'd *never* felt so alone in my life, and that light kept me going, gave me the strength I needed. This little heart is my connection to that."

ALEX

THAT OLD HOLLOW LONELINESS CRUSHED at Alex's heart, and she could barely contain herself from outright sobbing. What a horror to go through! Thank God he'd had something beautiful to hold on to. She wiped tears just as they left her eyes. What could this all mean?

"Let me show you something." She cleared heaviness from her voice as she lifted her layered hair to expose the side of her neck. "I fell out of a tree when I was seventeen. Was pretty high up. Got stabbed by a stick on the way down. I woke up on the ground, surrounded by bright light, and I heard a man's voice say, 'Don't worry, everything is all right.' In the end it wasn't terrible. Doc said it had to be some kind of miracle that I had no concussion and didn't break a thing. It did give my parents and brother a scare. Got grounded from trees and, well, pretty much everything for a while." She sniffed a giggle and cleared her throat again. "I hadn't thought much about the circumstances in a long time. Until I saw yours."

Aaron touched the spot—tender pressure, tracing to feel its outline. The small mark so close a match in size and shape to his own. What an amazing synchronicity! His breath hitched, and he put an arm around her, pulled her close and kissed her.

She leaned into him, and he moved his lips to her forehead and pressed them there. A few more sweet seconds before the impending tasks ahead.

"C'mon," he said. He collected their plates and stood, hand out to help her up.

As she got to her feet and stood next to him, she couldn't help but smile. A warm shiver rushed through her, leaving her breathless. She averted her eyes. Blushing, she shook her head and ran a hand through her long hair, hugged her shoulders, then looked back at him.

"What?" he asked.

"I'm just really, *really* glad you're still alive."

A soft glow lit his eyes and he gave her a half smile. "Me too."

CHAPTER 38

ALEX

"Just keep it to two small bags. We can always get some things along the way. And download anything important you want off your phone and computer. Consider those gone."

Alex took a break from packing and boxing and dropped into her desk chair. The sleek black face of her Android phone sprang to colorful life as she punched in her lock code, revealing the home screen wallpaper of Aaron resting against a pine trunk that she'd taken the day before.

Loaded with pictures, the phone was something she hated to give up—the camera quality was half the reason she'd purchased it. *Damn, this is the coolest phone I've ever had.* Even though it was a couple of years old now, the thought of having to destroy it and her personal laptop brought a pang. But better that than being tracked. She unwound a USB cable and jacked in. Several minutes later the phone finished downloading to the laptop, and she backed up all the files from the computer on twin drives. She stowed the flash drives in a protective case in her backpack along with her other and the SD card her brother had brought her.

"I know you need to make some calls. Here," Aaron said and handed her a cell phone. "Don't use yours anymore. This is yours for the next couple of days. Then we'll destroy it. Les will have another clean one for you when we get on the road if you want."

Alex took the phone as she looked up at Aaron from where she sat at her desk. She traded him back hers. "Wow."

"We just don't know what might already be monitored." His thumbnail slid into the edge of her phone's case, and he pried it open to pop out the battery. "For us, a lot of this will be old school and off the grid for a bit. We'll use tech sparingly and carefully along with it, till we get where we're going."

He left the room and she called after him. "When you said 'off the grid' on the ship, I kinda thought you meant something a little different than this."

"I did."

Alex finished packing and brought her bags out to the kitchen table. She would miss the cozy one-bedroom, her home for the past year. Most of the furniture would stay as it had come with the place.

Betsy's tearful hug hadn't had anything to do with her breaking her rental agreement. The place would rent out in a heartbeat. Betsy would miss *her*. Alex told her she would drop by for visits after her return, and Betsy had squeezed even tighter.

Her friend Lou would keep her few personal pieces and clothes and things she'd already boxed until she was ready to take them back at a new place. The two cats she kept sometimes, Sami and Mia, belonged to her friend Natalie. Alex wanted her own cats, but not until she had a more permanent place, so she got to cat-sit when Natalie went out of town on her frequent business trips. That worked out very well for the current situation.

The joint checking account she shared with Lou for their art and photography business was already taken care of. Her own personal one and her savings she cashed out and closed. Though she loved to drive, she hadn't purchased a car in the months she'd been here. She borrowed Lou's when needed, and Alex lived within walking distance of their shop anyway, so it was never a big deal. Now one less thing.

When she informed her brother of her decision to travel, he was excited for her but not as thrilled that she might be out of contact for so long.

"Enjoy yourself, but call if you have any problems," he'd said, and she'd assured him she would to ease his mind.

Lou and Natalie came over for a long lunch to hang out with Alex before she left and to hear all about what adventures she had planned for her travels. The suddenness of her trip had thrown them some, but she explained how she just needed the time away to regroup.

Dying to tell Lou the truth of all of it, she'd decided against that conversation for the time being. Too risky. With Aaron's agreement, she had elected to not mention him or Les to any of them at that point. The fewer details her friends and family knew, the safer they would remain.

Bags ready. Accounts taken care of. People contacted. Utilities canceled or transferred back to Betsy… All squared away, and it's only four o'clock on a Monday afternoon. *So weird!* Alex's imagination worked over what few details she knew, recent events, and what might lie ahead as she now had time to sit for a bit and examine this whole thing. Now it was all up to Aaron and Les. Tomorrow morning they would be on their way… somewhere. Aaron had gone out earlier before her friends arrived for lunch but was back now with his stuff and napping on her bed to recover lost sleep.

What have I done? Mulling over the decision now, in the quiet of her mind, her thoughts drifted to her family, her friends. Her jobs and routines. What had been her life. Her heart ached at the sense of loss and severe change leaving would bring. But she had to go with it. Events had all come together and led to this, and there was no way she was going to just sit back and play it safe. Let life pass her by. *He* was here. Now. Whatever it took, she had to move forward. She had to make it count.

An hour later, curled up in her oversized chair with the pillow Aaron had used the past two nights hugged against her chest, Alex dozed off. Entranced in his scent, she dreamed of the time when it would be him in her arms as she fell asleep instead of stuffed fabric. A sharp rap on her front door roused her awake.

Gee, thanks for interrupting. She got up and stretched away sleepiness, started toward it to answer, hesitated. Should she? A cold chill slithered down her spine. After what happened the other night, there was no telling *who* might show up at her door. At least they were knocking and not breaking in. Better check it out first. She tiptoed to a small window that overlooked the porch and peeked from the edge of the curtain.

A neatly dressed, stocky man occupied the exterior entryway. One hand rested on the porch rail. The other fidgeted with the contents of his front pants pocket. The khakis and turned-up collar of his navy-and-white-striped polo shirt gave the impression that he had walked out of a different decade. His short-cropped light brown hair standing stiff as a wire brush against the breeze, he fixated on her door, unblinking.

Crap! It wasn't some scary assassin type, though by comparison she might prefer that. His polished appearance belying his unpleasant personality, Chip Anders was waiting at her door. A friend of a friend's brother. Or something like that.

After much protest, she'd consented to the date. Just to be nice. New to her surroundings and trusting a friend, instead she should have put her foot down and stuck to her intuition. This one had been a good choice to stay away from. Self-absorbed and callous, he furthermore formed an instant dogged attachment and refused to leave her alone. Her poor friend even now remained apologetic to her for ever having introduced them, as Chip had become obsessed over nothing. Just that one outing—a strained couple of hours of a blind date with friends.

Really? *Now?*

She'd actually considered filing a restraining order against him, but he hadn't shown up in months and her hope was that he'd given up. She backed away from the window, fuming to herself. Maybe he would just go away.

No such luck as he knocked again, louder, and called out to her. "Alex, I know you're in there! I want to talk to you!"

She didn't answer. Arms folded across her chest, she gripped each elbow so hard her knuckles whitened. Teeth gritted. A bully and a jerk, his repulsive nature was the last thing she cared to deal with. Same as within the first five minutes of meeting him. Cursing under her breath, she felt her mood shade to gloom. Odds were, he wasn't going to just leave without a good incentive to do so.

Confirming her suspicions, Chip called out again even louder. "Alex!"

As she weighed her options, Aaron appeared at her side. The comfort of his presence sent a wave of relief washing through her and she filled him in.

"Answer it," he told her.

She edged the door open an inch. "Chip, what are you doing here?"

"I want to see you. I've stayed away like you asked. That should have given you plenty of time to think. To change your mind."

"No. And I told you, you need to just stay away. Period. Plain and simple."

Chip's haughty stare insistent, he planted his feet wide and set his hands on his hips. "I don't believe you really want that."

"Well, I do. Nothing has changed, and it never will. You need to go. Now."

"Aww, c'mon, baby. Let me come in and we can discuss this in detail." With that he shoved her door open wide and pushed past her.

"*So* not a good idea…," Alex muttered as he strode on in. *And by all means, just freaking invite yourself!* She crossed her arms again and scowled. In the past she would have gone straight to Betsy's or just plain not answered. Or maybe called the police so she wouldn't shoot him herself.

Chip strutted around the living area. He stopped next to a stack of boxes, his intrusive gaze coming to rest on the packed bags that now lay beside the sofa.

"Hey, you goin' somewhere?" A devious smile dimpled his cheeks. "You'll need some company for a vacation."

"She's got all the company she needs."

Intonation steady and calm, Aaron stepped from the hallway into view to stand between Alex and Chip.

The insidious grin vanished. "And just who the *hell* are *you?*" Chip's voice rose an octave to a near screech. Rapid blinking betrayed his cognitive struggle to retain an authoritarian presence while coming to grips with the unexpected situation of finding another male in the apartment. His mouth hung open a moment before he clamped it shut. He collected himself, squared his shoulders, and took a step toward Aaron.

"Man, don't. Just... don't. Really."

Though he appeared relaxed and his articulation remained civil, Alex noted Aaron's stance change, a subtle, almost imperceptible shift to defensive. He could convert that in an instant to a frightening aggression if Chip refused to think in a rational manner and attempted something stupid. Which Chip probably would, knowing him.

"What the...?" Chip's eyebrows shot up and he stopped in his tracks. At the direct challenge to his perceived superiority, a dark red crept up his neck. Fists clenched at his sides. Veins bulged at now crimson temples as he sized Aaron up. Looking past his adversary, he demanded again, "Alex, who the hell *is* this?"

"Don't look at her—look at me." Aaron gave him a flat stare. "It doesn't matter who I am. What matters is you were asked to leave. Politely. Now, if you don't appreciate polite and sensible, we can always try the hard way. But you'll be a lot happier and less sore if you go with polite."

Alex remained silent as the rage grew on her unwanted suitor's countenance. *Oh crap...*

Chip looked from Alex to Aaron, back to Alex, eyes gleaming, chin lifted. Lips twisting into lewdness, he gave her an extended once-over, lascivious stare flowing down her body and lingering a bit too long on places it shouldn't. Cocky now, he returned his focus to Aaron and snickered, readying for the reaction.

Aaron just crossed his arms and shifted his weight to one leg. One eyebrow lifted, he glanced down at the floor in front of him and pushed at a piece of lint with the toe of his boot.

The expected show of force not materializing, Chip's eyes widened and his mouth fell slack for a second time. He stood staring as Aaron gazed at him again, the latter's eyes passive, no trace of aggression.

"What…? Not gonna try to beat my ass? Avenge her *honor*?" Eager for the chance to prove himself in battle, Chip cut further. "Guess that just shows what kind of man you are. *I* wouldn't let someone do what I just did. I'd pound them so bad they'd never look at any girl again!"

AARON

YET YOU JUST DISRESPECTED HER as an example. Nice way to impress a woman.

"I'm sure you would." Aaron's initial hope that his presence alone would give this man second thoughts on further advances toward Alex vanished. That, angry or no, Chip would just leave. No such luck. The unfortunate truth was there would be no reasoning with this person.

Keeping his expression unassuming, Aaron couldn't prevent one corner of his mouth from a slight upturn. He'd seen too many men with this proclivity. An immature obsession with lust and greed. The desire to take by force anything they wanted. What next? That would be up to Chip.

"What a damn coward." His attempt at provoking a brawl thwarted, Chip chuffed a dramatic shrug at his inability to lure Aaron into a fight by nonphysical means. "No matter." He snorted and turned his attention back to Alex. "Fine! But this is *bullshit!* You know it!" He sucked in several sharp, seething breaths. "I'll be back. You'll see. And *you*… I'll deal with you." He growled out his threat, pointing a thick finger back at Aaron. In a huff, he pivoted and stomped toward the open door, shoulders slumping forward into a sulk. Chip slipped his hands into his front pants pockets, offering Alex a pout as he skulked past.

A glint of metal. Alex's mouth opened, but before she could make a sound in warning, Chip flipped open a blade and spun. Wild slashing exaggerated in a brute show of force as he lunged at Aaron.

Aaron's response was to take one step back and slap the knife away. He seized Chip's empty hand and arm, twisted them up behind the ruffian's back, and locked his arms on Chip's head and neck. Aaron's grip put Chip to his knees but wasn't tight enough to put him out. Aaron didn't want him out, just incapacitated and listening.

"I told you. Don't. This was your choice. Now, in a few seconds I'm gonna let you up. You're gonna go and not come back. You don't want to choose anything else. Got it?"

Chip jerked hard against Aaron's hold, but Aaron altered his grip ever so slightly, and after several seconds Chip let out a whimper. Another few seconds and he stopped struggling.

"We good?" Aaron pressed his captive in a now dangerous tone. "You really *don't* want to do this. Are. We. Good?"

A prolonged moment and Chip signaled acceptance. A single forced nod. The tension slackened from his body. He had no choice but to acknowledge defeat.

Aaron released him and stepped back. He moved to the door, putting himself between the exit and Alex.

Chip got to his feet and glared at them in silent protest, nostrils flaring, but this time made his way to the door and out onto the sidewalk. He stalked to a newer blue BMW parked at the curb. One look back and he ripped open the door, slammed it shut with a metallic bang. The engine revved to life, and the poor vehicle lurched away, squealing and swerving out of sight down the street. Tire smoke dispersed in the slight breeze. Quiet again.

Aaron shut and relocked the door. He laid a hand on Alex's shoulder. "Are *you* good?"

"Yeah." She appeared more rattled over the incident than she was admitting and rolled her eyes in attempt to hide her distress. "Well... maybe not so much. He hasn't shown up in at least six months. He's... been a pest before, even overly pushy, but I... I *never* saw him pull a knife. I've never seen that." Tears formed in her eyes at what could have transpired, and her hands started to shake. "Thank you."

Aaron pulled her close in his arms. "Here. It's okay. I've got you." He held her in silence until her breathing calmed and the tension in her muscles relaxed against him. "That's more than some obsessive crush. That's an escalation. He needs help. If he'd accept it." He eased her from his hold and took her face in his hands. "I'm so sorry. I should have just met him at the door myself and not had you answer at all."

He snuggled her to him again and rubbed her back in comforting apology. "He might not have pulled that knife if I hadn't been here. That was probably just for my benefit and to look tough, show off for you."

But Aaron knew better. He purposely omitted his own observation of Chip's true end goal for him. The venom in Chip's eyes hadn't been just for show.

Aaron kissed the side of Alex's head. "But you never know... and he may come back. But it won't matter after tonight."

CHAPTER 39

ALEX

"SO... YOU'RE NOT GOOD WITH arrogant stalkers, but you're willing to run off to who knows where with crazy ex-black-ops types?" Aaron's face was alive with devilry as he looked across the table at Alex.

It was a mixed bag for supper as they tried to use up much of her remaining food in the fridge. Thankfully, her earlier unease had fled, and she gave him a mischievous grin.

"Are you questioning my choices and motives?"

He swallowed a bite of food. "Just curious."

"You're funny."

He continued to stare at her as he ate, humor dancing in his eyes. "Well, c'mon. Let's have it."

"Oh. *Okay* then. You actually *do* want my opinion." She set down her fork, took a drink of her milk, and considered his question. "Well, for one, Mr. Psycho, you're not crazy. You're just that good. That's what I see anyway. And there's a big damn difference between confidence and arrogance." She searched his face. "You guys have that quiet confidence and *insanely* amazing skill set. You don't flaunt it, just do what needs doing. And you do good with it. You care."

As she talked, he stopped eating too, his full attention on her.

"Okay, this could get long, but you asked. And if you want my honest opinion, this is it." She smiled at him. "I trust you. And yes, of course there's a lot more to it than just that. But I wouldn't go anywhere with you if I didn't." Alex hesitated. There was so much more, but how much should she say? Her feelings had grown way beyond rationality. But then what was truly *rational* about anything that had happened to them so far? Oh well, now was as good a time as any. *Hey, he did stay even after seeing me lose my shit the other night.*

Might as well go ahead and see what happens. "On the ship, at the end, and all of it really… What you did? That was everything." She looked down at her plate and took a deep breath. "But you also ripped my heart out." She fiddled with the hem of her shirt. The whole of those final events of their voyage came crashing back. A tightness tugged at the back of her throat and her eyes stung. Before she lost her nerve, she rushed out the rest. "And then, a couple of days ago, you brought it back. I care what happens to you, Aaron, and even though I am curious, I really don't care what you used to do. I see who you are now, and that's what matters to me."

AARON

AARON TOOK IN ALEX'S CONFESSION, at a complete loss for words. Wow. His half joke of a question to her had gotten all serious. However, he did have to admit hearing those words from her, the sentiment in them, was something he needed. In just doing his job, and in doing what he felt had been the right thing, he had made an extremely powerful impression on her. That look on her face in that split second as he came to the decision to take Shane out was burned into his memory; the heartache of loss combined with a fierce determination had mirrored his own emotions.

Of course, his tackling a guy over the side of a ship and getting killed in the process to save people would in all likelihood make a sizable impression on anyone. But since he was used to the extremes, he hadn't anticipated just how profound an effect it would have on her to think *he* was gone.

The knowledge that she cared a great deal for him was why, in the end, he had let her know he was still alive. At first he'd thought that action would be enough. Just let her know and move on. But, right or wrong, the longing to see her had won out. He had to. To find out if he was just crazy and allowing his hopeful imagination to run away with him. After meeting her again at the pier, he knew better.

And now, after what she had just confessed to him, he had proof that their connection ran at a much deeper level for her too than she likely realized. She'd focused her eyes back on him, waiting. He had better tell her something before she got too concerned.

He scooted his chair back from the table, rested his hands on his knees, and took his own deep breath. "That," he said, "was a damn good answer."

ALEX

PREPARATIONS WERE COMPLETE FOR THEIR morning exit.

"You should go in and try to sleep," Aaron said as he sat on the sofa next to Alex. He nudged her shoulder with his. "I'll make sure everything's secure."

"Yeah, I know." She pushed back into his nudge with her own and looked over at him. "But I'll feel better out here. I won't be able to sleep if I'm not in the same room with you. And I don't expect you to understand that."

He gave her a warm smile and kissed the side of her head. "I understand that more than you think. But you'll be more comfortable in there, won't you?"

"I figured that for you the other night, but you slept on the floor." She smirked back at him.

"True." He glanced over to the window and door, looked back to her. "It's up to you. I won't need the couch if I'm gonna stay awake."

His gaze, though reassuring and protective, was pure heat, and she felt it all the way down to her toes.

"Okay." She got up and went in to grab a pillow and blanket off her bed. *If only there wasn't a need to keep watch.* Sleep had eluded her most of the previous night, which she'd spent alone in her bedroom.

And judging by Aaron's drowsy eyes and consumption of coffee, he hadn't seen much sleep either, even with his extra nap. She squeezed her pillow tight and breathed deep. The one he'd used earlier—it still smelled like him. They'd have more time soon. Hopefully.

Aaron was standing beside the sofa, stretching out a shoulder, when she reemerged from the hallway. Several inches of skin between the hem of his T-shirt and his sweatpants were exposed as he pulled an arm up over his head.

Oh yeah, we really need some downtime soon. She arranged her bedding and scooted in under the blanket. Aaron sat back on the edge beside her. Alex took his hand and hugged his warm fingers and forearm to her chest. He gave her a wink, rested his chin in his other hand, elbow on his knee.

What did Les have planned and where would that take them? Tomorrow...

ALLIANCES AND BONDS

CHAPTER 40

ALEX

THEY'D CHANGED VEHICLES TWICE AND now occupied an older-model Chevrolet pickup truck. By the sound of its engine plus the roll cage in the cab, there was much more to the aged brown four-wheel drive than met the eye. Late afternoon found them in a remote region of Montana. Had it not been for the overall situation, Alex would have appreciated the rugged mountainous setting much more.

Les drove, Aaron slept, and Alex sat between them, feet up on the dash to keep her legs out of the way so Les could shift. She nibbled at one finger, her brows knitted.

Les took note of her expression in the rearview. "Second thoughts?"

It took Alex a few breaths to register that he was speaking to her. She looked over at him. "Huh? No. *Definitely* no. Just... thinking."

"Well, you look fairly perplexed."

She frowned again as she looked out at the road ahead. "It's just... something Shane said to me when he brought me back up to see..." She trailed off, recalling events she'd rather not. "Anyway, I just thought he was being a jerk. But maybe it meant something. Thinking about it now."

Les glanced over at her again.

"He said it was part of the bargain that they kill Aaron and that I made the wrong choice." Bringing up that short conversation and the events of that moment left her with the beginnings of an irritable mood. She shook it off and looked to Les. "Do you think it means anything, or was it just him trying to mess with me?"

Les remained silent for a time before replying. "It actually could. Makes sense with what we've been hearing. The ones we feel were *actually* calling the shots with the pirates? That group is where the chatter's centered. There's one guy in charge, with a few decent semipro hired guns. Shane was, unfortunately, part of it. Seriously doubt he'd have been given carte blanche on the kill, but what you just said helps solidify what we been thinking." He glanced over to Alex again. "I won't sugarcoat it for you. I know you don't want that."

"I know you guys told me it would be, but... it's bad, isn't it?"

Les nodded back to her. "We think the guy at the top of this is someone ol' Psycho used to know back in the day. Not only is this guy bad news outright, always involved in questionable shit, but he hurts people. And"—Les nodded toward Aaron— "he's also got a personal vendetta against our friend here."

"Wonderful."

The hard, barren blacktop streaking by underneath their vehicle matched her weary gaze. The fact that her stomach was also performing sick gymnastic flips at the thought of all this didn't help matters. "Do you think Shane knew the whole time? That this guy was after Aaron? And that's why he was so, so… why he tried to kill him?"

Les met her gaze with a brief glance. "Nah. Shane always wanted to show off, prove himself better. He 'n' Psycho never saw eye to eye. I think he may've known at the end. In communications with the pirates, somebody bloody likely figured it out. Still highly unlikely he'd have had permission then to do anything himself. Take him out, you know. He just took advantage of an opportunity to torture someone."

Finding no words to respond to that insight, Alex turned her eyes to the road once more. Thoughts shifted to the past couple of months of her life and how things had taken such a sudden and dramatic turn. From working subtle changes into her everyday to gain more freedom in her work environment, making small yet decisive moves toward future goals, to that unplanned invite from her brother, and now riding in this truck. With *him*. Aaron. His well-being held the utmost importance. Whoever this Damien character was, whatever it took, he had to be out of their lives. And the how of that goal being accomplished didn't matter much to her at the moment.

Her mind had begun to wander to dark places when she felt Aaron stir next to her. Still asleep, he shifted position to lean over against her, one arm lying haphazard on her leg. She took hold of his hand, careful to not disturb him, and held it tight in both her own. Focusing on the feel of their entwined fingers and the sound from the big V-8 engine helped to drown out her scary speculation.

"You really do love him, don't you?"

Les's words broke Alex from her thoughts, and she looked over to see him smiling at her. More of a statement than a question, there was resoluteness in its sincerity. Neither she nor Aaron had said it, they hadn't even had a conversation about their relationship. She had yet to give it much thought. But she did. She wouldn't be where she was right now if she didn't. And it was obvious that Aaron held deep sentiment for her too or he never would have come to find her.

She smiled back at Les, her reply bringing her feelings to words. "Yes, I do. No apologies."

CHAPTER 41

ALEX

ANOTHER HOUR AND LES STEERED the truck off a back road. The narrow dirt drive they now traversed carved a winding path through woods and rugged terrain. Rocks and boulders littered the berm. The truck's beefed-up suspension absorbed much from the rough trail, but Alex found herself grabbing ahold of the roll cage rail above her head to steady herself.

A good distance farther and they pulled to a stop at a large gate. Its battered wood and metal construction, in sad need of maintenance, gave her the impression it could crumble apart in the slightest breeze. Could it even provide any decent barrier? Les pulled out a walkie. "Gate two. Party's here."

Aaron stirred next to Alex, raised his head off her shoulder, glanced around and peered over at her.

"Hey." She offered a warm greeting to his drowsy observation.

Upon his waking, the green tones and gold flecks in his irises showed more prominence to the gray-blue. The idea of seeing that on a daily morning basis brought a glow to her heart.

"Hey, yourself," he replied, his voice rough from sleep. He squeezed Alex's hand, stretched with a groan, and looked over at Les. "We here?"

"We're here," Les replied, and with that the gate clanged and began to move.

Aaron straightened up in the seat as the worn barricade parted in the middle to swing out, allowing them safe passage. As they crossed through the opening, Alex noted it was by no means old and decrepit, just made to look that way. The backside sported heavy-gauge steel with large, sturdy motorized hinges and massive vault-like pins that would throw together when closed and locked. Wow. Appearances.

A half mile or so farther and several buildings came into view. Nestled at the foot of a mountain, these too appeared aged and abandoned, arranged between pines and rocks. Weathered exteriors streaked with rust from metal-trimmed roofs, block walls mottled by peeling paint, their nondescript features would offer little to attract outside interest.

Les pulled the truck to a stop next to a couple of older-model cars parked between two of the eight structures. The powerful rumbling of the engine ceased. He opened his door, pulled the keys, and hopped down. Aaron exited his side and turned to grab Alex at the waist as she slid over the bench seat to get out. He lowered her the short distance to stand beside him.

Les walked around the front of the truck to join them. "C'mon," he said. "Meet the rest of the team."

Alex and Aaron shared a quick look. He took her hand, and they followed Les back through the cars and buildings.

Les led them to the rear of a windowless single story that melded into the hillside. As they approached a rusted door, a dull click sounded. He reached out and grabbed the handle. They followed him inside, and as the door closed behind them, it clicked again.

A long narrow hallway led to another door. That opened into a large and comfortable, if somewhat cluttered, room. Several chairs and two sofas were arranged together beside a small kitchenette and dining area. Multiple computer banks occupied nearly a third of the space opposite. Shelves piled high with books, documents, and binders lined one wall.

Two men spoke at a console, one sitting, the other standing bent, looking over his shoulder. The second straightened and called out in greeting.

"Hey, Care Bear!" The tall, slender man's longish dark hair swung to his loping gait as he trotted over to Les. Baggy jeans and metal-band T-shirt completed an overall laid-back look that made Alex think of a surfer dude or grunge rocker.

They clasped hands, and Les introduced everyone. The man who had approached them was Andy Parker. In addition to being former black hat intelligence, he was an avid gamer, and that term had become his nickname. By contrast, Mikey Duman dressed in neat and professional attire. Shorter, trim and compact, he stayed at his station, his dark, wavy hair and goatee brightened by the light from his console. He lifted a waggling hand in welcome. A genius with surveillance and possessing a remarkable IQ, he had picked up the informal call sign of Brain.

Andy veritably bounced with excitement to meet them. "I know all about you," he said to Aaron. "Really, *really* crazy shit, man!"

Aaron raised an eyebrow, giving him a dubious inspection.

"But it's good, dude." He turned to Alex. "Still trying to figure you out. I mean, it's all good, just getting started." He offered a somewhat uneasy grin as she tried to hold in a laugh. "We'll have to get you a code name too. I'll have to knock that one around the ol' hat rack for a bit." He finished with a finger tap to his head.

"Okay." Alex looked to Aaron, back to Andy, the latter's manner of speech further establishing the cool surfer impression for her. "I'm... excited to find out what you come up with."

Andy nodded at her, turned his attention to Les, more serious. "You need to see the new shit." He winced a glance at Alex in apology for his language, and she waved him off.

Les moved toward Mikey, motioning for Aaron to come with him. "What you got, Brain?" They stood behind Mikey at the console. "Hey, Gamer, go show her the toy box, mate."

Alex crossed her arms. The feeling that she was being put off on some distraction must have registered on her face.

"I'll fill you in," Aaron called over to her, adding in his reassuring wink. Satisfied that she wouldn't be kept in the dark, she turned her attention to Andy.

A wide grin spread across Andy's face. "C'mon. Don't know if you'll really appreciate this much, but it's pretty wicked."

Alex followed Andy to a door just past the kitchen area. Nimble fingers punched numbers into a keypad, and the door popped. He pushed it wide and led her past cleaning supplies and storage to another door, keyed a second pad. That door clicked, and he shouldered it open. He motioned Alex in as the lights snapped on.

"Oh... Oh wow." She surveyed the space around her and raised both hands to cover her gaping mouth.

Walls, shelves, and a wood-slab table in the middle displayed almost every weapon she could think of. Others she had no idea about. A large glass-doored cabinet stocked plenty of ammunition to match. She gawked at the immense assortment before her. *Talk about a candy store!* She turned to face Andy, wide-eyed and silent.

"Yeah, I know. Not really a girl thing, but it's pretty impressive." He gave her a hesitant look. "You… wanna go back out?"

Alex blinked at him. "Are you kidding me? Holy cow, this is awesome!"

She moved over to a shelf and picked up a pistol. This collection would provide the *perfect* distraction to keep her mind occupied and off what was being discussed in the other room. Momentarily anyway.

Pulling her gaze from the weapon in her hand, she looked back over to Andy. Oops—she had just grabbed without asking. "May I?"

"Uh, yeah, have at it." Andy exhaled and cocked his head as she picked up and examined several weapons, visibly relieved at her honest excitement. "Okay, dude, this is *so much* cooler than I expected. *Nice!* No awkward babysitting." He winced. "Uh, I mean yeah, you really know your stuff."

He shrugged at her laugh and went to join her. They spent the next half hour talking and checking things out, Alex picking out her favorites and Andy explaining some of the ones she wasn't familiar with.

CHAPTER 42

AARON

AFTER ANDY AND ALEX DISAPPEARED into the weapons hold, Les and Aaron went over the most recent discoveries from Mikey's and Andy's investigations.

"There's no connection to anything else," Mikey informed them. "That old unit and anything even remotely attached to it has been scrubbed. We back-traced every possible lead, back channel, question mark, and then some. This guy uses a different identity in outside circles as a more public face. But it's him. One hundred twenty percent."

"Hmm. Less complicated but maybe more dangerous with no one to keep him in check," Les commented.

Wondering aloud, Mikey nodded over to Aaron. "Man, after all these years? What would've given this guy any idea where you even *were*?"

"Shane. He would've reported back all the info he could to his crew so the rest would know what to expect when boarding the ship." Aaron shrugged. "That's why they knew everything about us. And Essex would've been in constant contact with them to make sure he stayed on top of things. Would've figured it out from what he was told by them. With a good enough description of us? Yeah. Man's nothing if not meticulous. And obsessive. It was likely just dumb luck. Just happened to be the job we were on."

"For as meticulous as he seems, his group sure is lacking on the tech side. Surprises me. Anyone with even a halfway decent set of skills should've picked up on that bug we sent in. Either they're just that negligent, or"—Mikey looked up at Les and Aaron—"they want us to *think* they're that sad."

ALEX

"I, UH, WE DIDN'T KNOW what you liked. It's just us guys up here most of the time. Here," Mikey stammered and handed Alex a box containing several brands of shampoos, conditioners, body washes, and lotions.

She peered in and back at Mikey. He scuffed his feet in an awkward little shuffle and only met her gaze on occasion.

"Thank you. Really," she told him. "But you didn't have to get all this. I'm really not that high maintenance." She giggled. "I could've just used whatever you guys keep on hand."

Mikey gave her a shy smile. "Okay."

"I do appreciate it though," she said, reassuring him. "And you'll be plenty stocked up for the future too."

He nodded. "Well, depending how long you guys stay." He turned to go. "Good night."

"Good night," she called after him.

She inspected the box again. What a thoughtful and sweet thing to do. *But good grief, there's enough in here to last me for two years!* More voices made her look up as Les, Aaron, and Andy entered the hallway and headed toward her. Aaron and Les carried their bags.

"...and cameras and sensors are everywhere!" Andy continued explaining to Aaron as they got close enough that she could hear. "Anything gets within a couple of miles, we know it."

They stopped to stand with Alex, and Andy inclined his head toward the door behind her. "Room okay?"

"Mikey just brought me here. I haven't been inside yet. But I'm sure it's fine." She held up her box of supplies. "Did you guys leave *anything* at the store?"

"We always get stuff at like five or six different places anyway when we stock up, so it's spread out. Makes it less noticeable. It's all good." Andy smiled and turned to leave. "See ya in the a.m.!"

"Yeah, see ya." Alex shook her head, smiling as he walked away.

"Well, guys, I'm down at the end if you need anything." Les handed Aaron the bags he carried. "They'll be up for a while. Mikey's next to me; Andy's across from us on your side. But he's rarely in there. Likes to game late and normally just hits the couch. We go through a *lot* of coffee up here." Les glanced from one to the other. "I guess I just assumed, maybe I should've asked? This good?"

Alex looked over to Aaron as he replied. "Yeah, man, we're good. And thanks."

"Don't mention it. See you kids in the morning." Les turned and strolled back up the corridor. "Ton of stuff to go over tomorrow. Go easy on him tonight. He'll need to sleep at least *some* of the time."

"Les!" she exclaimed after him as she felt bright pink color her cheeks.

He just waved back at her.

Aaron chuckled. "That'll teach me to nap on the road. What *did* you guys talk about on the way up here?"

Alex side-eyed a demure look at him, biting her lip. "Well, not exactly *that*." She recovered into a naughty smirk and called after Les. "He *did* sleep most of the way here, you know!"

Les just chuckled at her from the end of the hallway and waved again as he entered his room.

"Oh man, I did *not* just do that." Alex covered her eyes with a hand. She peeked out through her fingers at Aaron.

He just stood there grinning at her. A step closer, and his eyes flicked to her lips once. A brief *mmm* and shake of his head. He reached past her, turned the knob, and pushed the door open for her. "C'mon you. In."

Alex hugged her box of supplies, turned and went into the room as Aaron flipped on a light and closed the door behind them. She set down the box and looked around. "Hey... this is nice! I guess maybe I was expecting something really simple."

"Yeah, not bad." Aaron's quick visual inspection of the room brought a low whistle. "Damn, Les, you sure spared no expense here. This is great!"

Designed with rustic luxury, the room's only rival would be a higher-end lodge hotel suite. A walk-in closet and spacious private bath enhanced posh accommodations. Comfy stuffed chairs and sofa, LED flat-panel TV, and a solid walnut desk with a laptop occupied the living area. Natural twig-and-fabric paneled partitions provided privacy for the plush queen bed beyond, its four-poster canopy draped in linens that would form a cozy cocoon when released from rope ties. A compact yet fully equipped kitchenette completed the space. Located near the center of the building, however, the room was missing windows.

"Wow, you could totally live in here long term." Alex looked over at Aaron. "Wonder who they've had stay before?"

He deposited their bags beside one of the chairs and checked around, familiarizing himself with the layout, satisfying his curious and cautious nature.

"Don't know." He shook his head. "But yeah, thought it would be a bit more basic than this." He walked back over to stand in front of her. "Home, sweet home. At least for a while." Resting his hands on her shoulders, he offered her a comforting gaze. "How you doing with all this? Okay?"

Alex sent him a small smile. "Yeah. I'm good. Still just taking it all in, I guess. This is definitely nothing I would've expected a week ago." She took a step forward and hooked each index finger through his front belt loops. "Of course, just over a week ago, I didn't expect you to show up either."

Aaron chuckled. "Guess you just never can tell what kind of strange things are gonna pop up in your life."

She giggled. "No, guess not."

He gave her a more serious and engaging look. "Gonna say you're still good with that too?"

She cocked her head at him and raised an eyebrow. "Seriously?"

He laughed, pulled her close, and kissed her.

CHAPTER 43

ALEX

BATHED NOW AND IN PAJAMAS, Alex sat cross-legged on the bed, brushing out almost-dry hair. Water pattered in the next room; Aaron taking his shower. After several days of experiencing enough strangeness to fill a lot of people's lifetimes, she now found her nervous excitement returning. They were protected here. Some time to relax at last and just be them. The first time since their motorcycle ride that it had truly been just them. Alone, with no immediate threat, no readying for an escape or needing to be on constant vigilance for some attacker. The two days at her apartment were filled with so much prep and organizing to leave, that true emotions had taken a back seat to those more pressing matters. Well, at least since the night of her meltdown per Les. She smiled. Yeah, that had brought some stuff out. At least it had turned out beneficial. But aside from their obvious affections, she felt safe with Aaron. He wanted her there with him. A decision she knew gave him trepidation due to current circumstances, but a resolution he had come to, nonetheless. Given his choices to run or leave her behind and work out his predicament on his own with Les's offer of help, he had chosen her. Her stomach flip-flopped again, but this time from huge giddy butterflies and not extreme knots due to danger.

Now. Was she ready for this? What would he expect? He was not the type to push anything if she wasn't. But if she was, would he think less of her? Oh, this is stupid! Don't overthink it. Just by the fact that he seemed familiar in a way that still boggled her mind was enough to put her at ease. Mostly. She plucked her bottle of water from the bed stand and took in a large mouthful.

The bathroom door opened revealing Aaron in a pair of black sweatpants. He finished rubbing his hair with a towel and tossed it back inside to land on the rack. He looked at her and gave a quick eyebrow raise. "Hey."

Alex had seen him once on the ship without a shirt. This was, well… different. And better. Standing there, damp hair sticking out in multiple places, pants riding low on trim hips, he relaxed to one leg and leaned against the doorjamb.

Alex swallowed and choked on her water.

"You okay?"

Aaron dropped to her side and patted her back as she recovered from her brief coughing spell. She quieted and risked a sideways glance at him. Lower lip in his teeth, one upturned corner of the mouth, mirthful eyes squinted. Yep, she'd made a great impression.

They both disintegrated into giggles.

"Oh man… that's… embarrassing…," Alex got out between bouts of laughter. She hid her face in her hands.

Aaron quieted and pulled her against him. He kissed the top of her head. "Well, for what it's worth… thanks."

She hugged his arm and kissed his shoulder, tucked her head under his chin. After a time, she spoke. "I don't know why I'm so nervous. This is silly."

He released his hold and cupped her jaw in his palm, turning her head to face him. "No need to be. It's been a crazy few days. You need some time to decompress."

"I don't know that it's really just that," she replied.

"What then?"

He retained his mischievous expression. Speechless for the moment, she offered a resigned sigh. Those eyes… A thought flashed in her mind. That thing she had gotten used to but remained a constant question. "Can I ask you something? It might sound weird, but I just need to ask."

"Sure," he replied. The look on her face spoke to the unusual and brought a wondering look to his too. "What is it?"

Where to start or how to even formulate the question? *It's gonna sound weird no matter how you say it, so just say it.* "Okay. I… when we… whenever we touch, my skin tingles." She squirmed at how odd that sounded and started to ramble. "I don't know what it is, and I know that's really weird and I thought… I thought maybe it was a static charge on the ship, but it's never happened with anyone else and it keeps happening and I don't know what it is, but—"

AARON

HE STOPPED HER BY PUTTING a finger to her lips. *Hell, I thought that was just me.* Those thrilling charges, way more than normal exhilaration rushes of aroused feelings. Something else truly physical, yet… beyond words? Sensations he'd never experienced before either. *Well, I'm officially not… crazy.* He stifled a laugh at that one. He smiled as he closed his eyes a moment, opened them to meet her gaze. "Glad I'm not the only one."

"Really? Yes! So, I didn't just weird you out?"

He shook his head, all at once comforted and trying to hold in another laugh. "No. Not weirded out. Not unless it counts for me too."

Alex, nearly breathless, pushed out a question. "What do you think… that is?"

"Hell if I know. Here." He held up his hand, beckoning hers to join it.

She held her palm up to his, not quite touching. There was a warmth that grew between and expanded along his forearm.

He grabbed her hand and interlaced his fingers with hers. Focused on it now without all the prior external incidents to distract him, he was able to experience just how strange and wonderful this oddity felt. Warm and scintillating, it coursed through his hand and wrist, up his forearm. He studied his limb, half expecting it to glow. He looked back at Alex and offered a shrug. It was definite both were affected the same. Exactly what that was? Unexplainable. But it felt good. And… bonding.

"That's amazing," Alex whispered.

Aaron put up his other hand, and she slipped complementary fingers through his. Same response. He stretched out his arms in slow motion to pull her closer. Heat of her body radiated against his chest. Concentrating on that sent a rousing thrill through him. He leaned forward and kissed her. Warmth. Light. Comfort. And more. Tongues caressed each other, enveloped in a lightning of bliss. Like their first kiss at the pier. Also, the few since. But not quite at this magnitude. Maybe because they were alone now? No stress of defense or planning, no others around, or additional outward interference? Mind in a whirl, he pulled back from her and stared into her eyes. Spellbound.

Dizziness swept Alex, the sheer euphoria of the experience showing beyond compare in her entranced expression. So far... "Aaron?" His name in wonderment came with breathless question.

Aaron squeezed her hands in his. "Yeah. That's..." His mind worked over the possibilities. If just touching would produce feelings like this, and that kiss...

"What do you think about...?" Alex whispered, her implication matching his own current trend of speculation.

"You... want to find out?"

ALEX

ALEX NODDED BUT LOWERED HER gaze. Her insides writhed. Desire for him more than she could ever put into words, her soul and body ached to be as close to him as humanly possible. At odds with her heart however, her overthinking mind. Would he think her too easy and thus question her loyalty and trustworthiness? She bristled at her own inhibitions. That's just maddening! She knew him better than that. Though she'd never been one to jump into things fast, maybe it was just the illusion of fast because of the missed time after the ship and the whirlwind of a long weekend they had just come through. They were far from strangers. Doubtless they were together. To give herself, body and soul to him, embodied her highest commitment. Was it their lack of discussion of such feelings and future? Whether spoken out loud or not, his actions held the confirmation. He had gone out of his way to keep her with him and make sure she was cared for. He'd brought her here with him knowing full well this would be a long-term operation. No man would do that based on something superficial. And the emotion in his eyes as he'd voiced his decision to Les. Seeming too soon shouldn't even be a concern with him at this point. So why was it poking at her brain?

Aaron pressed his lips to her forehead. He dipped his head to find her eyes. "Hey. I won't rush you. You know that, right?"

She opened her mouth to reply and stopped. Why did she always have to be the good girl? But jumping in fast had never been her forte. And this one held a specialness to her she couldn't fathom. She didn't want to mess it up. And why in the world would that mess things up? Where had that ideal even come from? Social judgments? Because he'd been a perfect gentleman over the days at her apartment? Dammit! It shouldn't be this hard! Mental face-palm. Maybe she'd just built it all up too much in her mind. Everything about their relationship so far, even with all its unexpected and extraordinary circumstances, fit her... fairy tale. The truth of that now raced through her heart. "I do. I... dammit, why do I feel this way?"

"What way? Tell me."

Alex tipped her head back. The pale linen canopy and pine plank ceiling beyond held no answers. Lids lowered. *Ugh. Well, he is good with the psychology stuff.* She brought her gaze back to his. A sincere concern softened his countenance. *Just tell him.* Still no words came. Alex frowned.

"Just remember some of the talks we had on that ship deck. I am still here."

She pushed her shoulder at him and giggled. "Okay, yeah, some of those were pretty deep. And if I didn't scare you off with my paranormal stuff... guess my weirdness is a turn-on for you?"

An eyebrow hike and wink accompanied a smirk that widened to a devilish grin.

"Stop!" His playful acceptance eased her misgiving. "All right, here goes." *Oh Lord.* At least with all their talks and consummate friendship, he'd already experienced her sentimental, heart-on-her-sleeve side. He'd always offered great perspectives that helped her better understand perplexing thoughts. And there was their talk over dinner at her apartment. *You have spilled your guts to him about plenty already.* She blew out a breath. "I don't know where this hesitation is coming from. I know you. And I know what I want. I just... I don't want you to think that I... I want you to think the best of me. I don't just..." She squeezed his hands. "*This*, with *you*, means... everything." Her gaze lowered to his chest and its sparse coating of hair. "Maybe I just care too much. I want you to think the best, to know... that it'll always be you and only you." Her voice hushed. "I've known that for a while." Damp lashes veiled the impassioned charge of her admission as she refocused to his attentive gaze. "I feel like I'm falling so fast."

AARON

THAT SMALL LINE THAT FORGED between neat brows whenever she searched for words that eluded her. But she needn't search further.

Aaron couldn't help analyzing her at their first few encounters on the ship, and the profile his mind had developed remained solid. An easy jovialness in conversation, flirtation came only once she reached confidence in interaction. And not with just anyone. Kind and funny, she still kept reservations to a point, making sure the person she dealt with could be trusted in honesty. Cautious with the need to get to know someone before she would open up fully. And even then, she would hold back in observation.

Her playfulness with him had been sweet with just the right amount of naughty without going over the top. She would never throw herself at anyone, too self-respecting to act sleazy, too weary of being taken advantage of. The type of quality woman that would laugh at and walk away from a player. In general, a woman like that would be hard-pressed to participate in one-night stands or any frivolous relationship. Commitment of body and soul to another would be reserved only for a most cherished and loyal partner. To some that could come off as superiority, but it was only the wish for a more meaningful long-term experience than a quick fling could hold. The discipline to wait for what she wanted most.

Written through discord that now colored downcast eyes lay the burning desire to give herself to him crashing headlong into the ingrained reluctance to appear an easy mark and a fear of subsequently being discarded. She had solid core values. And she'd been hurt before. A tenderhearted soul, was she afraid to truly give her whole heart lest it be unrecoverable? No, that wasn't it at all. She'd already given it and wanted only to be perceived as respectable and worthy of the highest expression of love in return. She respected herself too much and deserved that respect and self-respect in another.

There also resided the shy little girl from childhood.

She might not grasp the subtle nuances of her personality, but her struggle at sharing their first physical intimacy endeared him to her even more. And made him want to be a better man. Also, bringing to the forefront of his mind just how much he wanted her only for himself. She would love completely. She had fallen for him. Did he deserve that?

His eyes stung, and he gave her a comforting smile. The world could be cold, and shame at some of his own conduct in the past began to surface. After the orders, after he'd left the devastation of that cruel life, trying to find his way in an unfeeling cocoon he felt due him because of it. But that was long ago and under completely different circumstances concerning all parties involved. When he couldn't bear sharing his true self with anyone. Long before he'd found this one. His one. He swallowed down the growing lump in his throat and squeezed her hands. "Don't feel weird about it. Religious and cultural beliefs, societal expectations, and moral values shape our thinking, and they often clash. And when something holds high value in your heart, you want to keep it sacred and safe. Honestly, having it bother you this much, well, that's damn inspiring, especially these days." *And to know you place that high a value on me...* He rested his forehead against hers. "Who knows, maybe even if we were both the biggest players out there, this connection we share would've negated all that and made us only want each other anyway. Just my thoughts. And if I was out for one thing, you'd know that by now. That's not me. And I know that's not you either." *Hell, I could tell that the first time I saw you on the ship.* "I wouldn't have you here if it was. And I could *never* be disappointed in you. *Ever.* Whatever you choose right now. I'm right here either way. Believe that. I don't think I could give you up even if I tried. This with you means one helluva... it means everything to me too."

ALEX

HIS HUSKY VOICE WAS SOFT and nearly shaking. Long lashes framed shimmering blue-green pools that reached inside her soul, his gaze unwavering despite the glisten of tears. He sucked in his bottom lip to halt its quivering.

Alex couldn't speak but leaned forward to kiss him again. Damp streaks traced both their cheeks to blend at ravenous lips. He wrapped his arms around her and trapped her hands behind her back, locking her against him. Enfolded in his embrace, she felt the aura around them energize with the singularity of their union.

Enticing heat from his bare chest and arms permeated the thin fabric of her T-shirt. Warm scent of freshly washed skin, hearts in unified cadence. Pure intoxication. She crushed her body to his. Sinewy biceps, the strongest steel, a tender armor to her cares, snugged her into his secure hold.

"Alex… I'm gonna do something that may piss you off."

"Uh…" What in the world was he saying? *Oh shit.* "What?"

He brushed his lips to hers again. "I'm gonna tuck you in for the night."

Was that some sort of slang term she'd been oblivious to in life, or was he being straightforward? The sudden shift in perceived direction caught her off guard. Yet again. He was good at that. "Um, okay?"

He smiled back at her and hugged her tight, disengaged one hand from hers, and leaned her back just enough to grab the top of the comforter and top sheet. He dragged them near her and lowered her onto her back.

Alex lifted her hips, allowing Aaron to pull the bedding all the way from underneath her. He took her leg and placed a soft kiss on her ankle before sliding both her feet under the sheet. He bounded up beside her, and she rolled to face him as he slid in on his side and pulled the covers up over them both.

"I'm gonna sleep with you. But actually sleep. Tonight. Hopefully." One corner of his mouth turned up, and the inner corners of his brows rose.

Alex couldn't help but burst out laughing at the playful light on his face and that quirky half smile, lower lip caught once again in his teeth. *Oh my God, this man is adorable!* She reached over to brush dampness from his cheeks.

How many times had she wondered at the extreme variances in his being? The efficient killer in defense, the smart-aleck joker, the childlike, intelligent, fun, and comforting partner with her. And while he could hide them well, he was becoming much more open in sharing his true emotions with her. She could find no words.

The chivalry of his decision relaxed her and brought her to awe, but at the same time she couldn't help the longing that swept through her. It just made her want him that much more. He could take her right now and she'd let him.

Those opposing aspects tore at her, but he *was* giving her exactly what she needed. His honor. His body in close contact with hers, his desire obvious, and yet he cared more for how she felt and what she would experience than acting on his own yearnings. Her admiration of his reverence for her was pushing her further into her own passion for him, and she ached to share herself with him and embody in that way the true love which he so richly deserved. What was it he had all but whispered the first night in her apartment as she lay against him on her couch? *In time.* She sighed into a smile. It would be worth it all the more. Enraptured in his presence and care, she snuggled up closer as he looped an arm around behind her.

AARON

AARON READ THE CONTINUED CONFLICT in her hazel eyes. Soft pink surfaces of flushed cheeks, smooth and warm under his fingers as he wiped away her drying tears. Well, it would definitely make for an interesting night to see if they could make it through and keep to his word. *Oh boy.* Maybe he shouldn't have said it?

No, this was something he needed to prove to her and himself. He could be honorable. He *was* honorable. Maybe that was more a thing he needed to convince himself of. And maybe he didn't *need* be in this particular situation, but he *wanted* to be. At least for this first night. For her. Tomorrow however… He'd plan something extra special for them. They were both ready.

They were intimately connected, closer than he'd allowed anyone to touch his soul since his childhood. Damn. What was it about her that made him let his guard down? There was something extraordinary with her, something sacred. Their initial physical intimacy should be nicer than just jumping into bed after a long day on the road.

He tangled his fingers into her hair. "You good?" he murmured.

"I'm good." Slender fingers drifted along his shoulder blade as she caressed his back. Her eyes glistened in the low light. "Thank you for being sweet."

Aaron chuckled and stretched up over her to click off the bedside lamp. "Don't think most people would call me sweet. But you're very welcome."

He slid his hand back into Alex's hair and brought her mouth to his. Her tongue entwined in urgency with his own, and that arresting, magnetic wave of whatever it was swept rational thought from his mind.

Her kisses, one place she *didn't* hold back. *This is incredible! Lord, I could get lost in these kisses.* He pulled back from her lips and rested his forehead against hers. *What is it about staring into the eyes of this woman?* "Can I keep you?"

Alex kept her captivated gaze steady with his. "You know you can."

CHAPTER 44

ALEX

"OKAY. THIS IS WHAT WE know." Les looked at the guys and Alex.

All five sat around the table to review information and work out a plan of action.

Les continued. "There is nothing we can find left of the original group except you and Essex. For this to work out, it's got to be so catastrophic that there's no chance of anyone spending much time even *thinking* about looking into it."

Aaron sat back in his chair and crossed his arms. "Honestly, the catastrophic idea is the best—take care of it all at once. I'd just rather not actually bite the dust on this."

"That's the whole point," Les said with a dry chuckle. "But I agree. Find a way to take him out that looks like you went too. Just on the off chance that he does have anyone left that we don't get. Though I doubt anyone else would care that much. Explosions are, of course, the best and most showy. And they can hide a lot. But we'll have to consider all options on how to best accomplish it."

Alex studied the center of the table, silent. Focus and positivity tripped over themselves in a rapid dash to the exit door in her overthinking brain. Though the guys were experienced in these types of operations and tactics, it all still came off as terribly uncertain and dangerous. Scary.

She pushed her chair back, got up, and walked to the other side of the room. Damp palms mashed across jeans-covered thighs. She hugged her shoulders. The aerial map on the wall in front of her disintegrated into a mosaic of muted colors. What they spoke of brought back to her too much of the ship. The why in their thinking made sense of course, but she just had to step away for a bit.

It had been hell enough then... but now? Waking in his arms this morning, last night's tenderness, and the promise of his intentions for some extra quality alone time for them this coming evening; the rush of sparkling warmth and the beautiful ache that accompanied those thoughts combined in a crash with the heart-crushing lump in her chest at the risks of the scenarios being hashed out at the table behind her.

Every single tiny detail would need to be applied with incredible precision to pull off their plans. Aaron's very survival depended on it. The hum of their voices reached her, but she didn't register much more of what was said. She bit hard on her bottom lip to stave off tears.

After some time, discussion came to a close. Chairs scraped across cement as the four left the table. Footsteps behind her. Strong arms wrapped around her in a tight hug. Alex took hold of his hands and pressed them to her, remaining silent. Aaron rested his chin on her shoulder, the warmth of his cheek and breath on her neck a sweet balm. He held her a few minutes before speaking.

"Hit a little too close to home, didn't it?"

A quick nod. The comfort of his body against hers now brought a safe sense of calm. After several more minutes, she turned around to face him. "I don't want to be all screwed up about this, I don't. But I can't help it right now. It's too much. It's just the same thing, the ship all over again…"

"Except this time we'll know what to expect."

"Will we? Really?"

"Yeah, we will." He gave her a brief smile. "We're not going into this blindly. Of course there are always wild cards, but we'll take the time we need, plan it down to the last detail. This discussion? It's just preliminary, a rough idea. Just a place to start."

Another nod and she wiped her eyes, trying to smile. "I'll get it together, really." *How am I ever gonna get through this?* She set her jaw. *I just will. I have to trust. Them and myself.* Contained apprehension morphed into a playful smirk. "But right now… I really just want to shoot something."

Aaron laughed and gave her a quick hug, rubbing her back. "You know, that's not a bad idea." He released her and took hold of her hand, leading her back toward the others. "Hey, Les. Range time?"

"Sounds like a plan." Les walked over to join them.

"Yesss!" Andy exclaimed and headed straight for the "toy box." "Hey, Brain, ya comin' this time?"

Mikey remained in the kitchen to make himself a snack. "No, no, I'm gonna hang here."

"C'mon, you hardly ever shoot."

"I'm good," Mikey replied. "Enjoy."

Andy waved him off as he punched codes and moved through the doors to the weapons room. The others followed, gathering various arms and ammo. They headed outside.

CHAPTER 45

ALEX

THE RANGE WAS CRUDE BUT well laid out. Close-up targets maxed out at about two hundred feet with marks at distance for rifles.

Alex and Andy fired various handguns for over an hour. Running out the last six rounds in her current magazine, Alex checked her pattern. Not too bad for that far. They'd need to walk out there and check it up close later. Andy hadn't fired yet on his last reload. Maybe he was just waiting for her to finish out hers. She glanced over at him and nearly burst out laughing.

"Uh, what?" she asked at his starry-eyed stare.

"Dude! You totally been hitting that two-hundred-foot one!"

"Yeah...?"

"With a handgun!"

"And...?"

"Well... I can't hit one that far with a handgun. Not like that."

Alex smiled at him. "Practice. But I always have. I still miss some out that far, but not too many."

Andy still gaped. "But that's like, less than a two-foot round... at two hundred feet? That's rad!"

Alex gave a humble shrug. "Thanks."

Of her last set, the center of that farthest disposable target liner *did* appear rather lacy upon closer inspection, even from this distance. A giggled snort escaped her when a good lower third of it flopped down to dangle in the breeze. Most, if not all, shots had hit their marks.

Lou would appreciate a field grouping like that. She'd take a picture of the riddled paper and show it to her... sometime. *Wish I could text you right now, girl.* She holstered her own favorite pistol, her SIG 9mm she'd just finished firing. *Many holes in targets... oh yeah.* Her accuracy bolstered her confidence in the face of the earlier vexing discourse.

She looked back to Andy and grinned. "And I feel a whole lot better now too."

Percussion still sounded from Les and Aaron picking off the long range targets, and she turned her gaze toward them

Andy nudged her arm. "You should totally try the rifles too. Bet you'd be good."

"Yeah, well, I don't know about that," she replied with a laugh. "But I'd love to."

Andy elbowed her arm again and started over. She followed. They waited in observation a ways behind until Aaron and Les reached a stopping point.

Andy approached them, Alex trailing a step. "Sweet shootin', guys!" He motioned to Alex as she stopped beside him. "She's over there pickin' off crap at the two-hundred-feet mark! Puts me to shame."

"We know." Aaron's teasing sideways smirk displayed admiration. Both he and Les had been watching her, probably curious how she would do as they hadn't seen her actually fire a weapon before.

"I think she should try something farther out." Andy grinned.

"We'll set you up. What suits your fancy?" Les asked her, indicating the rifles as he and Aaron got to their feet.

She shook her head. "I'm not sure. I really don't have much experience with rifles. What do you guys think would be a good fit?"

Les looked at Aaron.

"308?" Aaron asked him.

"Well, I know *you* sure like that one. But then what kind of bloody weapon *don't* you like?" Les replied with a chuckle. "Yeah, that would be a good fit for her. Solid and reliable, and it'll definitely reach out and touch someone."

Aaron handed her the rifle he'd been firing and went over with her what she didn't already know.

"Okay. Now this is just straight-up scoped, so you'll have to adjust your aim to compensate. At this distance, the round will fall some. Also, it's not windy here, but notice out past the blue car on the right? See how the weeds are blowing? It's past the shelter of the hills and we're catching a good breeze out there, and that's going to affect your shot too."

Alex peered through the scope at her target as she and Aaron lay on their stomachs on the ground. An old waxed canvas tarp underneath them gave protection from rocky soil. So far away.

She lifted her vision up and out past the scope, squinted back through it again.

"When you're ready, just relax, exhale, and squeeze."

The force of recoil jolted Alex's body as it punched against her shoulder. A second later, a puff of dust revealed impact about five feet before and to the left of her target.

"That's good. Now, notice where you hit. Remember where you aimed and adjust. Same drill. Relax, exhale, squeeze."

Another poof of dirt, closer but still too low, in front of her target. Alex shifted her aim up a bit and to the right of her first two. Sighting through the scope, she corrected just a little farther than she thought necessary. She let out a slow breath and squeezed the trigger.

Standing a few feet behind them, Les and Andy viewed the target area through binoculars.

"Bloody hell, woman," Les breathed.

"Oh yeah!" Andy bounced around and punched the air.

Alex bit her lower lip and rested her chin on her hand on top of the rifle stock. She looked over at Aaron, her cheeks dimpling at the expression on his face.

He shook his head at her, returned her smirk, and rested his forehead on his hands on the ground in front of him. A moment later, he looked back up at her.

"There's a lot more we'll get into besides target shooting, but… the wrong people find out about *that*." He extended an index finger out at the range. "They'll want to hire you."

"I'm not telling if you're not." She nudged him with her shoulder. "Besides, I work for you."

"I've got it!" They all turned at Andy's exclamation. He bounced on the balls of his feet, his springy exuberance uncontainable. "My nickname for her!" He paused and bowed for dramatic effect, gesturing wide in Alex's direction. "Hot Shot!"

AARON

AARON'S SECRETIVE INTENTIONS FOR THEIR upcoming evening were made evident throughout the rest of the afternoon in the knowing glances of their new friends.

"So, it seems our entire little encampment here knows something that I have a pretty good guess about." Alex's cheeks glowed a rouge frame to her sly grin. "And while that is kinda amusing, you didn't... actually give detailed plans, did you?"

Aaron laughed. "God no. I sure hope you don't think I'd do that. Not the kiss-and-tell type." His grin widened and he lowered his gaze. "I just maybe mentioned that, well, maybe they could all make it a late night for themselves?" He rubbed the back of his neck and peeped back up at her. "Like maybe several hours late."

A giggle escaped Alex. "Oh yeah, not subtle at all." She rested a hand on her cocked hip and combed the fingers of her other the length of the section of hair that lay in front of her shoulder before flipping it back. "Pretty confident there, aren't ya, sir?"

He stepped close enough that only a breath existed between their noses, vision locked on the beauty inches away. In any way she was willing, he'd make every effort. But first, food. He reached past her and turned the doorknob to their suite.

The space was candlelit, a table set for two. Canopy sheers of the bed had been set free from their ties to cozy an intimate refuge. Delicious scents of the awaiting meal drifted to them from the warm stove.

Alex turned to Aaron as he closed the door behind them and wrapped her arms around his neck. "You did all this for me?" Her eyes glistened with appreciation.

He winked at her. "Let me date you. At least one official date. Dinner. So far it's been far from anything normal in that department for us."

A smile lit up her eyes through her lashes. "If we count our hangouts on the ship, we've had quite a few. And the day we rode up to your property, I'd call that an amazing date." She stroked the hair at his nape and whispered in his ear. "And thank you. You certainly do know how to make a woman feel special."

He returned her embrace and whispered back to her. "For the right woman, I hope to always." He slid a hand behind her neck and head and kissed her. Maybe the food could wait...

STRATEGIC DEVIANCE

CHAPTER 46

ALEX

"THIS IS ACTUALLY THE REALLY rough part," Aaron said to Alex. "Psychological conditioning."

Les agreed. "You can be damn good with weapons and skills, but if you lack the mentality to make the hard decisions, if you hesitate, you get yourself killed. You get others killed," he said. "Hey, you guys get over here too." He beckoned at the two men at the computer bank. While their learned knowledge on this subject was extensive, it never hurt to refresh.

Mikey and Andy made their way over and sat on either side of Alex on one of the two sofas.

Les stood in front of them. Aaron reclined on one elbow on the adjoining sofa.

Alex struggled to keep her attention where needed and on topic, but it kept wandering to the other sofa and Aaron's seductive form. Legs slack in repose, fitted black T-shirt, well-worn jeans and unlaced tactical boots. His head rested on his right palm, fingers buried in tousled hair, his left arm draped along his side and hip to end with slack digits spread across an inner thigh. Just his normal easygoing self. Beyond inviting.

That carefree vision coupled with recent memory of this morning's shared intimacy consumed her imagination and thoughts. Over the past week since their "dinner date," she'd felt veritably obsessed with him. As if she hadn't been already. And he seemed the same with her, although he did a better job of keeping it more subtle than she around the others. When they were in private, however, they could barely keep their hands off each other. Spending hours at a time immersed in their pleasure and devotion, they'd kissed and giggled, shared secrets, and explored passion in waves heightened by that magically charged touch that bound them unlike anything either had felt before. At the moment, she needed to get her mind off his body. *Yeah, right.* That would take some serious mental work.

Would the others notice her current predicament? A lean forward to stretch out her back allowed her hair to fall across and veil her face. Aaron *had* to know what he was doing. How *dare* he look like that when he knew she should be concentrating elsewhere!

A rakish smirk and his index finger lifted off his thigh to point at Les. Dammit! Busted on another stolen glance. She flashed her eyes at him and buried her face in her hands, mashing knuckles into her lids. She *had* to refocus to the instruction at hand. Plus hide her captivated smile from Les and the companions who had just settled beside her. A deep breath. Poker face time.

She brushed back her hair, and her eyes were back on Les, who was still just getting started in his lecture. Basic firearms discipline and evaluations had made up most of their first week after arrival. Today's focus would be something new. The psychological aspect fascinated her, and her intent was to soak up every bit of invaluable information this training had to offer.

Les continued his talk for a while, going over a more textbook explanation of the topic. "You probably feel that, faced with a lethal force confrontation, you can pull the trigger and take out the opponent. Correct?"

All three nodded confirmation, though Mikey's response came less than enthusiastically. "Yeah, well, maybe… You know I don't do this stuff. I'm the computer guy."

"So am I, but you gotta be able to if you have to." Andy looked over at his friend.

Mikey glared back at Andy.

Les went on. "At some point, you *will* be faced with it. You won't like it. But you have to be able to handle it, take control of the situation." He turned a stern gaze on Alex.

She met his look, listening, intent, but experiencing a cringe in her gut as he questioned her directly. "Do you really believe you can handle that?"

Alex answered him with a slow nod. She had received some of that training before in a class, though only the basics. But she'd still always felt she could defend herself if needed and act. "Why? Do you think we can't?"

Les gave her a wry smile, and in a flash drew his sidearm on Aaron.

Alex was on her feet at once, gun drawn but pointed toward the floor. The hair at the back of her neck lifted and her core froze as adrenaline flashed through her veins, chasing away all those amorous warm fuzzies from minutes earlier.

"Can you make the *hardest* decision? Someone you know?" He challenged her, his intense gaze remaining fixed on Aaron.

"Les, this *isn't* funny! Stop it!" She had seen him reload earlier and for whatever reason had paid attention. "You're not chambered. Besides, we know you. We *trust* you. You're a friend…" She stopped, tickles of suspicion creeping in at the edges of her mind. That look he was giving Aaron…

Les's gruff reply was cold as ice. "Yeah… we bloody trusted Shane for the most part too…" With that, he racked his slide, chambering a round, the stare he had leveled at Aaron turning chill and blank.

"Aw, *fuck*!" Andy edged back on the sofa, bringing his legs up under him, ready to flee as he scooted behind Alex, toward Mikey.

Mikey's eyes were saucers riveted on Les.

Aaron regarded Les, his calm expression unchanged.

Though he retained his laid-back position, Aaron's jawline pulsed in a clench, and one muscle in his left forearm twitched. Alex raised her weapon to Les. Hers was still chambered from the range the prior day. This *wasn't* happening.

"Les, don't give me a reason to not trust you. *Especially* with this one. After Shane, I won't hesitate."

A thick, confused tension hovered in the silence for harrowing seconds.

"You just did."

Les locked eyes with Aaron, lowered his weapon, and reholstered it. He turned back to Alex. "But we'll work on that."

Alex stood frozen, mouth agape, and looked from one to the other. Color drained from her face. She eased down her own pistol.

"Holy shit, man!" Andy collapsed back to the cushion and rested his head in his hands.

Mikey bolted over to his computers without a word. Dropping into his chair, he busied himself at once, hunkered down behind one of the larger screens.

Hands now shaking, Alex holstered her weapon and sank to the sofa. The unfortunate kick of nausea began to rise as she struggled to reconcile her turmoil at this mental blow, and she found herself unable to either come up with words or cry. Staring at her palms, she felt her body start to tremble. The ways this could have ended so badly. *What the fuck?*

That condition remained temporary, and she was back on her feet in an instant. "What the hell was that? Just what the hell *was* that?" she demanded of Les, her fear and shock now having been replaced with a boiling need to understand why their "friend" would even hint at such an action. She also restrained an urge to provide a swift kick to an area of his body that would quite painfully demonstrate her disapproval.

"Just proving a point. Wanted to see how you'd react."

She opened her mouth to reply, but unable to come up with any decent rebuke, she snapped it shut. Fingernails dug into palms, and she turned on her heel and stomped off, slamming the door to the outer hallway behind her.

The main outer door remained in lockdown from night security, but if they knew what was good for them, they'd open it. A metallic click sounded just as she reached the exit, and without missing a beat, Alex rammed her hands into the smooth steel of the crossbar latch. The door slammed open and she marched outside.

A few seconds of pause; would they lock it again after it closed? It drifted shut. No click followed. She snickered to herself. "Yeah… *Whatever.*"

She stalked to the edge of the compound and plopped down on a large rock under a pine. *Asshole.* She kicked a small stone. Midmorning sunlight shone dappled points of brilliance all around her through the boughs. The air held a sharp chill. She ignored both and glared at the mountain.

AARON

AARON EASED UP FROM THE sofa and took the couple of steps over to where Les still stood. "You could've given me a heads-up on that."

"Yeah, I know." Les shook his head. "Just thought of it. Figured spur of the moment would elicit a more natural reaction. Sorry, mate."

Aaron nodded and after a moment threw Les a hard side-eye. "You do realize, had that been for real, your first shot would've had to have been the kill shot."

Les glanced away from him and over to the guys at the computer bank, who purposely ignored them.

"And then you'd be dead now too." He raised an eyebrow at Les, his gaze darkening. "In fact, the only reason you're not is because she knew, deep down, that *you* weren't *really* gonna shoot me. Somebody else? We'd be mopping." He gave Les another hard stare. "You did make her question it though."

Les sighed and looked back to Aaron. "Yeah." He shrugged. "At least we know she'd do it. Sometimes that emotional attachment can come in handy." He rubbed his face. "Maybe we can use that. Along with detachment training. It'll take some time... I'm thinking of something."

Aaron shot Les a dangerous look at that. *Don't screw with her, man. You're playing with fire.* He rested his hands on his hips. "You shouldn't have brought Shane into it."

"Yeah, well, I wanted a true, strong, gut-wrenching reaction. And that dodgy bastard *did* wind up with her gun on the ship."

"Well, no thanks to *us*, she had no reason to not trust him."

Les nodded. "And yeah, I know she's bloody pissed."

"To say the least." Aaron rubbed his hands through his hair, laced his fingers behind his neck, and gave Les a solid stare. "*Don't* do it again." He turned to go after Alex and glanced back at Les. "Damage control."

"Think she'll actually talk to you right now, mate?" Les's look was somewhat apologetic.

"*I'm* not the one who just pulled a gun on me."

Aaron rubbed one shoulder as he walked down the outer hallway. *Dammit, Les!* Had the man done more harm than good with his little test, or had it been a valuable training scenario? Aaron would find out soon enough. Les had come damn close to getting himself killed. The man knew it too.

In a matter of seconds, Alex had transformed from the giddy girl stealing seductive glances to a protective lioness ready to kill. She'd been a vision in her fitted Levi's and lace-trimmed white T-shirt, taking up that armed defensive stance; while it sent a wave of admiration and desire into the mix with the dose of adrenaline sweeping his bloodstream, the paradox lay in witnessing her unfaltering determination. She would kill or die to protect him. The perfect partner and teammate. The most devastating loss he could ever face.

Training her and enhancing her skill set for her own protection? A good thing. Training her to lend support to their upcoming operation? A plus. Putting her in a situation where, if things went bad for him, she *would* put herself in harm's way? Not the best option. He needed to discuss this with her. And Les.

Plus today was a whole different side to Les than Aaron was used to seeing. His friend sure used some strange methods to evaluate a person's mental capacity. That one had even caught *him* off guard. Aaron himself was usually the one pulling the crazy stuff, though that was more in line with reading other's intentions and utilizing his own physical talents. Les wouldn't harm him. But facing the business end of any firearm brought a general apprehension. Even with training to the contrary. No matter how calm he stayed inside, telltale signs of that unease could escape. The fact that Alex picked up on those minute reactions fast showed her attention to detail. Or was it her attunement to him?

Exiting the outer door, he squinted against the sunlight, his eyes finding Alex right away. Out beyond the buildings, seated on a flat-topped boulder, her back to him, she made no move to turn around. As he headed in her direction, he also noted the extra cold chill in the air. The moderate weather they'd experienced so far was about to take a turn.

ALEX

THE STEEL DOOR OPENED AND closed. Footsteps crunching over gravel and dried grass soon reached Alex's ears. Aaron walked around and stood in front of her. She continued to stare past him toward the mountain. If she looked at him right now, she'd burst into tears. He didn't move.

After a time, she asked, her voice small and quiet, "Did you know he was gonna do that?"

"Honestly, no."

She nodded, and he approached to sit with her on the rock. Looking out in the direction she was, he offered, "Pretty decent view."

"Yours is better." Her reply came immediate and terse as she referenced his piece of land.

He waited a few more minutes before speaking again.

"I know it seems harsh, but... an honest reaction tells a lot. That's what he was looking for, and that's what we got."

"Well, *yay* for you guys," she shot back, still gazing into the distance. Several more minutes passed, and she spoke, restrained but sincere. "Just so you know, right or wrong, if he would have shot you, I would have killed him."

"I know. So does he."

"And he needs to know—what he did? That can't happen again. I can say I *do* actually understand *why* he did it, but from here on out, it's up-front. No blindsiding."

"Yeah, he won't." He rested a sympathetic gaze on her. "We'll work with you. It'll be tough and complicated and frustrating as hell. But we'll be ready. We gotta be. And then it may get real bad before it gets better."

Recovered enough, she risked a peek over at him and quickly lowered her lids. Seeing him at the business end of *any* weapon was traumatic. How the hell was this all going to work? A deep sigh helped release what remained of her upset. She hugged his arm, resting her cheek against his shoulder. "This was some of why you said I might regret coming along."

"Some."

"Some." Another resigned sigh. "I know. And believe me, I'm still trying to get my head around just how what seems like putting you in *more* danger is supposed to get you *out* of it."

"Well, it's either that or we run for the rest of our lives and never call one place our home."

"Yeah, I get that. It's still just… just…" She trailed off as his words sank in, and she sat back and blinked at him.

Smile lines dimpled his cheeks, as her mind worked over his intimation to understanding. *Our* home?

"You… just said…"

"I know what I said."

A small squeal escaped her as Alex grabbed Aaron in a hug that nearly strangled him and just about sent them both off the rock.

He slapped a hand down on the granite beside him to steady them and held her tight with his other arm. "Well, you wouldn't be here if that wasn't the case, now would you?"

AARON

"OKAY, WELL, SHE'S EITHER A lot more resilient than I thought, or you give a *damn* good talk. I don't know if I should be impressed or worried."

Aaron didn't reply, just shot Les a sideways grin.

"Uh-huh." Les shook his head at Aaron. "Well, all the same, I'm glad she's better."

Upon the two coming back inside, Alex provided Les a warm greeting and grabbed Mikey to help her make lunch for them all. Cheerful chatter now elicited giggles from her shy cohort as they gathered various condiments, meat, and bread from the refrigerator.

Les, Andy, and Aaron stood over near the computers.

"Dude, what *did* you say to her?" Andy asked, also taken aback by Alex's quick recovery from Les's little experiment. And curious.

Still offering no explanation, Aaron only sent Andy a wink.

Andy waited, at last giving up on any answer. "Well, I would've been pissed for *days* if I was her." He glowered over at Les. "I'm actually still a little pissed anyway. That was *cold,* man." He shuffled off to go join Alex and Mikey.

Aaron put his foot up on the edge of a chair and leaned over to tie a bootlace.

Les glanced at him again and smirked. "Best bloody damage control *I've* ever seen."

ALEX

ANDY LEANED IN CLOSE TO Alex as she assembled sandwiches. "Okay, you *gotta* tell me. *What* did he say to you?"

Alex just eyed him, her face alight.

"Aw, c'mon. You *too*? *Really*? I mean, you were like *so* mad! And then you come back in here like nothing at all happened? You *gotta* tell me!"

"Andy, you're such a girl." She cocked her head at him. "And how do you know I'm not playing a psych job on you?"

"*Oho* no. I *know* it's nothing like that. I mean, you look like you either just won the lottery or got like the best Christmas present... *ever*!"

Alex smiled back at him. "Better."

Their meal finished, all remained at the table, engrossed in conversation.

Full of curiosity and after hearing more of the details of what transpired on the ship, Andy at last commented to Aaron. "That's crazy, man. You're a real revenant."

Aaron just shook his head and rested his chin in his hand.

In answer to Alex's look, Andy must have assumed she needed an explanation. "Revenant. You know, a ghost, spirit. Like that."

Alex nodded back at Andy as Les asked Aaron what they'd all wondered for some time. "Just how *did* you get out of that? You should've been blown to bits."

Aaron glanced around at their inquisitive looks and shrugged. "Simple physics really. Kick off hard, dive deep. Got just far enough under the hull and away. Maybe that grenade wasn't the greatest." He reached over, and Alex took his hand in both of hers as he continued. "Did get knocked for a pretty good loop though. It wasn't like I had that whole thing planned ahead or anything."

"But why didn't you let us know then that you were still alive?" Les asked.

"Well, once I realized that I was, I was still a little out of it at first. And I still wasn't sure at that point just what we were *actually* dealing with. Worked my way around the ships. Made sure. Then I thought it would just be easier to disappear. Fewer questions. And plausible deniability for the rest of you. So I hid out near the stern of our ship, and when we got close to shore, took a swim."

Les nodded his approval. "Overall good idea, I guess. It worked out."

Alex eyed Les. Shifting her attention back to Aaron, she gave him a bleak yet relieved sigh. "I know I don't understand all this yet. But I sure am glad you're okay."

Aaron squeezed her hand. "Maybe I've gotten a little too used to disappearing over the years. I shouldn't have this time. I'm sorry."

"You're here now. That's what matters."

"He's never been *okay*." Les grinned.

Aaron unfolded the middle finger of the hand supporting his chin and smirked at his friend from behind its uplifted rebuff.

"Yeah, I got that. Bloody insane loon."

The grin and raised digit remained in place, and Aaron arched an eyebrow.

Les returned a peppy hike of his own brows and laughed. "You did miss out on all the bloody debriefing joy though," he said as he finished his chuckle. "Never know too. If you hadn't done what you did, things might be a whole lot different now.

I'll bet our new 'friends' had lookouts dockside by the time we got there. If they'd seen you and jumped us then? That coulda been a real fiasco."

Aaron nodded to Les. "We'd have fought back in defense. Which could have resulted in… more casualties." He swallowed hard and cleared his throat. "Any confrontation at that point could've had a disastrous outcome. Plus there'd have been the additional aftermath of landing us all in a foreign jail as authorities sorted out the mess."

"Bloody mess indeed." Les turned his attention to Alex. "Since you're 'present' again, I'd like to know your thoughts on what I did earlier."

Alex shot him a black look. "I'll reserve what I could say for myself, because it's not real nice. But…" She gave a long pause before continuing. "I knew you wouldn't really shoot him. You came out to find us, help us, and brought us here. Why would you do all that just to end it?" She narrowed her eyes at him. "But don't think that makes it all okay. You're still not on my favorites list right now, buddy."

Les eyed her a moment. "Hmm. And what if maybe I had decided to cash in?"

He waited, judging her reaction. She just raised an eyebrow, giving him a look. He chuckled at her.

"But no. Good read," he said with approval. "You were thinking beyond the scope of the immediate situation, yet I know you were ready to act."

Alex didn't disagree.

"We're gonna get into something a bit tougher now," he said after a moment.

"Oh *great*," Andy interjected. "Worse?"

Les fired a hard look at Andy. "Yes. Mentally, worse. But lucky you, this will be more for her."

Alex closed her eyes. What could be worse than threatening, or pretending to threaten, Aaron's life? But this was all for the good of keeping him safe, right? What in the world did Les have planned *this* time?

She raised her lids to find Aaron's consoling gaze on her, and she gave Les a solid stare. "Whatever it takes."

Les nodded his satisfaction, steel-blue eyes sparkling, then turned to Aaron. "How you feel about getting shot for real this time?"

CHAPTER 47

ALEX

IN HIS ELEMENT WITH COMPUTERS and electronics, Mikey was more open, animated, and conversational. Alex spent several hours beside him later at his main station as he elaborated on some of the finer details of surveillance and spying. He also touched on the seedier aspects of the dark web.

Besides those two goons that had tracked her and invaded her apartment the couple of weeks prior, he informed her that she'd also been tracked through her social media and some online business accounts. Essex and team had monitored her location and whom she associated with, searching for any indication of Aaron.

The knot in her stomach threatened to make her vomit. She also had the urge to go take a very hot shower to wash away the feeling of being violated. She sighed. She *had* wanted to know. More grateful than ever to have always been discerning with posting media, she concentrated on Mikey's words to help squelch her disgust. It also kept her mind off Les's upcoming lesson.

Intrigued but hopelessly lost at some of Mikey's explanations, she voiced a thought. "Okay. I have a question. Well, maybe more of a request and question. Can you upload something, like say a picture to a website, and make it look like it was taken and sent from a completely different location?"

Mikey eyed her with mirth. "Well, sure! That's child's play. Where in the world would you like something sent from?"

His confidence and knowledge helped ease her discomfort. Alex giggled at his amusement. "Okay. I was just thinking. I sell photographs to a few different sites. I just figured I'd put that on hold for a while. But would it be possible, or even a good idea in our situation, to upload some over the next couple of days or weeks and make it look like I'm in another country?"

Mikey squinted before excitement consumed his features. "Oh man, I totally get you! And that is such a sweet idea!" Deft fingers flew over the keyboard. "They're watching two of those sites already. If they think you're traveling, they'll be chasing their own tails trying to find ya. And spread it out over the next few weeks? Yeah. This,,, will be fun!" His digits paused on the keyboard, and he looked back over at her. "We'll run it by Bear first and see what he thinks, but I figure he'll go for it. Whatcha got for me?"

Alex retrieved her camera and pulled the card, which Mikey inserted into his system. He brought up her gallery.

"You're not *actually* traveling, so your passport won't flag. But this will show up on your website and accounts, so it'll still make them look. Give those boys something to do!" He laughed.

"What ones you want sent, and what sites you want 'em to go to?"

Alex gave him the details, and he pulled up several of her scenic photos to the screen. "Step one, change any embedded data on where it was taken and the date. Step two... Where would you be?"

"I... don't know. I guess I really hadn't thought that far." She paused a moment. Any thoughts on her own travel planning had screeched to a halt when Aaron showed up. *Europe? Australia?* That's what she'd told the girls. "Based on the scenery, where do you think would match? What countries?"

"Hmm... Pines and mountains, flowers and rocks, and sunsets. *Some* of the sunsets can be almost anywhere since you don't have identifying markers in the foreground. The mountains and trees..." He switched screens and brought up similar photos from the web. "Best places for stuff like this to match? Austria. Or Germany. Maybe Finland. Ha, or even New Zealand. Those basic areas work. Heck, we can send you all over the place! And the sites don't care where you are unless they're wanting something specific. They're just buying photographs." He glanced at her, back at his screens. "A big plus in this too is you like photographing more off-the-beaten-path stuff, not the easily identifiable touristy stuff." He grinned and chuckled. "Flower wise, we'll do some quick research. For the trees too. Don't want to upload something that doesn't even grow there. You never know who might be knowledgeable on botany."

CHAPTER 48

AARON

SEVERAL DAYS LATER CAME THE more intensive firearms instruction. They used the indoor range set up in one of the larger adjacent buildings, which also served as a workout area and more storage. The weather had taken a turn for the worse with snow showers and high winds whipping outside. Les's training this time was to have Alex actually shoot both of them. He and Aaron explained to her in detail the heavy-duty body armor they both would wear. A lengthy discussion convinced her, for the most part, that nothing she shot would get through it. Andy, who had elected to come along, also made an attempt at reassuring her.

When targeting a suit mounted at the end of the range, Alex had no trouble placing accurate groupings and inspecting the results. No through penetrations. Easy enough. She'd been shooting at targets since she was five years old. But Les wanted to test her will, impress upon her what it would be like to target and fire on a live person. To *feel* the difference in emotion between inanimate object and human.

Les's idea behind that was as a means to better condition Alex for the real possibility of having to defend herself and shoot someone. Regardless of her earlier response to his front of turning on Aaron, just assuming she could fire in defense was not good enough. And targets were one thing. A real, live body would provide an altogether different mental scenario.

Les and Aaron stood about thirty feet away from her.

"Dude, you're twisted," Andy commented to Les.

"I know it's unorthodox. But she can handle it."

"I know she can, just should she right now?" Aaron asked, worried about dumping another tough psych job on Alex so soon after Les's last. She was strong, but would this leave her too shell-shocked and upset? *I'll take whatever he throws at me* had been her resolute statement to him that morning as they dressed for the day. Her unwavering independence, her will to get it done impressed the hell out of him. Regardless, this part was still very new and disturbing for her to have to experience. Let alone the fact that he would be one of the targets.

"It will probably be one of the hardest things you'll have to do," Les told her. "But when you do, it will help desensitize you, help you detach emotionally. Plus it will help with part of the plan we're coming up with for this mission. Do you understand?"

Alex stared at Les. "I *understand* just fine. It's just the actual *doing* it." She looked down at her pistol in her hands and muttered, "*Detach emotionally, my ass…*"

"The best way is to just aim and do it. Don't think about it, just do it. Then it'll be over." Aaron tried to encourage her, though he doubted he was doing a very successful job of it.

God, that despair in her eyes. Though he had long since dealt with his own insecurities and pain brought out in his training from those years ago, watching her trepidation now brought some of it back to mind. His young punk self, learning tactics and lessons no one should ever have to, too overconfident, not truly knowing what lay ahead for him at the time. And… the very first time he'd had to kill. He bit back the sudden urge to whisk her away, to tell Les thanks but no, thanks, and take her somewhere she'd never have any risk of experiencing a fraction of the hurt he knew all too well.

This situation was dragging up emotions for him he'd thought long gone. Why was this coming up so strongly now? On an average day, they were just memories without emotional attachment. Just the past. Stuff he'd gotten over. But no day was average anymore, not since he'd met her. Damn. So much for feeling he had his own psyche together.

For completely different reasons, they would be teaching her to suppress her own feelings of compassion and remorse. Exactly what had been done to him. Good for combat, horrible in the aftermath. It always came back. He clamped down on his thoughts and refocused. He'd get a handle on his own inner state later. Right now she was what mattered. Getting her through this. This would be nothing like the harshness he'd endured. And he would be here to support her.

"Well, it's too late. I've already thought about it. And too much." Shimmering eyes shone from her fallen face as she looked over at him.

"It's okay, really. Just go ahead. It'll be fine."

"You must really trust my aim," she said after stalling a few more moments.

303

Aaron thought back to the ship and his first encounter with Alex about her carry. As he'd taken her offered weapon from her with the grip in hand, his previous perception of her had solidified. Just the difference in how she'd carried herself showed she was aware and careful, displaying full knowledge of the importance and consequence of her concealed weapon. And she did know how to handle it. While still not knowing the quality of her shooting at that point, the simple dexterity in her actions had strengthened his impression and his confidence in her being armed. Add to that the accuracy she'd now displayed at the range. He chuckled and offered some more assurance. "We have seen you shoot, remember? I think we're pretty safe."

Les muttered over at Aaron. "Well, at least in *your* case I'm sure she'll be bloody careful."

"Should've thought more on that one before you set this up, huh?" Aaron smirked back at Les.

Les rolled his eyes.

Aaron returned his attention to Alex. "It'll be just fine. We trust you. We're ready."

ALEX

ALEX RAISED HER GUN TO target his chest. *Oh, this is just hell.* Stance set, aim accurate, she let her trigger finger inch back inside the guard. The smooth crescent of metal, so familiar and comfortable in a range or self-defense settings, touched pitiless and bitter against her digit. A sudden bleak chill clutched at her insides, her active imagination making its presence felt in dreadful images.

Her hands shook, and she withdrew her finger from the trigger. She bit down on her lower lip to keep it from quivering and squeezed her eyes shut. *Okay, you can do this. Stay positive.*

Focus! Their armor is the best in the business. You are a damn good shot, so you won't miss. You. Know. This. Her lids rose. A couple of deep breaths to calm herself, and her vision lifted back to Aaron. *Screw this.* She lowered her weapon.

"I'm not sure I can do this." She looked away, trying to blink back the droplets she felt forming at the corners of her eyes and to hide the dejection she knew clouded her face.

Les glanced at Aaron, stepped out, and strolled over to Alex. "Here, it's okay. I'll show you something that might make it easier for you." He spoke in a reassuring tone as he held out a hand for her weapon. "Let me see that."

She hesitated a moment, handed it over to him.

With an immediate twist, he turned and shot twice.

Aaron took a step back and dropped to his knees. Expelling a groan, he leaned forward to rest on splayed hands.

Alex yelped and clamped both hands to her mouth. *How dare you!* She glared at Les and ran to Aaron.

AARON

AARON SAT BACK ON HIS heels as Alex dropped to her knees beside him. He closed his eyes and drew a deep, slow breath. *Dammit. No matter how many times that happens, it still hurts like hell.* The impacts stung worse than expected, even with the heavier armor. He would have bruises.

Alex put a hand on his arm, and he opened his eyes to meet hers. The concern that showed on her face for his well-being stirred something in him every time he saw it, and he gave her a weak smile.

"It's okay. Really. Not like I thought it *wasn't* gonna hurt."

"You people are nuts," she said and hugged him. Rising to her feet, she offered a hand and waited for him to stand with her. "I think I've got this." She turned and marched back over to Les.

Les. As she approached, she held out her hand to him, folding her fingers twice. "Give it." She nodded at her weapon, keeping her eyes fixed on his, her expression deadpan.

He handed it back to her easy and made his way over to stand with Aaron. "Bloody hell, what have I done?" was all he murmured to Aaron as he turned back to face Alex.

Three quick shots made a nice tight grouping, and Les went down to a knee. He coughed and grunted as Aaron pulled him back to his feet.

"Now, you *had* to know that was coming," Aaron commented with smug amusement.

"Yeah," Les groaned and rubbed at his chest. "Worked though, didn't it?" He looked at Aaron. "She's gotta be loaded hot too."

"Well, I never checked. It's just what she's been runnin' through that nine." Something they *should* have checked. He'd been a little distracted...

They affirmed readiness for another round. Alex checked her mag, slapped it back in. "I have six left. Let me get through this. But... back up a few feet."

ALEX

ONCE THEY'D BACKED AWAY, ALEX sighted. *Them.* She closed her eyes, trying to steel her mind, to will away the sick prickles that corroded her reserve. The guys stood safe in their armor, but the understanding of what Les meant hit her. The *feel* of the difference. This was no longer average target shooting at some... *thing*. Some stationary piece of paper or wood, or even the armored vest on a lifelike mannequin. This was people. And... *Dammit, Les!*

Her lids snapped open. No hesitation. Each man received a grouping of three. Neither went down this time, though it had to hurt. She holstered her weapon and looked back across the room. She sank to her knees, buried her face in her hands, and sobbed.

CHAPTER 49

ALEX

ANOTHER FEW DAYS AND TWICE more they completed the exercise, though having changed out Alex's practice ammunition to lower-grain rounds. Andy also took a turn. Mikey flat-out refused, and they didn't press him further. Alex's alone time with Aaron soothed weariness from her soul, and his understanding and thoughtful tutoring of the emotional responses her psyche produced during training proved quite interesting learning.

By her third time out, she didn't cry, though tightness still pinched at her throat and stinging blurred her vision by the end. Not to mention her heart seemed crushed to the ground each time. Effective or no, that aspect of Les's conditioning would never sit right with her. Not with his choice of targets.

"When you can shoot us, it makes you that much more able to take out an enemy, someone you don't know. You may never need to, and I really hope to God you don't, but you need to be able to handle it if you do. To protect yourself and the people you're with. You just can't lose yourself to it."

Alex nodded at Aaron, then gave him a small smile and a long hug before he stood.

"Be back in a few." He walked to the coatracks, pulled on his winter jacket and gloves, and headed for the outer door.

Several minutes later, Les wandered over. "Doin' okay?"

"Yeah, I guess. I don't know," she answered as he sat beside her.

"It'll take you some time to process. That's natural."

"How do you handle it? It doesn't seem like it even fazes you guys at all."

"That's just time, training, and experience. We've obviously been exposed to this stuff way longer than you have."

Alex nodded, hesitant to ask her next question. Her words came low and soft. "And... when you do have to... kill someone?"

"The way I look at it, and I'm pretty sure he does too, is if they're trying to hurt people, then they've made their choice." Les looked at the floor in front of him. "We all deal with it differently." He shrugged. "Protection details are good in a lot of ways though. We just do what it takes to keep our people safe. It's mostly defensive." He looked back at her after some moments. "On a lot of jobs, we don't get into a situation or see any action. But occasionally, like on your trip? The unfortunate happens. We just have to handle it."

Indicating the outer door, Les continued. "Another reason we call him Psycho? He's probably the best and really only person I've ever known who can completely detach, take care of business, then turn it off and come right back. To separate and do the job, take out an enemy, and snap right back to helping get others out of harm's way. Not lose the empathy for others, not become lost in the combat. Not even a little. And it's real. But even so, there's always some distress there. If not, well, then we'd be just like the ones we're defending against."

Les flashed her a somber smile. "The other side, and he'll tell you this too, his biggest issue with any of this? Caring *too* much. I know he tries not to. But he does. And if something goes horribly wrong, like with Shane? He gets past it, but he'll hold on to it for a while. It's not so much having to take out an attacker, it's about losing an innocent life."

"But Mario... That wasn't Aaron's fault, or yours. Shane made his choice. And that's on Shane."

"I know that. You know that. And he knows that. But he was the lead for our team. Even with Shane being vetted, Psycho will feel the responsibility for what happened, whether he should or not."

Alex laced her fingers in her lap and squeezed her palms together. Mind focused back on the ship, she questioned Les. "Why does he take so many chances? Is it more so he won't have to put someone else in a bad spot, or does he really like it? Shane said he always chooses the dangerous stuff."

Les took in a deep breath, let it out slow. "I guess maybe because of the past. It's kind of an atonement. Aside from the fact that he's bloody good at it." Les rubbed his face and stared at the far wall. "Back when I first met him? I don't think he much cared if he lived or died at that point. At least that's what we all thought. Took some damn daft chances. Over time, he toned it down. Took on more of that controlled assurance you see now. And it took him some time to get back to himself. But he did." He stopped, as if gauging how much he should say, then looked back to her. "Has he told you any of it? About what happened before?"

"A little. I know there's a lot more, but I won't pressure him about it. I know things were bad. Whenever he's ready, I'll be there for him."

Les studied her. "Well, all I can, and really should, tell you is in that time, there were orders given that were, let's just say... sinister. It wasn't assignments they were initially told they would be involved in. Those guys got used for some really bad stuff. I think he feels if he can put himself in the risky position and keep someone else out of it, it may help make up for a part of that. Part of it's the skill and training too. He knows he can handle it. Part is in the protection of other people. It's definitely not the way Shane bloody told it, for any adrenaline rush or some kind of bravado."

They sat in silence for a time before Les spoke again.

"He didn't want you to have to go through all this. What we're doing here. And neither did I. Whether you *can* handle it or not, you shouldn't *have* to. We really had to weigh that against your safety, if you'd be safer here or left on your own, and what you'd go through coming with us. And since you are here, you have to be prepared."

Alex hung on every word as Les talked.

"He wouldn't have left you though. That night at your apartment? Man, you might have wanted to clock me to the floor, but I had to walk away from that look he gave me."

"What do you mean?"

Les shook his head at her, searched her eyes, a warmth lighting his countenance. "He was in love with you from the ship. He never said it, but I knew. I just didn't realize how much. For me, upsetting you was one thing, just figured it might be better for us all, including you, if he let you go. But after the way you mates both reacted independently? Yeah. I knew it didn't matter. He wouldn't leave you, and you would have found some way to force coming along to be with him. Sane or not."

So Aaron had fallen just as she had. At what point had Les picked up on it? Near the end? Earlier on with her increasing time spent with Aaron each day? It shouldn't have come as a surprise to her.

Alex stared back at Les, blinked to recover from his revelation, and gave him a sheepish smile. "Good read."

He chuckled at her use of his prior comment to her. "I've been hard on you on some of this, I know. I have my reasons. I care what happens to you, and I want you to be prepared for whatever we get into. I need you to be as ready as you can be. I need to see how resilient you are and how well you can handle it, to make it through. Like I said before, you do handle the crazy well too." He nudged her arm with his elbow and gave her a quick wink, then turned more serious again. "And… that guy that I've seen take out the worst of the worst, do more insane, crazy shit, do whatever it takes to keep people safe? Don't let that devil-may-care attitude he comes off with at times fool you. That man loves you beyond compare. He's real true-blue. And I wanted to see just how committed you are, how much you're willing to do, just how far you'll go for that. Because I care what happens to him too. He deserves good." He paused, steel-blue gaze reaching deep into hers again to cement his point. "I trust that bloke with my life and with the life of anyone I care about. All this? What we do, what we have done? Not everybody can deal with that. Not everybody can understand it, and not everybody can bloody live with it. But… I think you can."

Alex fought back tears at the sincerity in those words. Les's care for his friend, for her. And his veiled trials, aside from the intensive tactical trainings, to make sure she was loyal and committed? To some that admission might seem an affront. But coming from him, in this unique position, it meant everything.

Les winked again. "Grab a warm coat and go join him. He's just out there 'cause he likes the snow."

Alex smiled. "Me too." She leaned over and gave Les a tight hug. "Thank you. For all of it."

MIKEY

MIKEY AND ANDY VIEWED THE security camera feeds on the computer screen. Aaron and Alex slipped and dodged around drifts, throwing snowballs at each other. They ended up in a wrestling match, laughing and rolling as they played in the snow.

Mikey's voice was subdued when he spoke. "I really hope this thing doesn't go bad," he said, and Andy looked over at him. "If something happens to one of them? The other is gonna be messed up real bad for a really long time."

Andy put a hand on Mikey's shoulder, stood and walked away as Mikey switched over to check the weather radar.

DEPRAVED
REAQUAINTANCE

CHAPTER 50

ALEX

"ALL OF US THEY BROUGHT in, we were all screwed up in one way or another. Some a lot *more* than others. The damaged and the lost. I was just a delinquent kid, causing trouble, nothing to do. I bought their promises of making a difference. Being valuable. Seeing the world.

"Essex and a couple of others, well they came with some serious baggage. Pissed off from day one, picking fights just to fight or prove themselves. The operating objective was to provide us discipline, mental restructuring. Then get us trained, give us a purpose in life. Figured we'd just go along with whatever we were told to do without question. No matter how sick the orders were. Most did.

"Essex loved it. In excess. For whatever reason, he just liked causing pain. After… some things happened, I decided to make my exit. Had to plan it out over time. Told no one. If anyone had known, my parting gift would likely have been a blade in the base of my skull. Or worse. You don't just walk away from an operation like that. They don't just let you leave."

"Why does he even care? You said it's been like ten years… why should it even matter to him, to come after you now?" Was it worth any real attempt to understand Damien Essex? A myriad of unsavory visions clouded Alex's thoughts as she, Aaron, and Les sat at the table, discussing events to come.

"It's complicated." Aaron took her hand and squeezed. "And personal. I didn't approve of his methods. He didn't approve of my not killing everything in sight. But since he knows now for sure that I'm still alive and well, he'll never stop. He'll never let it go. He just won't. It's just the way he is." He shrugged, lost in thought as he rubbed her arm with his free hand. "Plus he's about as close to pure evil as I've ever seen in a human being. He's a sadist. He hurts people. Unfortunately, he likes that part of what he does more than any money."

Les nodded. "He really just needs to be taken out."

Alex bowed her head and stared at the wood grain of the tabletop, searching for relief in its well-worn surface. As time neared for their plan to execute, her concern for their safety skyrocketed with each new particular she learned about Essex. The current conversation wasn't helping her active imagination either. In dealing with the abomination this man presented as, how could events truly work out in their favor?

"This is like a bad movie… It's just stupid!" She looked back up at Les, to Aaron. "Isn't there *anything* else we can do? Can't we call somebody, call in anonymously and just let some kind of authority know where he is and what he is?"

"If that were a viable option, we'd do it. But it'll only get people killed if they confront him. And he'd just disappear again," Aaron told her. "He's that slick and he doesn't care. Then he'd be in the wind and we'd never know where or when he'd show up. We'll set this up and see if he follows. If not, there are a few... let's just say *places* an anonymous tip or two could maybe get results." He tossed a quick glance over to Les. "Maybe. But if he does follow, we gotta be ready. Because if he does, he'll be prepared for all-out war."

"Is that really a good idea though, bringing them in here?" Alex asked.

"Here it's just us and them. It's isolated. No chance of civilians getting caught in it. Anywhere else, we couldn't guarantee that," Les told her. "And we know here. We can set everything up here. They won't be familiar with it, and even if they do real good surveillance, there are always those little parts they'll miss, the intricate stuff only we know."

"Home field advantage," Alex remarked.

"Exactly," Les replied.

"Plus there's the arrogance factor. Don't get me wrong, Essex is no slouch. He's intelligent, genius level. Dangerous. A quick thinker." Aaron fastened his gaze on her. "But he's cocky. When he thinks he's got the upper hand, his arrogance will trump his skill every time. He'll screw up. That's where we'll catch him."

Les agreed. "We just let him think he's got the drop on us, that we're not expecting him at all."

Alex's voice was filled with dread as she spoke to Aaron. "It's the bait part I'm worried about. I'm sorry, but like I said the other night, it just creeps me out on a whole different level that he's so obsessed with you."

AARON

"I KNOW. BUT THE POINT is to make it look good. It's got to be believable or he'll know something's up. We need to come off as completely surprised and as disorganized as possible. And I am the bait. It's his sole reason for any of this." Aaron held her gaze, tried to reassure her.

Even though she'd handled all the training and weirdness pretty well, he knew it was still hard for her to come to grips with an understanding about Essex. To someone outside his profession and background, it likely *would* come off as illogical and incomprehensible for a man like Essex to even exist. Unfortunately, the part of the world Aaron had experienced provided for the development of such men, those with a cold, rapacious appetite for lust, violence, and destruction, who lacked the compassion for life that would keep that in check.

And now they had the opportunity to remove one of the worst examples he'd ever encountered. To eliminate this threat now would mean saving countless lives in the future. It was a chance that had to be taken for their own welfare and that of others.

Though their group was small and had come together from a wide variety of backgrounds and talents, in the past couple of months, their cohesion as a team had become solid. That aspect, their recent training along with the skill sets that Les and he possessed, would be a serious advantage for what was to come. Looking at things from that perspective gave him confidence.

Looking at it from the side that none of them should have to be in this position in the first place brought him concern. Of course this wasn't normal. Stuff like this just didn't happen in the real world. But here they were. And Essex had to be dealt with once and for all with as few put in danger as possible. He and Les would remain at the forefront of any action while keeping the others back as much as possible.

His preference before would have been to keep them all off the radar altogether. But running was getting old. It just extended the inevitable. This scenario would grab Essex's attention, Aaron meeting up with Alex in a remote location. Make it look like he wasn't on or paying attention anymore. An easy target. Aaron reached into his pocket.

"Here. It's your old phone." He handed the device and its battery to Alex. "We'll call them first on an untraceable one over a span of a week, using that number we got off those two from the apartment. Leave the bread crumb that they've found you. Then a couple more calls leading to this area. Then you'll call me here, from town, on your phone. They'll pick up that call on their surveillance, I'll come get you, and that will show them right where to go. We'll just wait and watch them then, all the way in, and when they do get here, we'll set everything in motion and it's done."

"How do you know he won't just grab us on the way, away from here?" Alex asked.

"Because, weird as it may seem, he draws energy from seeing others care for each other, knowing he will shatter that. He would rather wait until he thinks we feel comfortable and content, completely safe and happy. Enjoying each other. To destroy that connection, the love and joy, along with me? To cause the most shock and pain? In his mind, that is the ultimate achievement."

CHAPTER 51

AARON

PACING. SHARP MOVEMENTS. UNFINISHED TASKS.

For Aaron to be scattered ahead of any operation was unusual. Actually, this was a first. And something that could compromise their advantage. Initiation of the event was still a ways off, likely a few more weeks yet. He'd get it together long before then... *Dammit, where's my coffee?*

"Hey, mate. You missing something?"

Aaron half glanced up and continued stuffing items into a duffel. A grunted thanks as Les set the misplaced mug of coffee in front of him.

Les remained in place. "Anything you wanna talk out?"

Aaron stopped, fixated ahead. "I…" Knuckles whitened as nails dug into palms, and his arms dropped to his sides. "Aww, fuck, I don't know." He looked over at Les. "All right, so I do know. It's her. I…" He rubbed his jaw, his other hand now resting on a hip. "I don't know how to do this. I mean I do, you know. But I don't."

"All the time I've known you, you've kept everyone at arm's length. Even when you care, and I know you do a bloody lot, you never let anyone close. Not really. Now you're trying, and you don't know what to do with yourself."

Aaron yanked the zipper closed and pushed the bag off onto the floor. "Yeah, that's basically it." He shook his head, and a short chuckle accompanied the acute crossing of his arms.

Les scratched his head. "Well, ya gotta admit, you don't have the best track record. You're no angel, that's for bloody damn sure."

Aaron offered a tortured glare. "Don't fuckin' remind me," he muttered. He bowed his head and studied the tabletop. "I think that's a big part of the problem. How can she ever trust somebody like me?"

"Can she?"

"Hell, Les, you know she can!"

"Yes, I do. But *you* need to believe in what you already know."

Aaron kept silent and squeezed his lids closed. His next words came in a near whisper. "I don't deserve… you don't know the half of what happened before."

"She won't go anywhere. If that's what you're worried about. Hell, I don't think there's anything you *could* do that would make her leave. Beyond messing about or just outright sending her away."

"Well, I'm sure as fuck not looking to do either." His throat constricted, and he swallowed hard. To be honest, the thought of being with anyone else made him want to vomit. Alex's presence in his life had erased any question in that regard. No pretty face, no hot body, no intriguing personality could ever come close to the impact she imparted on him.

Even in heated discussion, her devotion struck him. Not needy or clingy, but a confidence of choice, a knowing that despite any differences or disagreements, she would choose him every day. Every night. Could it really be this good? Had he just gone too far and screwed that up?

Besides his tense movements and lack of concentration, he could feel his neck cord to the point of causing the muscles pain. His eyes burned at the harsh secrets pushing to the surface. He felt like he was losing control. And he'd never allowed Les, or anyone, to witness this degree of uneasiness in him. Ever.

Even when he and Les had first met, Aaron would head off any hints of what heinous affairs had come before with humor and a quick change of subject. He'd blow it off like it was no big deal and plain not discuss it. His way of coping at the time. Now he was being forced to face those shameful episodes on a level he'd never planned.

Les's voice broke in. "I have a cousin, has this wicked theory she's read about that when you meet the one, everything that's not truly who you are gets pulled up to get rid of. So it won't be in the way and cause problems, you know? Always thought she was kinda out there with all that. Fairy tales. Supernatural bollocks and whatnot." Les shrugged. "She believes it though. Maybe she's right."

Aaron's mouth twitched in a wry smirk. Weird as hell, but that fit. Les's insights, or rather his cousin's, were spot-on. Ever since he'd met Alex, it was like he kept putting himself under a microscope. That was new. He hadn't much cared one way or the other what anyone thought of him before. Now he found himself desiring to be the best person he could possibly be. Not that he was a complete ass most of the time or anything. Just sometimes…

"I want this too much. And it scares the fuck outta me."

"Don't let it. Just… be honest with her. I know there's shit you ain't never bloody told me. You don't need to give out details. But don't keep it locked up, mate. Not when it means this much. You need to know you can trust her with your best and your worst. Like I said, she ain't bloody goin' anywhere."

Aaron huffed out a sharp breath. "I don't know."

Les put a hand on his friend's shoulder. "I do. And deep down, you do too. You don't have to unload it all at once. But put a little more out there. See how she responds. I think you'll find out you never had a thing to worry about. She's got your back. And ease the fuck up on yourself."

"Yeah. But… what if I can't do normal? I don't want to drag her around through shit like this for the rest of her life. She deserves better. Better'n me."

"Okay then; do you trust her judgment? Do you think she's intelligent and makes good decisions?"

"Yeah, I do. Of course. She's a smart, strong woman. What're you getting at?"

"Then you should take a different view on this. She's an independent sort. You didn't just choose *her*. She chose *you* too. So there's that whole thing of your opinion of her making sound decisions and such…"

Aaron side-eyed Les, sarcasm caught in tight lips. *Yes, I get your point.*

"You're overthinking it, mate. Sometimes you're too intelligent for your own good. You know this stuff. Feel it and then let it go. You're being way too hard on yourself. What is normal anyway? We'll get through this. It'll be different then. I doubt she's the type who would want an average nine-to-five life anyway. If there's a little or even a lot of unconventional that happens, she'll roll with it." Les moved over and hopped up to sit on the table. "If you want to keep her, keep her close. *Trust* her with your secrets. You do love her, don't you?"

"God yes." Aaron leaned forward and rested his hands on the tabletop, eyes fixed on the worn wood grain once more. Les was right. When the hell had the best thing that ever happened to him become the most frightening? "I know she's the one. It's just… I've never experienced *anything* like this before." Rational thought eased back in as he shifted perspective to observe those feelings, something he should have noticed and allowed hours earlier, days earlier. Before it built up as a block in his mind. It wasn't fear of any situation of being with her. No, far from it; it was a fear of loss. Of somehow losing her amazing affection and friendship, and that soul-level, healing physical intimacy, a perfection the shadow depths of his mind were now telling him he didn't deserve.

"She's pushing herself with all this," Les added. "She could've opted out a long time ago. There's loyalty there. You guys have something beyond special. Those first few days in, when I pulled that stunt of drawing on you? I saw it then, and you did too. She'd defend you to the death."

Aaron sighed and looked over at his friend. "You're right. And that scares the hell outta me too."

CHAPTER 52

AARON

AARON DIDN'T NEED SECURITY FEEDS to review which direction she'd headed. The vision from the flat rock overlook came into his mind's eye as though he viewed the forested river valley himself. A good four-mile hike lay ahead of him.

She never left for a wander about their wooded location without giving someone, especially him, a heads-up. But his brooding avoidance of her all morning had accomplished its selfish goal. Why had he? Conflict within was eroding his natural ease with her. An ease they'd shared from their beginning. He did trust her with the deeper parts of himself. He just had to protect her from the really bad stuff. Or was locking that away just a defense for his own perceived well-being? Could he take that risk?

Angst about her immediate safety was kept at bay by the ability to sense what she saw and experience her deeper feelings. A relatively recent mutual realization, providing evidence for some uncanny tactile experiences, and one they'd been enjoying playing around with upon discovery. By visual reception, she was safe. The gut-wrenching emotional part left him the need to rush to her, wrap her up, and pour out his heart to her.

Rocky inclines and trails revealed little; she was getting good at the stealth exercises. Purposeful in eluding any follow. His gut lurched. *Way to be a complete ass, Donovan.* Traceable or no, she'd taken a path familiar to him from their walkabouts and a handful of picnic lunches, a couple of which had turned intimate. Recollection of those joy-filled adventures brought a piercing jolt to his heart. He *had* to fix this!

How bad had he messed things up? Alone time here and there was expected and healthy. Outright refusal to speak with her, allowing her to feel unwanted? Unacceptable. He'd achieved miserable failure by shutting down with her. A grand communicator, imaginative, creative, even persuasive in profession, all that aside, he hadn't even tried. Why? He'd have been better off to just fall apart in her arms.

Instead, he'd pushed her away, been a standoffish asshole. Demons of vile actions from another life were creeping up to steal a new and worthy reality. The very thing he'd hoped to avoid, he was bringing about. But that was fear's answer. And fear never won in his world.

He made enough noise that she would hear him and not be startled, though she'd know of his presence anyway. At the rustle of brush underfoot, she shrugged up a shoulder to dry shimmering streaks from her cheek. *Do NOT fuck this up.* He approached her back. Tentative hands reached for her shoulders. She stayed still, muscles going rigid under his fingers and sweating palms.

ALEX

ALL MORNING, NOTHING. NO GOOD-morning kiss, no sweet smiles, no touch, nothing. What had she done? Alex racked her brain for some trace of miscommunication. Aaron wasn't one to let things bother him without voicing it. Plus they'd made a reciprocal pact early on to make sure any misunderstandings were always rectified at inception. Surely he'd have said if there was some problem. But what was there?

Until recent days he'd treated her like she was his whole world, their openness with each other like two halves of a whole, two souls who'd known each other across lifetimes. Slow degradation of affection over the past several days was all she had to go on. It didn't make any sense. Had he changed his mind? After weeks of spending most of every day and night together in some form or other, had he come to the conclusion that she wasn't the one for him? At her wits' end, she'd left the buildings and walked, climbed their mountain trail, eventually arriving at this spot with its spectacular overlook of evergreen canopies and winding ribbon of river below. A good place to regroup and think. Or not think.

The soaked sleeves of her sweatshirt weighed cool on her arms, the plush navy fabric darkened in mottled blotches. Could one die of dehydration from crying? A water bottle hadn't figured into her equation earlier. She'd not even considered breakfast. What did it matter anyway? She grimaced and tossed a stone. *Oh, come on now, don't be all overly dramatic. Don't be* that *girl.* A few hours in peaceful nature were at least returning sarcasm to her wretched thinking.

He was on his way up. That tickle of warmth spread from her solar plexus and heart, a sensation she'd come to know well when he thought of her, a steady companion since the ship, in truth maybe even before. A feeling that surged when he focused. It had remained even with his increasing silence, a comfort though sometimes hurtful not in its essence but in its reminder of happier times.

She stiffened as his hands touched her, the reaction a response to her troubled mind. Despite that, he stayed put. Stalwart fingers massaged an affirming hold. She managed husky words through her sob-constricted throat. "Do you want me to go?"

"No."

A shudder ran through her as claws of doubt retracted their dank grasp. "Please…" Her voice cracked, and she clamped her teeth tight until she could speak again. "Please don't shut me out. It's the worst thing you can do besides…"

AARON

HE DROPPED TO HER SIDE and grabbed her tight in his arms, legs wrapping about her waist. "I want you. Only you. I don't want to hurt you, and I'm sorry."

She might try to hide some of it, but her soaked sleeves and puffy eyes told the story. *Do not EVER do this to her again!* Whatever it took, he had to make it right.

His words spilled out. "It's just… some things are coming up for me, things I'm not proud of. Things that I don't want to tell you. I got scared. There's so much… if you knew certain things…" He laid his forehead against her shoulder. "I don't want you to go."

"Does it affect us now? Us as us? Is there a reason you'll want to leave me sometime, someone else?"

"Absolutely not."

"Then you don't need to tell me. Only if you want to. I'm here, and I plan on staying wherever you are." She leaned into his hold and reached over to stroke his tousled hair. Her voice trembled. "I'm here for you. Even if you do tell me, you're stuck with me." The surrender of turmoil that radiated from him washed through and away from her like a wave. Peace returned in its place. "But please, please, don't *ever* stop talking to me. I don't care what you did. It happened before us. If it causes you this much worry about me and what I'll think, it's obviously not the real you."

Any reply got caught in the emotion that welled in Aaron's throat. Her words, the reassurance, her touch. Her body in his embrace again. At last he breathed simple words. "Thank you."

Reticent on the subject as a rule, Aaron did recount more incidents, almost confessions, over the next few weeks. Broken bits at first, progressing to greater detail and more revelation as he and Alex grew more comfortable with those discussions. Hints at situations that brought him the most anxiety to expose to her, though he said he would never say all of it. What he had gone through, some of the paths it had pushed him down after, poor choices in coping. What he thought might scare her away only brought understanding and compassion, more strength to their bond.

Fighting back her tears and anger at those individuals who took him to that place, with each story she held the space for him to release what he'd needed to get out for years.

"They trained us, watched and found what we were good at, then worked to bring those aspects out. That part was actually great. It was intensive and tough, but it taught us skills and to control our strengths. To know when to go so far, when to rein it in. They observed our thought processes too, got inside our heads. Tailored it to each individual. But what they were teaching us, they were doing to us.

"You think my grasp of psychology and analyzing behavior is impressive? They were far better. At least in the manipulation. We knew it was all off the record, that we'd be doing things that were dangerous, unpleasant... necessary. Necessary for the good. That ended up not being the case. A complete lie. Maybe necessary for *somebody*. But not anyone with a conscience. Or sense of decency in any aspect of the word. After a few missions that seemed reasonable, they farmed us out for... for..."

He rubbed his face and looked away for a few moments. When he turned back to her, he'd gotten his emotions back under control.

"What finally did it for me... We'd been sent out to... Well... Anyway, there ended up being a family there and... they shouldn't have been. Or so we were told. Anyway, Essex and Jacks, they... I couldn't let them... The others tried to hold me back. Broke Lenny's nose real good, an' Brax's knee was never the same...

"Well, I got hauled off and stuffed in isolation after. That mission, that's when I knew I had to get away. Or die trying. I was done. I planned it all out in my head over the ten days in that cell. Had learned a good deal about them too over time. I made nice and played good boy when they let me out. Two weeks later, I was gone."

At the look on her face, he took her hands in his. "It's okay. No more of that tonight. It doesn't get any better till that day I took off. And then it took a while for it to really get better with me. From an analytical standpoint, from what any professional would tell you, I did okay. On a true personal level... I don't know. Once I found something to channel that into, a decent purpose, well... You know what I do. Been tryin' to make up for a lot."

She withdrew one hand, wrapped her arm around him, and held him tight. Aaron returned her embrace before pulling the covers up over her shoulder. He kissed her forehead and nestled his head into the pillow. She tucked her head in underneath his chin.

"It's still a struggle. Sometimes it scares me," he added. "I know what I was trained to do. I know what I *can* do. But I do have the choice in how I use that. So I do the best I can with it. Try to help people…"

They lay silent for a time, content in each other's touch.

"Aaron?"

"Mmm?"

"You're a good man. Always know that's what I think of you."

He didn't say a word but tightened his grip on her, the hug for a moment so firm that she almost couldn't breathe.

CHAPTER 53

ALEX

A FEW MORE WEEKS OF training, planning, and surveillance. They were as ready as they could be for the engagement. Chatter indicated Essex's patience had worn down to a disturbing level at what seemed to him to be the unnatural disappearance of his quarry.

Andy took Alex along on a shopping trip and dropped her off at the nearby town's coffee shop.

"Wait fifteen minutes, then put the battery back in, plug in the charger, and call. Grab a coffee or something while you're waiting. I'll see ya back at base."

"Definitely my plan on the coffee. Thanks, Gamer." Alex gave him a quick hug and exited the car.

After a short wait at the counter for her order, Alex casually glanced around at the few patrons and scoped out a seat. Not a busy establishment during midmorning. Roast and the bready scent of pastries permeated the shop, providing a warm and inviting aroma. Mocha at last in hand, she made her way to a wall booth with a window, an outlet, and a decent view of the front door.

Time crept by, feeling at a veritable standstill. Playing over the details of the plan in her head, she prayed it would all work out. Such a dangerous position they were now in. Would the lackeys follow her? Or Essex himself? If so, they would in all likelihood be sealing their own fates. But the alternative of them out in the world, continuing to harm and murder others, was worse. Plus it would be *their* choice, Essex's and his henchmen's ultimate decision to track down and follow her trail, to invade the compound, to attack and force a defense. That man had put out a bounty for Aaron for a reason. A devious reason. Armed thugs had wound up inside her home because of it. And though Mikey's surveillance had assured her to the contrary, there were possibly others that could have tracked down her family. Essex had already escaped a maximum-security prison once. Aaron would always be at risk of discovery and life-threatening danger as long as Essex remained alive.

Snowflakes sifted past the glass, multifold, random bits of crystalline elegance dashing to the sidewalk. A gust swished them off down the street. How would she feel after this? How bad could it get and how *would* that affect her? Training or no, this was real now and ultimately upon them.

Alex sighed and blew on her coffee before taking a sip. Still too hot. She looked out the window at the sleepy small-town street. A nice little mountain community, likely close-knit, in complete oblivion to the danger that resided so close by. Essex's compound was as well disguised and hidden as their own, maybe even better, and just a few miles farther out in the opposite direction from town. Such close proximity, within just thirty miles of each other, and neither group had recognized the other's whereabouts until now? An odd coincidence? But there had been no reason to concern themselves. Although Les and the guys were aware of Essex's camp, they had just assumed it was some militia types and steered clear. More recent investigation revealed the truth.

Alex swallowed a larger sip of her brew, took a deep breath, and inserted the battery into her phone. She plugged it in and turned it on. The screen lit with life, and the short cheery provider tune sounded. Soon Aaron's picture appeared on the home screen. She ran her finger along the edge of the case. So he hadn't destroyed this phone after all. *Wonder if he looked through my photos?* She allowed a small smile to form. There was nothing in her gallery she'd be concerned about him seeing, plus she'd wanted to share more of her photography with him anyway. He'd never mentioned that most of the last ones she'd taken were of him.

How long would the device take to be detected? Probably not long. The guys had assured her she would only be monitored to find out where she went, but an apprehensive cloud still hung over her that maybe she would just be taken as bait to draw out Aaron. She relied on Aaron's keen sense of observation and the information he'd conveyed to her to keep those thoughts to a minimum.

Ankles crossed under her bench, she squeezed her feet together. Comforting pressure from the lump of her boot knife. *They better be right.* Aaron's knowledge of Essex and the man's methods was a huge bonus in this. Plus Les's tactical skills and the layout of the operation were meticulous. He was confident. And… Andy had not gone straight back. He would wait at a not-so-distant vantage point just to make sure.

Well, this is it. Alex dialed.

"Hey, you. You make it?"

"I made it. I'm in town. At the Caffeine Corral."

"Be there in a bit. Can't wait to see you."

"Me too. Bye."

CHAPTER 54

ESSEX

"GOT 'EM, BOSS."

"Send it all to my room," Damien Essex ordered his communications tech. He retired to his personal chambers to savor this most excellent news in private.

They'd spent months searching. Essex's handpicked surveillance team had produced multiple leads on their female target. All overseas. None panned out. But absolutely *nothing* on Donovan. No leads. No trace. Not a thing. *Had* his old teammate perished in Shane's suicide explosion? No. Though possible, Essex refused entertainment of such an obvious outcome.

That perceived violent end provided perfect cover for Donovan to disappear and reinvent himself, one of the man's trademark abilities. Would he go that far now, having lived outside their old directives for so long? Would his years of a new life and career choice make him complacent in taking precautions to hide his past? Aaron Donovan; back to using his given name. Even with possession of that knowledge, Essex had had a hard time tracking him. Donovan existed in an ever-mindful covert mode. A ghost at the edge of a dream.

A considerable upgrade to Essex's mundane hijackings and thugs for hire, this more than pleasant surprise of discovering his old adversary out of the blue had renewed his zeal and avarice. He'd kept busy with routine heists and the occasional hit, but killing people who meant nothing to him could never elicit an endorphin rush of proper magnitude. This delightful distraction would provide a fresh game of cat and mouse, a delicious eventual conquest. If and when they could catch up face-to-face.

From the search site before the confrontation, Shane had relayed detailed information of all on board back to Essex and his men. Essex found humor in Shane's fuming at the attraction between Donovan and the girl. He counted on that now and would use it to his advantage. If Donovan cared enough, if they'd gotten close enough, he would come out of hiding for her. The man was too much of a dreamer and a romantic. Their overseers had never been able to train that foolishness out of the boy.

No matter how much pain Donovan endured or how many horrors they'd all experienced or been party to, that infuriating mercy remained. The punk had gotten good at hiding it over their time together. Become adept enough at covering that vulnerability to escape the repercussions it brought from the handlers. But it was still there. Compassion. His weakness. That's what made him leave. And just as things were getting good. If not for that, those *special* assignments would likely have continued. Donovan had ruined it all.

Essex missed those missions. Trained for assassination, encouraged to use aggressive means with free permission to torture if need be with no consequence? Yeah, he missed it. And Donovan had been the one who was instrumental in gaining them access to their objectives. His niche in the operation. His ability to put others at ease, to get them to let their guard down, had opened the doors. Then Essex and some of the others could go to work.

Why couldn't Donovan just do his damn job? Why did he always have to let some infernal code of ethics get in the way? It all fell apart after the coward ran. No one else could ever pull off that deception quite as well. It was the reason they'd kept him on. That unnerving, innocent confidence he could bring to the surface and use in a con. That sickening, sweet likability that got them inside. The part that was real.

Essex would never show that kind of decrepitude, even if it paid. But watching Donovan forced into it, knowing it was a fake-out in those operations? That had been awesome, him using real emotion to bring authenticity to the part. To see the turmoil behind his eyes. Even so, that show of friendliness was beneath Essex. Only total control and strength counted. One could play at compassion, but the subject should see force right up front. Have a good scare before he went to work. Any flowery kindness could be enacted by someone else.

That someone else had been Donovan. Essex's nose wrinkled and he tightened his lips. *If he'd grown up in my house, he'd have had that nonsense thrashed outta him right quick. Gotten rid of all that goody-two-shoes crap. Wasteful trappings for weak-minded fools.*

Essex had often fantasized of being the one selected to rid their company of that softhearted ingrate. For Donovan to wear out his usefulness, to refuse an order one time too many. For the handlers to see the error in their judgment at last. How would it happen? Silently in his sleep? A stray round of friendly fire? Any number of unfortunate accidents could occur during an engagement. But no... up close and *personal* would be the most satisfying. He could view the life snuff out, the soul drain away into oblivion. And that would only transpire following a great suffering and loss of hope. Essex had longed to be chosen for that undertaking. And resultant assignment fulfilled, to be the one to dispose of the lifeless body. Ah, yes! A chill coursed through him. Exhilarated by his imaginings, a fresh swell of pride sent a burst of blood through his arteries. Hands clenched into fists and muscles strained in reflection, he imagined flesh and bone yielding under his powerful hands. The rush and reward of a job well done. He had to be the one. It was his right!

Alas, it never came to that. Unfortunately, strong-arming into certain situations, well, it just wasn't always as fruitful as securing the invite first. Contentious or no, Donovan had been pivotal to those mandates. A necessity. *If only Donovan hadn't been so damned adaptable!* That damn winsome smile and personality to match, coupled with a killer annihilation finesse. The perfect combination. He could have been so much more. Even when he pissed them off, it was like he possessed some kind of light that always brought him luck and favor from their overseers. A light that Essex felt the indescribable compulsion to extinguish.

Near the end, a horribly botched job brought Essex closer to receiving his wish. Part of the team injured, the objective derailed. All because of some damn kids! The handlers spent hours interrogating Donovan before tossing him into isolation. Ten days in a squalid hell.

His tune changed when he came out, and for the next couple of weeks, all orders were taken without question. The obedient pup. Had it finally worked? Had the man submitted to his destiny at last? That answer manifested in the form of a well-played diversion... and the pariah was gone. Slipped from Essex's grasp.

Now… after all this time, discovered at last! Essex stretched, his poise self-assured. What serendipity saw him deserving of this absurd fortune? Plus his assumptions proved correct; Donovan's survival skills remained on point, but he *had* come back for the girl. Another flaw in what could have been the perfect soldier of fortune. And he'd wound up *here*!

Even with a lack of conscience, Essex possessed the innate ability to gain a rapid and intimate understanding of the psychology of others. Another reason behind his selection for their old team. Intuiting someone's mental processes helped him establish how he could affect them, distract them, damage them before ever touching them.

And he knew Donovan. Smart and savvy, a likable sort when they had downtime or when he was tricking a target. He'd joke and play, and he could take what he dished out with the best. But he never took any real shit. And when they did get into a situation that required it? Damn could the boy be bloodthirsty! Still, he irritated Essex to no end with his concern for the well-being of others, his only killing when it was necessary. But Donovan was also one of the best, if not the ultimate best, Essex had ever met with tactical, hand to hand, and weapons. An intriguing contest lay ahead to be sure.

Essex would have fun with this. He'd use that girl to distract his prey. He'd make them suffer. In his imagination, he'd step into their lives, fantasize what it was like to be them. Their care for each other. Pure elation for him in the experience, to taste their combination of hope, of thinking they could win, to see a way out, the perceived light at the end of the tunnel, and then the terror behind their eyes when they came to the realization that all hope was a lie. That aspect gave him a rush like nothing else. He would use that love and fear to intensify the experience of taking the life. And that ultimate act gave him the raw decree of the power of life and death over another, that control he craved like a drug.

In charge of his own organization now, he could do anything he wished, and he relished in pleasurable thoughts of exercising authority over the one he never could. He would nurture every bit of unhinged gratification possible out of this. This one would be a hard-won kill... but worth every delectable second.

Now. The most recent recording. Essex replayed it over and over. The voices. Their excitement. The affection. Their heated anticipation of reunion...

His old teammate.

What incredible luck! Just when his frustration level had peaked, this beautiful gift almost literally dropped into his lap. He liked gifts. Especially from people he wouldn't even have to compensate, a couple of expendable losers hoping to make some easy cash. They wouldn't be missed. Those two he'd hired had made several calls this week alone. They had tracked down the girl from the boat. And of all the places she could go in all the world to meet up with Donovan? Right here! Right in his own backyard!

Essex chuckled. Probably some little romantic cabin in the mountains, a place his quarry expected to be safe and out of the way.

But was there a hidden agenda behind this sudden appearance?

One odd thing stuck out, especially after all the wild leads. That handful of calls made in the past week, though seeming local, weren't traceable. Only this last one. Those two amateur bounty hunters weren't that smart.

Could this be a setup? Was Donovan onto him? It couldn't possibly be this easy after all this time. Hell, what if the girl had never even left the States? That told another story. If that was the case, whomever Donovan had working tech with him was good. Not that the derelict couldn't have done it himself, he definitely possessed the skills. But that scenario would have just entailed a couple of good evasive deceptions and his disappearance. No, this someone had the acumen and capacity and also the time on their hands to really screw with Essex's team. Hmm, maybe they could be bought off. If they survived. But that was something for another day. First things first.

Essex flexed broad shoulders and powerful arms as he admired his reflection in the wall mirror. A pencil-thin dark mustache and buzzed hair completed his version of a severe military presence. A wide, toothy grin formed, an expression he displayed often. It confused people… paired with his crazed eyes and threatening build. But for the most part it was just that assurance of being in control of the situations he put himself into. And the intimidation factor was just so enjoyable. So he smiled.

Obsessed. Now *that* label Essex appreciated. Obsession gave him a definitive, focused goal, something big and exciting to look forward to. His heartbeat quickened with every devious detail slinking through his mind, what actions he could at last take, what games he could play, what distress and pain he could cause. This promised some real gut-wrenching, heartfelt satisfaction. An ecstasy. A kill extended not into just the physical extinguishing of bodily function but the slow burn disintegration of emotional well-being.

Psychological destruction. Attack, allow gain, beat down, permit a recovery. Repeat to the brink of perceived death. A vicious tease of ascending cycles of hope and defeat. His own little movie in which he embodied the hero to the outcome. Overcoming the injustices befallen him. Triumph at last. In the end, to finally eliminate the one person who did not appreciate things his way, who challenged him at every turn, on every mission they'd participated in. The one who held him back and caused him nothing but vexation. Never allowed him to showcase his own leadership skills. Caused the degradation and destruction of the unit… which ultimately resulted in Essex's stint in prison.

What amazing dumb luck to find the man again on some random hijacking job! A deep, exhilarating breath and another wide grin. The pleasure of this kill belonged solely to him now. As it should. Anticipation swelled at the thought of showing Aaron Donovan, in a very personal way, that crossing Damien Essex amounted to one of the worst choices the man could ever make.

Essex snickered as he pulled on his favorite camo jacket. He could indulge in these enticing fantasies all day and find gratification. Time now to take action and bring them to delicious reality. To at long last bring his adversary to justice. Striding out of his private quarters, he returned to his command center to speak with his surveillance tech.

"Check out where they go. I want to know *everything*. Every move, *every* last intimate detail. We'll give it a few days, maybe a week or even two. Let them settle in, get comfortable. Be happy. Be in love!" He arched an eyebrow to accompany his derisive chuckle. "Then we'll give them a sweet and tasty little welcome-to-the-neighborhood surprise."

CHAPTER 55

ALEX

LES'S FOUR-WHEEL DRIVE AND a large portion of the weapons, tech, and personal gear sat stashed away from the compound, hidden and remote. Outlying sensors detailed Essex and team streaming en route. Present company outfitted tactical gear and armed themselves to the teeth.

"Uh, guys?" Alex leaned on the desk next to Mikey as he monitored cameras. Her furious waving beckoned the rest over to see.

Andy bent in close to the computer screen. Its harsh light enhanced the growing paleness of his face. "Shit, man, did they bring the whole damn county?"

Three large two-and-a-half-ton trucks accelerated up the dirt road toward the main gate. As the vehicles passed the outer surveillance cams, the images showed multiple figures inside each, ready to deploy. Dust clouds dispersed behind each stout vehicle, wispy apparitions sneaking into the trees like silent intruders. Still a mile out, their ominous presence demanded respect.

"He does seem to attract a fair amount of scum," Les commented.

He and Aaron walked over to join them at the computer.

Aaron glanced at the screen and went back to loading his mags as he rested against the desk next to Alex.

"Wow. Guess so." Les whistled at the display and the trio of trucks charging up the road. "Maybe I *shoulda* turned your ass in for the dough if he can afford *that* many guys."

Aaron kept loading and grinned as Les dodged a couple of steps away, out of Alex's reach.

Les chuckled again at the dour smirk she gave him. "You know I'm just kidding."

MISDIRECTION OF THE GAME

CHAPTER 56

ALEX

"DRAW THEM IN BUT STAY out of the heavy stuff. We'll handle that."

Smoke-gray clouds cast a barricade to sunny independence beyond. The storm crept closer. Alex and Andy lingered near one of the buildings visible to the entrance drive. Andy tapped away at his smart phone, conversing with Mikey as the latter surveyed their area by cams. Brain relayed information to all as needed through earpieces, and both hers and Andy's prime instruction now came by him as events set to unfold. General communications with Aaron and Les ceased for her as both men set for frontal defenses.

Alex shivered against the increasing wind. Stratus clouds lowered to swallow up the last vestiges of blue on the horizon, forming a cold and desolate blanket. The usual jubilant appearance of initial snowflakes rushing past her face went almost unnoticed.

Trucks rumbled into view around the last bend in the drive. Her focus jerked to the present. She locked eyes with Andy. He shoved his phone into a pocket, and they ran back out of sight, into the complex.

"Think they'll buy we were scared?" Alex asked, panting.

"Don't know," Andy replied. "But they're still comin' either way."

ESSEX

A SQUEALING OF BRAKES AND a cloud of dirt. Three trucks rolled to a halt just inside to block the main entrance. As they'd made the threshold, two people standing next to one of the buildings perked up and ran.

"Hold up, boys," Essex ordered.

A sharp contrast to his assumption of some cute romantic cabin hideaway, his surveillance led him to this place, this old run-down group of buildings in the middle of nowhere. An unusual choice. Not many girls would put up with a dump like this. Had to be something *else* to impress her enough to stay. He cackled to himself. Maybe Donovan had gotten too used to the hellholes and decrepit locales that would describe the majority of their missions' settings. No matter. Still unsure on the total number of occupants, he figured there couldn't be many. Essex would put his plan into action anyway.

His mind worked over what might transpire in these initial minutes. What would happen now? There was no explosive ordinance. No shots. *Just a few more…* His attention darted to the two they'd observed upon arrival, scrambling between buildings farther in. Essex smiled. No ambush attack and people running scared. His surveillance team detected no signs that these people had any clue what was about to happen to them.

He himself remained unconvinced of that. Aaron Donovan was sharp. If the man had *any* idea he was even *remotely* being hunted… But… maybe he was too preoccupied with other "interests." Maybe Essex had surprised him after all.

He keyed his walkie. "Light it up."

An armor-clad commando stepped from truck two. A moment later, an explosive whoosh sent a streak of crimson-tinged smoke between the two front buildings. Concussion and fire bloomed, shooting out and around, a near-instantaneous transformation to black acrid smoke that drifted off in the stiff breeze. A screeching creak and the gutted body of an automobile slammed to the ground.

That should give them something to ponder on. "Okay. Spread out. If you can capture, do it. If not… just make sure you leave Donovan alive. That one's for me."

The man with the rocket launcher sauntered back and leaned against the side of truck three. The first two trucks emptied as Essex and his select squad hung back.

LES

LES WAITED BEFORE TRADING ODD shots with the second truck group. *Hadn't figured them to roll in and just bloody fucking torpedo the place right off!* Dammit, that was too close to where Alex and Andy should have run to. Near enough to his building, he'd also caught debris and heat at his rooftop position. He muttered another curse aloud. *Sure hope to hell ol' Psycho's still standing. Can't take down this whole brigade myself.* Faking missed wild shots, he still took out two as they all scattered and scrambled for cover. Plus placed a nice hole through the second truck's engine block. No one exited the third truck. It should contain Essex and a more elite team of fighters, waiting and observing.

The group from the first truck remained tight-knit, five of the eight in a rough tactical formation, the other three spreading out.

ALEX

WIND RATTLED A PIECE OF smoking sheet metal that lay near Alex, its warped skeletal form rasping as if moaning its demise. She lifted her head to peer through disheveled hair. Awareness of her body; no real injuries, just knocked flat. An explosion out of nowhere and *way* too close for comfort. Was this whole thing going south before it even got started? Wisps of foreboding wormed their way through her insides. She pulled herself up from frozen dirt and grabbed Andy's hand to help him stand with her. They traded a grim look.

"Fuck, man," Andy said and slapped at his head to knock some insulation from his hair. "What a twisted shitstorm. That wasn't s'posed to happen."

Alex offered agreement. "We need to get out of here."

Gunshots. She turned back toward the front of the compound. That should be Les engaging the intruders. Any distant hope for humble withdrawal on the part of said assailants fled at movement glimpsed through residual smoke. She grabbed Andy's arm and pointed.

"Go!" she urged him and made a quick dive to hide near a barrel.

He retreated to a pile of tumbled pallets.

One thug neared. The helmeted head swiveled as the man stooped and bowed, poking around corners and into nooks. Alex's position provided a good view of his actions. He hugged the side of the adjacent building as he hunted. A tire stack loomed in front of him. He kicked it over and swung in his rifle, dangerously close to Andy.

I have to get him away from there! She jumped out and ran to cower near a car. The man's attention flashed straight to her, and he re-aimed his rifle as he stepped to the center of the driveway.

"Get up!" The hood's cheeks puffed out in glee behind his face shield. Maybe he expected a first capture would move him up in ranking. He ordered her to stand and surrender again.

His enjoyment met an abrupt end as Andy took him out.

"Freeze!" Another slinked in from the side to hold Andy at gunpoint.

"Shit. Didn't see that one comin'," Andy mumbled and side-eyed the man pointing an assault rifle at his head. The explosion had cost them precious time. They shouldn't still be out here…

"Drop it!"

Andy turned and lowered his weapon.

Two light thumps echoed. Blood oozed at the assailant's collar. The goon swayed a moment and collapsed.

Assuming the invaders would wear full armor, which most did, they had trained to target open chinks. Intent on Andy, the man hadn't noticed Alex. His jugular paid the price. Smoke dissipated in the wind from her silencer.

"Good work, guys." Mikey's voice crackled in their earpieces. "Now get the hell back here. Move!"

CHAPTER 57

AARON

THE OTHER FIVE FROM THE first truck continued a stealth advance back into the complex. Clearing one section, they rounded a building... and came face-to-face with Aaron.

He stood silent, head bowed, a pistol in each hand pointed at the ground.

They stopped short.

He regarded them from under his brow. Bunched together, their formation all wrong. Too obvious they were in it for the thrill and the money. Not the elite team. Somebody *really* should have told them...

"You guys *really* don't want to do this..."

The man at the front snickered. He flipped up his face shield and had the audacity to wink as he licked chapped lips. "Oh, but I think we do." He puffed up his chest and growled out his demand. "Drop your weapons."

Aaron's reply came way too calm, and he inclined his head farther at the order given. "Okay then…"

Fingers released. Before the pistols touched earth, Aaron dropped, grabbed one, and fired, twisting on his side to kick the other hard. The forward hireling lurched to a halt in midstep, a single bullet to his windpipe driving out all prior cockiness. He fell in a heap, choking and grasping at the hole in his ruined throat.

The kicked pistol slammed the second at his kneecaps, tripping him to the ground. Aaron was on his feet and moving as the other three hesitated. Not bothering to aim, the panicked third snapped off a quick burst.

Aaron twisted around him, elbow smashing the side of the man's head. He snatched the rifle from flailing hands, swung it baseball-bat style, stock end into the fourth intruder's face. Gloves protected his hands from the hot barrel, and he tossed the rifle at the fifth man.

Five tried to swat the firearm away, and before he could re-aim, Aaron spun and delivered a crushing kick to his jaw. His neck came apart with a pop and the hireling collapsed. One, Four, and Five lay dead.

Number Two, recovered from the hit from the flying pistol, regained his footing and grabbed Aaron from behind. Large muscled arms flexed, the bear hug contracting in Two's attempt to crush the breath from Aaron's lungs.

Aaron squirmed for escape. Arms pinned to his sides, he fought for purchase to throw the captor off-balance. Movement to his left. Three struggled on hands and knees, shaking off the blow from Aaron's elbow. The man scrambled to his feet and grabbed a loose rifle.

Aaron rammed his head back, crunching Two's nose to a blood-spurting pulp, and spun with the screaming assailant still at his back. Three's wild rounds killed Two as Aaron dropped. His kicked pistol rested there. He grabbed it, twisted out from underneath Two's falling body, and took out Three with a double tap.

ALEX

ONE OF THE EIGHT FROM the first truck remained. Mikey warned Andy and Alex as the assailant closed on their position, having heard the shots from Aaron's fight. Andy and Alex caught that action as they skirted the end of the building, away from their own attackers. Left in awe, they rushed on after observing for only the thirty seconds or so it took Aaron to dispatch the five. They now searched for a suitable ambush point.

This side of the building offered little in the way of hiding places. Mikey screamed at them to take cover. The last intruder from truck one caught up. A barked order to disarm. The two turned, too slow to comply for the man.

"Do it now!" he growled.

Andy dropped his pistol. Alex hesitated.

Their attacker's head made an unnatural jerk and twisted way too far to one side. The hand contracted, arm swinging wide, landing several wayward shots into the roofline of the building next door. He fell forward, face-first to icy earth. Aaron stood in his place.

Aaron jogged over as Andy retrieved his own pistol from the ground. Light snow started to fall, and the wind picked up again.

"Guys okay?" Aaron asked.

Both nodded. Aaron laid a gloved hand on the side of Alex's neck, pulled her to him, and wrapped both arms around her, holding tight, rubbing her back.

"You guys shouldn't still be out here," he told her as she returned his embrace.

Les's words surfaced in her mind, of Aaron's ability to switch in an instant from the job to empathy and back. From taking out six assailants in less than three minutes to loving on her. Being told of that was nothing compared to experiencing it in reality. She squeezed tighter. He kissed the side of her head before letting go.

Pistol in hand, Aaron reached down, snagged the dead assailant's assault rifle, and tossed it to Andy, who shouldered it. "Let's go."

The three crept low along the side of the building, back toward the sound of Les firing and the others. Aaron led, Alex behind him, Andy bringing up the rear. Aaron held up a fist to halt them as they neared the fray.

He huddled them close. "This is where it gets hard."

ESSEX

"Okay, boys, it's time."

Essex and his remaining group of six monitored the situation from the truck. Long enough. While still not entirely certain how many he was up against, there could only be a handful at most. However, they had managed to take care of most of his rookie team.

That was the test. To allow him to see the extent of just what talent he faced. Plus the intimidation factor his large force played on his prey. Fatigued now on both physical and mental levels guaranteed they'd be less able to deal with his fresh reinforcements. Why play fair, right?

From the head cams his men wore, he witnessed most of what he needed. Aaron Donovan of course, and true to form, maybe even a bit better than he remembered. A sniper who also proved damn good at hand to hand. The girl, cute, but much more than met the eye. A decent shot. She'd killed one and kept it together. Another guy, and while not possessing the combat skills of Donovan or the sniper, a body with a weapon. And still alive. Maybe one or two others he'd not observed.

Essex spoke with two of his men. "Grab the girl. That'll bring the rest in line." They nodded and all exited the truck, spreading out. Essex brought up the rear, striding confident, bearing conviction that he now possessed full control.

ALEX

AGAINST THEIR WISHES, AARON SENT Alex and Andy back to the relative safety of the main building and Mikey. Locked down, more secure and partially underground, it also held the beginnings of their escape route.

One last open space remained before the structure. A whirl of wraithlike black in her peripheral vision made Alex skid to a stop.

Two armed thugs materialized in their path, and without breaking stride, one leaped into a spinning twist. Alex grasped at Andy's arm as he ducked, too late; the boot heel to the back of his head dropped the young man without so much as a whimper.

The nonjumper grabbed for Alex. A meaty hand clamped on her arm.

A quick twist and she slipped her sleeves, leaving him holding an empty jacket. He cursed and thrust it to the ground as she backed away. Rifle shouldered now, he crept closer, arms outstretched, stalking her. Her hand inched down her thigh to her holster. He snickered.

Movement to the side; Andy's attacker had her covered, rifle aimed and ready. A glance beyond him at her immobile friend on the ground. She needed to get them away from him. Would they shoot her? Who knew? *Dammit!* She turned and sprinted for the corner…

Several distinct reports, their corresponding dirt sprays inches in front of her toes, brought her to a halt. She backed toward the wall. The two closed in. *Well, that went well.* Her hand moved to her pistol grip. *Even if I can take out the one, the other's gonna shoot.* Her mind chased for options. No further time for a plan. Her attacker closed the distance.

Disarmed. Held at gunpoint with her own pistol. The cold steel of the barrel tickled her ear. *Fucker.* The disgusted stare she offered him only made him smile. A violent shove up against the wall, a rough, gloved hand firm against her throat. Cement block ground against her shoulder blades. *Too bad I can't glare him to death.*

The hand tightened, constricting her airway. He leaned in close. "We're not supposed to kill ya… but he didn't say you had to be in perfect shape."

The arid stare and putrid breath warned that if she tried escape again, consequences would be injurious even if not deadly. He eased his grip and let his hand slide down her chest as she gulped air. He smirked and glanced at his cohort. With that, he backhanded her.

Alex shrieked and sucked in an icy breath. Dazed, she winced as a flash of stars briefly obscured her vision. Her eyes blurred and stung, but she refused to let tears fall. Was her cheekbone broken? A metallic taste seeped between clenched teeth, and a throbbing, hot ache spread to envelop the right side of her face.

The experience of being hit like that was one she had never before known. And she was glad of that—it hurt.

"Now maybe you'll be a good girl." The thug pinning her sneered. He wrenched her away from the wall, a crushing handhold clinched on her arm.

These guys had proved *much* quicker and more highly skilled than the others they'd encountered. And more brutal. Gritting her teeth, Alex looked back at Andy on the ground as the two men led her away. *Please be alive.*

CHAPTER 58

AARON

TWO MORE SHOTS, ANOTHER TWO down.

His current position under heavy fire plus several henchmen converging on his rooftop vantage point, the time came for Les to move. He grabbed his rifle, and as he ran, he shouted to Aaron, who'd shown up to help even the odds.

"Psycho!" He tossed two full pistol mags just as Aaron finished dispatching one assailant, then continued toward his next location.

Aaron caught one in each hand, jammed them into pockets, and ducked as a knife sliced the air where he'd stood. He came up under, grabbed the man's wrist, ramming his shoulder, snapping the elbow. He continued into a twist, flinging the screaming assailant over his back to slam to the tarred roof deck.

The man lay whimpering where he landed. He clutched at his arm, eyes wide, and looked past Aaron.

"Psycho. Hmm, why didn't *I* think of that one? I *like* Psycho. But it *is* fitting."

Aaron didn't respond, just stood his ground, his attention now on Damien Essex.

The man sauntered from the rooftop access door. Square chin lifted, shoulders back, chest expanded in a puffed-up showing of superiority, at last the orchestrator of this invasion made his entrance onto the scene. Caught up in all the preparation, the training and planning, Aaron hadn't taken into consideration what seeing his old adversary face-to-face again might do to his own psyche. Bitterness rose in his throat and his jaw clenched tight. A hollow, unclean tension washed through him. Before it could get a grip, he let it go. It was just a reaction to an unpleasant memory. Nothing that would serve him now.

The intimidating figure of Essex continued his arrogant swagger, at last coming to a stop, hands resting on hips. Head cocked, he provided Aaron a lengthy once-over.

"Figured maybe somebody'd offed *you* a long time ago." Essex winked. "But kudos to you for being able to stay hidden and off my radar all this time." The large man sneered the mock compliment. "And alive."

Aaron shrugged offhandedly. He needed to reload. There was likely a gun or three trained on him.

Almost in answer, Essex spoke. "These boys won't shoot you. I told them *not* to. And they *know* the consequences for disobeying *me*." Essex grinned wide. His eyes shifted to the victim of Aaron's defensive move, and he addressed the wounded guerilla. "Haul your ass to the sidelines, Smith. You're a spectator now."

The man scrambled to unsteady feet and slunk over to settle against the second-story wall, cradling his shattered arm.

Essex dismissed him and refocused on Aaron. "Too bad for you, your little protection detail ended up in the middle of something I was after on that ship. Might have missed you again. And then poor ol' Shane? Really thought you might've bought it too when I heard. But I knew better than to take *that* at face value. You were always *so* good at squeaking out of those impossible situations. And I cannot express just how *very* pleased I am that they *didn't* kill you on that errand. I've looked forward to this opportunity for so long it would've been a tragedy if they had." He shook his head and spoke as if scolding a child. "And then you come up with a girlfriend? My hunch played correct. Shame, *shame* on you, Psycho. Didn't our handlers teach you anything? Don't you know? That's the *ultimate* distraction. That'll make you let your guard down every time."

Aaron kept silent. *Man sure is a talker.* But one question did tug at his mind; just where had the rest of the truckload with Essex disappeared to? No shots from Les's new position yet. Hopefully Alex and Andy were back with Mikey now, where he'd sent them, safe from this, away from the vicious menace that was Damien Essex. But where were those missing henchmen?

For Aaron's part, he'd just as soon shoot Essex in the head and be done with it, but empty pistols and ammo in pockets were not conducive to a quick draw. Essex wouldn't shoot him and wouldn't let anyone else. The man desired more than anything to beat him to death with his bare hands. That was his style. And he would take his time. But that was Essex's intention. Aaron Donovan had other plans.

LES

"ANDY… ANDY! *GAMER!*" LES SHOOK the man, and Andy groaned as consciousness returned.

A basic assessment showed no lasting damage, just a nasty bump. Blinking, Andy looked around and sat up, Les supporting him. He rubbed a hand across the back of his neck and winced.

"Ow." He locked eyes on Les. "Alex…?"

Les shook his head. "They got her." He helped Andy to his feet. "I'll get her. Get back with the Brain and finish prepping."

Reluctant to abandon any search to retrieve Alex, Andy began to argue, but Les silenced his protest. Andy took off once again for the main building.

Expending precious time, Les managed a quick covert operation to take care of three of the six from Essex's truck. The remaining were headed for the roof. He moved off to collect his rifle and get into position.

AARON

A SMALL THUMP FROM BELOW. Smoke snaked up the side of the building near a corner, ebony wisps curling over eaves and dancing in shifting winds as they disappeared skyward. Essex glanced that way but continued his monologue, undistracted. The crackle of his radio brought him to pause.

"*Excuse* me just a second," he said, mocking sincere apology as he keyed the walkie to listen. His eyes bulged. "Superb! The more, the merrier! Come on up!" He smiled over at Aaron like the Cheshire cat and actually remained… *silent*.

This can't be good…

Two armed mercenaries escorted Alex onto the roof, ushering her out just past the access door to where the second-story section of the building rose up. One stayed with her, the other moving over to stand with a third, who arrived carrying a rocket launcher. She glared daggers at her captors as though she could burn them down with her thoughts.

They never made it to the main building…

No matter how well thought out or controlled a situation, there always existed the chaotic element, a surprise twist, an unanticipated move by the opponent. The exploded car that altered the original retreat route. The extra time to maneuver a different path. The resultant opposing leverage that now upped the stakes. Also, why it was never a good idea to become too attached…

Aaron couldn't hide the grief that ravaged him.

The man guarding Alex leaned in close to her ear, his whispered utterance disgusting based on the look she gave him. If tearing her chaperone to shreds were an option, she'd have done it.

Essex smiled. "Thought you might appreciate that."

The calm that Aaron had maintained up to this point melted into controlled, chaotic rage that he barely contained. A cold vise twisted his insides. He'd known the risk to Alex, having her involved in this operation, but seeing her held captive and being unable to help her tore at his soul. Though near impossible, he had to remain detached—he couldn't let her dilemma consume him. If he didn't keep his own ire in check, he could lose any advantage he might find. He had to keep it together. And also find a way to get her off this damn roof! Aaron met Essex's stare head-on, though that was *exactly* what the man wanted. Maybe Aaron would give him a whole lot *more* than he wanted.

Essex performed a deep bow. The big man loosened his gun belt and tossed most of his weapons to the roof deck.

"That's what I want to see." Essex gloated, his words echoing Aaron's assumptions. "That's more like it. You know, I could've turned you in, but I rather want you all to myself."

That remark was sure a strange one. *Turned me in? To whom?* Aaron tried to let go the unease those words brought him. Likely Essex was just spewing attempted confusion, trying to throw Aaron off his game before their battle even got started. But still. He pushed down any seeds of worry for later. More immediate things concerned him at present.

Essex resumed his talk, now making sure Alex could hear, describing his intentions for Aaron in agonizing detail. Aaron had forgotten about this side of the man's grotesque talents. He kept his eyes on Essex's movements, on occasion glancing over to Alex. The grisly words were, without a doubt, having their intended effect.

"Now to decide." Essex crossed his arms and tapped his chin with a finger. "Just what *shall* I do to you?"

ALEX

NIGHTMARISH VISIONS. WHAT HORRORS THOSE words conjured in her mind! *Just shut up!* The awful descriptions of wounding and torture pervading her ears spoke to insanity. What kind of fiendish mindset could come up with that? Though just an attempt to mess with their heads, it was the worst audible torment Alex had ever experienced. She fought to ignore what Essex was saying. Her brain took a run of its own however, still cycling through an imagined sequence of events of what Essex wished would transpire.

The thug next to her chortled. "This'll be great! Front-row seats." His harsh voice dripped with an evil excitement, in part to bring her additional distress but also because of his legitimate

372

pleasure in seeing his boss in bloodthirsty action. "Been saving up for this. Man's gonna feel some real *pain* before he dies."

Alex threw him a sidelong glare. *Really? You can shut the hell up too!* Her blood boiled, reddening her face. She had to do something. Just standing here at the mercy of these sickening remarks made her skin crawl. Readiness wound her muscles into coiled springs. Could she get away with it? Would it make things worse? Did it matter at all at this point what she did? They'd take no immediate action to kill her.

Based on what she'd been told about Essex, his final agonizing revelation for Aaron would be to kill him with the knowledge that they were keeping her. One last cruel attrition. Her guard had just informed her as much with his own lurid twist. But bonehead here had let go of her arm, assuming she would stay put. Nowhere to go. A scared little girl…

Alex spun. She snatched the rifle barrel and shoved it aside, drew back to punch, the picture in her mind's eye of her fist crashing clear through his ugly head. His reaction to force his gun back to bear too late, the whites of his eyes expanded a split second before impact. She opened her fingers, and the heel of her hand smashed straight up into his nose.

Blood spurted. His head snapped back. Staggering backward, his skull impacted the block wall with a crack. The incredulous stare glazed over. Soundless words floundered for escape from carnage-covered lips. Knees buckled. He slid down in slow motion, eyes rolling back in his head, unused rifle coming to rest across slack thighs.

Maybe she'd killed him…?

Essex stopped flapping his lips, and he and Aaron both looked at her, in startled question.

Aaron arched an eyebrow and murmured, "Holy shit…"

Payback. "No more shitty comments from the peanut gallery," she muttered and rubbed her hand. As she turned back to face the scene, she wiped her hands on her pants to remove the unsavory collateral of her action. Silence. A look up to see all eyes on her. *Um, enjoy the show?* Sarcastic comments were all that came to her flustered mind. She spread her hands and shrugged, leaned back against the wall, and folded her arms. Not even a glance at the dropped weapons near her feet. The other two henchmen rushed to guard her. A close yet safe distance, rifles at ready, *they* would not make the same mistake.

"Humph!" Essex grimaced. "Oh, I *like* this! Well, well, *well* now. Maybe we have more fun *here* than I expected. And one of you throw a coat on that woman! It's damn cold out. What are we, heathens here?"

One of the guards dropped to the motionless man sprawled on the ground beside Alex and stripped off his upper body armor and jacket. She made no move to cooperate in receiving the extra covering, and the man ended up just draping it over her shoulders from the front.

Perverse intrigue glossed Essex's features. "Fighting skills. Fiery stubbornness. Refusal of my *more* than generous offer of keeping her warm. Mmm, and that smokin'-hot body, tactical outfit be damned! Even more alluring in person than on surveillance." A lingering appraisal and he licked his lips. "Maybe…" He delivered a long pause as he turned a sly smile back on Aaron. "Maybe the question here *really* is not what do I do to *you*… but what do I do to *her*?"

AARON

OH JESUS, DON'T EVEN *go there…*

Every fiber of Aaron's being confined corded tension. Ready to deliver as much damage as conceivable once Essex got around to making a real move, he struggled to neutralize whirling emotions. This had to be just about the worst mental scenario imaginable in which to ready for a fight.

All that time they'd spent in training Alex on the psychological aspects, here he stood smack in the middle of his own cognitive chaos. Dammit, he should never have allowed her into this mess! What if? *No. Don't think about it. Keep your head in the game, son.* He tilted his head, cracking his neck. A stress reliever. Like that would work. His blood might as well have run as ice in his veins.

Essex gave a show of overdramatic slowness in unsheathing his large, scarred knife. He reveled in the art of the tease. "And here is what we carve with, ladies and gentlemen." The ugly blade curled and swooped through the air in front of him, his arm and fingers commanding artful displays of dexterity, the weapon moving as an extension of his black soul. "Anticipation at its best." Battle imminent, his tongue skimmed his lips again. "Haven't had anyone actually worth challenging at this game for a long time."

Essex's steroid-fueled size and strength could be to his advantage, but he'd never been quite able to match Aaron's speed. Aaron just needed to make sure he didn't allow the big man to get a good hold on him.

Aaron pulled his own knife, folding it back against his forearm. *Here we go…*

ALEX

OH MY LORD! WHAT IS it with these types of guys? These arrogant assholes who think they're all that… and just have to show off, string it out, make a show of torture? Where is Les, and why doesn't he just shoot Essex?

Were she able, Alex would do it herself. And she'd add a few extra bullets too. Just because. Aaron must be out of ammo, or he would've already done it. While possessing amazing skills as a fighter, Aaron was efficient and no show-off. He would just take care of business.

Unless… what if it was his concern for her and what her guards might do if things didn't fall in their boss's favor? Great. She had no choice but to just stand and watch. And hope.

AARON

AARON REMAINED SILENT AND SET. Essex circled. The torturous commentary continued, though the object of cruel intentions had switched from Aaron to Alex. Aaron blocked it out, ignoring the horrific words, intent on the man's actions. Stopping at Aaron's back, Essex spouted one last nasty comment.

Aaron spun and ducked, grabbing Essex's slashing arm as the man sprang forward. He dropped to his back, kicked his feet up and caught Essex in the gut, using the big man's momentum to flip him over. Aaron jumped back to his feet as Essex twisted away, regaining his own stance.

Really? Well, that was a way-too-obvious shit move. Either Essex is slipping… or just playing stupid. A few more head-on attacks that Aaron deflected with ease. At this rate he would just need to defend and his opponent would wear himself out.

Essex's skills were *infinitely* better than this. *What's he doing, trying to fake me out? What's he waiting for?* From years ago, ages ago, it all started coming back. Essex pretending to be average, clumsy, drawing in opponents, making them overconfident, making them let their guard down, only for the man to unleash his real level of skill and crush the unsuspecting's body, willpower, and hope in a barrage of calculated attacks they could never have believed him capable of.

Dragging it on and on until at last, satisfied and bored, he finished it in some profoundly disturbing manner. That's how he'd built a reputation. That's why he was feared. And Aaron now recognized where Shane had picked up some of his tendencies.

He knows that I know that. Why bother using that on me? And then it hit him. It wasn't just for him. Essex enjoyed the psychological effect his toying was having on Alex.

Stupid son of a…

Essex lunged.

Aaron sidestepped, swatted the knife, and shoved Essex hard on the back, sending both brute and blade to the rooftop.

Essex rolled, regained his feet and weapon. Poised in a wide crouch, he curled his fingers. "Come on!" Enlivened eyes gleamed with the ruse.

Aaron backed off several feet and threw his own knife down to lodge in the roof deck in front of him. He stripped off his jacket and tossed it over the side of the building. Both gloved hands raked through damp hair before his arms dropped back to his sides to shake out coiled tension. He glared at Essex from under his brows.

Just… fuck you. Deep breath. *Keep a handle on this—you know better. Don't let him get to you.* Weight relaxed to one leg, hands coming to rest on hips, and he cocked his head. "This is fuckin' stupid, man."

Essex straightened to full height. He eased his stance and laughed as he tapped his blade against his palm, eyes aglow. "Ah, so you *do* remember!" His sick grin revealed true intent as he nodded toward Alex. "Thought she might appreciate something a little milder before we get to the good stuff." He glanced from one to the other, spreading his arms wide. "Aw, c'mon!" Shoulders lifted in dramatic showmanship to accompany faux incredulity. "She should at least *think* you have a chance here. She's gotta have *something* to root for, doesn't she? You and *I* both know how this is gonna end. But it's still so enjoyable to see her keep that *tiniest* sliver of hope alive for you till the bitter end, isn't it? I think it keeps things that much more interesting.

You see, it doesn't pay to care. Love can always be used against you. It is, however, entertaining to watch others be torn apart by it."

True. It can be used against you. But it can also give strength. I'll take my chances. And what is life worth without it anyway? Aaron transferred his gaze from Essex to Alex. Her defiant eyes sparked with dread and worry. But also her confidence in him. She had seen what he could do, and he knew she relied on that now to keep it together, to keep her sanity. What Essex had done for sport to distress her had not entirely gone to his plans. Aaron set his jaw, giving her a slow nod that she returned. At least she wasn't just terrified.

Each receiving the other's understanding and assurance, Aaron focused again on Essex. The wordless, intimate encouragement he and Alex had shared didn't go over well with the big man. Essex uttered a deep growl and flexed his arms, his face contorting from demented enjoyment of anticipated torture to outright madness. Now it *would* get bad. Their true skill level would come into play, and it would take everything. Better than stringing this out. Attention locked on Essex, Aaron performed a slow-motion kneel and plucked his blade from the roof. *Let's get this done and over with.*

Essex circled. Stalking. Thick fingers massaged the knife grip, itching for the connection with flesh. A predator fixated on the long-awaited meal. The pounce. An intricate set of fast-paced attacks ensued, forcing Aaron to scramble to stay out of reach of that dangerous blade.

Shit! Well, at least I know for sure what I'm dealing with. This was the treacherous fighting style from those years ago, though beyond sparring opponents, the only recipients of that pent-up destructive fury had been the mission objectives. Or anyone who got in the way.

They both had the years and mileage since, but Essex was still quick. And tricky. Aaron ducked and rolled. A kick back caught Essex with a solid boot to the thigh. Falling hard, Essex managed to twist, and the knife slid across Aaron's shoulder as he rolled away. That biting draw across flesh turned to dampness on his shirt. It wasn't deep, but still. *Do better.*

Back on his feet, he backed off a bit as Essex regained his, the big man's eyes beaming at having drawn first blood. Aaron would still force Essex to attack, make him have to work just that much harder.

Several more attacks. Labored breathing increased for both. A growing fatigue, though minute, displayed in Essex. Could there be an opening to end this soon? Or was it a well-laid trap? They locked together, a dangerous embrace, each striving to drive their blade through the other's face, fateful grips struggling to eliminate life, or at least inflict damage.

"Had enough yet, boy? Ready to give up?" Essex's hand contracted, gripping shirt fabric and what lay underneath. He snarled in Aaron's face. "This shit body armor won't save you in this contest!"

In answer, Aaron headbutted him.

Nose crushed, Essex howled and shoved Aaron. He backed off, flipping blood from his face. Crimson droplets splashed to the roof deck. He cackled. In a flash, he closed on Aaron again.

Aaron spun and sliced Essex across the back of the neck as the big man slid by him, then jumped back, only just saving his lower extremities from Essex's broad blade. Very close. *Too* close. Essex at once sprang back in and grabbed Aaron, searching for the kill.

Aaron twisted hard. He wrenched from Essex's grasp, flung him aside, and delivered a devastating blow to the side of his head.

Essex collapsed to his hands and knees. Attempting to shake off the lightning of pain that bombarded his skull, he wobbled as he got his feet back under him. *"You little fucker! You won't take me!"* He rocked back on his heels.

Aaron moved in to end this deceitful game.

"Maybe I should have told you what happens to *her* if you kill *me!*" Essex spouted through clenched teeth.

A stifled whimper sounded from across the roof.

The tip of Aaron's blade halted, millimeters from the top of Essex's skull. Momentum interrupted, he stepped back, well out of reach of the large man. His gaze jerked to Alex. Enfolded in the grip of one of the captors, a large hand wrapped tight on her throat, one arm held twisted too far behind her back.

Essex's implication ripped at his heart. With it rigged like this, there was no way he could win. No way he could finish Essex and keep Alex safe and alive. *You dirty son of a bitch.* Essex couldn't see the anguish that crossed Aaron's features. Aaron rested hands on knees, catching his breath. A short reprieve. Time to think. *Where* was *Les?*

Essex's draconian enjoyment ruled this game. The fiend would just keep at it. If any kind of decisive play presented for Aaron, he could not act. Alex would die. Okay. Fine. Just keep on, buy the time with his pain, take the beating. At some point a real opportunity *would* present itself.

A resigned sigh. Aaron swiped at his eyes, straightened, flipped his knife. Catching the handle, he gripped it, blade back against his forearm once more. He nodded at Essex. Satisfaction dressed the big man's face as he jumped back to his feet. If Essex wanted a show, Aaron would give it to him. He had more than enough incentive to keep Alex and himself alive.

LOYALTY AND PERDITION

CHAPTER 59

AARON

AARON STOOD FAST NEAR THE edge of the roof. Thick black smoke rolled up in billowing waves behind him. Imperative now that he find a way to end this soon as Essex's gaming attempt to wear him out was achieving some success. Fatigued muscles screamed for rest. Various places would soon show purple where his attacker had landed blows. An old shoulder injury renewed its presence.

A risked glance in Alex's direction. She stood once more against the wall, the unwanted coat crumpled at her feet. Too stubborn for her own good. The two guards stood, attentive and ready to execute orders, the injured third settled next to his downed cohort, pistol lodged in his good hand. She ignored them, her arms folded in front of her, hands gripping her shoulders, anxious gaze riveted on him and his antagonist. Being witness to this encounter was taking a decided toll on her too. *This is just ridiculous!* If only she didn't have those two assault rifles pointed at her...

Motion. A sudden lunge by Essex. Jarred back into combat mode, Aaron made a lateral dodge to evade the flashing blade. The hasty move cost him precious footing. In a blink, Essex switched from a torso-aimed attack, taking advantage of Aaron's stumble and twisting low for his legs. Just catching his balance, Aaron leaped straight up. The wicked knife dissected empty air. Without the expected solid contact, a now unsteady Essex pitched sideways and crashed to the roof.

To avoid his landing placing him right back in harm's way, Aaron kicked off from the man's bulky shoulder. A loud huff issued as his boots struck Essex's muscled flesh.

Essex rolled and swiveled. A burly hand shot out to grab at Aaron's ankle. The fiend blundered a decent grip but held on just long enough to pull Aaron's foot and trip him.

Aaron slammed facedown on the roof deck. Impact knocked his breath from him and sent his weapon flying. The knife bounced just beyond reach. He scrambled and kicked, gulping air, fighting to fill straining lungs. Pain that had shot across his chest subsided. *Thank God no broken ribs.* Meaty hands grasped at his legs.

Essex clawed and dragged, at last gaining a firm hold on one pant leg. Aaron responded with a twisting kick. His boot smashed Essex's cheek, but the man just grunted a curse and held on. With a second blow producing similar results, Aaron tried rolling to twist out of the hand lock. In answer, Essex yanked and rammed down his elbow. Aaron stifled a yelp as the large joint pummeled just above his knee, and he bit down against the resultant surge of pain.

Legs now trapped under Essex's advancing bulk, he fought to keep the man's knife from causing him irreparable harm. He slapped away the slashing blade twice. A third deflection brought a scorching sting when the edge raked along his forearm. Essex couldn't gain decent leverage in his current position of crawling forward on his belly, only able to raise his weapon arm so far, thus sparing Aaron worse injury. Still, it left Aaron with a deep laceration from elbow to wrist. *Dammit!* In stark contrast to the burning wound, blood tickled as it oozed from the gash. It dripped from his right elbow and began to slowly soak the side of his shirt as he struggled.

Essex crawled farther. "Let me see your eyes!" he hissed. "I want to watch the light go out when you die!" With that and a burst of incredible power, Essex reared up, both ample hands clamped around the grip of his knife.

He drove straight down at Aaron's throat. Pinned on his back, Aaron instinctively shot his arms up to halt the big blade. Essex bore down with all his upper-body strength to drive the dagger home, intent only on doing severe bodily damage to the man he held captive.

Aaron pressed him back. Sharpness trapped flat between gloved palms, sides of his hands jammed against the hilt, Aaron's grip held safe from most damage the honed edge could effect. He fought with all he had to keep that large point from penetrating him.

The blade inched closer. Essex, holding the upper position, retained advantage. And the added ballast. The savage growled and grimaced as he compressed his weight down on his quarry.

"I *always* win! *Always!*" Saliva and perspiration dripped from his ruddy face. "Time for you to end!"

Trapped on his back, sweat-soaked and bloodied, Aaron was no match for him, remaining as he was, stuck under this beast. The muscles of his arms and chest were tasked to near collapse with the exertion of holding back the thrusting, crushing mass.

The ruinous tip of that knife indented the neck of his shirt. Sharp steel pierced the material and pricked at his skin. He couldn't maintain this tension much longer.

I can't go out like this... And Alex... Fuck no! Not happening! With the big man's concentration fixated on sinking the blade, Aaron managed to work one leg free. Boot heel planted... just enough leverage...

With a twist to the side, Aaron shoved as hard as he could and rolled, throwing Essex.

Essex's pupils dilated as he found himself catapulted by a strength unexpected from his intended victim. Battling to steady himself in midair, he toppled to the side and crashed in a cursing heap on his back. Squirming and screaming, he tried to right himself. Blinded by desperation now and his fury at a perceived failure, he lashed out with his weapon arm and swung hard. A solid strike. Sadistic, sated crowing escaped his lips.

White-hot agony exploded along Aaron's left side. A piercing jolt of cold steel. The blade had sunk just below the bottom hem of his vest. *So much for the damn body armor.* He sucked in a ragged breath and gritted his teeth against the impact, biting back his own scream as Alex's echoed across the rooftop. She wouldn't take seeing that well... *Please don't move, hon...*

Hoping vital organs and anything else important had been missed, he scrambled away before Essex regained equilibrium. The giant blade plunged hard again, this time planting deep into roof sheeting as the maniac failed in his attempt at another blow.

Aaron snagged his knife on the way and staggered a retreat to near the building's edge. Breath coming in rasps, he tried to retain some semblance of control. He took stock of his injuries. The bleeding from his forearm had slowed. A brief inspection of his side revealed the stab wound, just above and to the inside of his hip bone. It appeared more superficial than it felt, though still a sizable incision. *If only that damn vest had been an inch longer...*

Precious blood leaked in a stream to saturate his waistband. He lowered his shirt and pressed his hands firmly to help stanch the flow, swallowing hard against the resultant blitz of pain. Training had taught him suppression techniques, but following this grueling contest, those were proving elusive.

Those conditionings of the initiates, as they'd been termed, included enduring arduous tortures. The purpose told them being twofold; to learn control of their own pain for survival and to teach what various injuries would do to anatomy, making them more efficient at information retrieval. Aaron's personal opinion was that some of the handlers just enjoyed abuse. Regardless, he had learned, and he drew from that now.

The severity of sensation from his wound lessened from sheer will or natural endorphins. Or shock. Remaining ever mindful, he kept a wary eye on Essex. The big man reestablished his footing, rotated his shoulders, and made quite the show of stretching and swinging his arms.

"Aww, come on! You can't give up now. We're just getting started!" Essex spread his hands in invitation back to the fray. "This is so enjoyable!" He turned his attention to Alex. "Nice show, eh? Quite the performance." He grinned.

With a gaze into her furious eyes, a covetous look swept his features. He raised his blade between them. Stained with Aaron's blood, he gave it a slow rotation, once more pervading an emotional torture. The brute's expression personified that of a famished animal. Fixated on the red metal glistening in front of him, his eyes closed and his tongue skimmed the entire length of one side. Blade sliding down past his open mouth, he lifted his lids to meet Alex's horrified stare. Blood dribbled off the end of his tongue. He licked his lips clean and shrugged.

Offering her a slight bow and a wink, he said, "And I am so glad you let him come out to play."

Aaron took in the scene before him. Why, oh why, had he ever allowed Alex into this mess? Tumultuous emotions radiated from her, mirroring the revulsion clouding her face. Though excruciating, this little display from Essex did at least show him something. Essex was growing tired too. This short garrulous break was nothing but a bid for recovery time. Not that Aaron didn't appreciate the respite as well. But now, stepped back in observation, he could read the heaviness plain as day.

ALEX

THREE MUFFLED THUMP-CRACKS. THE guards to either side of Alex jerked and collapsed at her feet. The man Aaron had injured earlier slumped to one side. Claret splatter painted the wall. She yanked her vision from Essex to the now prone bodies on the ground beside her—and *eww!*—their partially missing skulls! Helmets were no match for that kind of ammunition. Les... *Yes!*

A welcome jolt of hope kicked through her. In that split second, she looked back to Aaron, then knelt and grabbed her pistol off the guard she'd taken out earlier.

Without hesitation, Essex dropped his blade, produced a grenade, and pulled the pin. He spread his arms wide, his bellowing laugh echoing across the rooftop.

"This is what I *live* for!" He flipped the pin away and pointed a finger at Alex. "And just what do you think you're gonna do with *that?*"

Alex kept her pistol aimed. *Not this again!* An insidious reminder of the ship, that final heartbreaking event. But this time she was armed. She stood her ground.

Essex glanced back over to Aaron with an evil sneer. "This little lady's got some backbone! Wonder if she'll stay as graciously in your corner once she knows everything?" A contemptuous giggle and he relaxed his stance, giving Alex a sympathetic gaze. "Let me tell you a little story, my dear, a tale of enlightenment for you that I'm fairly sure you're not aware of. Your 'boyfriend' here? You see, he's just like me. A ruthless, cold-blooded killer. Trained by the same people, part of the same elite team back in the day. The things *he's* done? Oh, the stories I could tell you. You think you're with someone honorable? You think you're protecting something *good*? You really should allow me the opportunity to prove to you just how *very* mistaken you really are."

Alex just stared back at Essex. *No more bullshit.* "Guess you didn't get the memo that I was actually on the ship too?" She eyed him. "I know what he does. And I really don't give a crap about anything you have to say to me. Or what you think you know or don't know. So just don't."

"Ah. It's not just about killing a few bad guys and saving some people. There's a *whole* lot more to it, to why I'm even here. You *have* to be curious. You can't just *not* want to know."

"I know more than you think. And I know all I need to." Alex took a step toward Essex, never wavering from her target. What she'd witnessed in recent hours had pushed her way beyond any fear. "You can't tell me anything I'd believe, not coming from you anyway."

Essex's expression softened. "My dear, just why do you *really* think we were chosen for our previous operations? Because we are talented fighters? Because we can overcome almost any physical situation we're thrown into? Oh, *so* much more!" His eyes narrowed, taunting her, and he tapped the side of his head with a finger. "You may not believe *me*. But I bet you *have* believed every *single* thing you've ever heard from *him*. Haven't you? There's a talent there that most don't possess. The ability to convince most anyone of anything based on a quick psychological profile. It doesn't take much time. And it's a means to an end. I'll guarantee that, just like me, he knew who you were and *exactly* how to manipulate you within the first few minutes of meeting you. How to lie straight to your face and make you believe. Make you believe *anything*! Beyond a shadow of a doubt. You'll find we are both very, *very* skilled at that."

Raising an eyebrow, Alex provided Essex a mocking frown. Seriously? What her antagonist failed to realize was that over the past couple of months, Aaron had confided a good part of his past to her. Nowhere near everything, but enough for her to understand the haunting reality of it. The way those events tormented him proved he could never be a willing part of anything so disturbing. He'd left it for a reason, and that decision had shown her so much more of the truth of who he really was.

Essex went on. "You believe he loves you? I've seen that play before too. Setups to get us close to our targets. Extremely easy to pull off. And, to reiterate, a means to an end. You'll wake up one day and you'll realize fully that what I've told you here today is true. He doesn't love you. You're just a stepping-stone with benefits. Just a cover to hide a true identity. You are being used, my dear. You're too trusting. The sooner you come to terms with that, the better off you'll be." His beady eyes took on a suggestive glint. "Not bothered yet, girlie? I can recount for you as many of his racy details as you'd like."

"Don't!"

"Oho *ho*!" Essex howled out at the uncommon desperation pervading Aaron's cry. "*There* it is! A reaction at last! I'll break you yet!" He spun back to face his prey. "So *that's* what it takes! You really *haven't* told her everything, have you? Oh my God, man! Do you even know who you really *are*? You were taught and trained to perform and betray and not feel a damn thing! All those entrapments and lies? You know you loved it. You've played so many roles I'm amazed you even remembered your real *name*! *Nothing* about you is real!"

Essex's insinuations sent a sick cringe cascading through Alex. Not to mention the crushing wave of hurt and disgust that crashed into her from across the roof. Her mouth went dry. This was the taboo part of Aaron's previous life, what he'd been so averse to telling her about. She clamped her teeth tight against the burn of welling tears. No! This loathsome fiend would *never* get to her like this!

So what if Aaron hadn't told her? He hadn't because of his own regret at any abhorrent actions, not because he wanted to hide secrets from her. It all sank in now. He desired faith and trust from her and couldn't bring himself to admit what he felt might diminish her regard. And with all they were to each other, he deserved her faith.

Alex looked past Essex. Aaron, stricken and close to tears. It was too obvious their attacker had pinpointed that deep torment. Whatever treachery Essex had referred to wasn't in Aaron's true nature. Regardless of what any facial expression might tell her or what he might have to do, Aaron's eyes always held truth for her. They pleaded for her belief in him now. She let the hurt flow out of her. They would get through all that later. Right now her strength was what mattered. For them both.

She returned her attention to Essex. "Wow. Well, that's intelligent. Stand there and tell me *you're* a professional liar, then expect me to *believe* you? And what a sad story. Yeah. Not sorry. Not buying it. I know better. Besides, if I believed everything some idiot tried to tell me about others, I wouldn't know some of the best people in my life. And just going by what you said about me? Epic fail on your part 'cause you obviously don't have a clue about who I am at all."

AARON

AARON YANKED HIMSELF OUT OF his visceral reaction. The *one* facet he'd avoided or kept vague. Would she still find him trustworthy if she knew those lurid particulars? How could he prove to her an undying loyalty, one of the very things he respected most, if he had committed acts so completely opposite that quality? No matter if it was on orders and not by choice. It still mattered to him. He'd done it. He would have to address that aspect now.

Dammit. The one thing Essex just *had* to pull up to get to him. And it worked. He clamped down on any further emotional response. No more satisfaction for their aggressor to continue probing. He also paid close attention to Alex's subtle reactions to their antagonist's words. To his relief, she seemed unaffected now, or if not, she hid it well.

And she genuinely impressed him. She kept it together and held her own in conversing with the intimidating and scheming Essex. Her quick pickup on that man's rhetorical subterfuge in her time on this rooftop showed. That observation helped provide her the steady calm that he'd hoped for her in the outside event she wound up in this extreme a circumstance. And her look to him following Essex's last remark? More reassuring instead of questioning. Many would give consideration to Essex's version of the truth. Or at least falter. She had not. That brought him a confidence boost he hadn't envisioned he would need.

Attention back on Alex, Essex scrutinized her for the smallest evidence his words were causing her doubt. The doubt he needed for distraction. Any small fracture in her will. Unable to discover such, he sniffed with disdain.

"Hmm. So sad. And such a waste. You really *have* been well deceived in all this. I would like to have thought you were smarter than that." He shrugged. "Oh well. Your choice then. And your loss. I do apologize for my diatribe here since we've met. I can see that my deleterious comments have tainted your perception of me. But I'm the only one who can ever tell you the truth. The *real* truth. I know deep down that you know that."

Alex just shook her head and shrugged back at him. "Seriously. Just stop. I *really* don't care."

Essex threw back his head and howled. "You can never have what you think you want! He'll never stay away from it. The violence. The control. It's a necessity! We can't leave it. I love it! He loves it! He's just like *me*! They made us killers. You think you can have that little house in the burbs with the white picket fence? With this one? Think again."

"Whoever said that's what I want?"

"Damn unshakable little…" Essex switched up tactics again and shot her a demonic grin. "*You're* not gonna shoot me," he scoffed. "You can't do it! You're not made for this. You don't have it in you." He took a step toward her.

Alex remained a rock, weapon trained on him, sure and steady. "Dude, I can hit a two-foot target at seventy-five yards. *Damn* sure I can hit an asshole at thirty feet."

Her calm delivery and snide comment gave the man pause, and the smile drained from his face. His cool demeanor cracked. "Go ahead then," he challenged. "Go ahead! *Shoot* me! I drop this, and I take him with me." Turning and taking a step toward Aaron, he tossed over his radio. "Call your man down!"

Aaron glared at Essex. He then let his gaze flick across their surroundings.

How to get Alex off this rooftop and out of danger? At least calling in Les would buy some extra time. *Think, man! What the hell have we trained for?* They would all be in the same space now. What if? With a resigned sigh, Aaron bent down, wincing at the pressure that simple action put on his side.

He picked up the radio and keyed it as he straightened to standing. "Bring it in, man."

Several strained minutes passed. Essex hummed a tune as he flourished the hand holding the explosive in front of him.

Les appeared at the doorway and scanned the rooftop. Close quarters were never his preference for confrontation, but Aaron knew Les would make it work. Essex with that grenade; sadly familiar. Alex locked on her target. Aaron saw his own haggard weariness reflected in Les's eyes the closer his friend got to him.

Les walked at a guarded pace over to stand with him. "Bloody hell, man," he muttered to his cohort. "What're you thinkin' now?"

Aaron shook his head. What would present that he could work with? With a live grenade in play, it would have to be efficient. And fast.

Essex turned an evil, contented smile toward Alex. "Now you're stuck," he purred. "No way out of this one. I guess in the end, I wind up with *two* gifts today. One I've desired for some time. And this new one that I've just discovered?" Essex gave her a ravenous once-over as he let his words sink in. "I do believe with the correct persuasion, you could be a capable asset to my, uh... habitation? Yes. Definitely. You'll be very, *very* well cared for." He gave her an offhand foul chuckle and returned his attention to Aaron and Les.

"I guess I should say thank you," he said to Aaron. "A girlfriend wasn't such a bad idea after all. Very nice choice, my friend. *Very* nice." He chuckled again, knitting raised eyebrows. "Oh, I'm sorry. I guess it still isn't working out so well for *you* though. As I said, I *always* win."

Eyes locked on Essex, Aaron retained his focus. *Just ignore his words...*

Les looked at his friend, over to Alex, ending back on Essex. "She'll kill you," Les stated. "You take us out, you're a dead man anyway."

Essex laughed. "I highly doubt that. She's no killer. Come on! Look at her! When it comes down to it? She won't."

"Well, all I can say is don't piss her off. She bloody shot me."

Essex offered Les a quizzical eye. "Really? Well, you look fairly alive to me. At least for the time being."

Aaron arched his back and flexed abdominal muscles, employing the most subtle motion possible, testing the wound to his side. Pain rocked him, but he judged the injury stable enough for physical action. If he had any decent luck. With the big man's attention now on Les, Aaron took his eyes off Essex and met Alex's. The edge on her side wasn't far from her position, only a few yards behind, and he shifted his eyes there to indicate direction. Giving her his slow nod again, he shifted his own footing backward.

"Aww, you're scared. Rightfully so," Essex said as Aaron's movement caught his eye. "I guess I should expect that from a coward who's used to running. Don't worry. This is almost over. I must say, it has been enjoyable. Much more so than I would've expected. But as they say, all good things must come to an end." He gave a slight bow, smiled, and took several steps back from the two of them.

CHAPTER 60

ALEX

ALEX SAW ESSEX'S ARM FLEX back to toss, saw Aaron grab the back of Les's coat and pull him backward. *How do we get out of this?* Had she read the correct intention in Aaron's look? The cool steel of the trigger tickled at her finger. It wasn't exactly a plan, but it should work and at least get them out of harm's way. Alex adjusted her aim and fired.

Her shots impacted and sent both men off the rooftop, over the side. They disappeared into swirling smoke.

Essex's arm and the hand that secured the explosive halted midswing. Rapid blinking as his mind came to grips with the images he'd witnessed, and his jaw rose and fell several times before emitting coherent words.

"Wha... what the...? Why the hell would you...?" He stared over at her like an unruly child who'd just had a favorite toy taken away. "No, no, no, no, *no!*" he screamed.

He turned and ran to the edge. Smoke drifting around the corner was too thick now to see, and it drove him back, choking. He coughed and gagged as he stumbled away. Her sudden concern that he might still go ahead and toss the grenade after them ended as he scowled at her. Of course he wouldn't. He couldn't watch, wouldn't be able to observe his cruel handiwork.

"You bitch! You *bitch!* How *could* you! You can't rob me of this!" All but spitting his words now, he stomped across the rooftop toward her. "You *can't* take that away from me! It's *my* right! Mine!"

Oh crap! Assuming Essex also wore body armor under his fatigues, she went for the head shot.

Alex rapid-fired twice. With almost superhuman reaction timing, Essex twisted away and his head jerked as at least one of her bullets impacted the side of his skull. A strange, unintelligible howling escaped, pulling back his lips as he staggered backward. Unstable now in his footing, he teetered in place.

Yes!

The grenade slipped from his fingers as he groped for the wounded scalp above his left ear. A deep graze peeled flesh from bone. He fumbled, pushing hanging skin and hair back into place, all the while screaming out disjointed obscenities at her. Blood coated his hands. But had her shot penetrated?

As the grenade rolled past his reach, he shrieked and dropped to his knees, grappling at the gun belt he'd relinquished earlier before the fight. His hand closed on the grip and he yanked the pistol from its leather.

Shit! Should've triple tapped. Why the hell didn't I? Dammit...

With a grenade that could go off at any second, there was no time for a decent re-aim and additional shot. That explosive should take care of him anyway. Alex turned and sprinted across the roof, ignoring what might happen behind her. Rounds peppered at her heels. She tossed her pistol over as she dove for the edge, grabbed the rain gutter, and rolled off. Just before she dropped and lost Essex from her line of sight, he kicked the grenade away. *No!*

Detonation. Debris rained down on her as she hit the ground and rolled. On her feet. *Don't think. Move.* She grabbed her pistol. Sharp aches in her feet and one shin from the jolt of landing, she ignored them and swatted at falling embers as she ran. Around the corner, past the burning crates. A bonfire to distract, it had now ignited the side of the building beneath the block exterior.

Flames sprouted from crackling eaves. She skidded to a stop. Broiling heat against her face threatened to drive her back, but she stayed. Where *were* they? A tightness formed in her chest. Had something else happened? They should have landed about here, but there was no one. Aaron's jacket. She snatched it from the ground and took several steps back, her eyes flicking in a frantic search. *Guys, where the hell are you?* Her attention lowered to boot prints. Several crimson impressions marred disturbed snow...

Alex yelped as her shirt constricted about her neck and shoulders and she found herself being yanked backward.

AARON

THE ROOFTOP WAS NOT HIGH, but both Aaron and Les were grateful for the snowdrift that helped break their fall. They rolled out, gaining their feet as gunshots echoed from above. An ear-shattering explosion rocked the building.

"No..." Aaron halted in his tracks and looked up.

Embers and bits of cement and smoking wood fell all around them.

"It doesn't mean…" Les touched his friend's shoulder.

Running footfalls sounded from beyond the building's edge. Les grasped a still-dazed Aaron, shoved him behind some barrels next to the adjacent building, and jumped in behind. They crouched and hid from view of the figure that sprinted around the corner.

The familiar female form ran up and stopped short. A slight limp to her gait. Her jaw set as her overbright but alert gaze made a hasty sweep of the area. She bent to the ground. Aaron put a hand to his mouth, lowered his head, and rubbed at his eyes as he let out a shuddering sigh. He stepped out and grabbed her, pulling her down with them.

ALEX

READIED FOR SELF-DEFENSE, ALEX relaxed at once at the sight of the two men before her. *Oh, thank God! You guys…* A whimper escaped her. They were alive and here. She seized Aaron in a hug and reached out to take Les's hand. Both gave her a quick squeeze.

Secure in his arms, Alex ran a tentative hand down Aaron's side. "Are you okay?" she whispered. Her fingers met with the damp fabric of his shirt.

"It's not as bad as it looked," he breathed into her ear. "Really. I'm okay."

She sat back and attempted a positive countenance. His reassuring answer rode the voice of a man in dire need of release. The unrelenting physical exertion was pushing him to breaking, not to mention what looked to her like severe injuries.

Alex swallowed against the growing lump in her throat. "That didn't look okay."

Inner ends of eyebrows rose toward the center of a furrowed forehead, a slight upturn of one corner of his mouth; his now-familiar look of apologetic concern at her care for his well-being. He took her chin in his hand and caressed it with his thumb.

She lowered her eyes and pressed her lips tight in her teeth to prevent the bottom one quivering. He could take a lot, and he might be fibbing to keep her from worry, but she had to believe what he told her. Meeting his gaze again, she nodded her acceptance.

"Let me see that." Les shook his head as he yanked open a cargo pocket and took out a med pack. "Bloody hell, man. All I ever do is patch you up."

AARON

AARON EYED LES BUT DID as he was told and peeled up his shirt. Blood seeped from the two-inch gash, a sticky grim mess all around. He caught Alex biting back tears as she backed up to allow Les room.

"Gotta give you somethin' to do," Aaron grunted to his friend. He winced and held in most of a groan as Les cleaned the area and applied antiseptic. Clenched jaw. A quick eyebrow raise to console Alex. Clotter and a wide bandage followed.

"There. That oughta keep your arse held together a bit longer." Les shoved the med pack back in its pocket. "Not many left. Don't know about Essex. Think we can take 'em and not have to blow this place?"

"Maybe." Aaron completed a mental count as he lowered his shirt. "Probably only two or three plus him if he made it. Might as well."

"Pretty sure he made it." Alex cleared her throat and swiped a hand across her cheeks. "Right before I went off the roof, I saw him kick the grenade. I didn't... I didn't triple tap. I hit him in the head; he went down at first. I thought... I should've..."

"You got off that roof." Aaron brushed his fingertips along her jawbone. "That's what's important."

Alex nodded and wiped at her eyes.

"Okay? Well, he may be injured, but that doesn't mean much with him," Aaron said as he took stock of his weapons and remaining rounds. He began reloading.

Les did the same and looked over at Aaron. "You got her loaded hot again, don't you?"

Aaron looked at Les, then Alex. "Yeah. Better takedown power if she needed it."

Alex scrutinized them. "You *were* farther away this time."

Aaron winked.

Les rubbed at his own chest. "Yeah, body armor to the rescue. Let's go."

They emerged from the cover of the barrels. More vehicle noise from the front of the complex. A fourth truck rumbled in. Armed men spilled out as it screeched to a stop behind the others. Late to the party but more trouble all the same. Les shook his head. "Never mind—it's no good. Let's get back to the boys."

CHAPTER 61

AARON

SNOW WHIPPED PAST. THEY SLUNK around a cinder block corner. As her adrenaline began to subside a bit, the biting wind made Alex shiver.

"Here." Aaron took his recovered coat from her hand and laid it across her shoulders.

"But—?"

"I don't need it. We've got gear stowed, remember?"

Alex nodded as she slid her arms into the jacket. Aaron grabbed her hand, and they moved to rejoin Les. The three stayed low and hugged the side of the building.

"He saw you shoot me, shoot us, but he'll have to make sure. Should buy us a few—"

The bullet impacted the block wall mere inches in front of Aaron, spraying him with debris and making them all duck.

"Shit!" A stray thug had discovered them. And they were *way* too exposed.

"Move!" Les shouted as Aaron began return fire.

"*Shitty* shot," Aaron muttered under his breath, thankful for the man's poor aim.

Les squeezed off a few rounds just as they made the corner. Under fire, their assailant ducked back into an open door of the adjacent structure.

"You guys go. I've got this," Aaron said, and before either could protest, he took off at a dead run. He disappeared through the door to pursue their attacker.

"Aaron! Dammit!" Alex yelled as Les grabbed her hand, pulling her around the corner and toward their destination.

Aaron chased the shooter down the corridor, each in turn trading shots and ducking into doorways for concealment and cover. The long hall turned several times, and the man would soon clear an upcoming exit... too close to the others for comfort. The penalty for failure now would be the continued danger to Alex and Les.

Right before the final bend in the long, darkened hallway, the assailant dodged over a threshold just as Aaron rounded the previous corner. Aaron sprinted and dropped, twisting into a slide. Several rounds pocked the wall above and behind him, their sprays of ashy explosions showering grit.

Skidding low past the opening, he double tapped and slammed hard, feet first, into the corner wall. Pain in his side flared. A distinct thud sounded from inside the room. *Won't be a threat now.* He jumped up, pressing his back into the corner. A peek under his shirt hem revealed a soaked bandage and fresh trickle from the stressed knife wound. *Fuck it.* Time to move. He ran to the end and exit, back to his destination, and with any luck Alex and Les.

ALEX

"GRAB WHAT YOU CAN AND go. Ten minutes max. Plan F."

Les's words rang heavy. Andy saluted and jumped into action. He and Mikey grabbed packs and stuffed various remaining items from their workstations. No matter how much preplanning had gone into this turn of events, a sense of frenzy still hung in the air.

Alex stood, mesmerized by the sudden flurry of urgent activity. Had all gone as planned, they'd have already escaped to the safety of the truck. What now? *What do I do?* She blinked at Les as he handed her several loaded mags for her pistol. She stowed them in pockets. "What's plan F?"

Andy ran by them just as she'd asked the question. "It's when everything is fucked!" He sprinted to the supply room and disappeared through the door.

She turned back to Les, who gave her an affirming nod.

A volley of shots rattled the outer hallway.

"Everything's transferred and deleted," Mikey called over from the computers. "I'll leave the cams up. Just shoot it when you're done."

Les acknowledged. "Go. I'll contact you guys later. You know the drill." He looked at Alex. "Go with them. They'll get you out."

"But…?" Alex's stomach felt lodged in her throat, and she could barely form a clear thought. *No! How do I do this?* A burning crushed her chest. She couldn't just *leave…* Aaron wasn't back!

Gunfire cracked again from the hallway. Loud banging on the armored steel door.

Mikey checked the camera. "It's him. And he's got company."

Mikey keyed the release, and the door crashed open. Aaron scooted inside and backed against it, slamming it closed against the thwacks of a good dozen or so rounds. Mikey keyed the lock to buy time, but it wouldn't hold long.

Aaron holstered his pistol and jogged over to Alex and Les. Mikey took one last look at the computer screen. The hall video showed three men with assault rifles approaching through smoke before one aimed and took out the camera.

"So much for that," Mikey muttered. He went to join Andy by the storage room door.

Alex grabbed Aaron in a hug, which he returned with a crushing embrace. Gunpowder, blood, and sweat, chest heaving to regain breath. The extended physical exertion was taking its toll. She half expected him to collapse in her arms.

"You gotta go," he whispered in her ear. He squeezed her hard and stepped back.

"Aaron, I—"

"Don't." He cut her off. "Me too. But tell me later."

His brow wrinkled and a flash of suffering crossed his face as he brushed his hand across her bruised cheek. Inside and out of the cold now, the wound throbbed. It would swell more soon. She nodded, blinking wetness from her eyes as he stared into them.

"Go with them now. We'll handle the rest." He grabbed her again, held her tight, and kissed her forehead before releasing her. "Follow the plan. We'll meet you after."

MIKEY

A HIDDEN TUNNEL AT THE rear of the supply and weapons room formed their way out. Along with another that Les and Aaron would follow in time, the long, narrow underground passage led almost a quarter mile out, away from the complex. The two were intersected by another shorter one to provide multiple exit options if needed.

Mikey, Andy, and Alex moved at a jog. Not far along their route, a loud thump pounded the corridor, followed by a magnifying low rumble.

"Shit! Look out!"

A growing fissure breached the ceiling above them. Alex, walking just ahead of Mikey, paused and turned back at his shout. Right underneath! He shoved her hard to push her from danger.

Andy's attention jerked to the widening crevasse. He grabbed his friend by the collar. The unexpected yank tangled Mikey's footing and he tripped. His pack flew from his grasp. He stumbled backward against Andy, and the two fell to the floor in a jumble of limbs. The pack containing the detonator and spare radio flopped to the ground.

The chasm expanded. Pebbles and sand transformed to a choking avalanche of roaring debris, and they all scrambled for safety. The ceiling rocked the ground as it collapsed in a thunderous crash.

"How did that happen?" Andy coughed and waved as dust settled.

Mikey sat stunned for a moment. "Dunno. Somebody probably blew something up." He crawled closer to the rubble in front of them, which now formed a complete blockade of the corridor. "Alex!" he screamed. Could she hear? Was she buried? Or was she alive and well on the other side? *"Alex!"*

She called out, "I'm here! I'm okay!"

"Good!" Mikey shouted back. They could just make out her voice. He yelled louder. "Do you see the bag?"

"No!"

"Shit." Mikey looked at Andy. Without the detonator, they couldn't trigger the explosion set. And with the forces closing in when they'd left, Les and Aaron wouldn't stand a chance without it. Andy started to search on their side, but Mikey stopped him. "It was way closer to her."

ALEX

ALEX COUGHED AND PUSHED A chunk of cement off her leg. Dirty and bruised but no serious injuries. Just a stinging cut on her right ankle. She rotated the foot and pressed it against the floor. Only a minor ache. Good. Walkable. And Mikey and Andy were alive! *Thank God.*

She scanned around and pushed at the bottom of the pile, clawing aside dust and smaller debris as she continued to dig. Rocks. Cement. Rebar. Shards cut her hands as she shoved pieces aside. *Oh God, help me. This is hopeless.* Her finger snagged a dirty strap. She pushed and dug faster. The top of the backpack emerged.

"No, wait! I see it! Hold on!" She yanked a couple of times, and the strap broke. A rock was pinning it fast. She sat back and kicked. The rock shifted. She scrambled back in and clenched her fingers into the canvas. Another couple of hard pulls and the bag came free. "I've got it!"

Mikey told her what to look for and what she would need to do. She dove in, rummaged through, and came up with a sweatshirt. Wrapped in the middle, the detonator and radio.

Andy hollered through rubble. "Channel's already set! We can't do any good now! We'll let them know!"

AARON

"THERE'S NO TIME. IF WE had another hour, maybe a little less… but if we don't blow it soon, Essex gets away. And you know he'll go after them. Just because."

Les's statement, though truthful, hurt all the same. Mere minutes after Mikey, Andy, and Alex had made their escape into the passage, an unexplained blast leveled nearly half the main building. A good portion of the exit corridor collapsed around Aaron and Les, leaving them trapped in a small space halfway to the outer door. They struggled with debris for around twenty minutes, coming to the agonizing conclusion that heavy equipment or some miracle could provide their only hope of escape. Les nodded and Aaron returned it. They wouldn't make it out, but at least the other three would.

Aaron kicked hard at a piece of cement block, leaned his head against the wall behind him, and stared at the broken ceiling. *So fucking unfair!* He closed his eyes.

Alex, smiling and happy on the ship, laughing at his stupid jokes. That adorable shyness she'd tried hard to suppress the first time they'd talked and now whenever he caught her watching him. Daydreaming. The way her lips pouted when she lined up a shot. The peculiar electric yet comforting soft touch of her skin against his, delicate fingers entwined in his hair, kisses that reached into his very soul. Shared experiences, a depth of connectedness that no words could truly describe; a heaven he'd never dared dream existed in this world for him.

Heart-shattering intimacy. How she curled up to him at night, long lashes nestled on flushed cheeks, her soft breath caressing his face. Gentle curves of her body illuminated in subtle sheen in their darkened room. Being with her burned away all that was before. All the pain. All others. Nothing existed but her. His peace. He would build a life with her. A future…

Her fierce and protective strength that would surface in the presence of danger, especially when it came to defense of him. Her curiosity and softness as she pointed out the intricacies of wildflower blossoms. Their shared love of the natural world. Watching her blow on hot coffee as they relaxed together on her favorite rock, those mornings when weather permitted, just meters from where he now sat trapped. She never could drink it too hot.

Sitting with her on the front porch of a future home. Crisp mountain air, fresh and clean, scented with pine, the cold making her snuggle deeper into his arms. Good coffee. Warm blanket. Watching the snow fall. Together. The promise of a new life.

That unforgiving knife of regret wrenched at the pit of his stomach. *Why does it have to end like this? Right when it's just getting started!* Was this the price he had to pay, a reckoning for the horrors of a previous violent life? To lose this beauty and joy, the providence of truth and goodness that had finally found him? He pressed the back of his skull and shoulders to the crumbling wall behind him. Jagged points of broken block knifed against his back and head. He dug in his heels and pushed harder. Fingers contracted into closed fists, so constricted the fingernails cut into his palms. No physical pain could ever surpass the sensation of loss that tore at him now.

Oblivious to the passage of time in that moment, he was roused by Les's hand on his shoulder. Aaron opened his eyes, an acknowledging nod to his friend all he could produce as an answer. Those beautiful visions and the heartache that flashed through his being disintegrated into present reality. Dragging out his walkie to confirm the location of the others, he started when it crackled first.

"Care Bear? It's Gamer. You guys read? Psycho?" Aaron looked over at Les, keyed it to answer.

Andy relayed their current predicament. "We all still got ways out, and she knows what to do. See you on the other side, guys."

Andy keyed out, Alex remaining on her radio with Aaron. His voice came raspy from dust and trauma as he spoke to her. "Follow the plan. Don't worry about us." He glanced over at Les again, seeing the resolve in the other man's eyes. "It'll be okay. We're right where we need to be, right where we planned." He winced as he lied to her. "Set your timer. Blow it in exactly fifteen, then get out. Just like we planned."

"Promise me you'll be okay."

The clear crack of anguish in her voice sounded through the static of the transmission. Aaron swallowed hard. Meeting Les's gaze and trying to keep his own voice steady, he keyed his radio. "Promise."

CHAPTER 62

ALEX

ALEX BRUSHED THE BACK OF her hand across damp cheeks. Waiting. So close now, she could practically feel it in her bones. This would all be over soon. She checked her watch. She trusted they were all in position... Now.

The small switch clicked under her thumb. Seconds ticked. A thump and rumble. The first distant blast. Another and another. As successive thumps reached her ears, she rushed into motion, crawling through the debris of the damaged tunnel toward the light at the end.

AARON

CONCUSSION FROM THE SECOND STAGED blast rocked damaged walls, raining chunks of cement block and grit down on them. More fell from the ruined ceiling near the collapse. Dust swirled in eerie waves around the one emergency bulb that had survived and lit their small tomb. Shadows danced. Blackness presided near the top of the debris pile. An illusion? Its shape remained steady. Aaron squinted. An opening.

He met Les's gaze with determination. "This ain't over."

They scrambled up the pile, hands and feet digging, sliding, grappling their way to the top.

"It's not big enough!" Les yanked at obstructions that blocked their escape, ignoring the sharp edges cutting into his hands.

"Here, back up."

Les moved away as Aaron wedged his back against a large portion of broken wall and kicked hard at a mass near the hole. It tilted. He struck it again. A third time and it took a sharp shift. They struggled and shoved to topple it on over, then pulled themselves through one at a time.

Rough sliding down the heap on the other side. They reached the floor and ran to the end of the corridor. The now-damaged door stood half-open to the space beyond, heavy black smoke and red-tinged embers trailing across outside in a hellish cloud.

Automatic-weapons fire thrashed the ground near their feet as they ran before a deafening explosion took care of that. They sprinted to the far side of the complex and behind the last building there. Pressed flat to the back wall, they leaned heavily into the coolness of the block. A small respite. Though way behind schedule, a brief window remained.

"Think we can make it?" Les asked, attempting to catch his breath.

"No one can say we didn't try." Aaron offered half a smile.

They ran.

ALEX

ALEX CLAWED HER WAY OUT into sparkling snow, spots of dust dotting impressions left by her hands and knees. She brushed herself off as she stood. Hours of suppressed fear swept to the surface and joined with intense relief that this horrible mess of violence and destruction neared its end.

Dirt formed a light mud film on her knuckles as she rubbed tears away. She wiped them on her pants. Would things ever go back to any semblance of normal? Not a chance. But at least they could start a more peaceful life.

A small smile lightened her features as she trudged her way toward nearby fencing to watch. Just to make sure. A few bits of snow still clung to the broken barbed wire. She brushed off one icy section with a finger. A chuckle escaped tight lips. The weather-beaten and twisted metal of that fence reflected the current state of her insides. Her vision lifted. Uphill from the compound, she had a clear view of the mayhem and devastation below.

Essex and two more of his henchmen stood huddled, trapped on the roof. His perceived high ground. Walls of fire grew around them. Did he still intend to escape? One man held the recovered rocket launcher. *Well, that explains the explosion that screwed up the tunnel.*

No sign of Aaron and Les. Good. No Andy or Mikey either, but of course they continued well on their way out the alternate tunnel. That passage supplied the only hidden escape for Aaron and Les too, a much better option than fighting their way out the front. It all depended on perfect timing. Everything set into motion now could not be stopped. The explosions built on themselves and would soon consume the entire complex.

Motion caught her attention and nearly stopped her heart. *No! Not* where they should be. *Not* where they *said* they would be!

Why are you guys still down there! She tracked Aaron and Les across to one of the only remaining outer buildings yet untouched by the blasts. As they disappeared behind it, her sight was drawn back to Essex. He too had spied them. He snatched the rocket launcher from the man next to him, hoisted it to his shoulder, took aim…

Seconds later, the building he targeted exploded…

That detonation paralyzed Alex in place. The following explosion brought the ultimate end to Essex and his men. Ejected several yards into the sky, their arms and legs flailed helplessly as the three cartwheeled in cartoonish fashion. Slow motion, falling, back to the conflagration. Consumed. Gone. Two more blasts, the last one shaking the ground enough that it chased Alex farther away.

Slipping and scrambling through snow, she stumbled her way clear of any perceived danger and turned back. The entire block of remaining buildings erupted into orange-and-crimson carnage. Rabid white-yellow flame transformed to angry black clouds hundreds of feet high, bits and pieces of construction rent to streamers cascading from devilish smoke. The inferno raged before her, heat driving her back even farther…

Alex screamed, dropping to her knees in the snow, her anguished cry drowning out sounds of explosions that still reached her ears. She sank forward into icy flakes, silently sobbing, the frozen crystals melting to her face and hands doing nothing to diminish the agony that constricted her soul.

Strong hands lifting her, pulling her, half dragging her.

Soft powder.

Truck.

Alex curled in the seat, weeping into folded arms until sleep overtook her at last.

WHAT
DREAMS

CHAPTER 63

ALEX

ALEX WENT HOME. TO LOU'S home. With events still too raw, she couldn't share details, just left it as her trip had not gone as planned. Lou held space for her to cry and unburden what she could from her troubled mind. Unable and unwilling to talk about most of it just yet, she didn't contact her brother or other friends. They needn't worry—there was nothing to be said until she knew everything for sure.

The plan to eliminate Essex had worked to perfection, if only in that the man and his mercenaries were gone. Zero chance of their survival. They would never harm anyone again. Andy and Mikey got Alex to the truck, and after driving for several hours, stowed it and changed to another vehicle for the remainder of their journey back.

Desperate to get in touch with Mikey again, she still had to wait a week to retrieve the key. Time would provide an extra barrier to any unsavory characters making a connection and tracking her down. Not that any remained with reason to, but the delay had been set up as precaution nonetheless.

That week had stretched an agonizing span into oblivion.

"Good morning!" The hotel desk clerk greeted Alex as she approached. "How may I help you?"

"Hi." Alex's heart pounded as she returned the greeting, faking a relaxed smile. "Do you have a package for MaryAnna Sommers?"

The slender, red-haired girl flashed a bright smile. "Let me go see." She turned, heels clicking to the end of her counter, and disappeared through a door.

Would it be here? Alex tapped her foot, halted it midway up, and shifted stance. She wrung her hands, wiped damp palms on jeans-covered thighs, and leaned forward on the counter, gripping her elbows. *Wow, the nerves... Calm down! But what if there's nothing here?*

The girl reappeared in the doorway, speaking as cheerfully as before as she click-click-clicked her way back over to Alex. "Right here. Here you go."

Alex let out a breath and attempted to conceal her shaking hands as she took the small tan package, biting back too wide a grin when she read the code name, a variation of a character from a favorite childhood television show.

She thanked the clerk and turned to go. "Have a great day!"

"You too!"

A brisk walk to Pier 7 and fresh coffee in hand, Alex chose a corner table near a window. She leaned back in her chair, glanced around, took a drink, and slid her thumbnail the length of the taped cardboard to slice the small box open. There was a key, and a note written on the back of a free trial membership card from the local gym. LOCKER 71.

Alex smiled, hope causing her breath to catch in her throat. Yes, this had been discussed ahead of time, but just the fact that these items remained in play meant something to her. *If there was no reason, there would be no key, right?* She tucked the key and the card in her pocket and finished her coffee. Time for a workout.

Later that day Alex entered the gym, changed and stowed her clothes in locker seventy-one. She spent an anxious hour trying out various stations just to make it look good. At least working up a sweat helped to calm those nerves. A little. After showering, she collected her street clothes plus a phone and charger from the locker. She dressed, left the gym, and made a hasty trip of her walk back to Lou's.

Lou had an evening out planned and wouldn't be home for hours. Alex plugged in the phone and waited. Once it was on and charging, she keyed in her birth date to open it. No messages. She checked the contacts list and giggled. Brain. Gamer. She'd waited long enough. She sent Brain a simple *?*. Her foot tapped again, and she nibbled at a finger. *Come on, guys, please answer!*

Fifteen minutes. Setting the phone on the counter to continue its charge, she wiped at her eyes and stepped over to her chair that Lou kept for her. Aaron's jacket lay there. She slipped it on, brought the collar to her nose and lips. His scent, ingrained in the supple, worn leather, enfolded her in its own assuring hug. If only it were his *real* arms. Nonetheless, it helped her feel close to him. She slumped into cushioned upholstery and curled up. *This is absolute hell.* Had Aaron and Les made it? Were they okay? Mikey would surely answer her, wouldn't he?

Overwhelmed with racing thoughts, she attempted to focus and center herself. Worrying and wondering would not help. Quieting her mind at this point though proved near impossible.

She pulled a fleece blanket over herself and sighed. Minutes stretched.

Wouldn't she know? If Aaron hadn't made it, wouldn't she *feel* that? Silence enveloped her, and she brought his presence to mind. Within seconds a warmth grew in her heart space, a soft and comforting sparkle, almost as if he were sitting right there with her. Several times during the past week this perception had occurred. Sometimes with her specific intention, as now when she thought of him, others out of the blue, snapping her mind to him.

The same had happened after the ship, though at the time it just seemed an oddity, another rarity to go along with that electric rush when they touched. Every time, the connection to him formed, as though he thought of her from some distant place and their hearts merged. A distinct longing, it made her smile and tear up at the same time. It always did. Along with these recent occurrences came the essence of the pier and his forested property. Was that because of the strong memories of those places? Hopes for a future?

Again, in experiencing this now, the strength and closeness of their bond, these unusual sensations, wouldn't she be able to tell if he wasn't alive?

Star Wars.

The theme tone split the silence and jolted her back to present. *What the...?* Phone! She leaped from her chair, flinging the blanket halfway across the room, and ran to the counter.

Mikey: "u got it."

She hopped in place and held in a squeal. What to reply? "what do i do?" she sent back.

More minutes passed. "comic palace in 20."

"omw." She grabbed the phone and charger and her backpack and rushed out the door.

Several patrons meandered the store, reading or thumbing through boxes on counters. Alex had visited the place once before. The worn yet cozy seating area still occupied a room off to the side. She scanned around, hoping she hid any desperation, and headed that direction.

One man lounged in a chair, a stack of comics and magazines next to him on a milk-crate stand. He glanced up as Alex passed. To her relief, he buried his nose in haste back inside his comic as she caught him checking her out. In no mood for idle chitchat, her only interest at present lay in seeing the guys again and finding out what information they had for her.

Having arrived early, she walked to a far chair where she could view the front door and windows to wait for Mikey and Andy. Would their ensuing conversation be just to confirm the horror her eyes had witnessed? As Les said, explosions are showy, messy, and can hide a lot. Had there been another escape route? She checked the phone.

"Hey, Hot Shot."

Andy's greeting gave her a start. He and Mikey walked toward her. They must have already been inside when she arrived. *Sneaky cusses.* She stood, and as they stopped in front of her, she grabbed both in a tight hug. They returned it, the shared bond between them a comfort now that they were back in each other's presence. After a long embrace, they moved to a sofa. Alex and Mikey sat together, Andy on the coffee table in front of them. So many questions, above all one.

"Have you heard from them?" Alex asked.

Andy and Mikey glanced at each other, the latter in the end breaking the silence. "We heard from Care Bear, but he won't tell us where he is."

"But they made it? They're okay?" Alex struggled to keep her voice low.

The two men exchanged another glance, and Alex's heart sank.

Andy spoke to her. "We aren't sure. He only contacted Brain once and just said he would be in touch. That was four days ago."

Alex put both hands over her mouth. *Please, please, please! Tell me! There has to be more!* She craved information. Her urge to scream at them wouldn't help. Her body trembled. So glad to know about Les. What about Aaron?

"We don't know—we just don't. He didn't say."

She set her elbows on her knees and buried her face in her hands. This was not the place to make a waterworks scene.

Mikey laid an arm across her shoulders. "Come with us."

Mikey and Alex walked together. Andy trailed a few steps behind to answer a text he'd received.

"Where are we going?" Alex asked. Being back in the company of these two, plus the curiosity and action of heading to a new destination, alleviated her racing mind. Some.

Andy laughed out of nowhere. He grabbed her shoulders from behind, gave a quick squeeze, and trotted up beside them. "As they say, never put all your eggs in one basket." He met her gaze, his now-cheery face a stark contrast to just minutes earlier.

Wow. Must have been a great text.

"Where you think ol' Care Bear hung out to watch out for you guys anyway? Got a little old warehouse over on eleventh."

Alex nodded. She'd never considered much about where Les would have stayed in the days before showing up at her place. "Okay. Cool."

Several blocks later found them near their objective. Mikey checked the surveillance cams and sensors on his phone a couple of streets out. He nodded an all clear.

Still so covert in their actions. Alex rubbed her nose to cover an amused smile. But, after what they'd all been through, it made sense. Plus they still had jobs to do. *What could they be up to now?*

Andy led them to a side entrance obscured in part by a wild, tangled tree splitting a crack near the foundation. The metal door creaked on rusted hinges.

Darkness engulfed them but for the flickering exit sign above. Smells of dust and old grease lingered from days gone by. A bright sliver seeped from below another door across the expanse. Their footsteps shushed on cement, echoing into inky rafters, and her eyes adjusted to the dark as they made their way over.

Opening the door revealed the light. Alex blinked against it, her pupils adjusting again. They entered a living area and workspace similar to but on a much smaller scale than the mountain compound. She stopped and waited just inside the room.

Mikey and Andy walked on in, and the latter whispered something she couldn't hear to his companion. Mikey grinned and stole a tiny glance at her before taking a chair in front of a computer.

Andy called back to her as he crossed the room. "Make yourself at home."

He walked to a door at the rear and opened it a crack as she sank into a stuffed chair.

"Hey, Bear, we're here."

Alex sat straight up and gawked over at Andy. Her mouth fell open. *Les is here? And…?*

"Andy…?"

He turned back to her as she started to stand and motioned for her to stay put as he walked over and plunked onto the sofa across from her. He couldn't hide his grin, and Alex's offhand notion was that he would totally suck at poker. But then, more than likely, so would she. She spread her hands, eyed him, and shrugged. *What?* He just shook his head and beamed at her.

The door he'd spoken into creaked. Les emerged. Fatigue clouded now gaunt features, revealing a man who looked as if he hadn't slept well in weeks. His left forearm bore a cast, he walked with an obvious limp, and a row of stitches stretched an inch and a half across his forehead. He shuffled over. Reaching the sofa, he dropped down beside Andy. He stared across at her, his eyes narrowed but alive with intensity. Not a word was offered.

A tightness vised her chest and throat. *Oh God no...*

But there was Andy, still trying to hide his stupid, silly grin. It occurred to her in that moment that it was Les who had sent Andy the text.

Had it not been for Andy's expression, Alex would have succumbed to despair right then and there. "Is anybody gonna tell me *anything?*" she blurted out.

"You need to take a walk." The sullen cast to Les's leaden voice grated at her ears. His eyes all but looked through her.

"What?"

"Take a walk."

The sting of being put off and unwelcome knifed her. Except for Andy's grin. She frowned and stood, crossing her arms. What the hell was happening? Where was Aaron?

Les got to his feet and stepped over to her. "Take a walk," he repeated. He pulled a folded envelope from his pocket and handed it to her. "You don't need to be here for this."

Alex blinked back tears. She swallowed against the burgeoning lump in her throat. Why would no one tell her anything? She stared at Les and he stared back. *Just tell me!* Trembling lips pinched together as she crushed her jaw tight, eyes ablaze in challenge.

He nodded at the envelope in her hand. It was folded in half, and she spread it out. Her first name only on the front. Her heart skipped several beats as it seemed to fight itself on whether to jump out of her chest or crash to the floor. She put a hand over her mouth. This could be the best news ever or the worst nightmare.

She looked back into Les's intimidating stare. "He's not here, is he?"

"No, he's not here. Just... take a walk."

Alex looked to Andy and Mikey, and neither would meet her eyes now. Her bottom lip quivered. She turned abruptly and bolted out the door before they could see her cry.

CHAPTER 64

ALEX

ALEX SPRINTED THREE BLOCKS BEFORE stopping. There was an old bench near one of the stores, and she slumped onto its worn seat, mental exhaustion overtaking her. Labored breath hitched as she fought off outright sobs. What could be so bad that the guys didn't want her in their presence to read it? Had Les written her that Aaron was gone and just didn't want to say it to her face and watch her fall apart? *Oh God.*

But, no, her handwritten name, though oddly scribbled, still bore Aaron's distinct characterizations. *Aaron* had written whatever lay within. Had he decided he really was too much a danger to her to remain in her life? He couldn't possibly just... *Might as well get this over with.* She wiped her eyes and slid her thumb inside the envelope to pull it open. A small, folded note. She opened the paper. The writing was a little sloppy, but it was very evident whose it was…

PIER 7 COFFEE & SUDS

Are you freaking kidding me?

She brought the hem of her shirt up to dry soaked cheeks before letting out an exasperated chuckle. "Les, you're an ass. But thank you."

Alex stood and turned in the direction of the pier. Eight blocks away. *Oh Lord, I'm a mess!* A search of her backpack produced a lone saved napkin. She swiped it over her face, blew her nose, and tossed it in the trash can beside the bench. *As good as it's gonna get right now.*

She shouldered her pack, started walking, and shoved the note and envelope into a jacket pocket. *Oh, the heck with this.* She took off at a run, only stopping for the traffic lights.

Pier 7 was packed, just opened for the dinner crowd. Alex burst through the front door, ignoring the several surprised looks she received, and zigzagged her way through to the pier. Between tables and patrons out back…

Wood decking. People. Laughter. Gentle waves lapping at supports, a carefree backdrop to lively conversations. The scents of salty sea air and fried food mingled. Seagulls squawked as they rode the breeze. Orange sunset. *More* people…

Alex continued to weave her way through the crowd. Wow. Party tonight? She squeezed beside a group near the rail and continued. Halfway to the end. With a resigned sigh, she moved on. It would just never be fast enough right now. Pausing and waiting on a couple to slide past her, she felt a weird vibration against her side. The inside pocket of the jacket. Her hand closed on the phone from the locker. She swiped it open and checked the message: "all the way."

Alex grinned. Her heart raced, and she could barely breathe. She clamped her jaw tight on a squeal. Just. Get. There. She moved. A break in the crowd. Ten feet. More people. They were at least beginning to thin out now, and she felt less like a squirming sardine.

The last fifty feet, and in an odd twist, only a few random individuals occupied the remaining space. A fisherman... A couple at one corner...

AARON

THE SUN DIPPED TO THE horizon. Perfect setting. Les and the guys would send her on the right path. Would she follow it again? Should be getting close enough now. *I really hope to God she doesn't hate me for doing this again.* Aaron took out his phone to text, stuffed it back in his pocket, and smiled. If she showed up this time, there would be no question. Not that there was, but events over the past few weeks could have been the hardest test of all.

They had all taken a real beating on this one, and not just physical. She had born witness to more of the extreme violence and talents of his profession than she should ever have had to. He rubbed his neck, checked his watch, and looked at his damaged hand. It would take some time but would heal. At least he was a good shot with both.

He settled in to wait.

ALEX

ALEX JOINED AARON AT THE rail. She focused on the sunset. She couldn't speak. She couldn't look at him. If her knees didn't give out at any second, she would consider herself lucky. His arm brushed against hers as he removed his sunglasses. No way could she hold back tears now. She dropped her pack at her feet.

Just breathe. Gathering as much of her wits about her as she was able, she turned to face him.

A black eye, a couple of healing cuts on his nose and right cheek, and his left hand was wrapped, pinky and ring fingers immobilized in a splint. A different black jacket as she still wore his other. Jeans and boots. Gleaming with tears, his kaleidoscopic blue-green gaze connected with hers...

Those brief seconds of eye contact said everything needed. Alex grabbed Aaron around his neck and shoulders as tight as she dared. He'd put himself through so much. How severe *were* his injuries? Possibly worse than he'd admit, based on Les's appearance at the warehouse. The snug hold he gave her however, lifting her from the deck, told her she could provide a more secure grasp, and she did.

At last in his arms again. Where she belonged. The comforting heat of his body against hers was like sunlight to her soul. He set her back down, tucked his chin into the side of her neck, and they just stood and held each other.

Minutes later, Aaron rubbed Alex's back. His solacing arms contracted about her even more, enfolding her in an all-encompassing euphoria before he released his hold. Alex lingered in the embrace a few seconds longer. *Not just yet.* She pressed herself into him before stepping back.

AARON

AARON CRADLED HER FACE IN his hands. "Just let me look at you." Her familiar musky vanilla scent intoxicated him. His gaze traveled over the contours of her chin between his thumbs, the rose-colored cheeks, the way her sun-kissed hair fell around her forehead and ears. A lingering respite on soft lips, coming back to take comfort in those deep hazel eyes. Everything he needed lay there. Home.

"Always hold on," she whispered to him.

Aaron grabbed her again and crushed her to him. She slid her hands inside his jacket over the soft flannel of his shirt and around to lock at his back.

"Oh God, honey, I will. I will forever," he whispered into her hair.

She snuggled in tighter.

CHAPTER 65

ALEX

"I GUESS I HAVE MY answer then."

Alex tilted her head at him. *Answer?*

"The first night? You said after we got through all the crazy to come back out here and ask you if you still want me around."

Alex giggled as she recalled that conversation. It seemed a lifetime ago. "Yeah," she replied to the question implied. "You do. I do."

He eyed her. A corner of his mouth quirked up under his narrowing gaze. "I do, huh?" A humorous frown. "Damn." He glanced around the pier. The crowd had thinned significantly, and he was able to spot a waitress cleaning up one of the tables near the restaurant. He turned back to Alex. "Wait right here."

Aaron jogged up the pier, his minute limp a tell he hid some pain from her. He stopped and spoke with the waitress. She checked inside her apron pouch. Another waitress exited the building, and the first one called over to her. That girl rummaged through her own apron, went back inside. Returning to the pier, she walked over to Aaron and handed him something. He thanked her and headed back toward Alex.

Aaron strode to a stop in front of her, quieting his breathing from the hike up and back the boardwalk. "Didn't really think this through ahead of time."

Alex gave him a quizzical frown. "What?"

Aaron reached out and brushed her chin with his thumb and index finger as he searched her eyes. He turned his attention to her left hand and took it in his right. He caressed it for a moment. The objective of his trek up the pier became evident as he clamped the capped end of a permanent marker between his teeth. He pulled off the lid and proceeded to draw...

Aaron released her hand. Alex inspected his artwork. A single if slightly wobbly line drawn around her ring finger, a small heart connecting it on top. For what seemed the hundredth time this day, she gulped down the lump in her throat. Stable breath hard to come by, her eyelids fluttered.

"Like I said, I... really didn't think this through... It's been official for me, I think since the first time I saw you, and we'll make it more official..." He recapped the marker.

She just stared, eyes wide, as in a trance.

That simple hand-drawn black line... the meaning it symbolized. All essence of time and surroundings vanished. Alex blinked at him, and tears rolled down her cheeks. Was it really possible for a person to survive this, having their emotions ripped from one end of the spectrum to the other all in one day?

"That's... that's just about the most... I... I don't think I've ever even *heard* of that before!"

She grabbed him in a tight hug again. All reserve left her, and she sobbed on his shoulder.

AARON

HER LOCK THREATENED TO COMPRESS the air from his lungs. Aaron returned a secure hold to her quaking body. This was by far beyond any positive response he desired. His own eyes squeezed shut, he nuzzled the side of her neck.

"Whoa. Okay. I guess I'll take that as a yes."

The sunset had all but disappeared, now just a sliver of tangerine and purple on the horizon. Only a handful of people remained on the pier besides them, many of the rest having filtered back inside to see the band. Alex held Aaron's hands, careful of his injured one.

"How long do you think it'll take to heal? And how's...?"

He followed her line of sight as her eyes shifted focus to his waist. Releasing her hands, he tugged the hem of one side of blue plaid flannel out of his jeans and pulled it up a couple of inches to show her.

Only an angry rouge track remained to mar tanned skin, its roughness and swelling already beginning to subside. In the end, the damage from Essex's score held the good fortune to go no further than a painful, visible reminder and the requirement of a few internal and surface stitches via Les. Another scar in the making. Alex laid a tentative palm to his side and returned her eyes to his, her touch a soothing comfort not only to the wound on his body but also to his soul. He shrugged in a lighthearted gesture as he took her free hand again to reassure her.

"Les fixed me up pretty good. I heal fast." A wink accompanied a lopsided smirk. "It'll be fine as long as I keep the strenuous activities to a minimum for a while."

Alex regarded him through her lashes as he lowered his shirttail. "Well, we'll just have to be extra careful with you then."

A devilish laugh and grin answered her. He rotated his hand as he let his gaze pause on it, a throaty sigh forcing the several shameless comments that came to mind into submission. "As for this, pinky's broke. The other one's sprained real bad. I don't know, couple more weeks or so maybe?"

Alex nodded. "Guess you won't be writing much for a while, huh?"

Aaron chuckled. "Didn't know if you really noticed."

She giggled at him. "Well, of course, silly. I'm a bit more attentive than that. And I didn't think you wore your main holster on that side just for style."

A slight bow of his head and a squeeze of her hand in appreciation of her observations and humor. He glanced around the pier, out at the ocean, returned his eyes to her. "What now?"

"Give me that." She took the marker from him.

Aaron stopped her as she reached for his hand. He dug a fingernail at the end of the taped wrap.

"Wait, no, I can work around—"

"Mmm-mm…" He now had the end of the unrelenting tape in his teeth to tear it open. Success at last. He unwound the wrap, removed the splint, and presented his hand. "That'll work better."

Alex shook her head at him. With great care, she took his hand in her own. The familiar digits appeared as before, with their slight bends and large pads, but a catch developed in her throat at the fading purple-and-yellow discoloration the bandaging had concealed. She blinked and swallowed. Delicately and slowly she drew her own tiny heart and black band around his bruised finger. "There. Now we can wrap that back up."

"Not just yet."

Aaron eyed her drawing. A match to his, though much neater in form. That small return gesture with the deepest of meanings. He could understand why she lost it with his. He cleared his throat and glanced away, blinking back dampness from his own eyes. Damn.

Okay, son, get it together. He looked back to her, his knowing smirk not a bit successful in warding off the tears. They rolled down his cheeks and he bit his lip. She was back in his arms in a heartbeat. Right where she should be. Just a little longer. *We gotta get off this pier.*

He brought a hand up to rub his eyes and laughed to clear his head. "Okay. So I guess it's official—you like being stuck with my sorry, crazy ass. *Now* what?"

Alex stepped back, playfulness lighting her features. She cocked her head and put her hands on her hips. "Hmm. You *did* put me through a lot more hell over the past couple of weeks." She trapped her lower lip in her teeth. "And you're definitely gonna pay for it." The dimples at the corners of her mouth deepened in elvish charm. "Better have something *real* good in mind to make up for that."

Aaron laughed, eyes flashing, and laced his fingers behind his neck, wincing as he forgot about his hurt ones. "Good one. That's a good one." He nodded at her, producing his half smile. "You bet I do. Where do you want to go?"

Alex stepped forward and looped her arms around his neck. He moved his hands to her waist as she brushed his lips with hers and pressed her forehead and nose to his. "Home."

Aaron kissed Alex. "You up for a night ride?"

"Absolutely."

CHAPTER 66

ALEX

FINGERS INTERLACED ON HIS BELLY, the warmth of his body pressed against her, Alex leaned into Aaron's back, holding tight on the back of his motorcycle. The winding road and blurred outlines of trees whizzing past told her where they were headed. Higher elevation brought a chill to pine-scented air.

Tall lodgepoles and sugar pines inked black silhouettes against starlight above. Aaron parked the bike and led Alex by the hand through the dark. The crunch of their footsteps on pine needles and twigs echoed into shadowed mountain wilderness. The hoot of an owl sounded in the distance.

Away from the light pollution of civilization, stars shone with an intensity Alex hadn't seen for some time. Their brightness filtered down through the trees to light the way and gave an ethereal glow to natural shapes on the forest floor. Chill air frosted breath, ghostly wisps in the sable of night.

Aaron stopped and clicked on a flashlight. A fire ring stacked with wood lay in front of them, brush and forest debris cleared well away from its stone-lined edge. He handed her the light. "Hold this."

Several clicks from his lighter produced a glow in old pine needles and cones. The flames intensified, their orange-tinged flickers illuminating Aaron's face. Alex switched off the flashlight and handed it back as he stood. Dry kindling crackled. A tent cozied nearby between a couple of immature ponderosas.

"Well," Aaron said with a shrug, "it's not exactly a house with a fireplace yet, but…"

Alex took hold of his hand and hugged his arm. "It's perfect."

Morning serenity and cold air. Aaron knelt at the campfire to stir and rouse the coals. Fresh kindling and dry pinecones crackled to life under newly added logs. They'd be ready for making breakfast later. Smoke drifted skyward in a thin wispy column against the windless peace of sunrise.

Alex sat just inside the tent door, blanket wrapped snug around her. She giggled at Aaron when he shivered and pulled his leather jacket closer about his chest, tugging at the long hems of his sweatpants to hook over and cover bare toes.

"I won't be out there long," he'd told her. The cost of choosing to throw on only a couple of items of clothing before venturing out into the chill.

He shrugged back at her, his quirky grin dimpling red cheeks. He'd be back in soon enough to get warm. All the events from her first moment of seeing him on the dock at the ship, to this moment in time, swirled through her head. Would life ever be normal again? Not a chance. Would unusual circumstances arise from time to time? Excellent probability. Did she care? Not at all. He was worth every precious, crazy second and more. Another smile touched her lips.

She reached over to open her backpack and pulled out her notebook, the journal she'd started on the ship. Those few first records, quite a few since during the stay at the mountain compound, but nearly forgotten in recent weeks as everything unfolded into insanity. She ran a finger over its worn edge, removed her pen, and before she began to write, took a look back at her first line entry…

Boy, have I got a story to tell…

A FINAL NOTE

I sincerely hope you enjoyed reading this book as much as I enjoyed writing it. If you did, I would greatly appreciate a short review on your favorite book website. Reviews are crucial for any author, and even just a line or two can make a huge difference. Thanks so much,

R. Jayne Revere

To get updates and exclusive content, please join me on my website at: www.rjaynerevere.com.

ABOUT THE AUTHOR

 R. Jayne Revere grew up in the rural Midwest. Stories of adventure and thrills always captured her attention, as well as those where attraction develops under unusual and chaotic circumstances. Putting her active imagination to use, she combines those elements along with a hint of the mystical in her books. Nature photography is another creative outlet for her, and her love of the natural world always finds its way into her fiction.

When she's not writing or dreaming up her next story, she can be found on outdoor adventures, traveling, and enjoying time with her awesome family and friends and adored cats.

She appreciates a good coffee, and like her character creation, Alex Thomas, she *can* hit that two-foot target at seventy-five yards.

If you love a good high-stakes action/thriller with a healthy dose of romance and a touch of the supernatural, you're in the right place.

Stay up to date with R. Jayne Revere: www.rjaynerevere.com